To Now And Forever

To Now And Forever

AVERY VOLZ

Tivshe
Publishing

Library of Congress Control Number 2022920621

Paperback ISBN 978-1-954175-79-2
Hardback ISBN 978-1-954175-80-8
Electronic ISBN 978-1-954175-81-5

Distributed by Tivshe Publishing
Printed in the United States of America

Cover design by Fay Lane

Visit www.tivshepublishing.com

Also by Avery Volz

To the One I Love

For my parents, first and foremost, as my #1 supporters.

For the me I was when I started this project, and for the me I am now three years later.

Chapter One

FEBRUARY, 2082

Two things would have made this tea better: another spoonful of honey and if Blake Walker could take a hint. He was seated across from Abigail Reeves, his white button-up shirt so crisp and flawless, it was almost suspicious. Abigail wondered if he spent his time holed up inside his house and ironing his clothes. But okay, for a man in his late seventies, Abigail had to give him some credit. She was eighty-one and couldn't care less about wrinkles in her shirts anymore.

Blake touched the thick rim of his glasses. They made his bright green eyes appear two times larger. "I mean, hell, I was a history teacher for thirty-five years." His voice was gravely and broken, probably from all the vape pens he carried around like gym rats who carry those gallon water bottles. "Let me tell ya, Gail. Teaching high schoolers sucked."

He paused to look around the café, green eyes flicking this way and that. Abigail took the opportunity to sip her tea and finally say something.

"I can't imagine. I had terrible experiences in high school."

Blake may have been a scatter-brained old man with no intention of reading the energy in the room, but his empathy was still in its twenties. He looked back at Abigail with his nearly-non existent eyebrows arched in concern.

"What do you mean?"

Blake had probably been cool in high school, Abigail decided. He had probably been an athlete who partied on Friday nights and spent Saturdays cleaning up those Friday decisions. He'd probably had his equal share of letdowns, but he probably hadn't almost lost the love of his life to an abusive alcoholic father. He probably hadn't been suicidal and probably didn't spend his time overthinking every detail of every decision down to its bedrock. He probably hadn't spent every day wanting to disappear into a vortex of nothingness. Then again, maybe he did. It wasn't fair to assume anything these days.

"I just grew up pretty quickly," Abigail offered.

Blake nodded, his usual goldfish attention span now locked in and razor focused.

He was in love with Abigail and had been since he'd met her in the narthex of their shared church three years ago. He was vocal about it too—no interest in wasting his precious time. So whenever she was in the mood to crack open another bit of her shell, Blake was ready to observe and listen. Funny thing was, he had no chance.

"I'm sorry," he murmured, reaching out to cover her hand in his.

It was a kind gesture, and they *were* friends. But it had no effect on Abigail's heart.

"How about you let me take you out to dinner?" he suggested with a grin so big it tried to take over his face.

Abigail pulled her hand away and flashed a coy smile. "No thanks. I'm busy."

This was their game. Cat and mouse like a couple of bored college kids. Age was just a number.

"Doing what?" Blake challenged.

"Writing."

"Forgive me. I didn't know you were a bestselling author." Seventy-eight and the guy still had a whip for a mind.

"It's a letter," she corrected him.

"For whom?"

"None of your business, that's who." Her mind, unfortunately for Blake, was still a tack, too.

They grinned at each other, passing dares with their eyes. Eventually, Blake gave up like the sore loser he was, and sighed.

"Will you ever give me a chance?"

Abigail pursed her lips. "Maybe in fifteen or twenty years."

Blake chuckled at the joke. "Fair play."

"Back at ya."

"Okay, Mom. I got my drink, let's go." Aliana Reeves helped her mother out of her seat. "Hey, Mr. Walker."

"Hey, kiddo."

Abigail turned back to Blake and nodded once. "Have a great rest of your day."

He shook his head, and that already massive grin continued to grow. "I'm gonna charm your heart someday, Abigail."

"Don't waste your breath." She blew him a kiss. "It's always belonged to someone else."

Chapter Two

SARATOGA SPRINGS, NY—ALBANY, NY (2031)

If I clenched my jaw any tighter, it would've snapped. I was pinned between my father and Colton Reeves at the kitchen table of my childhood home, scarfing down a plate of steaming lasagna just to keep my hands busy. Talk about the epitome of tense situations. Jamie, my father's girlfriend, sat across from me, twirling her fork through the noodles with an easy smile. I was sure she felt the tangible tension in the air that was strangling me with its gnarled fingers, but if she did, she didn't show it. Colton took a bite of his food and complimented Jamie for her cooking. Dad stared at him like a seething dragon. In fact, I swore I saw smoke curl from his nostrils.

"So," Dad said, finally leaning forward and spearing his lasagna with a fork. "You're a Penn State graduate, Colton?"

"Yes, sir. Graduated with my bachelors in architectural engineering."

"Mommy, I don't like this," my five-year-old son Gavin murmured from across the table. He gestured to his lasagna distastefully.

I gave him a look. "Honey, that's not nice."

"And I assume you have a good job?" my father continued, glaring at Colton over the rim of his glass.

"I'm a glazier for a company in Clifton Park. I install a lot of glass." He shrugged.

"Seems interesting."

"Mommyyy."

"Gavin, eat it," I insisted. "This is your dinner."

"I don't like the way it looks!"

"It's noodles and sauce, buddy! It's basically mac and cheese with a different color."

The reason I was so tense was because this was the first dinner with my father where Colton was at my side since we'd broken up nearly fourteen years ago. And Dad wasn't exactly Colton's number one fan, not after Colton had dumped me as a reaction to his own father's violent abuse and then three years later failed to admit his feelings for me after stealing my virginity. But one global pandemic, a failed marriage, and a near-fatal car accident later, that was all water under the bridge. To us, at least. My father, on the other hand, held more grudges against my boyfriends than a woman on her period.

"I didn't like lasagna when I was little either," Colton told Gavin with a kind smile. "But it's one of my favorite foods now. If you give it a try, you might really like it, too."

Gavin blinked at him and then glanced down at his food again. And just like magic, he started eating forkfuls.

"Thank you," I mouthed at Colton.

He winked at me and squeezed my hand under the table.

For someone who had been through enough trauma to last three lifetimes, he sure was handling this tense dinner with ease. Then again, this probably felt like a cake walk to him. I hoped my dad caught that little interaction with Gavin and added it to a pro-Colton list.

"Clifton Park isn't far from here," Dad pressed on. "I always thought you were the person who wanted to get as far from Saratoga Springs as possible."

What's that supposed to mean, I wanted to throw at him. But that made me sound twelve, not twenty-nine. I held my tongue.

"I'm sure I said that when I was young." Colton laughed softly. "But it's a great place to live. I have a job, the people are nice. I really can't complain."

Dad nodded and continued to aggressively chew his food. In all honesty, there wasn't anything he could hold against Colton now. What was he *supposed* to do? Accuse him of all the stupid things he'd done as a clueless kid? That would've made Dad the bad guy.

"We're having apple pie for dessert," Jamie said, and Gavin leapt for joy in his seat. "I know this is a special occasion."

"It's something," Dad muttered into his cup. He looked away and took a few gulps of soda.

I ignored him and smiled at Jamie. "That sounds great. Thank you."

"Colton," Gavin said.

"What's up, buddy?"

"Are you coming to my birthday party tomorrow?"

"You kidding? I wouldn't miss it for the world! You're gonna *love* the present I got you."

"What is it?" My child's eyes glimmered in excitement.

"It's called a You'll Find Out Tomorrow."

And Gavin erupted into laughter because Colton was the coolest person in the world to him. I wanted to flap my arms in the air and scream, *See, Dad? He's more of a father to Gavin than Evan was!*

Evan...the name still left a sour taste on my tongue. But I hadn't talked to him in years, and sometimes I wondered if he'd forgotten we had a son together. In this situation, Colton was the swoop-in savior. *See, Dad?!*

Two slices of apple pie later, my stomach was full and happy.

Gavin was going on and on about how he'd recently conquered his fear of jumping into a pool. He talked with his head held high like he'd won a shining trophy.

"Well, we better get going," I said when my son paused long enough to take a drink. "We have a big day tomorrow and *someone* still has to wrap a few last-minute presents."

Gavin squealed.

"Thanks so much for coming over," Jamie said. She pulled me in for a hug and then did the same thing for Colton, which warmed my heart. I hoped Dad took notes on Jamie's welcoming, friendly, *forgiving* personality. But that might've been wishful thinking.

"See you tomorrow, buddy," Dad enclosed my son in his arms and squeezed him tight. He shook his hand through Gavin's hair, too, which always made the golden curls lose form and dangle down above his eyes.

Then my dad came right for me.

"Bye, Dad," I mumbled against his chest.

"See you later, sweetheart." The tension rose four notches. "Goodbye, Colton."

"Have a good night, sir."

Outside, the humid July air was a lot more manageable. Gavin skipped to the car and climbed inside after I unlocked it.

"That went well," Colton said with a sort of *thank God it's over* kind of tone.

"Really? Because I felt like I was gonna melt."

He opened the passenger door for me, and I jumped into the car.

Gavin talked the entire way home, which was only ten minutes, but it felt like an eternity that night. I'd been exhausted the last few days, juggling Gavin's birthday preparations, practicing new music for the Saratoga Strings orchestra I was a part of, and mentally preparing for this dinner. Now that one item had officially been checked off the list, I wanted nothing more than to collapse into bed.

Colton veered the car down our winding street and killed the engine in the garage.

"Buddy, go straight upstairs and brush your teeth," I muttered, trying to rub the sleep out of my eyes.

There was still so much to do tonight.

"But, Mommy, I wanna play with the dinosaur that Aunt Mary sent me."

"You can play tomorrow with all your friends."

"But—"

"Gavin."

"Okay, okay!" He jumped out of the car, stomped up the two wooden steps, and slammed the door behind him.

"He's pretty ambitious," Colton said with a small smile.

"You have no idea."

The silence that followed was the kind of quiet that could drown you in sleep if you let it. I could feel my bones sinking into the passenger seat. My eyelids suddenly weighed twenty pounds.

"I can stay if you want me to," Colton whispered. "Help wrap presents so it'll get done faster."

I forced my eyes open and grunted. "Nah, you don't have to."

"Gail." Something in his voice made me turn back to look at him. "I haven't seen you this exhausted since the week of our finals during freshman year of high school." I smiled in spite of myself. "Let me stay to help."

"Okay," I said after a moment.

Gavin was scream-singing his favorite song upstairs, and his voice reverberated through the house's foundation. Colton actually doubled over in laughter.

"You should record this," he said, "and play it back when Gavin's eighteen."

"Same thing my dad did to me. Guess it's time to pay it forward."

Colton and I settled down in the living room with light blue wrapping paper, tape, and too many gifts to count. It was a wonder my wallet wasn't in tears.

"So, how're you holding up?" I asked after wrapping a race car track.

Colton's eyes darkened just the tiniest bit, like they always did when I mentioned his anxiety. It had gotten so much worse over the years that I'd known him, but that was to be expected. He'd been beaten bloody by his father at sixteen, nearly overdosed at a party when he was twenty-one, and almost died in a car accident at twenty-eight. Colton was a breathing miracle with a million-dollar smile, but that didn't hide the fact that his hands never seemed to stop trembling.

"I'm okay right now," he assured me with a neutral expression. "You help to take my mind off things."

I watched him wrap for a moment, watched his jaw clench and his fingers twitch. There must've been a tornado in his mind. Either that, or the constant threat of one. But he wasn't battered in my eyes; he was absolutely perfect.

"Colton, why don't you—"

"Mommy! I'm ready for a bedtime story!"

"Be right there, buddy!"

I finished wrapping a tie-dye soccer ball and pushed myself up to standing. The sight of the ten other unwrapped gifts made me want to rip all the hair from my scalp.

"Go," Colton said, reading the look on my face. "Be with your son. I've got this."

And then, as if just realizing my first love was sitting on the floor knee deep in shapeless sheets of paper, I closed the distance between us and pressed my lips to his. These lips were like home to me. They were remnants of a sweeter, safer time.

"Thank you," I whispered.

He flashed me a heart-shattering smile.

I didn't know what chaos was until there were twelve little boys rocketing through my living room and screaming at full volume. I felt the need to bubble-wrap the cake and every expensive thing I owned for fear they'd get destroyed before the party ended at four.

The living room was packed with parents I hardly even knew, but I was making a conscious effort to throw myself into conversations with them. Social anxiety be damned.

"Is Gavin your first born?" a woman with piercing blue eyes asked me.

"Yeah." I cringed as one of the boys slammed his toy car down on the coffee table and sent two coasters flying off in different directions.

"Eli is my third," the woman went on, oblivious to the circus around her. "Had my first when I was eighteen. Can you believe it?"

"That must've been hard."

"Oh, it was. I had to put everything else on hold just to raise her. But there's something so amazing about a child needing you, you know? I loved it so much I dropped out of college to have more." She laughed and it sounded like the squawk of a bird. "Now I have a twelve-year-old, a nine-year-old, and Eli just turned six in June."

I nodded politely. "That's amazing."

"Are you thinking about having another one?"

My stomach instantly deflated. "Uh, no. I'm not."

"That'll change!" Another squawk-like chortle. "I said the *same* thing."

I was about to answer her when a flash of light caught my eye.

"Oh no, honey, don't touch that!" I lunged to retrieve a glass candle out of a boy's hand. He was about to throw it like a football.

"Kids," a woman with frizzy black hair muttered with a tight smile. "They think the world revolves around them." She was sitting on the couch with her feet propped up on the coffee table and a half-empty glass of wine in her hand.

I stared at her for a moment, my right eye twitching. I had *just* scrubbed that coffee table spotless.

Colton took my hand. "Gail, could you help me in the kitchen for a sec?" Once we were alone he murmured, "I sense that you're about to punch a wall."

"Just a little," I hissed.

He rubbed my shoulders until the adrenaline in my veins faded into exhaustion.

"This is hard," I said. "Having kids is so hard. I *just* cleaned the house, Colton. Yesterday. And now these boys come in and mess it all up! You know the back foyer's covered in mud, right? It rained last night and the yard's still muddy. The boys didn't take off their shoes. I *told* them—"

"Hey," Colton gripped my shoulders. "Breathe."

"I don't know how."

"Like this." He inhaled through his nose, puffed his chest out like a balloon, and then exhaled through his lips.

I involuntarily copied him.

"It's three o'clock. You've got one more hour. And then as soon as this party's over, I'll clean up so you can go take a bath and relax."

"No way." I shook my head. "I'm not asking to do that. It's my house, I can take care of—"

"You know it's not illegal to ask for help, right?"

Sometimes I wondered if Colton was so forwardly helpful because the tedious tasks kept him out of his head. He'd been going to a therapist for two and a half years now, and I recalled him saying he was supposed to "actively pursue normal activities." How that helped him cope with trauma, I wasn't sure, but if it worked, it worked.

"Fine."

I grabbed a handful of Doritos and stuffed them into my mouth, munching aggressively.

"Also," Colton said, taking a Dorito for himself. "You're turning thirty next week, and I think you should go out."

"What?"

"You know, get together with Erica or someone and go out for the night. Have some fun."

"I can't just take a night off. I'm a night staff member for Gavin's park program, I have to plan the outdoor activities for vacation Bible school, there are three pieces of music I have yet to learn, I haven't even *touched* my violin in—"

"Do you hear yourself?"

My mouth froze, and I stared into his sympathetic eyes. Okay...maybe I did sound a little insane.

"Going out would be nice." I nodded slowly.

"Exactly. So, after everyone leaves, go take a bath and call Erica. I'm sure she'd love to hear from you."

Erica Trevins was my best friend from high school. These days, she was living in New York City as the manager of a vintage boutique on Fifth Avenue. She was also the kind of person who would drop everything to celebrate a friend's birthday.

"Okay."

Footsteps stampeded down the hall, and twelve little boys burst into the kitchen at once. Gavin elbowed his way to the front.

"Mommy, can we eat cake now?"

"Cake, cake, cake, cake!"

Who knew twelve toddlers could be so overpowering.

"Of course!" I hoped my smile didn't look forced. "Colton, can you grab a couple plates?"

∾

"Aw, yeah! Turn it up!" Erica hollered.

The Uber driver cranked the volume up, and "Blinding Lights" by The Weeknd blasted through the speakers.

"God, I haven't heard this song in *years*!" Erica shouted.

It was one of our all-time favorites.

I felt like a celebrity. The sequined tube top hugged my torso like another layer of skin, and the lacy jean shorts exposed my lean legs that I'd spent months shaping in the gym. My hair was curled into rippling rivulets. My lashes were smeared thick with mascara, and my lips were a shining blood red.

Thank God Colton was kind enough to watch Gavin for the night. I leaned my head back against the leather seat and inhaled the sultry evening air that was seeping in through the cracked windows. This was *my* night. I was going to live. All those pesky tasks on my to-do list could wait until tomorrow.

Our Uber drove the forty-minute ride to Albany, which at night, was a neon city of electric blues and shimmering golds. At a quarter past nine, we arrived at a bar that seemed to be vomiting purple light.

"Drinks are on me," Erica insisted as she handed the Uber driver his tip. "I got paid last week, and my poor wallet's getting overweight."

"How tragic."

Inside, rough wood floors contrasted the glimmering bar top —all of it washed in the deep purple lighting from above. There was an occupied pool table in the back and a full house of laughter and loud, intoxicated conversations. Erica and I sat down, and I craned my head to see the blackboard menus above the mixers.

"What can I get you ladies?" the balding bartender asked.

"Can I get a mojito please?"

"And I'll have a Black Box Chardonnay," I added.

"Aw, *there* she is!" Erica slapped my arm. "Miss dirty thirty!"

"Please don't ever say that again."

"How's it feel?"

I smiled. "Really good actually."

"If there's one thing you deserve tonight, it's getting fucking wasted. Hey, excuse me!" The bartender turned back to Erica. "Just keep the drinks coming, buddy."

Halfway through my third chardonnay, my head was spinning, and I was dying laughing at just about everything.

"And my husband was like..." Erica stopped to hiccup. "He was like, 'The next time we have role play, *I'm* choosing the theme.'"

We must've sounded like hyenas because I was slapping the table and squealing so loudly my throat was starting to get sore. Erica took another sip of her drink, and her eyes shifted to something over my shoulder. She grabbed me and pulled me close.

"Don't look now, but that guy over there has been checking you out for like fifteen minutes."

I turned around anyway, only to lock eyes with a roguishly handsome brunette. He looked like the kind of guy who could be on the cover of People's edition of *America's Sexiest Man Alive.* He looked like the upcoming British actor that every girl swoons over. I smiled at him, but didn't engage.

Erica's eyebrows pinched. "What the hell was that?"

"What?"

"A *smile*? Get off your ass and go talk to him!"

I tossed back the rest of my drink. "No."

She straightened in her seat like my answer had electrocuted her. "What are you? Some type of Mormon? That guy is *hot.*"

"Erica," I chewed my straw. "I'm back with Colton now, remember?"

Another visible jolt. "Gail, you turned thirty today. *Thirty!* You dated Colton when you were what, sixteen? I get the whole first-love-forever thing, but you've matured past him. In case you haven't noticed, there are other people in the world. Like *that guy!*"

I turned back around and caught Movie Star's eye again. His smile was crooked and annoyingly attractive.

"You never let yourself meet new people because you're always holding onto the past."

"That's not true."

"Wake up!" she slurred. "Do you really wanna relive your high school days?"

"No, but—"

"Colton is *the* representation of your high school days. If you let yourself, you could find someone so much better than him. You deserve better."

"Colton is an amazing person," I hissed, glowering as hard as I could.

"You're in love with the idea of him, Gail!" Erica's voice was thick with impatience. "You don't love *him!* Everyone knows getting back together with an ex is like a ticking time bomb."

I could physically feel my heart break. It was like a branch snapping in half in my chest, the sensation rippling through my body like a hurricane. All I could do was stare at her in disbelief. I hadn't realized she'd felt so strongly against my reconciliation with Colton, but wasn't alcohol infamous for exposing true feelings? Then again, maybe she was right. Maybe I was stupid for holding onto something from my past, even though I swore this time would be different.

A terrible mix of dread and embarrassment attacked my stomach, and I was pretty sure I was about to throw up. I swallowed the sour bile, whipped out my phone, and ordered an Uber. Then I snatched my purse and stomped out, leaving Erica alone at the bar.

Chapter Three

SARATOGA SPRINGS, NY

My bow sailed across the strings, seesawing back and forth. A rush of harmonies flowed from my violin, slashing the silence into tiny broken shards. My fingers skipped along the fingerboard, moving faster still. I had no idea what I was playing, but the rush of climbing and falling down the scale always gave me goosebumps. It was a form of therapy — way cheaper than sitting down with a psychologist and hashing through my problems.

Erica and I hadn't spoken since my birthday. And in the three weeks since then, I'd immersed myself into practicing for the Saratoga Strings' first performance of the season. I'd joined the orchestra in an attempt to find solace after my brutal divorce. It was no secret that my violin was like an over-the-counter drug, but not even it could fully calm my mind sometimes.

I constantly replayed my conversation with Erica in my head, desperately trying to decode her words and mine. *You're in love with the idea of him, Gail! Everyone knows getting back together with an ex is like a ticking time bomb.* That right there was the scariest part. Because she had a valid point. I didn't know anyone who had successfully stayed together with an ex after so much time. Was I foolish for thinking it was possible?

I set my violin down on the couch and pulled up Colton's contact on my phone. We had some great conversations over text. He was funny and witty and kind—everything I wanted in a man. So, what then was the issue?

The front door slammed open, and Gavin stepped into the house, dropping his enormous superhero-themed backpack by the coat rack.

"Hey, buddy! How was your first day of first grade?"

"Mr. Petran is *super* funny, Mommy. He told us about the time his pet snake got loose in the classroom, and they had to get everyone out of the building." Gavin cackled excitedly.

"Well, did they get the snake?"

"Mhm. Mr. Petran also said that he'll let students take the snake home for a weekend! The snake's name is Winter 'cause she has, like, white specks on her back."

"I don't know about taking care of a snake," I said.

"It would be so fun, Mommy!"

I scooped my son up into my arms and planted a kiss on his cheek. "Wanna help me make some chocolate chip cookies?"

"Yeah! Is Colton coming over?"

"Do you want him to?"

"Yes!" He nodded slowly, blue eyes bulging for emphasis.

Something in Gavin's eyes lit up every time he talked about Colton. That was a good sign, wasn't it?

Four hours later, we were all sandwiched together on the couch, watching *Cars* on the old Disney Plus.

"This movie came out when I was young, buddy," I told Gavin.

"It was one of my favorites," Colton added, grabbing up a handful of popcorn.

Gavin was mesmerized. He stared at Lightning McQueen like

the car was a Greek god performing miracles. And when Mater scared the tractors, Gavin laughed so hard he had the hiccups for ten minutes.

"That was awesome!" Gavin shouted when the movie ended. He hopped off the couch and pretended to drive a car all around the living room.

I checked the clock. "Okay, Mr. Nascar driver, it's time for bed."

"Can't!" Gavin looped around the coffee table. "I'm about to win the race!"

"Your bed's the finish line. Don't let 'em catch up to you!" I called.

He sprinted down the hall and rocketed up the steps. Colton laughed and offered me the rest of the popcorn.

"How was work today?" I asked him as I clicked the TV off.

"I had to install new windows at this house in East Glenville. The house was huge. I was there all day, but it looks great." He shrugged.

I stared at him for a moment. "You don't seem enthused with the work you're doing."

"I am," he disagreed lightly. "I just...I'm thinking about looking for another job. Honestly, I haven't thought too much about it yet. But my boss is a real dick. I work my ass off all week, but I don't get paid as much as my one coworker who does squat. Jaxson won't give me a raise though."

"That's ridiculous."

He pressed his lips together and shook the popcorn bowl.

"You should look for something around here," I suggested. "Just Google glass repair jobs in Saratoga Springs, and I'm sure you'll find something."

He smiled, and his laugh was just an exhale through the nose. "I'll keep that in mind, thanks."

For a moment, we listened to the water turn on upstairs.

Gavin must have been brushing his teeth. "So, how are things with Erica? Any luck?"

I'd briefly mentioned our fight to Colton but purposely left out the details. I believed my exact words were "It's just stupid drama."

"Haven't talked to her," I muttered. "She said some pretty...untrue things."

"Like what?"

The words froze on my tongue. *Getting back together with an ex is like a ticking time bomb.* "She was just trying to get under my skin."

"Don't let her," Colton said. "How long have you guys been friends?"

"Fourteen years."

"Exactly, so don't let this blip break you guys for good. It's not worth it, trust me."

I sighed because like usual, he was right.

"Erica, it's me. Listen, I'm sorry. It was immature of me to just run out of the bar like that. I really need to talk to you, so if you could just...call me back, I would really appreciate it. Please." I hesitated and then pulled the phone away from my ear to end the call.

I was standing in the hallway at the rec center. Through the open double doors, the Saratoga Strings were tuning their instruments. I could hear my conductor's deep, hearty laugh like he was standing right next to me.

"Did she pick up?" my good friend Veronica asked once I sat back down in the violin section.

"Nope."

"Geez, *what* is her problem?" my other friend Seth huffed. "It's not even her place to judge. Like, I got back with my ex three times before it finally clicked in my brain that he's a shallow prick. You live and you learn."

I'd met Seth and Veronica on my first day in the orchestra. They were both violinists like me, except they'd been playing for far longer. Fortunately, we didn't have any secrets in our close-knit friendship.

"I don't know," I sighed, flipping through my sheet music. "I'm not innocent either. I mean, I left my best friend at the bar. That's class-A bitchiness."

"With good reason though," Seth insisted.

Veronica leaned toward me. "Have you at least apologized?"

"I left her five voice mails! I said I was sorry in all of them."

"Then you're clearly the bigger person."

That phrase made me want to scratch my skin off. The whole thing just felt too ironic to me. A bigger person wouldn't have stormed out of a bar in her drunken stupor.

"Good afternoon, everyone," Tod Niles declared. He took his place at the podium and picked up his baton. "First of all, welcome to our new recruits! Your auditions blew me away. I'm so happy to have you all here. Let's give them a round of applause."

The new head of the viola section smiled as we all clapped. She looked to be right out of college as I had been, but I couldn't remember her name. Jessie? Jesabell?

"As you all know, our selections for the fall concert are Mosier's 'Waltz of the Wicked,' Thomas' 'Phantom Waltz,' and Newbold's 'The Haunted Carousel.' These songs are..."

I stopped listening when I felt my phone buzz in my pocket. Thinking it might be Erica, I quickly shifted my violin to the other hand and ended up banging my bow against the metal stand. Tod broke off mid-sentence and glanced at me.

"Are you all right, Miss Ferr?" Tod asked.

"Yes." I smiled tightly.

I reached into my pocket to retrieve my phone, feeling utterly dismayed when it was just some random number. My skin caught on fire; I could feel every pair of eyes trained on my face.

Tod was smiling. "Do you need to step out?"

"Nope." I shoved my phone back into my pocket and pinned my eyes on the sheet music in front of me.

"As I was saying," Tod continued. "We're performing the week of Halloween, so we will all be dressing up—"

"Don't freak out," Veronica whispered to me. "Erica's going to have to call back sooner or later."

"What makes you so sure?" I muttered out of the corner of my mouth, still staring at Tod.

Veronica shuffled her sheet music. "She's your best friend, isn't she?"

I thought so.

"Guys, we should all dress up as sexy vampires for the performance," Seth interjected.

"I'm wearing a witch hat," Veronica disagreed.

"How predictable."

I shrunk down in my seat and tried hard to tune them out. I didn't want to talk about Halloween costumes in the middle of August, especially when I felt like I was losing one of my closest friends.

Gavin sat bent over his placemat, arm whisking back and forth as he scribbled in the outlines of cartoon characters on his children's menu. "Look, Mommy, I'm making the doggy blue."

"I love it, sweetheart."

When Gavin smiled, I turned back to glance at Elijah across the table. Eight years after graduating college, we still carved time out of our schedules to meet for lunch. His fiancé Brie was my good friend from high school, and they technically had me to thank for their union since they met at *my* wedding. Brie sat next to Elijah now, sipping her sprite.

"So, Colton had to work today?" she asked.

"Yeah, unfortunately." I set my elbows on the table and leaned forward. "He's trying to get a new job though, hopefully something a little closer."

"Does that mean he's moving in with you?" Elijah wanted to know.

My stomach turned to ice. Though it seemed like such a logical question, my brain hadn't even considered it. "Um...no. I don't think so."

"Why not?" Brie smeared a pat of butter over her slice of bread. "You guys are pretty serious, right? You were serious even in high school."

"What do you mean?"

She blinked at me like the answer was obvious. "The whole school thought you two were going to get married. That breakup shocked everyone."

"And this is *the* Colton, right?" Elijah asked. "The one that's had your heart forever?"

When he put it like that, it was impossible to conceal my smile. "The very same."

"Props to you." Brie nodded. "It's hard to love someone that long."

It was like flipping a switch in my soul. Her comment set my teeth on edge, so I reached for my ice water and nearly downed the whole cup. When did my relationship open for public speculation? It *wasn't* hard to love someone that long. In fact, fourteen years was the equivalent to one day for me. That was how Colton made me feel.

"I have a chicken alfredo here," our waiter said, materializing out of thin air.

"That's me." Brie raised her hand.

"And a chicken Caesar salad for you," the waiter continued, placing the meal in front of me.

I thanked him and noticed the twinkle in his rain gray eyes. He looked to be about my age. He had a full head of raven black hair, a slight stubble stretching down his jaw, and a smile that put all male models to shame.

"No problem." He flashed me a grin and sauntered off.

I could feel my cheeks burning as I speared through a chunk of lettuce, and I didn't have to look up to know Elijah was staring into my soul. He could read me like a psychic reads the palm of a hand.

"Gail," he said, twirling a fork through his spaghetti. "I know you and Colton are back together, and I'm sure you're incredibly happy—"

"I am."

"But...didn't his dad have like PTSD or something?"

I bit off part of a cucumber and stared at him. "Yeah, so?"

Elijah suddenly looked uncomfortable. "Well, this past summer I was working with a reporter who was doing a study on mental health, and we interviewed a guy who suffers from terrible PTSD. He said he swears he got it from his dad."

I cocked my head at him. "That doesn't make any sense. PTSD results from personal trauma."

Elijah sighed, and it sounded like he was breaking bad news to a child. "More and more research is coming out about the genetic link. I mean, look at Holocaust survivors. Their kids and grand-kids are more likely to suffer with higher anxiety and PTSD."

"So, what're you saying?" I asked, feeling my heart start to kick. "That Colton's gonna be just like his dad?"

"No! I mean, it's a possibility, but—"

"Oh my God." I sat back in my chair, feeling utterly nauseated.

Gavin glanced over at me, chewing a mouthful of mac and cheese. He'd only had the meal for three minutes and already, there was cheese smeared all over his mouth. To distract my thoughts, I grabbed a napkin and wiped his face.

"Relax, Gail," Brie said nonchalantly. "That might not even be the case."

"Colton's been through more trauma than anyone else I know," I muttered, dragging the napkin over Gavin's cheek.

"Gail, I really don't think—"

"All right, let's say he *does* end up like his dad," Brie interrupted. "What would you do?"

I stared at her, horrified and speechless. "I-I—"

"Would you leave him?"

"No!" The answer was automatic, like a preprogrammed response in a robot. But was that true? Colton's mom hadn't wanted to leave his dad, but after a while, his outbursts became too much to handle. God forbid Colton lost himself, was I strong enough to carry him?

There were moments when I noticed his light fizzling out, noticed a sluggishness in his steps and an angry scowl every now and then. But I figured those things were just normal. He'd been through a *lot*. Too much. Didn't he deserve to be angry and upset?

"See?" Brie shrugged. "Then what is there to worry about?"

Forty minutes later, we had split the bill and Brie offered to carry Gavin across the parking lot.

"She looks pretty happy with a kid," I elbowed Elijah. "Hint, hint."

"Oh, no way. Not yet." He laughed as his face glowed pink. "I'm not ready to be a dad."

I shrugged. "All in due time."

"Anyway, I saw you eyeing up our waiter," he said—the master of subject changes that he was. It was meant to be a joke. I took it as a jab.

"All I did was acknowledge his existence."

"I'm just kidding. I know you and Colton are like this." He crossed his fingers.

I stared at his hand and his kind, brotherly smile. The gesture conjured up a new thought.

"We are," I answered Elijah. "Because he's familiar."

"Meaning..." Elijah prompted me with his raised eyebrows.

"Familiar as in I've known him my whole life, and he is my best friend," I explained as we stepped down from the curb. "That's why going back to him is the smartest decision I've ever made. I don't care what anyone thinks."

"Good." We waited for a red Toyota to pass and then crossed the parking lot to my car. Elijah continued, "That's a valid point. Seems like you made the right decision."

"Yes. Believe it or not, I've grown up a little bit in the past fourteen years. I can make my own decisions now."

"That so?"

We were momentarily distracted by Gavin's squeal as Brie flashed him another silly face. I welcomed the distraction. This whole week, my brain had been bombarded with thoughts of Erica and how much I missed her. She was entitled to her own opinion, but what I had said was the truth: Colton *was* my best friend. He was the only one who could fill my stomach with butterflies on a daily basis. In other words, America's Sexiest Man From the Bar and Mr. Attractive Waiter could not compete with Colton Reeves.

As I realized this, a heavy stone plummeted through my torso and crushed my organs. Erica and I had been drunk. The petty, unfiltered, fired-up type of drunk. There was no way our friendship could disintegrate over a couple glasses of alcohol. Words were words, but Erica had always been there for me in the past. Her actions were louder than a few chardonnays.

"Hey, Elijah," I said as we all piled into my car. I needed a topic change. "That thing you said about how PTSD might be hereditary."

"Yeah?"

"What else do you know about that?"

"Erica, it's me again." I told the voicemail machine, staring out the window at the sheeting August rain. "When you get the chance, please call me."

"Still no answer, huh?" Colton asked, looking up from his phone.

"Of course, not."

I sat back down next to him on the couch, and for a few minutes we listened to the patter of rain on the roof. Colton sensed my unease.

"You're quiet. Tell me everything on your mind."

I met his stunning gold-green eyes, and before I could stop myself, I leaned in and kissed him. He immediately kissed me back, curling a hand around the back of my neck and pulling me closer. It was only seconds before my heart was screaming for him, and I put both of our mugs on the coffee table so our hands could be free to roam. I grazed the skin of his toned arms and sighed when he gently bit my lip. I realized then that I could lose myself in him and it wouldn't even matter.

"Where is this coming from?" he asked with a grin in his voice.

"What do you mean?" I pulled him on top of me and kissed him again. "Gavin's at his friend's house, and I'm sick of practicing my music, and you're off work today. It's the perfect opportunity."

I nearly had all the buttons on his shirt undone when he caught my hand and pressed a gentle kiss to my forehead. It was his way of suggesting, "Let's slow down."

In reality, Colton whispered, "I'm not one to pass up a chance to kiss you like this, but you've been out of it the whole day. Why don't you tell me what's really going on?"

Three heart beats passed before I sat up and heaved a sigh. It was now or never.

"When Erica and I went out on my birthday, she wanted me to talk to this other guy who was there at the bar. I didn't," I added quickly when his lips turned down questioningly. "She started saying stuff about how I'm missing out on the opportunity to meet other people because I'm...holding onto the past."

I clenched my teeth at that last part. Colton shifted on the couch, and I could see his jaw tightening like a wire. He let go of a long breath.

"I understand considering new opportunities," he murmured. "I did that a lot in college. It almost killed me."

I opened my mouth to respond, but he kept talking.

"Maybe other people think I'm an idiot for only loving one woman my entire life. But I don't give a shit." He said it so matter-of-factly, like he'd already given this a world of thought and didn't need to spend another second on it.

"You can't predict the future," I reasoned without knowing why. "Something might break us apart. The last thing I want is for you to end up like your dad and for me to end up like my mom."

Total silence.

I wasn't even aware that I'd been thinking about my mom the last few days, thinking about her callousness and her selfishness. But who was to say that wasn't part of *my* future? The world was a cold place. It was not an excuse for her to leave, but maybe her actions were more justified than I thought. Life was hard.

Except now that I'd spewed that thought, Colton looked like he was about to puke or punch a wall. Or both.

"Why would *that* happen?" His voice was barely audible.

I swallowed loudly. "Elijah interviewed someone who did research on a genetic link for PTSD. It's a small percentage, but there's a chance that...given how your dad was abused when he was your age, his trauma response could pass on to you."

Colton's eyes filled with terror. "Is it guaranteed?"

"No!" I said quickly, placing my hands on his shoulders. "There are probably sex differences and other outlining variables that we don't know about. But...hasn't it ever crossed your mind?"

"No, it hasn't actually." His tone was cutting. "Because I promised myself I would work my ass off to *never* be like my dad. If that means medication and therapy for the rest of my life, then so be it, but I will *not* be turning into him any time soon. And there is no way you could end like your mom," he insisted. "It's impossible. Your heart is twenty times bigger than hers."

Something about his words stung my eyes with tears.

Colton took a calming breath and reached for my hand. "I will *never* hurt you again. Even *if* severe PTSD and depression is what fate has in store for me, I'll handle it. I've dealt with worse things. I'm not going to be a drunk who beats his own kid."

My breath felt fragile.

I wanted to believe him. *God, I wanted so badly to believe him!* He was the love of my life after all. If I had to watch him waste away, it would poison my heart for good. I wouldn't survive that a second time. I squeezed his hand.

"Move in."

His head snapped up. "What?"

"Quit your job in Clifton Park and move in with us. Veronica's brother is an architectural engineer right here in Saratoga Springs. I could get you an interview."

"Seriously?"

"I'm sick of being away from you." I brushed away the last of my tears. "We're a magnet for back luck, Colton. Bad things are going to happen. Inevitably. But I want you there with me every step of the way."

"I will be." He nodded like it was a period to the end of his statement.

I leaned forward and kissed him, slower this time, savoring it. The couch vibrated when my phone lit up, and I glanced down to check the screen.

"Oh my God," I exclaimed. "It's Erica."

Thirty minutes and two apologies later, I had my friend back. Turns out, if someone is meant to stay in your life, they will.

Chapter Four

SARATOGA SPRINGS, NY (2032)

Gavin was thrilled when Colton moved in the following January. I liked to believe that Gavin knew I was in love with this man, but I also got the feeling my son thought Colton was my best friend and that we just liked to have sleepovers.

One morning, Gavin wandered into the kitchen, lugging his backpack and grumbling about how much he wanted to skip school to go sledding.

"The snow will still be here when you get home, buddy," Colton said, drumming his fingers on the counter until the Keurig filled his cup with steaming coffee.

"I hope so." Gavin frowned.

I set a bowl of Whole Mini Wheats in front of him and offered a warm smile. "Eat up."

Colton put a lid on his cup, and I tried hard to keep my eyes off the pressed shirt that was buttoned at his elbows. He'd gotten the job as a new landscape designer, and I thanked Veronica's brother a hundred times over for the interview opportunity.

Colton had a meeting today, but I wanted nothing more than to strip him out of that outfit and pull him into our bedroom.

"On the bright side," Colton said, retrieving a crisp bagel from the toaster. "Today's Friday."

"Are you still going over to Andre's tonight?" I asked Gavin.

"Yup. We're gonna stay up all night and mess with his sister," he replied deviously.

"That's not very nice," I chastised.

He shrugged. "Amy took Andre's action figure. We gotta get her back."

"What's the plan?" Colton wanted to know.

"Water guns," Gavin grinned.

Colton reached out to high-five him, but when he turned to see my expression, he cleared his throat.

"Don't go crazy, okay?" he told Gavin. "What's one action figure in a world of other cool toys? Does Andre have any cool dinosaurs or...?"

Gavin thought for a minute. "No, but he does have a monster truck!"

Colton flashed his palms. "There you go! Between you and me, I wouldn't bother going after Amy. When she realizes you guys have the cooler toys, she won't even want the action figure anymore. You guys just have a good time and she'll come around."

When he winked, Gavin's eyes sparkled. Mine did, too. How did I get so lucky to have a man like this walk into my son's life?

"What time are you heading over?" I asked, pouring a glass of orange juice.

"Andre said five," Gavin slurred through a mouthful, milk dribbling down his chin. He wiped it away with the back of his hand.

I caught Colton's eye, and he watched me wistfully.

Today was the Saratoga Strings' luncheon. So while Colton was dressed in a handsome button-up and matching Calvin Klein dress pants, I was wearing my favorite red dress with the sweetheart neckline. Colton couldn't tear his eyes away from it.

"Sounds good, Gav," I said, patting my son on the back. "Have fun."

"I think we're gonna have fun tonight, too, right?" Colton asked.

"What're you guys doing?" Gavin wondered.

I opened my mouth to answer, but Colton beat me to it.

"We're going to play board games all night long," he insisted.

I covered my mouth to stifle a laugh.

"Board games?" Gavin made a face. "That's boring!"

"Oh, trust me. It's the opposite of boring."

He turned to grab his coffee cup and winked at me. I swallowed my laughter and cleared my throat.

"If you're done, buddy, put your bowl in the dishwasher and go brush your teeth. The bus will be here soon."

Gavin grunted. "Andre and I will have *way* more fun than you guys."

When he left the kitchen, Colton and I burst out laughing.

That night, after Gavin was safely at Andre's house, Colton and I cracked open a bottle of wine and sat on the couch, joking around like two lovesick teenagers.

"I kid you not, Gail. The basketball came out of nowhere. *Bam!*" He slapped his forehead. "Hit me right in the freaking face. I'm telling you I couldn't see straight for a week and a half!"

I giggled at his reenactment.

"It made my sophomore year at Penn State very interesting. I'll tell you that." He snorted. "I'm just lucky my friend Levi was there to drive me to Urgent Care."

We lost all track of time. Talking with him was like walking on air. It made me feel like I was floating into the atmosphere and getting ready to dissolve into a million colorful pieces. The wine helped.

When our laughter faded away, I leaned back into the couch. "This still blows my mind."

"What does?" he asked.

"This." I gestured between the two of us. "You. I feel like...this is just a dream or something. I never thought you'd come back to me."

Colton's eyes dropped to the carpet. "Me either honestly. I still have moments where I feel like I'm about to fall apart. Like if I shut my eyes, I'll wake up at my dad's house, and he'll be standing over me with his belt. Or...if I get behind the wheel, some dumbass is gonna total my car and kill me." He swallowed and stared into the bottom of his wine glass.

"One time, Beverly had a party in college, and I got so high, I blacked out. I don't remember what I did or...what I said. But I woke up the next morning in the upstairs bathroom with my head on the side of the bathtub. There was some random girl next to me and prescription bottles were everywhere—"

He choked on his voice, and I placed a steady hand on his shoulder. Beverly had been his girlfriend in college, but even as an adult, she walked around like there was a spotlight constantly dangling above her head. I hadn't seen her in two years, not since the day of Colton's car accident. But truthfully, if I ever saw her again, it would be too soon. Colton jumped at my touch, and his body tensed for a moment before he cleared his throat.

"I've almost died like, four times, Gail," he said hollowly. "And it scares the *hell* out of me t—to think about what might've happened all those times." He drew a shaky breath. "But...when I'm with you, all of that darkness disappears. I'm me again. Does that make sense?"

"Yeah, of course."

"I like who I am with you. You have a way of bringing out the best in me, and I've never found that in anyone else."

I recognized the desire in his face. His eyes brushed longingly over my body, and he leaned toward me, seemingly under an invisible magnetic force. I reached for him, craving that electricity. Our fingers intertwined, his warm ones thawing my cold ones. And then my heart was pounding again.

Colton had taken my virginity while we were in college, and back then, his movements were calculated and soft. Now, his lips were impatient. He kissed me hungrily, and I returned the favor. I tugged at his shirt until he removed it, and when he pressed his body against mine, a moan slipped from my lips. This deep, delectable, heavenly connection was the best feeling in the world. Having Colton's strong arms encircle my waist was enough to make me surrender.

In one swift motion, he scooped me up off the couch and raced for the stairs. I had to laugh at his haste because for a split second, it felt like we were teenagers again.

He carried me to the bed, and I realized that clothes were disappearing from my body one by one. I pulled Colton back to me and kissed him feverishly, feeling my head start to swim at his closeness.

In every kiss, every motion, there was a promise of forever. Every time my name rolled off his lips and his off mine, we were saying, "You are my world. Don't ever leave again." He was the light and the darkness. He was all the chemical elements in one form. He was a beautiful mixture of fire and water. He was a vibrant rainbow with each color in stunning clarity. These sheets were our oasis, and he was the love of my life.

The tiny clinking noise could have easily been a part of my dream. My eyes twitched once or twice and then relaxed when the silence resumed.

CRASH!

I jerked awake and sat up in bed with my heart flattened against my ribcage. It was quiet again, the silence thick and glaring. My breath was clenched between my teeth. Seconds later, something else shattered on the floor downstairs.

Colton shot up, his hands desperately clasping at the sheets. He was drenched in sweat and barely breathing.

"Colton," I hissed.

His eyes snapped to mine. That was when another crack resounded through the house. Both of our heads whipped toward the door.

"Someone's in the house," Colton muttered. I had never heard his voice so raspy. He said it under his breath like he was talking more to himself than me.

"Hold on." I caught his arm as he swung his legs out of the bed. "What if it's..."

I was about to say Gavin when I realized that Andre's mom would have called me if there was a problem. Gavin would not run home and take a baseball bat to every valuable thing we owned downstairs (that was what it sounded like). Another crash made me flinch out of my skin. Colton shook my arm off and stood up.

The weight of the situation hit me like a brick. It was a fear I had never experienced before: gut-wrenching and cold. Fight for your life.

Colton grabbed the lamp off the bedside table. He held it up like a weapon, but it looked so awkward and bulbous. *Was he going down there?*

"Colton," I whispered.

He must have seen the frozen terror in my eyes becaues he gestured to my phone. "Call 911."

"You're not leaving this room," I insisted, crawling to the edge of the bed on four numb limbs.

He swallowed. "Abigail, if someone is in our house, I'm not going to let them walk away without broken bones."

My stomach roiled, and I fought the urge to vomit right there on the carpet. Rustling and heavy footsteps sounded from some-where downstairs. I gnawed on my lower lip as Colton slowly opened our bedroom door. The hallway was dark, save for the tiny night light at the top of the steps, and Colton stepped out to peek over the balcony. For a moment, we drowned in dead silence until his eyebrows furrowed. I started to cry when he pressed a finger to his lips and moved toward the stairs, the lamp clutched tightly in his grasp. My body was on fire; every nerve ending was trembling in fear. As soon as he reached the bottom step unscathed, I sprinted quietly back to our room and pulled my phone out of the charger. I shut myself in the bathroom and dialed 911.

"Are you in a safe location?" the operator asked after I sobbed through an explanation.

"I am but my boyfriend isn't." I was shaking so hard, even my words sounded wobbly. "Please hurry."

"Help is on its way, ma'am."

I brought the phone away from my ear when I realized it had been too quiet for an unnatural amount of time. My house was fairly large, but not large enough to where Colton wouldn't have encountered the intruder by now, and that was sure to cause a ruckus.

"Please hurry," I said again and then turned the volume down on my phone.

Too quiet. Way too quiet. Sweat trickled down my skin despite the fact that I was only wearing a loose T-shirt and under-wear. And it was freezing outside. I moved on Jell-O legs toward the bathroom door and inched it open to find my bedroom completely empty. No sounds resonated from downstairs at all. My heart pounded so hard, it hurt, and yet I tiptoed toward the hallway anyway. Exiting my bedroom was like easing myself into a bath of ice-cold water. My spine turned to liquid.

The bottom of the stairs looked like a pitch-black abyss.

There was no way Colton would have been able to see down there. I needed to do something. Thinking quickly, I retrieved the spare flashlight I kept on a small desk at the overlook.

I pressed the flashlight to my chest, the coldness seeping into my skin and raising goosebumps on my arms and legs. I started down the stairs. Finally, my feet touched hardwood floor, and my entire body became an ice cube. I tried to squint into the darkness. Moonlight crept in through the blinds, but it was too slim and only illuminated small slivers of the floor. I considered whispering for Colton, but I didn't know where he was, and I didn't want to attract someone else. I took one step forward, blinking hard to see my surroundings. My toe nudged something hard, and I realized it was the edge of the couch. Shaking head to toe, I clicked the flashlight on and what I saw electrified my body raw.

Picture frames, glass vases, books, and candles littered the floor. Flowers were crushed and smeared. Our flatscreen was smashed through, sporting a spider web of cracked glass. Blankets were strewn across the couch and on the ground. Coasters dotted the floor. My mouth was a dry desert. My jaw practically unhinged in shock. And then I remembered the hundreds of dollars of rainy-day money we kept in a cookie jar on the counter. I turned and sprinted toward the kitchen until my foot slammed down on something sharp, and I yelped in pain. I lost my balance and fell straight onto the floor, banging my head during the collision. When the stars vanished from my vision, I noticed a tall, dark figure looming over me. My heart leapt into my throat.

"Don't move," the stranger said in a harsh baritone.

I'd dropped my flashlight when I fell, so I could hardly see the man's face, but when something cold pressed my cheek in and I heard the heart-stopping cock of a gun, I screamed.

"Abigail!"

The gun pulled away from my face as the intruder spun around fast enough to dodge Colton's swinging lamp. More glass shattered in the near distance, and I screeched, crawling for safety behind the bookcase. A stabbing pain attacked my foot. I felt down around my heel and sliced my fingers on the glass caught in my skin.

A gunshot exploded.

"Colton!" I screeched.

I burst out from behind the bookcase and spotted two figures wrestling in the living room. One threw a punch that the other avoided, and then they crashed down on top of the coffee table. It was a horrific symphony of grunts and snarls. Despite the searing pain shooting up my foot, I sprinted to the kitchen for a knife. When I returned, Colton had the robber in a choke hold against the wall. I could tell by the silhouettes — the intruder was taller, yet Colton had him sputtering for air. I blinked rapidly, wondering where the gun had gone.

I gripped the knife hard as the stranger kneed Colton in the gut and escaped his grasp. But just as he was about to attack Colton, sirens wailed in the near distance and blue and red lights flashed outside the windows. The intruder tensed and turned toward me. I could just barely make out the glint in his murderous eyes. He rushed toward me, but before I could slice him with the knife, he shoved me against the wall and sprinted through the back door.

Everything was murky then: the front door opening, the cops swarming through the house, Colton taking my with an expression like he was scared sick. He asked me something, but I couldn't hear it.

My lips moved, and it took me a whole minute to realize I was muttering, "My foot. It's my foot."

"This might pinch a little bit," someone said. It echoed in my ears, and I felt like my brain was floating in the ocean. Until an intensely sharp pain streaked through my foot.

I choked back a scream as the sharpness spread through my skin like an untamed wildfire. At one point, I bit down through my lip and instantly tasted the gush of blood.

"Okay, all done," the voice assured me. I realized then that she was a paramedic, and the tweezers in her hands were for the glass in my foot. She wrapped my foot in gauze, and I winced again.

The lights were on now, so I could see her face clearly, and she looked to be about my age with fiery red hair and porcelain, blush-stained cheeks. Once she was done with my foot, she moved to my arm, and I grunted when she pulled glass from it.

"I'm sorry," she murmured. I couldn't tell if she was apologizing for the pain or that my house had just been robbed or that I'd been traumatized beyond belief.

She cleaned the wounds on my arm and my face until they were bandaged up.

"Where's Colton?" I asked in a shaky voice.

"I'm here, Gail," he said from across the room.

Even from here, I could see the bruise blossoming around his right eye, the gash stretching down his arm, and the blood smattering his cheek. A paramedic was tending to him as well.

I suddenly remembered the gunshot and sat bolt upright. "Were you shot? Was he shot?" I demanded from the paramedic, eyes bulging, voice hoarse. "Were—"

"No, Gail." Colton shook his head slowly.

A cop stepped between us. "Miss Ferr," he said calmly, pressing his hands against his hips. "My name is Officer Cowen. Good news first: our men chased down the suspect and took him into custody."

My heart swelled with relief.

"It seems that as Mr. Reeves here was fighting him off, the guy dropped his gun. We already packed it away for evidence. It's just lucky neither of you were killed."

A noise startled me, and I spun around to see two other cops photographing a bullet hole lodged in the door to the den. I covered my mouth to keep the vomit from boiling up my throat.

"Very lucky indeed," Officer Cowen insisted. "Unfortunately, the bad news is, well..." He gestured around the living room at the mess of destroyed household items. Tears set my eyes on fire. "I'm so incredibly sorry."

I didn't even know what to say. I just stared blankly at the mess, lips quivering in disbelief. *What just happened? Did that really just happen?* No matter how hard I tried, I couldn't stop thinking about the cold barrel of that gun pressed to my cheek. I could've been dead; he could have blown my head off.

My voice was lodged in my throat like a golf ball. I just sat there, sputtering, not forming any coherent speech. And I must have been shaking, too, because the paramedic placed a steady hand on my shoulder.

"Thank you for your help," Colton said. His voice was more like a wheeze, completely void of energy.

I glanced over at him just in time to see a tear ooze down his black and blue, bloodied face. And then I started to cry, too, because for the first time ever, I was sure I finally felt a small amount of the extensive fear he'd felt his whole life.

Chapter Five

SARATOGA SPRINGS, NY

I t's okay. Take your time."

I sat in the teal polyester armchair, picking at my cuticles like I had a serious vendetta against them. My hands were shaking, but I tried my best to hide it. Gianna's eyes still flickered down to my hands despite my best efforts.

I forced myself to talk. "I just...don't understand how something like this could happen. Our neighborhood is like one of the safest—" *Ouch!* One of my hangnails yanked free, splintering pain through my finger. Gianna looked down at my hands again, so I folded them together in my lap and cleared my throat. When I spoke again, my voice shuddered. "I'm scared now."

Gianna nodded sympathetically. That was one of the many things I liked about her. She didn't criticize *or* pity.

She had been my therapist now for a little over a month, and at least three times a session, she tried to persuade me to talk about the robbery. Tried to get me to recount what happened and assign names to the overwhelming feelings that were constricting my brain. But even after all these weeks, the words still fell flat on my tongue. I could only repeat how scared I was—for my son, myself, Colton. And I still felt that gun pressed to my cheek every day. That wasn't really something I could just spit out and dissect.

"How are the house house repairs going?" Gianna tried.

"We saved everything that *could* be saved," I answered. "We had to cough up about three hundred bucks to get a new tv. Had to buy all new candles and coasters. The sliding glass door needed to be replaced 'cause he...broke through it." I swallowed and started picking at my cuticles again. "The picture frames off the mantle were destroyed, but the pictures were okay. Thank God."

"That's certainly something to be thankful for. How do you feel now that the repairs are made?"

I shook my head and kept my eyes glued to the floral carpet at my feet. "I–I can't even sit on the couch without thinking about..."

The problem wasn't so much that I couldn't name my feelings; it was more that I didn't *want* to name them. One moment I was remembering the intimidating shadow of the intruder and then I was shaking, which led to the realization that our home invasion was more like a cherry on the cake for Colton's PTSD, and I felt stupid for sitting in a shrink's office trying to battle my *own* hysteria when *he* was probably having a panic attack *right now*—

"Gail."

My eyes locked with Gianna's, and she raised a concerned eyebrow. I must've looked ready to explode because she sighed and set her clipboard on the desk beside her chair.

"Gail," she said again, leaning toward me, "no one is forcing you to do anything. What happened to you and your partner is scary and unfair." She ticked the adjectives off her fingers. "It is in your right to feel upset, and it's normal to not know what to say."

"It's Colton," I whispered. Another hangnail yanked free.

Gianna blinked. "Your partner."

"Yes."

I felt the dam puncture, and I spilled my guts in a rush, explaining everything from Colton's abuse to the way he held his bruised knuckles to his face the night of the break-in and cried. When I finished, Gianna nodded with an empathetic look in her eyes.

"And now I'm scared because...I just got him back, and I love him beyond words, but I don't know what to do. I feel like his whole life is just bad luck." My fingers were a bloody mess by now.

Gianna released a sigh like she'd been holding it in for sometime. "What about you though?"

I recoiled immediately, rolling my eyes and shaking my head. "It has nothing to do with me."

"It has everything to do with you," she countered slowly. "It seems like you've been suffering right along with him. When was the last time you checked in on your *own* mental health?" She gestured to my fingers.

"I'm fine," I insisted.

"Abigail. If you don't help yourself, how are you ever going to help him?"

The statement managed to sew my lips shut.

"Unfortunately, we're out of time for today, but I want to give you something. Consider it a worthwhile homework assignment." She fished around in her file cabinet for a moment before retrieving a piece of paper and handing it to me. "It's a check-in with tools to help you become more aware of your emotions."

I stared at the sheet numbly. "Gianna, I'm thirty-years-old. I think I can get a handle on my emotions."

She shrugged. "Maybe. But just because you're an adult doesn't mean you have to have everything figured out." She smiled at me then and clicked her pen. "I'd like to see you back next week."

Gavin pushed his plate away, scraping at the silence in the kitchen.

I blew a strand of hair out of my face and looked up at him. "What's wrong?"

"I don't like casserole," he whined, jutting his lower lip out.

"It's your dinner. Eat it."

"Nooo."

He knew something had happened, but he didn't quite understand when Colton explained the situation. My son was still a kid. To him, the world was a playground. Villains only existed in the movies and in his comic books. So when I cracked down on his time spent outside and away from the house, he became fussy. It had been like this all week.

"Gavin," I said, frustration boiling under my tone. "I clean up after you, I help you with your homework, I read to you every night, and I do a hundred other things for you before I even have time to do anything for myself. So, the least you could do is eat the dinner I cook for you."

"You didn't let me go to Andre's today."

My fork came down, crashing loudly against my glass plate. Colton touched my arm, a warning.

Yes, my son was innocent. Intruders and cold guns and thousands of dollars in house repairs did not exist to him. But his innocence, his *life*, was what I had to protect. He was the most important person in the world to me. I would not live with myself if something ever happened to him. He just didn't understand that yet.

"I told you that I want you home earlier now," I said.

"But why?" Gavin pushed.

"So that you're safe."

"But I'm okay, Mommy!"

I swallowed loudly. My fingers were starting to tremble. "Eat your dinner please."

"Nooo!"

My anxiety breached. "Then go to your room! God! There are

kids your age who are starving, Gavin! Do you understand that? They're *starving*. Hungry. You don't understand how lucky you are."

Gavin's face turned pink in an instant. His wide blue eyes filled with a mixture of confusion and sadness. He leapt off his chair and bounded up the stairs. Seconds later, his door closed—a bullet to my heart.

Colton cocked his head at me in disbelief. I spooned through the casserole instead of meeting his eyes. My jaw was a tensed wire.

"What the hell was that?" Colton asked, flashing his palms at me.

"He doesn't want to eat, then he doesn't eat," I mumbled.

"Abigail, the kid is six-years-old. You cannot take your anger out on him."

"I'm not! All I ask is that he comes home after school. That is not a big ask."

"It was here, Gail," Colton says, grilling me with those sharp green eyes. "The asshole broke in *here*! Last time I checked, Gavin was a lot safer at Andre's!"

I pressed my hands to my face, feeling my heart start to kick at my ribcage. I didn't want to have this conversation. I didn't want the memories shoved back into my skull.

"Stop."

"It's the truth," Colton said.

"How are you so calm?" I demanded, slamming my palms down on the table. "We were almost killed in the living room!"

Colton scoffed. "How's it feel to finally join the club?"

"You are unbelievable!" I yelled. "You walk around like you have everything under control when you're literally traumatized on the inside!"

"Maybe I'm just used to it!" he hissed.

"Do you hear how *fucked up* that sounds? *Do you hear it!*" I gestured maniacally to my own ears.

"I didn't ask for this, Gail!"

"I didn't ask for it either!"

Colton leaned forward. "It is not my fault he chose *this* house to break into!"

"I'm worried for my son's life! It makes me nauseous, Colton, thinking about what could've happened that night."

"Stop thinking about what *could've* happened and start being grateful you're alive."

"Why aren't you scared?"

"I *am* scared!" he bellowed, arching his eyebrows for emphasis.

This conversation was too much. It was too heavy, dripping down over my body like a poisonous, foul-smelling oil. It burned. I felt sick to my stomach. I stood up and snatched my plate off the table.

"Don't walk away," Colton said. "We need to talk about it."

I dropped my plate in the sink. "I can't."

"They caught the guy, Gail," he reasoned, dragging a hand down his face. "You need to accept what is and try to heal."

"What do you want me to say?"

"I want you to open up to me," he said. "Tell me what you're feeling. I know it's scary, but if we aren't on the same team, it'll be harder."

I shook my head. All I could feel was that damn gun pressed against my cheek, the barrel promising instant death. Instant separation from everything I loved. Worst of all, from Gavin. He didn't even know his real father. He couldn't lose his mother.

"I can't." My voice was barely audible.

I stormed out of the kitchen and locked myself in the bathroom but not before my breath got locked in my throat. I gripped the counter and forgot how to breathe. My heart felt like a jackhammer hyped up on crack, and for a split second, I wondered if I was having a heart attack. I didn't know what to do. *All I could think about* was that tall shadow looming over me in the living room. The freezing barrel of the gun pressing right into the hollow of my cheek. The *sound* when he clicked it—

My face was turning a dangerous hue of red. I pressed a shaking hand to the faucet and splashed cold water on my face eight times before my airways decided to open the tiniest bit. I dropped to my knees and sucked air into my lungs. My chest actually *hurt* from how fast my heart was beating. I didn't know how long I sat there gasping, but when I finally mustered the strength to stand back up, my flustered reflection told me I had developed a serious problem.

You're losing it, Gail.

My phone vibrated in my pocket. It was my father checking in on me for about the hundredth time today. When we told him what happened, he burst into tears right in front of us. He had crushed me in his arms, thanking God with every breath that we were okay.

"Thank you for saving my daughter," he had told Colton. Instead of a handshake, he'd hugged him. I could have been thrilled about that if my thoughts hadn't been swarming with the fresh trauma of a house invasion.

I didn't have the strength to respond to my dad right now. Physically, yes, we were okay. Emotionally, I was scarred beyond words.

～

I couldn't stop bouncing my leg. The lights in here were too bright; the voices were too loud. And for the first time in my entire life, my violin felt foreign in my hands.

Veronica leaned forward in her seat, staring at me with bulging eyes. "Are you all right, Gail? You look like you're going to be sick."

"Good afternoon, ladies and gents!" Tod Niles called before I could form an answer. He looked especially chipper this morning, sporting a gleaming smile.

I'd known Tod for two and a half years now. Ever since I moved back to Saratoga Springs and joined his orchestra, he had pushed me with music I'd never played before and opened his arms to each and every one of us. This was home. But it didn't feel safe right now.

"I hope everyone had a nice month off for the holidays and new year. I'm always thrilled to be back though, you know?" He smiled at Lester, the cello player who was as much a fossil as the instrument he played. Lester grinned in return. "Plus I'm very excited because now we get to start prepping for the spring concert. You know what that means...movie scores!"

"Will this be *Star Wars* 2.0?" Calvin Demono asked. A few bows even jabbed the sky in favor of his statement.

I squeezed my clammy hands together.

"That performance was pretty incredible," Tod mused. "But I never do repeats."

"Okay," Seth whispered from the row behind me, "either I'm hallucinating or you're literally shaking. What's wrong, Gail?"

"Can I get a drum roll please?" Tod declared as he pressed a stack of papers to his chest.

Sixty-five bows tapped excitedly against the music stands, and to the ordinary ear, it would've sounded like a crescendo of cheerfulness. But to me, it sounded like glass vases dropping, picture frames cracking, a gun clicking against my face—

I stood up and made a beeline for the doors just as Tod revealed the score we would be playing. Excited shouts exploded from the room, but I was still able to hear Tod call my name before the doors shut behind me. The bathroom was down the hall, and I sprinted like I was in a track race going for gold in the 100 meter dash. By the time I shoved my way into a stall, the acrid taste of vomit was already hot on my tongue.

Not a full minute later, the door banged open.

"She's in here!" Veronica yelled.

Two pairs of footsteps clapped against the tile as they raced down the row of stalls.

"Gail, are you okay?" Seth demanded.

I was hunched over, pressing my palms against my knees, and breathing like a dog who was exhausted from the heat. Thank God I'd worn my hair in a bun today; rinsing puke out of my ends didn't sound very appealing. Then again, nothing sounded appealing right now.

"Gail?" Veronica urged.

I inhaled slowly through my nose and immediately wished I hadn't because of the putrid vomit smell. I flushed the toilet and opened the stall door.

"Oh, you look like hell," Seth muttered. "Was it something you ate?"

I shook my head. "No, it's—"

I froze when I caught a glimpse of myself in the mirror. My skin was practically glowing green.

This was too much.

As if I hadn't embarrassed myself enough, I started to cry. Veronica immediately wrapped her arms around me.

"What's bothering you, Gail?" she asked, expertly keeping anxiety out of her voice. "Is it still about the break in?"

I didn't know why, but the fact that she even had to ask that annoyed me.

"Yes!" I tried to hold most of it in, but I couldn't help the jerking of my shoulders or the tiny squeaking sobs that escaped my lips. "I've been going to therapy and doing everything Gianna says! I've even followed the emotion check-in homework she gave me." I paused to hiccup. "Why does it still get to me?"

Seth put a hand on my shoulder, and I'd never seen him look so worried in all the time I'd known him. "You're not a robot. Healing takes time."

"Colton seems fine," I muttered. "Well, he *acts* like he's fine.

We sort of had a fight about it the other night." More tears leaked down my cheeks.

Veronica stepped back to look into my eyes. "Maybe he fakes it because it's the only way he knows how to heal. Everyone's different. You went through something extremely traumatic, Gail. It's normal to feel anxious."

"I just want things to go back to the way they were. I don't want to be scared to sit in my own damn house!"

"I know, I know," Veronica murmured.

A few seconds dragged by, and then Seth shrugged. "Have you considered medication?"

I scoffed. "What, taking a pill to make me numb?"

"It wouldn't make you numb," he disagreed. "It would treat your feelings."

"But not the causes," I countered.

"No, but that's what therapy is for," Veronica jumped in. "Take the medication to help you calm down, stay in therapy to learn how to live and cope."

I narrowed my eyes skeptically. I'd never taken medication in my life—not even when I was in college and suicidal. I learned to adapt then, and I could learn to adapt now.

"I shouldn't have to take a pill for something my body should be able to do naturally."

Veronica and Seth looked at each other, and I couldn't decipher what unspoken message flowed between them.

"Sure," Seth said. "A cancer patient shouldn't have to take medication for something their body should be able to do naturally either."

I stared at him, knowing I'd just lost the debate entirely. Because *dammit*, he was right. A cancer patient *couldn't* do that. And neither could I.

I ran two fingers under my eyes, drying away the last of my tears. "Okay fine. I'll talk to Gianna about it."

Veronica hugged me again. "Good."

After a moment, I remembered the rest of the orchestra's excitement.

"What score are we playing?"

"*Pirates of the Caribbean.*" Seth's smile was a mile wide.

"Colton will love that," I said weakly. "It was one of his favorite movies when we were younger."

When my hands finally stopped shaking, I left the bathroom with my friends and kept my eyes glued to the carpet. I didn't know what was going on with me, but the way it made me act was embarrassing. Why couldn't I, as a fully grown woman, not keep it together? I felt my stomach squeeze at the thought of what my peers would think of me now, but by some miracle, no one even looked up when we reentered the playing hall. They were all happily plucking away at our new music.

Tod raised his eyebrows at me with clear concern written in his wrinkled features. I nodded and waved the matter away with a forced smile. I didn't need my conductor worrying about my mental health, too. If I was going to take the initiative to start medication, then I would do it quietly so that I could heal in peace.

～

Gianna scribbled something into her notebook. "And when was the last time you had a nightmare?"

"Last night," I muttered.

That was nothing new; I'd been waking up in a pool of my own sweat almost every night for weeks now. Colton hardly slept either, but I doubted that my jerking awake at three am really made him feel any less alone.

"How's your son?"

"He's doing well."

I had tried extremely hard to lessen the bite in my tone when he was around now. Colton was right. He was just a kid.

He still needed to be a kid. As long as he was safe, nothing else mattered.

"Well, that's great." Gianna nodded.

For the first time in all the weeks since I had started therapy, *I* was the one to break the silence.

"I want to try medication."

Gianna stopped writing and looked up at me over the rim of her glasses. Her lips parted like she was about to say something, but instead, she exhaled and sat back in her armchair.

"I'm curious as to why you changed your mind."

I swallowed the golf ball lodged in my throat. "I think maybe if...medication treats my symptoms, I can treat the causes here with you."

Her smile bloomed out of nowhere, curling upward until her lips couldn't stretch anymore. "That right there was probably the bravest thing I've heard you say. You should be proud of yourself, Abigail. Just being here and having the guts to admit that is half the battle." She wrote something on a sticky note. "Of course, I'm not a medical doctor, so I can't prescribe you medication. I suggest doing some research and talking with your doctor. She'll probably prescribe some type of SSRI."

I nodded again. "I'm just ready to feel better."

I noticed then how much I liked her smile. It brightened her heart-shaped face like the sun coming out from behind the clouds. "Believe me, Gail. You're closer than you think."

Colton strode into the living room and clicked on the fireplace. Then he slumped into one of the chairs adjacent to the couch and tilted his head both ways until his neck cracked. The loud pops made me clench my jaw because I hated when he cracked his neck, and quite frankly, we weren't on the best of terms right now anyway. Ever since our talk in the kitchen, we'd hardly said anything to each other besides the monotone *Good morning. How was work? Did Gavin eat? Good night.* Honestly, it was sad. And I wasn't in the mood to play the blame game right now. I was just tired.

I stared at him out of the corner of my eye, watching how he scrolled through his phone with a listless expression. Anyone else would have thought he looked bored, but I could spot the twitch in his jaw like it was a glowing sign on the highway. He knew I was watching him. This was how we worked.

"Colton," I said, taking a sledgehammer to the silence.

He looked at me instantly, like he'd been expecting me to say his name.

"The doctor prescribed me Sertraline."

"Sertraline." He repeated. "I took that back in college."

"What was it like?"

He shrugged. "It worked pretty well. I didn't really have side effects at all. But I know it can increase risk of suicidal thoughts."

An ice cube sliced through my torso.

I didn't like to relive those terrifying months in college when I was thinking about ending my life. As far as I'd come since then, the memories still made me feel like a walking bulls-eye for my anxiety. It took years of journaling and counting blessings to get that scary underlying desire to go away. I never wanted it to come back. But I didn't want to suffer in fear anymore either.

"It's not guaranteed," I reasoned.

Colton walked over to the couch and sat beside me, placing his hands on my shoulders. The gesture was completely unexpected, and I flinched under his grip even though his hands were soft. In fact, he was hardly touching me.

"If you feel anything while you're on that medication, and I mean *anything*," *If you start to consider again,* his eyes screamed, "you tell me, and you're off that pill."

We stared into each other's souls. His hands never left my shoulders. I was the one to lean in first.

The kiss was desperate, almost selfish, as if we'd been secretly craving a moment like this for days. When I pulled away, his gold-green eyes gave my stomach goosebumps. It didn't matter how often I looked into them; they always made my heart stutter.

"I miss you." The words rolled off my tongue like a breath.

"Pretty sure I miss you more."

"What's for dinner?" Gavin asked from the hallway.

We jumped six feet apart, and Colton ran a hand through his hair. I cleared my throat.

"Leftovers, buddy. Chicken and green beans."

Gavin's eyes flickered between us for at least five seconds before he nodded and bolted up the stairs.

"Where are you going?" I called.

"To get my new action figure! Andre's letting me have it for the day! I wanna show you!"

Colton chuckled and planted a kiss on my forehead. Sitting there in his arms, I felt safer than I'd felt in weeks.

"We're gonna be okay," he whispered, caressing my arm to ease the erratic beat of my heart.

"Yeah." I exhaled. "I think we will be."

⁓

Two months later, during a monstrous yet soothing April rainstorm, I sat staring at a picture of Erica and her husband Spencer. Their smiles were like the sun and moon with matching pairs of dimples for each. His arms encircled her waist so perfectly; his chin fit just right on her shoulder. They were literally the definition of soulmates, so the invitation really shouldn't have been a surprise at all.

I dropped a Sertraline tablet on my tongue and swallowed it down with lemonade.

"What're you looking at?" Colton asked, glancing over from the sink where he was scrubbing sauce off a pan.

I stared at the picture second longer and then sighed. "Baby shower. Erica's pregnant."

Colton dried his hands on a dish towel and took the photo from me. "Wow. That's amazing."

I sank my teeth into my lower lip and placed my chin in my hand. Colton noticed my expression.

"What're you thinking?"

At first, I was planning to lie and say nothing, but Gianna would've had my head for that. I tried to think back through the paper she'd given me with all the tools for being more aware of my emotions. One bullet point was to speak my mind, even if the words came out in a tangled knot.

"I'm thinking about how normal their lives are. I mean, they got married. She's a graphic designer; he's a cardiologist. They're having a baby."

Colton nodded. "So?"

"Doesn't it make you wonder about our lives? Where we'd be right now if none of the shit ever happened? Like if your dad hadn't hurt you and the intruder chose another house?"

Something shimmered in Colton's eyes. "We aren't normal, no."

The simplicity of his words made me want to itch my skin off. It was like he understood exactly what he'd said, but the weight of it didn't hold any merit in his brain. Was he *that* desensitized?

"Colton, you freak me out sometimes," I muttered.

"Is that because I'm not a cardiologist who wears designer clothing?"

That made me smile.

"No." I reached for his hand and threaded our fingers. "It's because we really are magnets for trouble."

Colton sighed and stared down at our hands. "I wish I could give you normalcy and peace."

His face had obviously healed by now, but I could still visualize all the bruises. They were like invisible words that would show up if I shined the right light on them. I was the only one who knew they were there.

"Even though we're magnets for trouble," I said, "losing you for real would hurt a hundred times worse than all the bullshit we could experience in this life."

"For the record, a lot of things scare me, too." He inhaled, and his chest inflated like a balloon. "I always thought that when I got older, all my fears would disappear. Turns out, life is just one big scare-fest."

I smiled again and kissed his knuckles. "What doesn't kill you makes you stronger, right?"

"Funny you should say that."

"Why?"

He looked at me. *Really* looked at me. "Because thank God I survived. Otherwise, I wouldn't be able to say this." His smile was so soft. "Marry me."

My heart skidded to a stop. The world skidded to a stop. My mouth fell open.

"Life is one ugly, unfair jackass, but it's totally worth it because of you. And I know that I'll never find another girl who sees through me like you do. I understand it's a big ask because I'm a freaking magnet for trouble for literally *no* reason." When he stopped to laugh, I laughed, too, and blinked back the tears that were boiling in my eyes. "Life is clearly too short to waste time. So, Abigail Ferr...will you marry me?"

I wrapped my arms around him so fast, he staggered backward, and we almost toppled onto the floor. "Took you long enough to ask, dammit."

Chapter Six

MARCH, 2082

If this were a normal first day of spring, the sun would be glittering; the grass would be lush and green; the sidewalks would be filled with people walking their dogs and powering through runs and walking couples linked arm in arm. Instead, the ground was coated in two feet of snow.

Abigail glared out the window, watching the flurries twinkle and cascade down on the earth. She never liked snow. Everyone else would argue that it felt like they were living in a giant snow globe, which was true to some extent, but Abigail felt *trapped* in that snow globe.

Stupid groundhog, she thought with a grim expression. *Damn thing's a liar.*

"Look on the bright side, Mom," her daughter Aliana said an hour later during their phone call. "It gives you some more time to cozy up and write!"

"I would've liked to sit outside on the porch to write today." Abigail took a swig of orange juice and swallowed her Prozac pill.

She remembered when she used to take Sertraline for PTSD

in her thirties, and she remembered the glorious day when she felt well enough and was allowed to come off of it. But nearly fifty years later and following the heart-shattering death of someone she loved more than life, her psychiatrist was back to prescribing her pills.

"Your body reacts well with it," she remembered Doctor Breckbaker saying. "It's an SSRI. It'll help with the depression."

Abigail stared into her cup of orange juice now, frowning.

"The snow won't be there forever, Mom," Aliana replied, forcing Abigail back into the present moment.

"Easy for you to say. You live all the way in Miami."

A shuffling noise sounded through the phone.

" — to your grandmother." Aliana's voice came back at full volume. "Hold on, Mom, Kota's here. He just got back from college last night."

More shuffling and background noise, then: "Hi, Grandma."

Abigail instantly perked up. "Hey, sweetheart! How are you?"

"I'm good, I'm good. School's gettin' stressful, but you know how it is."

"You're not still coughing from the Pulmonem Fever, are you?"

"Nah. I was down bad for like a week, but I'm feeling better now."

"Good."

Abigail smiled. Hearing from her grandchildren was the most exciting part of her days now. She adored hearing their stories from college, watching them attempt some trendy ridiculous dance on social media, and listening to them talk about their love lives.

"You still dating that nice girl, Finnley?"

"Yep."

It was so obvious Kota was smiling just from the mention of her name. His voice always got smoother and higher when someone brought her up. They'd been dating for six months now, but Abigail knew it was bound to last longer than that. She hadn't seen her grandson this excited about a girl since his schoolboy crush on that famous actress back in 2068.

"Good," Abigail said. "I like her."

"Me, too." She heard his smile grow. "Anyway, are you still writing?"

Abigail turned away from the phone to cough into her elbow —loud, bellowing coughs that shook her body to the core. They hurt, and they made her throat feel like sandpaper. When the spell passed, she blinked a few times and brought the phone back to her ear.

"Yes." She cleared her throat. "Yes, I am. The letter's coming along beautifully."

There was a pause on Kota's end. "Grandma, are you okay?"

She took a sip of orange juice. "I'm fine, sweetheart. In fact, I turned the news off this morning and read a book instead, so I feel great."

Kota hesitated, and when he spoke again, his voice was guarded and cautious. "Greeaattt. Well, I gotta go. Finnley's gonna be here in ten minutes, and we're going out to lunch."

"Have fun. I love you, sweetheart."

If Abigail could talk with her grandchildren all day, she would jump at the chance in a heartbeat.

"Love you, too, Grandma."

The phone was handed to someone else.

"Okay, Mom," Aliana said. "Are you just going to for the rest of the day?"

"What else do I do?" Abigail said through a rasping laugh.

Aliana could only chuckle, but it seemed forced. "Did you ever talk to the doctor about your coughing?"

"Mhm. Went about a month ago. She told me to hydrate and stay aware of it."

"Maybe you should go again. You've been coughing a lot more."

"My next appointment isn't until July. They want to get me in for an EKG again."

"Are you having problems?"

Abigail shrugged though her daughter couldn't see. "Just some irregular beats every once in a while. Nothing serious." When Aliana didn't say anything, Abigail pushed the conversation along. "Oh, I forgot! I have to get going. Elijah and I are Face-Timing this afternoon to catch up."

"That's great! Tell him I said hi!"

"Will do, will do." Abigail looked at the stack of papers on the kitchen table and felt her heart swell eagerly. "Until he calls though, I've got some more writing to do."

Chapter Seven

SARATOGA SPRINGS, NY (2033)

August. It was my favorite month of the whole year. Lavender colored sunsets engulfed in a sweet, gentle heat. The remains of sunflowers blowing you kisses from the side of the road. Days spent journaling on beach towels, listening to Colton and Gavin splash around with each other in the pool. The two-diamond ring secured to my finger.

"One diamond for you and one for me," Colton had explained from down on one knee when he proposed for real. "Best friends and soul mates."

We spent the year planning the event: cake tasting, dress shopping, circling potential dates in our calendars, designing invitations. I was about to have the wedding of my dreams.

It was so different from the one I'd had with Evan. I had been entirely distant during that planning period that when the wedding actually arrived, it felt more like a lucid dream. *This* was so clearly a reality.

On the day of the ceremony, the church was adorned in gold. Muffled conversations and laughter drifted from the sanctuary and up the staircase to where I waited. My gown fanned out around me, pooling at my feet. The bouquet shook in my hands, but I wasn't nervous. I hadn't seen Colton all day, thanks to the bad luck that would prevail if I had, so now my heart was stampeding in all directions. Had it not been for the elegant heels I was wearing, I would have been bouncing around like a kid.

Speaking of kids.

"Gavin, sweetheart, come here," I called.

He turned and approached me with glowing cheeks. In his hand was the velvet pillow that held Colton's and my rings. When we'd asked him to be our ring bearer, he took the job with his chest puffed out in pride. Now, he looked nauseous. I knelt down to be eye-level with him, careful not to step on the skirt of my dress.

"You look so handsome," I complimented, straightening his tiny bowtie.

His wide blue eyes stayed trained on the rings. "I'm nervous, Mama."

"Don't be nervous," I said. "You'll be absolutely fine. And I'll be waiting right up there for you."

He nodded, and I brushed my hand across his cheek.

"You look pretty," he whispered back. "I think Colton will really like your dress."

I laughed and pulled him into my arms.

A gentle hand touched my shoulder. It was Dad. I had to giggle at how uncomfortable he looked in his tux with his graying hair combed back. Dad was a shorts and T-shirt kind of guy; dress clothing was not in his vocabulary. Fortunately, he was also good at setting his discomfort aside. He smiled down at me and then reached out to give Gavin a high five.

"It's time," he said, peering meaningfully into my eyes.

I squeezed my son's hand one last time and then stood up. Immediately, Erica and Cara swarmed around me to straighten the skirt once again, and Erica adjusted my veil.

"You know," Dad said as he led me to the edge of the staircase. Music flowed from the sanctuary. "It's not every day that people marry their high school sweethearts. That's a rarity." He turned to face me. "But despite everything that happened between the two of you, I think you and Colton really were meant to be together."

My heart smiled. "Thanks, Dad."

He nodded and cleared his throat. "'Course, you know you can always come home. I mean, I'm not going anywhere. And even though you're marrying the boy you grew up with and it feels like you were just kids yesterday, you'll still always be my little girl."

"Always."

He planted a kiss on my forehead just before the music shifted, and I looped my arm through his.

Planning a wedding had turned me into something of a perfectionist. In the weeks leading up to the ceremony, my anxiety was through the clouds. I'd worked closely with Gianna on monitoring my emotions and behaviors: picking at my cuticles, snapping unintentionally in conversation, and sleeping restlessly. The fear of the break in and the memory of the intruder's gun was always fresh in my brain, but it was less of a tsunami now and more of a normal wave. Colton and I had been through so much. We deserved to be happy together.

Cara and Erica, my two beautiful bridesmaids, went ahead of me and then I was descending the staircase. The steps led into a tiny corridor, no bigger than a walk-in closet and the lights from the sanctuary beamed up ahead. I heard the pews creak as my loved ones rose to greet me, and the music swelled joyously. But it all disappeared the moment I entered the room. The people, the lovely string quartet, the bright lights—it all vanished. I'd locked eyes with Colton.

He was stunning.

The clean sharpness of his suit, the wave of his gelled hair, the clarity of his luminous eyes. My heart screamed for him and nearly towed me down the rest of the aisle. Colton skimmed my dress, and his eyes shimmered with tears. He even pressed a hand to his mouth in awe, and I would've done the same had my hands not been occupied elsewhere with the bouquet and my dad's elbow.

Finally, *finally*, I made it to the altar. My father kissed my forehead and then slid my hand into Colton's. At the touch of Colton's skin, my body set on fire. Electrical pulses sent every nerve ending ablaze, leaving me breathless. We held each other's gaze while his fingers enclosed around mine.

Pastor David greeted the church. "We are gathered here today to celebrate the union of Abigail Ferr and Colton Reeves."

Our names echoed off the church walls—a perfect combination of syllables. Through the ceremony, Colton gave my hand gentle squeezes of reassurance. We recited our own vows, and then my son was walking hastily down the aisle. He seemed to have calmed a bit, but he was still clenching the pillow like it was a full glass of water threatening to spill over. Chuckles rang out from the audience. I blew him a kiss while Colton swooped to take the rings, and more laughs sounded when the two of them fist bumped.

Colton turned to me and slowly slid the ring onto my finger. The sun rays pouring in through the windows touched the two diamonds and reflected the light, creating a silver kaleidoscope on the marble floor.

When Pastor David asked if I took Colton Reeves to be my lawfully wedded husband through all circumstances, the words "I do" slipped past my lips like a breath. I felt myself drowning in Colton's beautiful eyes, and I knew he was lost in mine.

We'd dreamt about this moment as kids. We had sat on his couch and discussed our would-be vows. Practiced the perfect angle to kiss so that the audience's hearts would melt. We had discussed every detail down to the style and make of my dress.

"Then I pronounce you husband and wife," Pastor David announced.

Seemingly in slow motion, we leaned forward, and if our teenage selves could've been there, they would have burst out of their seats to cheer wildly. They had been so young, so in love.

Our lips touched, and the world exploded into a gush of color and happiness. Our loved ones shouted and cheered at the top of their lungs. Colton smiled against my lips.

No amount of fantasizing as a young girl could have prepared me for that moment because getting to marry my first love was like returning home after a trip to Jupiter. I kissed him fiercely, feeling our hearts *finally* intertwined for good. This was passion. This was pure. This was love.

$\approx$

Our first dance was a series of uncomplicated steps and twirls, seeing as neither of us were exactly professional ballroom dancers. People cheered anyway.

Twenty minutes later, Erica stood at the microphone with a glass of champagne. Her husband Spencer was seated close by, holding their one-year-old daughter, Catrina.

"And I just feel like—" Erica stopped to drag a finger under her teary eyes. "I feel like I met you guys yesterday, and here you are. Married." Her lip quivered. "That's a romance if I've ever seen one."

A resounding agreement swept throughout the room, and Erica blew us a kiss before returning to her seat. She had given the final speech, and after listening to all the tear-jerking reactions to our marriage, I was more than ready to rest my head on Colton's shoulder. But then he stood up from his seat.

"What're you doing?" I asked.

"Giving a toast to my amazing wife."

When he accepted the microphone, people went nuts. Ashton

in particular, his best friend from high school, was going absolutely berserk. I had to laugh at that.

"Can we take a moment to admire my beautiful bride over there?" Colton gestured to me.

I smiled as people turned to me and hollered.

"It's an understatement to say that I got lucky to have Abigail in my life. When we were freshmen in high school, she saved me from a failing grade in English." Laughter filtered the silence. "When we were sophomores, she was the best girlfriend I ever had. Unfortunately by twenty, we were broken up, but the thought of her saved me from an addiction. At twenty-seven, her love was the only thing that kept me fighting for my life after a near-fatal car accident. And when we were thirty, I finally asked her to marry me."

More shouts, more whistling.

"I feel very undeserving of her love," Colton continued. "I mean, I was just a normal guy who happened to be partners with an angel in English class." He paused to smile. "My heart hasn't belonged to anyone since."

His words sank through my flesh and into my bloodstream, traveled through my many veins, and seeped straight into my heart. They left goosebumps on my skin like Colton just kissed my entire body.

His eyes were locked with mine as he spoke, and when he raised his glass, everyone copied him. "To the one I love...here's to now and forever."

A collective silence followed as everyone took a drink and then cheers erupted from the crowd.

"I love you," Colton mouthed to me with a gentle smile.

"I love you, too." The truth of it filled my eyes with fresh tears.

Ashton and the other groomsmen bombarded my husband, hollering and jumping on each other like teenage boys.

"Wow," Elijah said when he sat down and offered me a powdered brownie from the sweets table. "What a speech."

I nodded, unable to find the words to describe the joy I was feeling.

Elijah smiled at me warmly. "I guess everything does happen for a reason. I'm happy for you, Gail. You two really have something special. It's like magic. You don't see that every day."

I felt my cheeks turn scarlet. "Thanks. He's just..."

"Perfect?" Elijah suggested.

"Well, no one's perfect," I reasoned. "But Colton's pretty damn close."

"That's how I feel about Brie." His eyes strayed across the room, and when he spotted her, I could practically see his heart spark.

"Planning to propose anytime soon?" I wiggled my eyebrows.

"Trust me." He laughed. "You'll be one of the first people to know."

The sounds of laughter and conversation settled between us, and I peeked over at him. I was going to miss these talks with him. I would miss his calming presence. Sometimes I thought back to the night of the freshmen party at the Curtis Institute of Music and nearly felt sick at how much time had passed. How much we'd been through since the night we met. Sometimes the very concept of time scared me.

"What happens now?" I murmured.

He glanced at me and grinned. "Well, usually the bride and groom plan a honeymoon after the wedding. Any place in particular you've always wanted to visit?"

"Venice," I answered immediately.

As I said it, I felt a little twinge in my heart. I would have thought that after everything that happened with Evan, I wouldn't want anything to do with the Italian city since *he* had promised to take me there one day. But the dream could be resurrected, especially now that I had Colton with me.

"That'd be a nice place to get away," Elijah agreed wistfully.

"I guess I won't be seeing much of you anymore."

His eyes flickered back to mine. "Nah, you'll still see me. Can't just marry someone and get rid of me that easily, come on."

The remark was meant to make me laugh, but I would miss him and all my friends dearly. It was time to go our separate ways for a little while again. That was how life worked.

"We don't have the money for Venice yet," I said, "so we'll be around. Promise you'll come visit."

"I promise."

He even lifted his pinkie to swear.

"Hey, Elijah," Colton said as he approached us through the crowd.

Elijah looked up at Colton and they high-fived.

"I guess it's time I take Brie out for a dance," Elijah said. "She's been waiting all night." He flashed me his signature grin and then waltzed off toward his girlfriend.

Colton sat back down, and I immediately pressed into him. His rich cologne permeated the air, and I inhaled deeply.

"Gavin's really loving the dance floor," Colton murmured fondly.

I looked up to see my son jumping crazily to the bass of the music. He had even found a dance partner: the daughter of one of our friends from high school. They held hands and spun around in a circle so fast, I feared Gavin would topple over.

"Sheesh, today it's Ella's daughter, but tomorrow Gavin will be all grown up with an actual girlfriend."

Colton tightened his arms around me. "Let's not worry about that right now. He's having a good time. Just let him enjoy himself."

The reception carried long into the night. My husband and I sliced into the large, elegant cake and then spent the rest of the evening on the dance floor. Even though I had removed my heels hours ago, my feet were already calloused and sore.

"Don't worry," Colton whispered during a slow dance. "I'll carry you home."

"Such a gentleman." I laughed.

"You know me."

I caught Sandy's eye as she swayed with her new husband Sean not four feet away. Her smile made my heart melt.

"I know I've said this a hundred times, but I've really missed your mom," I said, turning my attention back to Colton.

"She's missed you," he replied. "She hasn't shut up about you since high school. Not that I minded."

I giggled, and he spun me in for a dip. Just as I spun into him, he stole a quick kiss.

"Take me to Venice," I murmured against his lips.

"Done."

I narrowed my eyes. "That was easy."

"I'll go anywhere as long as I'm with you," he answered with a content shrug.

The festivities gradually winded down as it got closer to midnight. Colton and I had to break our conversation several times to say goodbye to our guests.

"We have to save up for a trip to Italy," I continued eventually. "So let's start tomorrow."

Colton kissed me again, and there was a promise beneath his passion. "I'm on it."

Chapter Eight

SARATOGA SPRINGS, NY–VENICE, ITALY (2040)

By the time we finally had enough money for a trip to Venice, Gavin was fifteen and tall enough to look me straight in the eye. His deepening voice had been on a rollercoaster for the last year, and every time it cracked, I had to bite the inside of my cheek to keep from laughing and spare his reddening face.

A growth spurt was a growth spurt. Gavin could eat a whole horse and half the farm now if I let him, and then he burned it all off with an hour's jog around the neighborhood, which I was reluctant to allow at first. But over the years, our little slice of the community had returned to a quiet, kid-friendly environment—no potential intruders for miles. Still, I made Gavin turn his phone's location on while he was out.

He ran fast and often. Some nights I could hardly catch him from the time he set his dirty plate in the dishwasher to when he was tying his sneakers and bounding out the door.

"Do you want to try out for cross-country this year?" I asked him one evening after he got back.

"Nah." He stuffed a handful of Cheeze-Itz in his mouth and looked at me from across the kitchen. "I wanna keep playing soccer."

He'd been an offensive player in soccer for years, and as a freshman striker in high school, he'd already scored three goals this season. His coach had approached me after the last game and admitted that Gavin had some serious natural talent.

"I don't know where he gets it," I'd answered, scrutinizing my son from across the field.

"Well, if he keeps it up, I could see him starting for varsity as early as next season," the coach continued.

I repeated that to Gavin later, and he was euphoric for fifteen minutes straight until I sent him to finish his homework.

When my son wasn't jogging, or consuming all the food in sight, or kicking a soccer ball, he spent hours up in a treehouse at Andre's house.

"What do you think they're doing up there?" I muttered. I could see the treehouse from my own kitchen, and I swore it was staring back at me with batting eyelashes and an innocent grin.

Colton shook his head. "God only knows with teenage boys."

"*You* were a teenage boy once," I quipped.

He cleared his throat. "Exactly."

I didn't want to believe Gavin was growing up. I didn't want to believe fifteen years had passed since I was groaning in the hospital room and breaking Evan's hand.

Evan.

I also didn't want to believe that it had been fourteen and a half years since Evan had confessed to cheating and our marriage had crumbled like a castle of toothpicks. Fourteen years, and somehow, it still felt like yesterday—much like all the emotional trauma I'd experienced since then. Time was a very funny kind of medication, and Gavin was my time capsule.

Watching him get older was its own kind of poison, but he was also becoming a smart, funny, and kind young man. His hilarious comments surprised me every day. Perhaps the biggest surprise he threw at me was, ironically, turning down our trip to Italy.

"That's your honeymoon," he explained over dinner. "So, it should just be you two."

"You're saying you *don't* want to go to Italy?" I couldn't wrap my head around it.

"Is this because of a girl?" Colton asked.

The corners of Gavin's lips pinched, but he shook his head. "No. I just think you guys should enjoy your time together."

"That's...very kind of you," I said. And mildly suspicious for a teenage boy.

He shrugged. "I can probably just stay with Grandpa and Jamie. Or Grandma and Sean." He looked at Colton.

"I don't know, Gavin. I don't feel comfortable leaving you here for two weeks."

Gavin rolled his eyes. "I'll be fine, Mom."

It turned into a bit of an argument as the months passed by. What was Europe if my son couldn't be there to sightsee as well? He shot back, insisting he had no desire to sit on a nine-hour plane ride just to visit a crammed city with dull colors. His words, not mine. And I figured out pretty quickly that arguing with a teenager was worse than arguing with a brick wall.

"Are you *sure*?" I asked for the twentieth time as we pulled into my father's driveway.

"*Yes*," Gavin hissed and jammed his AirPods back into his ears.

Dad came outside and waved at us with a gleaming smile. As he'd aged, he had become more like a golden retriever, always ecstatic when I returned home. Jamie came out as well, moving much slower as a result of her hip problems. I hugged her carefully.

"We're gonna have a great two weeks," Dad exclaimed, taking Gavin's suitcase from him.

"No parties." I grinned.

"Oh please," Dad said. "I'm the party animal. I love getting black out drunk every single weekend—"

Gavin hunched over and laughed so hard, he snorted, which had us all dying in a second flat. With the exception of Andre, my dad was the only person who could make Gavin laugh this hard, and when he started, it was contagious. A crinkle formed between Dad's eyebrows as he howled. His laughter faded into a hyena-like wheeze, which brought tears to our eyes as we struggled to breathe. Colton even dropped to a squat in the driveway, pressing his face in his hands as his shoulders bounced up and down. This was how our family worked: the joke itself was mediocre compared to the laughter that it created.

I pressed a hand to my stomach, flinching as it tied itself into a double knot. "I can't breathe!"

Colton stood up. His face was almost a pale purple from laughing so hard. "Oh my gosh." He paused to cough and chuckled again. "If I laugh any harder, my breakfast will come back up."

"All right, all right. Get on the road, guys." Dad's voice wavered from his laughing. "You don't wanna miss your flight."

Gavin looked like he was trying to suppress laughter now, his lips twitching uncontrollably. I pulled him into my arms. "Be good, do you hear me?"

"Crystal clear."

He waved and followed Jamie inside for the cookies she'd promised.

"Text me when you land," Dad said. "Is Elijah still going over to get your mail and stuff?"

"Yep. Talked to him last night. We're all good."

Dad sighed and wrapped his arms around me. "Have fun, sweetheart. You, too, Colton."

"Yes, sir."

As Colton backed the car out of the driveway, my heart

twinged a little. I'd never been away from Gavin for longer than a weekend. A part of me wanted to turn around and take him with us anyway. But at the same time, I was also craving alone time with Colton. Even though it had been years since the break in, I still struggled to let loose with Colton sometimes, afraid that I'd be woken up by the sound of shattered glass. But with this trip, I was determined to take my life back once and for all.

"Psst."

Something nudged my arm, and I jolted awake. Colton sat next to me with a battered copy of Christian Webner's new thriller still perched in his hands.

"Are we in Italy yet?" I murmured dreamily.

"Not yet. About another hour. But I thought you might want something to eat."

The flight attendants had provided packs of pretzels, and I ripped one open greedily once I realized how hungry I actually was. Colton brushed crumbs off my shirt and chuckled.

"What?" I demanded through a mouthful.

"I just love you," he replied and leaned in.

His closeness always did funny things to my heart, and I stopped chewing when his nose touched mine.

"I can't wait to explore in Italy with you."

I swallowed. "Me either."

"Let me rephrase," he said with an impish grin. "I can't wait to explore you in Italy."

When I gave him a light shove, he laughed again because he knew my heart was pounding now.

I chowed through another pack of pretzels and let Colton talk me into playing a few games of Person, Place, or Thing—a game from our childhood. I had just correctly guessed Angelina Jolie when the pilot came on the intercom to announce that we would be landing shortly.

When we finally arrived, I hauled Colton through the airport and out into a land of sunshine and crystal blue water.

The balmy air kissed our skin, and I could already feel my hair frizz. But the air smelled so sweet, like the wind was tinged with vanilla. I squinted into the distance, and there across the water sat the city of Venice. It's jagged, sand-colored buildings were perched so close together that even from this distance, it looked like a massive clutter of shapes with the occasional spire reaching up to stab the sky.

Colton and I were guided onto a boat among several of our fellow passengers, and I felt the spray of the water brush my face as we soared toward Venice.

Colton was already snapping pictures, and for a fraction of a second, I wondered what type of filter Evan would use on his photos if he were here with me. But that was a closed door. A stupid thought not worth feeding.

I could only gather about five words from our boat guide's broken English: "Welcome to the floating city."

Our boat zoomed under a wide arch and right into the heart of Venice, where timeworn structures surrounded us on all sides, as aged and gorgeous as fine wine. The warm tones of the buildings stood out against the cool, pale sky. Gondolas and other boats sailed past us, and I wondered where the people were heading. The possibilities seemed endless in this culture-filled city.

Colton squeezed my hand. "What do you think?"

"What do I think?" I breathed, gazing around in awe. "It's incredible."

Later when we arrived at the Hotel Montecarlo in San Marco, Colton held the door open for me. His smile seemed three times brighter now that we were in Venice. I walked into the lobby and before I could even register the glowing chandeliers or the gold and red tiled floor, I pulled my hair off my neck and basked in the air conditioning.

Clink.

I pulled my wine glass away from Colton's and downed the last of my wine with a smirk. For the last half hour, we'd been discussing old TV shows that we started five years too late.

"I thought Bryson was dead!" Colton exclaimed.

"That's what they want you to think."

"Leave it to *Dead Bolted* to twist all of your theories up in a knot."

I pretended to zip my mouth shut.

The sun had since disappeared, leaving behind a thin ring of fiery orange to soften the horizon. We were eating dinner at the Algiubagio Restaurant, and the terrace was surprisingly empty for a Sunday evening. But I didn't mind. The water was now black as midnight, illuminated only by the soft glow of candles on the tables and the silver beams of moonlight. A warm breeze blew through the area, playing with my hair.

"I want to say something," Colton murmured, setting his wine glass down.

"Please do. I love when you get all poetic."

"I assure you this is not poetic. It's crazy how we're in Italy right now, and all I want to do is just look at you."

His hand grazed mine, and the thrill I felt was only enhanced by the wine that had my mind buzzing.

"I love you, too," I said.

"Thank God for this moment."

We drank to that and then sat quietly for a moment, gazing out into the dark water.

"When did you become so religious?" I asked.

"What do you mean? I love going to church with you."

"No, in general," I clarified. "'Cause neither of us were close to God as teenagers. What changed for you?"

He sighed and gave me a look like, *take a wild guess.* "Life really sucked, Gail."

I tensed as the memories faded into view like a slow poison infesting my body. His father's abuse, my depression, my divorce, his car accident, the break in—*God, it was like a funnel!* My hands started to tremble. I'd worked hard in therapy to recognize my triggers and stop my anxiety from escalating. But sometimes it felt impossible. My dinner nearly crawled back up my throat at the thought of how much we'd survived.

"Sometimes I wake up and I just think...wow, I could die today." Colton's eyes had this strange distant look in them that made my entire soul lunge toward him.

I grabbed his hand and squeezed it hard, ignoring his small grunt as my nails dug into his skin. I didn't loosen my grip. I needed to feel him, feel his skin and reassure myself that I would feel it forever.

"You're never gonna die," I insisted.

His eyes cut to mine.

Sure, it was a childish thing to say, but thinking about how little time we had here on earth made me *feel* like a small child— totally at the mercy of the massive universe and its beautiful yet diabolical plans. Sometimes life was simply that: scary.

Fortunately, Colton could read my mind.

"I'm right here, love." He placed his other hand on top of mine. "When you kissed me in that hospital after the car accident, I felt a hundred times more alive than dead. God used you to get to me and shake some motivation back into me." Colton shrugged. "That saved my life."

The tension ebbed from my fingers as he spoke, and I glanced out into the rippling water, watching the reflection of the candle-light dance on the dark surface.

Even though I was Christian now, a small part of me still felt that death *was* final. Once you left this earth and ascended into Heaven, there was no coming back. I assumed most people wouldn't want to come back, but what did that mean for me and Colton? Could you sustain romantic relationships in Heaven? Would I recognize Colton among the billions of other souls? Or was life our only chance to feel something like this?

"Hey," Colton said, calling my attention back. "Let's not think about that now. We're on our honeymoon for crying out loud. It's time to have *fun*."

I swallowed the lump in my throat and nodded. "You're right."

"Besides, I don't know how much longer I can go without taking that dress off you."

My lips curled upward. "Colton Reeves, what a risqué thing to say."

He shrugged.

"Well, I don't think you'll have to wait much longer," I whispered, trailing my fingers up his hand.

Colton grabbed the arm of the nearest waiter. "Check, *per favore*."

∼

It was the most exhilarating, fascinating week of my life.

Colton and I spent our time sightseeing across the Canale Grande and snapping pictures at Ponte di Rialto—the famous bridge that connects San Marco and San Polo. We visited St. Mark's Square and went straight for Doges Palace. We took romantic gondola rides and kissed under silk-colored moonlight.

One evening, Colton towed me to the middle of our room, snaked an arm around my waist, and started to sway in time with the classical music he was playing on his phone. The gold flecks in his green eyes were especially vibrant tonight, and I couldn't stare long enough.

"Why are we dancing?" I giggled.

"It's on my Italy to-do list."

"Ah."

We swayed slowly, in no rush to skip through a dance and separate.

For a brief moment, I feared this was all a dream. I was frightened that when I woke up, Colton and our beautiful Italian oasis would vanish, and I would be stuck back in Cara's lake house—the one I'd stayed in right after I'd walked out on Evan. Or maybe when I woke up, I'd be stuck in the living room staring at the mess of shattered glass and picture frames from the home invasion. I tightened my grip on Colton's arms.

Focus on the now, Gail. Focus on the now. I repeated Gianna's words until Colton was fully in front of me again.

"Gail?"

"Yeah?"

His lips twitched and a crease furrowed his brows.

"What is it?" I asked.

His jaw clenched ever so slightly and then his eyes touched mine again. "Do you ever...think about having another baby?"

I stared at him. "I don't know."

He nodded and then drew me in for a twirl.

"Why?" I had a hunch, but hearing him say it would be better than me imagining it.

"I've always wanted to be a father. And I love Gavin so much, but...having my *own* son or daughter." His eyes sparkled.

"It's a gift." I nodded, remembering my little baby as I held him for the first time in the hospital.

"And if I'm being honest," Colton added. "A small part of me always wished I could have a baby with you. Even when we were teenagers."

I snorted. "We were a little young, Colt."

"We aren't now."

I would have been lying if I said I'd never imagined it, too.

There was something very appealing about having Colton's DNA mixed with mine; the thought brought on a range of emotions. Of course I'd imagined Colton as the father of my children at one point. That's what you do when you're young and in love—you plan a future, no matter how far-fetched and unachievable it actually is. And for a long time, I had to stop those dreams and push them away so that I could handle my own life. But this love unexpectedly came back from the dead, so why couldn't those old dreams be resurrected, too?

"I wanted you to be the one to do it," I whispered, and then realizing I'd vocalized my thoughts, I quickly glued my eyes to the ground.

"What do you mean?"

After drawing a deep breath, I said, "I wanted you to be the one to...give me a child. I think because I knew that I would be safe with you. Of course, at the time, you were *all* I knew, but...I wanted to take that leap with someone I genuinely loved and trusted."

Colton bent me into a dip as the song drifted toward its end.

"But you were meant to have Gavin," he said. "You were meant to meet Evan, fall in love, have a child, and break apart."

I never liked being reminded of my dark past, and even Colton talking about it set me on edge. It wasn't his fault; if anything, it was mine. The past was just an old ghost I hadn't come to terms with yet.

"So, your point is..."

"It's just like how my dad was meant to be an asshole, and you and I were meant to be apart for all those years," he said.

"Why?"

"Well, I had to learn how to be myself instead of changing every five seconds to roll with the crowd. And you had to pursue music and get to know yourself better. Beverly and Evan were important people for us at one time in our lives, but they weren't meant to stay. They taught us some hard lessons, and it was our job to learn from them. Gavin's just a wonderful thing that came from that relationship. But we couldn't be with each other for that amount of time because we had to learn those lessons on our *own*. Basically, we had to forget the past to move forward."

"Until the past came back," I said.

"It always does. But at the right time."

I could feel it suddenly—another door opening up in my mind, another possibility. This one shined brighter than all the other possible futures I'd ever considered.

"Why bring it up?" I asked, trying to break the ice.

Colton's grin could have dimmed the sun. "I'm always open to the idea of having a kid...if you want to. I would be there every step of the way. You don't ever have to worry about me leaving again. I'm yours."

"That's good to hear," I replied. "But I don't want to move quickly. I really just want to let this feeling sink in."

I pressed a hand to his cheek and caressed the patch of skin under his eye. He blinked and leaned into my hand, letting his features soften.

"I completely understand."

We didn't discuss the matter for the rest of our honeymoon, but it never left my mind. Through all of our cultural tours of the city, I entertained the idea of having a child with Colton.

What would the kid look like? Would our child inherit Colton's breathtaking eyes? It was so fun to think through that I couldn't stop. Gavin would come to love his baby brother or sister. They would be best friends. It was a pleasant thought. But *nothing* was more appealing than the thought of sharing such an intimate moment with Colton. When I considered the act of conceiving a child with him, my skin prickled with goosebumps.

By the end of our second week in Venice, my fantasies had gotten the better of me.

"You act like I haven't been by your side this whole trip,"

Colton managed to say as I kissed him hungrily on our last night in the city.

"Do you need an invitation?" I asked and swung my leg over his hips to straddle him.

He melted underneath me, succumbing to my actions almost immediately, and that was when I realized that we *could* do it— right here, right now. Or at least *try*. But just as his hands started to roam, a tiny voice in the back of my head spoke up.

Not tonight, it advised. *I'm not saying never, just not tonight.*

My subconscious was right, of course. I couldn't think straight when my head was filled to the brim with lust. Thank goodness that tiny voice was a mighty one.

Later, as I laid against Colton's chest, I reminded him of how much he meant to me.

"You mean the world to me, too, Gail," he whispered, gently stroking my arm.

It sounded like he'd said something more, but I was already falling asleep, and his words were lost.

I wasn't in a particularly good mood the next day, having to trade my paradise for the camped seats and tasteless food of an airplane. The only thing pulling me home was Gavin.

"Don't worry, we'll come back," Colton assured me.

When we finally got to the airport we had an hour to spare, so after wolfing down some hotcakes from McDonalds, we wandered into a gift shop. It was filled with priceless nick-nacks, all designed right in the heart of Italy, and I settled on a stained-glass sculpture of a dolphin leaping over waves. I planned to give it to Gavin.

Just as we checked out and made our way toward the boarding gate, my phone rang. I didn't recognize the number.

"Hello?"

"Hi, is this Abigail Ferr?" a woman asked. The voice didn't ring a bell at all, and I cleared my throat.

"It's Reeves now, but yes. Can I ask who's speaking?"

"My name's Cindy Blockhouster, I work the front desk at North Carolina Specialty Hospital. We have a woman here who checked in about two weeks ago and was sick with a very high fever, and we believe she may be in relation to you?"

I glanced at Colon, who was watching me with a weary look.

"Okay," I said hesitantly. "Who is she?"

"Her name is Jacklyn Novalous."

It was an uppercut straight to the gut.

"Y-yes," I breathed into the phone. "That's my mother."

"Ah," Cindy said. "Well, we were just wondering if you'd like to be present when they take her out."

I shook my head, feeling it cloud with confusion. "Take her out? What do you mean?"

"Oh," Miss Blockhouster said, sounding flustered all of a sudden. "She passed away last night."

My face dropped its expression, and the coldness immediately regained its hold on my body.

"Abigail?" Colton asked, alarmed. "Who are you talking to?"

All this time, I never knew where she was. All these years...I never even heard from her. It shouldn't have really been a surprise that she would go back to North Carolina—her home state. But it stung to realize that she'd never called to check in. Not when I graduated, not when I got married, not even when I gave birth to my son. It dawned on me then that she never knew Colton; she didn't know if I was happy or not, yet she didn't bother to ask. She'd become a terrible person. So why was I being crippled by the loss?

Because once upon a time she *did* care...

Colton said my name again and gripped my shoulder.

"My mom's...dead."

Apparently, it wasn't Miss Blockhouster's place to comment

on any funeral preparations, so I had no clue whether I was even invited or not, but I doubted it. I boarded the plane in slow motion, and then, for nearly ten hours, I was alone with my thoughts. Colton tried his best to soothe me, but I had so many confusing emotions that all I could do was just stare out at the sky and attempt to lose myself in the clouds.

My mother...the person who was supposed to support me through every step of my life, was gone. I really hated her for it, hated her for not calling to make amends before she died. Did she not regret leaving me all those years ago? Clearly not. I had found peace in that storm; I grew up and forgave her, but for what? Maybe we were never meant to make up...as sad as that was.

I didn't sleep that night. The sky was pitch black; it was like flying through an inky mist, and the claustrophobia feasted on my stomach. I reached into my carry on and took a Dramamine pill, careful not to wake Colton. He slept so peacefully. I wondered if my mother was resting the same way or turning over in the morgue, though it was hard to tell. Because I would probably never know.

The most information the hospital could give me was that she'd contracted a deadly virus, most likely a flu or the Pulmonem Fever, and couldn't win the fight. Apparently, Pulmonem Fever cases were skyrocketing in North Carolina recently, and my own mom happened to be taken as a victim.

I stared out the window at the dark sky and shook my head.

Life was just not fair sometimes. I hated myself for thinking this because I'd been hurt by my mother, but she didn't deserve to die like that—writhing in her sickness.

When the sun finally came up, my limbs were stiff as boards. My neck whined in protest, no matter which way I turned my head, and my tongue was bone dry.

Colton's eyes finally fluttered open, and I was grateful. I'd felt very lonely throughout the night. It wasn't that he didn't offer to stay up with me, but I could see the exhaustion in his eyes and sent him to sleep instead.

"How are you?" he asked in a sleep-groggy voice.

"Confused," I admitted.

He sighed. "I would be, too."

A thought dawned on me, and my stomach performed another summersault. How was I going to tell Dad? Did he get a call from the hospital as well, or was I going to have to break the news myself? *Yeah, the woman who abused you in your last marriage—she's finally dead. Might as well just pop the champagne.*

I wanted to cry, but my pride wouldn't let me, and I felt sick for that. Nobody deserved to go out like my mom did, and deep down, I knew she would be missed—by me *and* my father, whether we admitted it to ourselves or not.

So maybe it was best not to say anything. I didn't want to dig into my mother's new life—whomever she'd met, whatever she'd done, I didn't want to know. All I knew was the woman she had been for me: a kind role model, turned callous killjoy.

"It's okay, love," Colton said.

I nodded, not trusting myself to speak. I would either yell or cry, and our surrounding passengers didn't need to witness that. It wasn't their business anyway.

For one fleeting moment, I questioned God. I had just had two of the best weeks of my life. Why did my mother's death need to be slammed in my face at this exact moment in time? Maybe it was because we'd left Venice. Out here in the normal world again, anything was bound to happen. But I sighed and immediately renounced my judgment of the Lord's plan. If I'd learned anything, it was that *that* wasn't worth fighting.

"Do you think she'll have a normal funeral?" I whispered.

Colton shifted to look into my eyes, but when he tried to speak, no words came. Eventually, he shrugged and a look of remorse contorted his features. "I don't know."

I sighed and reached into my carry-on to retrieve the sky-blue journal. I'd brought it in case I wanted to jot down the adventures from this trip, and now they were overflowing in my brain.

I started with our arrival, listing everything from the boat guide to the crystal-clear water. And when I finally made it to the news of my mother's death, I wrote down every emotion that crossed my mind. And finally, under my list of memories, I scrawled:

Jacklyn Novalous-Ferr was only my mother for fifteen years. Then she left, and after all of this time, I still don't know why. But regardless of her cruelness, a part of me hopes that she is at peace now. God, please save and forgive her.

Colton watched me curiously, and when I glanced over at him, he gave me a nod of encouragement.

Drawing a deep breath, I closed the journal and placed it back in my bag. The closing of the notebook was significant, I decided. It meant that I was ready to move forward and deal with whatever emotions came my way. Because there would be emotions—powerful ones. But I'd survived loss before.

The pilot came on to announce that we were nearing the airport in New York, and I gazed down at the floating landmass with longing. It was actually good to be home.

Chapter Nine

SARATOGA SPRINGS, NY—NEW YORK CITY, NY

I f there was ever a moment where everything was right in the world and my mind was quiet, it was when I was on stage with my violin. There was something so satisfying in feeling the cool metal of the strings press into the flesh of my fingers as I played. Creating such intricate melodies from muscle memory was like my own personal superpower.

Today the Saratoga Strings was performing *A-Flat* by Larry Moore at the Fall Festival. The song's fluttering undertones and mischievous harmonies kept the audience's attention under careful lock and key. My head was bobbing in time with the rhythm, and I caught Veronica's eye as my fingers skipped up the fingerboard. She was grinning as well. For a short piece, this composition sure packed a punch. At the end, we all performed a dramatic down bow, and the audience went nuts. Tod spun around and bowed before stepping to the side and clapping for his orchestra as we all stood up.

This moment—the crowd's roaring energy—*this* was the

driving force underneath life's monotony. The intense feeling of accomplishment and gratitude.

After I had exited the stage, Colton materialized through the crowd. The streets were blocked off to make way for bounce houses and blow-up obstacle courses. Vendors took to the sidewalks, and families crowded at picnic tables to enjoy the sweet autumn air.

Gavin and Andre appeared beside Colton, lost in a conversation that seemed very important, judging by Gavin's rose-colored cheeks.

"She's here! Might as well do it, bro," Andre was saying.

I pulled Gavin into a hug and decided to ignore his hesitancy to be in my arms. "What's this about a she?"

"No one," Gavin answered, tossing a warning look at Andre.

Andre only grinned. "Just a girl he likes."

"Shut up!" Gavin hissed.

"What's her name?" Colton wondered.

"You're too young for that," I chastised, and all three of them looked over at me. "You boys are fifteen. Your only concern should be keeping your cleats clean after soccer practice and keeping your grades up."

Gavin waved my comment away like it was an ineffective dad joke and turned back to whisper to Andre. But I could feel Colton's questioning gaze trained on my face.

"—at the hoops," Andre told Gavin and pointed toward the basketball hoops before he saw me watching and dropped his hand to his side.

"Hey, uh, we're gonna go shoot some hoops," Gavin said. His eyes were already scanning the area behind my shoulder. He was looking for someone.

I could have told him the sky was deteriorating, but it wouldn't have phased him. Whoever this girl was, she had to be something special.

"What was all that?" Colton asked after the boys jogged off.

"What do you mean?" I put my violin case on a nearby picnic table and sat down.

"What's with the *you're-too-young* stuff?" Colton sat down across from me. "You and I were sixteen when we dated, Gail."

"That was different," I muttered, waving goodbye to Seth and Veronica as they bolted toward a jewelry vendor.

"How? Gavin's getting older. He's bound to experience it sooner or later."

"He's just got a lot on his plate right now with school and starting varsity for soccer. A girlfriend would just be a distraction."

The sounds of the festival grew louder as the space between us grew silent. Colton didn't take his eyes off my face, but for some reason, I couldn't look at him.

"I didn't think of it as a distraction when I played volleyball in high school."

"That was different," I said again.

Colton shrugged helplessly. "Honestly, Gail, sometimes you make no sense at all."

I knew my logic was faulty, but there was a reason rooted deep in my bones. "I don't want him to get hurt like I did."

The statement was so unexpected that even the raucous festival faded into gray this time. My cheeks flushed pink, and I whipped my head to look at Colton. He was staring back at me with his jaw flexing uncontrollably. I hated that look. It meant he was shouldering all the blame even though it wasn't all his.

Taking a deep breath, I added, "Heartbreak just sucks, you know? It sounds stupid, but I wanna protect Gavin from that."

Colton looked away for a moment, and I watched the gears in his mind churn. I knew he was thinking of what to say and how to say it. A piece of my heart frowned.

"Everyone experiences heartbreak sometime in their life," he said slowly before glancing back at me again. "It's *part* of life." His lips twitched to say something more, but he closed his mouth instead. It didn't matter though because his eyes were filled with an old and familiar apology.

"I know that," I reassured him. "But I'm worried about how Gavin will deal with it."

"You mean like—"

"I buried my feelings when you and I broke up. That almost killed me." I shook my head and shivered against the chill of a breeze. "I won't let Gavin do the same."

"He won't," Colton answered immediately. "Because we'll raise him to face his feelings."

A playful squeal erupted from a bounce house and instantly drew my attention. My eyes drifted to the basketball court, and I searched for Gavin. There was no girl with him. He was just dribbling a ball and sidestepping Andre.

"Gail, why is this getting to you?" Colton asked, gently touching my arm. "You just killed it on stage. You should be happy."

I let go a deep sigh. "I am happy, but my anxiety's been terrible recently. And I miss my mom." That last part made my throat constrict the tiniest bit. Ever since that flight back from Venice, my hands had hardly stopped shaking. That was the downside of being a violinist. As soon as you got off stage, reality set back in like an impenetrable fog.

Colton nodded. "Have you written in your journal lately?"

"No, but I really need to. I just can't shake the feeling that something bad is about to happen."

"You think too much. How about I buy us some ice cream and we take a walk around the vendors?"

"You do know the way to my heart," I relented.

He smiled and kissed my temple.

～

We left around five o'clock, and I couldn't resist Gavin's request for Mission Barbeque. Andre tagged along with us.

"Okay, but think about it," Andre called as he stomped up the porch steps, one arm secured around the bag holding my precious barbeque sandwich. "Call of Duty 4 *is* the best. You got the insane multiplayer feature, the awesome map designs—"

"Andre, honey, put the food on the table."

"—and the freakin' missions, man!" He dropped the bag in the center of the table and gave Gavin a pointed look.

My son was already halfway into the mountain of fries, slathering them in ketchup.

"Hey," I said. "Prayer first."

Gavin sighed, closed his eyes, and led us through the fastest prayer ever spoken. It was over in a matter of seconds and then he turned toward Andrea again.

"Call of Duty Black Ops 4 has multiplayer, and it's still superior."

I sighed and took a seat beside Colton.

Andre was scowling. "You're wrong."

"Actually, you're *both* wrong," Colton interjected. "Madden is by far the best videogame to ever exist."

I cleared my throat against the swell of their argument and reached for my sandwich. I knew I could wolf it down in a matter of minutes with how hungry I was. I was only two bites in when my phone started ringing.

"Your opinions are all wrong!" Gavin yelled, holding up his hands and refusing to argue further. This just egged Colton and Andre on.

I sucked ketchup from my fingers and excused myself from the table. My phone was flashing an unrecognizable number, and I felt my brow furrow before answering.

"Hello?"

"Hi, Gail."

Every ounce of air left my lungs. I whipped my head behind

me to see that my husband was still occupied with my son and his friend and then stepped into the living room on wobbly legs.

"Evan," I hissed. "Why are you calling me?"

"Why do you think?"

I raised my eyebrows in disbelief, stunned speechless. There was no way he was calling to get me back...That couldn't be what this was about.

"You're not—"

"I didn't call for you." *Ouch*. I could almost hear his eyes rolling. A stretch of silence followed before he said, "I want to know how my son is."

I could hear Gavin laughing at the table—so carefree, so innocent, so unaware.

"He's fine," I said in a strained voice.

"No, I want details."

"You should've thought of that when you were my husband."

"I'm not the one who took our son and ran."

My body started quivering again, and I could feel the cortisol leaking through my veins like a stimulant drug. And I was in the living room of all places, where the intruder was, where I almost—

Too much! my anxiety screamed. *This is too much! Get out!*

"Will you meet to talk with me?" Evan asked.

"No, absolutely not." My heart was dust by now, swirling in the tsunami of adrenaline inside me. My brain was on red alert, blinking with a shrieking siren. Vaguely, I thought about how sad it was that my life had come to this—that one tiny thing could rupture my feelings of security.

Was I okay?

"Abigail," Evan said, clearly losing patience. "Let's be honest with each other. If the situation were reversed, you would want to know, too."

Damn his reverse psychology. I hated that almost as much as I hated him. But he was right. I would give anything to know how my son had grown, what activities he'd taken up, who he was surrounding himself with. But my stubborn side wouldn't let me give up that easily.

"Aren't you in Ohio?" I challenged.

"Nice try, but I'm in New York City for a job."

"Oh, is posing as a professional photographer just to have sex with random women your new occupation?"

"Why would I cheat on my new beautiful, loving wife?"

Acid clawed its way up my throat. "Fuck you."

"No thanks. Been there, done that. But I'm not calling to fight, Gail," he said firmly. "I want to know how my son is, and you can't keep the information from me. Come out to the city and let's talk."

"You don't want to meet him yourself?"

"You took that opportunity away from me, remember?"

I frowned. If he really wanted to see Gavin, he would've put up more of a fight. It would be best if Gavin stayed home. But why now?

I resisted the urge to punch right through the wall. Or no, not the wall. I wanted to punch the living lights out of Evan. I had just lost my mother, and my anxiety was its own monster. I didn't need to deal with this right now. But of course, Evan was right.

"I can't just leave home," I argued.

"Why not? That's a bullshit excuse."

I bit down on my lower lip until I tasted blood. "Fine! When should I meet you?"

"How about Friday in Times Square? We can go to a restaurant and talk there."

"Careful, Evan. What would your new wife think?"

"She already knows I'm doing this. Text me when you're on your way."

And with that, he hung up.

I didn't know what I was feeling, but I was shaking. My mind reeled, thinking up a hundred different scenarios as to how this could go. But I was already concocting a plan. I would lie and tell Colton I was going shopping with Veronica, and—

Are you crazy? the logical part of my brain screamed. *Don't you dare lie to Colton!*

I put my face in my hands as the first trembles of a headache threatened from behind my eyes.

Lying to Colton would kill me. But I couldn't tell him the truth. He would just lash out and remind me of how terrible Evan was. That was no secret. But reverse psychology was powerful, and I couldn't resist picturing myself in Evan's shoes—completely in the dark as to how my kid was doing. That would kill me more than lying.

It took twelve deep breaths before my emotions could shut their mouths. I clenched my hands into fists and walked back into the dining room. Colton was educating the boys on the videogames *he* used to play as a kid—Grand Theft Auto and Halo—and my reappearance made him all the more eager to prove his point.

"Oh, Gail, remember when we were young and we used to play Red Dead Redemption in my basement?"

"How could I forget? Your mom had to come downstairs and force us off the Xbox." I swallowed, surprised to hear the level tone of my voice.

"I didn't know you were a gamer, Mrs. Reeves," Andre said.

"I wasn't really, but my boyfriend was on the weekends."

That made them all laugh, and I chuckled as best I could. It was better to make them think nothing was out of the ordinary; it might just make the whole operation that much easier. Then, the only thing I would have left to worry about was the guilt of lying to Colton.

And unsurprisingly, he didn't bat an eye when I told him I was going shopping with my friends. In fact, he was just his usual chivalrous self.

"I can come if you want, to help hold bags and stuff."

"Thank you." I kissed him. "But I'll be all right. I don't expect to buy the whole store."

"I hope you're serious," he said, tossing a nervous glance at my wallet on the table.

I grabbed his head and crushed my lips to his, praying that he could hear my thoughts. That he would understand why I had to go and sit down with my ex husband. He would say something like, *You're too good, Gail. That prick doesn't deserve to know.* But there was so much Colton didn't understand. For starters, he himself didn't have a kid.

"Be safe," he whispered against my lips.

"That's the plan."

It was *freezing* in New York City. I wished I would've worn an extra coat because my sweater was so thin it might as well have been a layer of skin and not of wool. I pushed my way through the crowds and tried to keep my hands balled up in the pockets of my jeans. Despite my efforts, warmth simply avoided me.

Evan had agreed to meet me at a restaurant in the heart of Times Square, and as I approached the door, I felt my insides churn. I truly did not want to see him at all; this was bound to be a nightmare. I knew the very sight of him would sicken me. Funny how people you once loved could turn into monsters.

"Dining alone?" the hostess asked.

I scanned the booths until I spotted him, and my heart folded in half. He was him but in an older man's body, sporting a goatee now and larger arm muscles.

"No, I'm meeting someone here," I told the hostess and walked past her.

One conversation. It was one conversation about our son, and then I was free to go. He couldn't hold me captive, and I wouldn't *be* held captive.

Those disgustingly familiar sapphire eyes snapped up at me. "Hey, Gail."

I sank into the booth, scowling as hard as I could.

"Oh come on, lose the bitchiness. Like I said, I want nothing to do with you."

"Ditto," I spit at him.

His passive-aggressive gaze hardened into a look of disgust. "You don't make anything easy, do you?"

"Says you."

Evan pinched the bridge of his nose. "Still living in the past I see, but that's typical for you."

It took every ounce of energy not to slap him like I did the night he confessed to cheating. "We're here to talk about our son, in case you forgot."

"Enlighten me," Evan said.

I dropped a stack of pictures down on the table. They were Gavin's school pictures, from preschool up to the ninth grade. Evan picked them up and stared at them with a peculiar look in his eye. It wasn't quite affection; more like basic intrigue. I scoffed at him.

"Would you look at that," he mused. "Kid's got my eyes."

I didn't answer; I just let him look through the stack while I tried to swallow the bile that was bubbling up my throat.

"Tell me about him," Evan said.

I explained that Gavin was a natural born soccer player and that he had a kind, compassionate heart. I talked about his excessive appetite and his love for running and cheesy war videogames. I even mentioned Andre. Basically, I wanted Evan to know that Gavin was doing just fine without him. But my ex-husband smiled.

"Sounds like he's growing up to be a good kid. He'll go far in life, no doubt."

I nodded and dropped my eyes to the table.

My brain couldn't wrap its gnarled hands around this. How

did I go from loving this man to despising him with every fiber of my being? Would I ever get tired of hating him? Would that negative energy burn me out for good?

"How's your family?" The question just fell from my mouth like an unexpected hiccup. My heart blazed anxiously, and I looked back up at Evan.

His eyes were still trained on the pictures. "They're good. Dad retired from the police force last spring. Mom's still baking. Gracie's in high school. Laine and Taryn just had their third kid." His voice was distant as he squinted at Gavin's eighth grade school picture.

I swallowed. "And Dani?"

Evan finally looked up at me. "She's a successfully published author. Published her fourth book last May."

Pinpricks attacked the corners of my eyes. I felt my soul swell at the thought of her pursuing her dreams. *Dani*. The little seventeen-year-old with the massive dream and boxes of journals. She'd wanted so badly to be a writer, and now she was one.

"That's amazing," I replied, my voice hollow and miles away. I almost sounded like the old me.

Evan nodded. "Look her up on Amazon. She's doing really well." He smiled at the picture of Gavin on the soccer field.

Something was different this time in the *way* Evan smiled... like he was proud of Gavin. Like he wasn't just a blurb of the past that deserved erasing. It made some lone plug in my brain finally reach its outlet, and the spark of electricity was something along the lines of closure.

I didn't feel the touch of a smile until Evan asked, "What?"

"Gavin's just a good kid."

Evan's sapphire eyes flicked back to the picture he was holding —the one of Gavin as a baby, sobbing his little heart out during his first time meeting Santa. "I believe it."

I swallowed, trying to figure out why there was a burning

lump in my throat now. "Will you please tell Dani that I'm proud of her?"

"Mhm." Evan wasn't really paying attention to me, which snapped me back to the present moment.

Oh, right.

This wasn't 2023. We weren't dating, and Dani wasn't around the corner with her spiral notebooks, and I wasn't driving back to Philadelphia to the apartment I shared with Cara. Sometimes life could be so strange. It didn't matter that I was happily married now. One look at Evan—Evan, who had taken a machete to my heart—and suddenly, I was sick on nostalgia. Not for our relationship though, I decided at that moment, but for my youth. I twisted my hands together and looked around the restaurant to distract myself.

Eventually, Evan sighed. He slid the stack of pictures across the table to me and leaned back in his seat.

"I'd like to meet him."

The statement was an instant uppercut to the gut. Flashing sirens screamed in my brain. Evan's right eyebrow arched ever so slightly as if to say *Earth to Gail! Answer me!* So I did.

"No."

Evan blinked. "No?"

"No."

He placed his elbows on the table and sunk his midnight eyes into my soul. "What gives you the right—"

He was interrupted by the waitress standing at our table. Poor girl had a crazed, *please hurry up, I have a hundred tables to attend to* look in her eye. For her sake, I kept my order short with a Sprite and small Caesar salad. Evan took three whole minutes on deciding what he wanted, which made me want to shake some empathy into him.

Okay, yeah. This definitely wasn't 2023. How could I have been so in love with someone like this?

When the waitress sprinted to the kitchen, Evan glued his gaze back to me. "What gives you the right to not let me see my own son? Does he even know about me?"

"You lost that right when you slept with another woman while we were still married."

"Okay, you wanna split hairs?" He shrugged sharply. "You were in love with someone else."

"For the love of God, Evan!" I grilled him with my glare. "I loved *you*."

"Yeah, like a virus loves its host."

My mouth fell open. "What the hell is that supposed to mean?"

"You know what it means," he hissed. "You *used* me."

I stared at him for the length of four heartbeats, but just as I opened my mouth to respond, he cut me off.

"I was gonna say that I regretted cheating on you, but God, you make it so hard to feel bad! You're so self-absorbed, you can't even verbally admit that if that other asshole—what's his face—would've shown up, you'd have left me like *that*." He snapped and reached for his drink. And while he chewed a piece of ice, all he could do was shake his head at me. "I'd rather screw a random girl in the back of a bar then come home to someone who can't even own up to the fact that she's a toxic bitch. You use people, Gail, 'cause you can't ever be fully satisfied."

My body instantly went cold. "Shut up."

"You might have your whipped husband fooled, but not me. I know who you are deep down and you should really hate yourself for it."

I had to suck in my next breath because his statement wrapped my lungs in a chokehold. We held each other's eyes—his sharp and glaring and mine nearly popping out in shock. The words that I said next crawled out from a dark abyss in my brain.

"I never want to see your face or hear your voice again. Stay away from Gavin and stay the *fuck* away from me."

His cheek twitched the tiniest bit as I snatched the pictures and scooted out of the booth. Our waitress was scrambling toward us, and when she spotted me, her eyebrows instantly furrowed.

"Is everything—"

"Put my meal on his tab," I muttered. It was all I could do not to lose it and punch someone.

The sun had already set, so I shivered on the dreadfully long walk back to my car. I couldn't tell if my stomach was twisting because of hunger or humiliation, not over what I'd said—Evan deserved that—but about what *he'd* said. I wasn't bulletproof. His words really, really hurt.

I pushed through the bustling crowd, desperate for the solitude and silence of my car. I nearly sprinted to the parking garage, trying to make it before the tears started. But running in twenty-degree weather was like moving through an ice cold ocean; my vision was already blurring.

My knees felt weak. My heart jackhammered against my ribcage. My lungs were sore. I couldn't catch a breath with the wind that kept shifting this way and that. All the while, I knew my anxiety was chasing me through the crowd. I tried my absolute hardest to escape its claw-like grip, but just as I sprinted into the car garage, it took me in its hands and threw me to the ground.

You're a toxic bitch.

You should hate yourself for it.

I gasped for breath. It was amazing how someone could put all their effort into tearing you down and making you crumble with despair. Even though those things weren't true, my anxiety *liked* to claim otherwise. I didn't want to feel this way. I didn't want to be taken down.

For a split second, I considered going back to find Evan just so that I could tear him apart piece by piece until he was nothing more than a pile of flesh and bones. My blood warmed and curdled at the thought; revenge would be so, *so* sweet. He had it coming, too, after the way he'd treated me. How easy it would be to give into these delicious desires; for one moment I entertained the thought...

But no. He would get what he deserved eventually because Karma had his name written in bright red ink.

I climbed into my car, not as angry but terribly hollow. I felt weak, and strangely, I missed my mom. I stared out the windshield for a few minutes and tried to make sense of my emotions. Giana had taught me that being mindful of what you were feeling helped to take the edge off. The key was to *let* yourself feel, then when your emotions were in check again, maybe you could allow your brain to have a say.

The beige wall of the car garage stared back at me, and I saw so many faces in the gritty texture: Evan's, Gavin's, my mom's, Colton's. They all looked at me expressionlessly, like they were waiting for me to do something. I wiped my tears on the skin of my arm and glanced up into the rearview mirror. Just a little puffiness under the eyes and a red nose. By the time I got back to Saratoga Springs, no one would know that I'd cried. I sighed and pulled out into the bumper-to-bumper traffic of the city.

I felt my temper rise again.

I was angry with myself over what I'd done. Coming here to meet Evan had been a total mistake. Shame on me for actually thinking we could have a civil conversation like adults. As I predicted, I felt guilty for lying to Colton, and on top of everything else, my stomach was growling like a deranged animal.

At an infuriatingly long red light, I fished through my purse for something to eat and retrieved half a protein bar. Then, afraid I would lose myself in a panic attack, I whipped my phone out.

"Hello?" Elijah answered on the fourth ring. He sounded happy. Distant laughter and music echoed behind him.

"I fucked up."

"Huh?" He must've held his hand over the speaker because his next words were muffled. "Yeah." His voice got louder. "Sorry, what'd you say, Gail?"

"I fucked up!" I screeched, feeling my fingers start to shake on the steering wheel.

"What are you talking about?"

"I went to meet Evan in Times Square to show him pictures of Gavin, and we ended up fighting, and I want to kill him." I was crying again.

Elijah didn't answer for a long time. Or maybe it was only a minute, but the silence felt endless to me. Eventually, the sounds in the background faded, and Elijah's voice turned cautious.

"What happened?"

I explained everything in a rush of wobbly words, and when I was done, the silence crept back in.

"Why'd you lie to Colton?"

That made me freeze. I didn't know what I'd been expecting him to say, but it was not that. Which was stupid because it should have been the most glaring red flag.

"Well, I thought that...he would be mad at me, and..."

"And?" Elijah urged.

"This didn't need to be a fight."

"Why would it have been a fight?"

Sometimes I forgot that Elijah was so wise and knew exactly what questions to ask to make me rethink every choice I'd ever made. It was an incredible quality but not when I was the one being questioned.

That very realization right there almost made me slam on my brakes.

"I don't know." My voice sounded far away like it was in a different realm. Maybe a part of me had come detached and was analyzing my decisions from an objective view.

"Well," Elijah said. "I can't blame you for going to meet Evan. He's Gavin's dad; this was bound to happen sometime." He paused, and it sounded like a car drove by him. "But I think you get caught up in this very...black and white way of thinking about things. Like, there's no gray area in the way you approach choices.

You were either going and lying to Colton to avoid the confrontation or you were going to stay home and forget Evan called. It seems like there was never an in between."

I stared blankly at the ribbon of road in front of me as he spoke.

"Confrontation scares you, so you'll do everything in your power to avoid it. Is that in the ballpark?" Elijah sounded genuinely curious.

I was speechless. My mind had instantly gone blank, blown to shreds by this short, dead-on evaluation.

"Hello?"

"Y-yeah," I stammered. "You're just...a genius. Please quit journalism and go be a psychologist."

"No thank you." Elijah laughed. "Stuff with the brain freaks me out."

The guilt came on quickly and heavily. "I'm literally a grown woman, and I don't have this stuff figured out yet."

"There's no rush," Elijah said. "Life is all about growing."

"Well, then why do I still not want to tell Colton?"

"Maybe you're scared to pop that bubble of safety. You guys have been through a lot, and if I were you, I'd be tired of the bullshit, too."

"Safety as in no conflict?"

"Safety as in being on the same team about things," Elijah clarified. "But what's the harm in communication?"

Heartbreak, I almost said. It danced on the tip of my tongue.

"All I know is that right now, I'm exhausted," I deadpanned.

"Sounds like it." Elijah pulled the phone away to talk to someone, and his distant laughter was as clear as silver wind chimes.

"Where are you?" I asked.

"Brie and I are at a bar with some of my old college friends from California. I haven't seen them in months." The grin in his voice was so wholesome.

For the first time all night, I smiled. "I'm happy you get to see them."

Elijah burst out laughing over something I didn't hear, and I knew it was time to hang up. I'd intruded enough on his evening.

"Thank you, Elijah," I said.

His laughing died down. "Yeah, Gail, if you need anything, just call me. It'll all work itself out."

"Sure thing."

Not five minutes after I ended the call, my phone started ringing again. It was Colton. I tried to control my breathing as I pressed the phone back to my ear.

"Hey." My voice was only slightly shaky.

"Hey, love. Gavin just went upstairs to bed. How was your trip? Did you buy anything nice?"

It was then that I realized I hadn't purchased any proof of my so-called shopping trip. *Dammit.* "No, I didn't see anything I liked."

"Wow, I thought New York City was the place to shop." When I didn't answer, he just cleared his throat. "Well, how far are you?"

"About an hour away."

"Okay. I'm going to bed 'cause I have a meeting tomorrow at nine. Our plans just got cleared to build a park out near Blue Street. The project's called Witker."

"Why?"

"'Cause my boss' wife just passed away from cancer, and their kid always loves to go to the park. Witker's their last name."

"It sounds like you have an eventful day tomorrow."

"Oh, I'm so excited," Colton gushed.

I couldn't return his enthusiasm. A part of me was mad at him for having to go to bed; I wanted to sit on the couch with him and drink hot chocolate and explain everything. That kind of conversation just couldn't take place over the phone.

"Well, goodnight, Gail," he said. "I'm glad you had fun today.

I'll see you in the morning."

"'Mkay," was all I could manage.

After I hung up, I wanted to bang my head on the steering wheel. If a relationship didn't have communication, what was it? Dead. Had I not learned that the hard way? And this relationship was too important to lose again. It took all my strength to draw a deep breath. Forget Evan, forget the asshole who trailed me the entire way down the highway, forget my stupid anxiety. I would tell Colton and everything would be okay. It had to be.

I drove in silence and my mind eventually calmed, as did my grip on the steering wheel. I exhaled and massaged my temple, where I felt a headache forming.

"God, forgive me," I whispered.

I pressed my fingertips to my temple again and tried to ignore the burning sensation in the pit of my core. It was loss, and I knew the feeling well.

"I just need peace." Though I said it out loud, my voice was barely audible.

For the rest of the drive, I allowed myself to drown in the silence. When I finally got home, I invaded the fridge and heated up some rotisserie chicken along with steamed broccoli, which I inhaled in less than five minutes. Then, with exhaustion clouding my brain, I climbed the stairs.

Colton was sound asleep on his side of the bed—one arm propped behind him, and his head lolled off to the side. His bare chest rose and fell in a slow, steady rhythm. The sight thawed my cold, pessimistic heart and made a smile blossom on my lips.

I tiptoed through the room and got ready for bed as quietly as possible. And then I crawled in beside Colton and brushed a curl of hair off his forehead.

"I love you so much," I whispered, gently pressing a kiss to his cheek.

He stirred and shifted to place a protective arm around me, and the gesture made my heart cry.

Chapter Ten

SARATOGA SPRINGS, NY

As the days passed by, I didn't hear from Evan again, and I prayed that it was over for good now. More so, I hoped that he was rotting in a box under a bridge, but truthfully I didn't know...nor did I care. Instead, I redirected my focus to my violin, my sky-blue journal, and my son.

Gavin seemed happier than usual. There was a blush in his cheeks now that never seemed to fade, and he walked with a bounce in his step. Several times I caught him checking his phone and turning away to quickly type a response, but each time I inquired about it, he just shrugged me off. Did he think I was born yesterday? I knew those signals like the back of my hand; I'd done the *same* thing to my father. As much as I hated to admit it, I knew the time had finally arrived. My son...had a crush.

After rehearsal on Thursday evening, I came home to find him bent over a textbook at the kitchen table. Except his attention was glued to his phone.

"Science?" I asked, leaning over his shoulder to peer down at his notes. "God, your handwriting is appalling, Gav. Has anyone ever told you that?"

"This is biology," he said. "And yes, my teacher did...once or twice."

He scrawled down a few more vocabulary words from the text and copied their definitions.

"This sucks. Who even cares about a nucleus?"

"Your cells do," I answered.

He rolled his eyes.

Gavin's phone buzzed again, and his hand twitched to answer it.

"Who are you texting?" I asked as innocently as possible.

He shrugged. "Just a friend from school."

Right, okay.

I wandered into the kitchen to cook some spaghetti. "Is this friend a girl or a boy?" I called.

I forked through a lump of congealed noodles, waiting for his response but there was none, and when I peeked back at the table, Gavin was grinning down at his phone, completely unaware that I'd said anything.

"A girl then," I said to myself.

Colton came home late that night since he'd had to help work on the blueprints for the park they were designing. Exhausted, he dragged his feet through the house and only grunted a few answers when I asked him about his day, which kind of made me angry. I confronted him about it, which led to a five-minute argument over why he supposedly didn't need to answer because he was tired. Gavin witnessed the whole ordeal, gave us a funny look, and left to go to his room.

"Hey," I said after a long stretch of silence.

Colton looked up from his bowl of spaghetti. His eyes were fatigued yet still offering a challenge, as if daring me to pick a fight with him again. I wanted to do the opposite.

"I'm sorry," I murmured. "I think we're both just tired."

Colton sighed. "Probably. I'm sorry, too."

Unfortunately, this was far from a peace offering.

By the coming weekend, we were nitpicking everything about each other. He chewed too loudly, but apparently it wasn't as loud as my practice with the violin. He hogged all the blankets, but I apparently hogged the entire bed. And God forbid he couldn't watch one episode of something on Netflix before bed.

Through all of our bickering, Gavin just disappeared to his room. In the moment of a heated argument with my husband, I didn't notice his absence. But when he reappeared for dinner or to go downstairs into the basement to play videogames, the sight of him made me feel guilty. He looked just as upset as us.

I didn't know where the tension was stemming from between me and Colton. I hadn't gotten the chance to explain what happened in New York City only because he never offered me a chance with his long work days and his stress level with the park blueprints. As a result, we were both standing on the edge of a cliff, one nudge away from a massive argument.

The following Tuesday, Colton and I arrived home at the exact same time. He simply nodded at me before walking inside. I sank into a chair at the kitchen table with a cup of tea, hoping it would relax my tense muscles. That had been a stupid wish.

"Oh, Veronica called the house phone," Colton said dryly.

"When was that?"

He shut the cabinet door and turned toward me, his face carved of stone. "She called for you yesterday, and when I said you were at the store, she told me to ask you if you wanted to go shopping today."

A knot of fear dropped through my stomach like a jagged glob of ice.

"And I thought to myself, *wow*, this girl really likes to shop! I mean, was New York City not enough?" His glare seared me open. "And she had *no clue* what I was talking about."

I set my mug down and tried to make sense of my jumbled

thoughts; in my defense, I thought she would at least call my cell phone to ask me something like that. *The* one *time she calls the house phone...*

Colton crossed his arms and shrugged. "Where were you?"

Ready or not, here it comes.

"I *did* go to New York City," I said slowly. "That part's true. But...I didn't go to meet Veronica and Seth."

"Clearly."

I exhaled. "I went to see my ex-husband, but it's *not* what it sounds like, I *swear*," I insisted when Colton turned away from me.

His face had gone dangerously pale and he was leaning over the sink like he might be sick into it. I knew that feeling of betrayal, too, but this wasn't *that*, and I had to make him believe me. The only question was would he?

"He wanted to see how Gavin was doing. He called me the night of the fall festival and forced me to go to the city so that I could catch him up on Gavin's life—"

"Forced you?" Colton scoffed. "No, you had a choice, Abigail. You didn't have to listen to him, but you did. You went. You chose him." His voice cracked on the last word.

"No!" I argued. "I went because if I was in his position, it would kill me to not know how my child was doing! That was the only reason I went, and you're right. It did turn out to be a mistake, 'cause he said some *awful* things to me."

A moment of glaring silence filled the space between us. This was ten times worse than our tiny, futile disagreements. This was a *fight*, with a legitimate cause. And like usual, it had been my fault. Colton leaned over the sink, shaking his head. His palms were pressed on either side of the counter, and his face was a mask of disbelief.

"Why didn't you just tell me?"

"Because I knew you'd act like this," I answered.

"What?" he shouted, whirling around to face me. "Like a husband who's just concerned for his wife's safety?"

My mouth snapped shut, and I took two deep breaths before attempting to speak calmly. "Colton, I did it for Gavin."

"No, you did it for Evan. I know we don't talk much about him, Gail, but you should've just told me. I would've gone with you."

"You didn't need to," I said. "After he called me a toxic bitch, I told him to never speak to me again and walked out."

This took Colton aback for a moment. "He called you a *toxic bitch*?"

"Look, I take full responsibility for my actions, and I'm sorry I lied to you. But I had to do it for my own wellbeing."

"I was worried sick, Abigail! When Veronica didn't know what I was talking about, I went crazy! I didn't know where you'd gone or what happened or...why you lied to me. I mean, did you even stop to consider what this might do to me?"

"Of course I did!"

"YET YOU STILL WENT!"

The door slammed shut, and Gavin strode into the kitchen just to drop his backpack into a seat, pull the Cheez-It box from the cupboard, and glare at both of us before stomping to his room. I reached out for him and felt my lips part to call his name, but my throat closed around the words.

The memories replayed behind my eyes, almost like they happened yesterday: I was a freshman in high school, and I was nervous to go home because my own parents had been fighting nonstop. That day Mom smoked in the kitchen...I could almost smell the putrid odor like she was right here in my house. I remembered feeling terrified and helpless, calling out to Katy for help. Just like Gavin might call out to Andre. I didn't realize I was shivering until Colton placed a hand on my shoulder.

"Abigail."

I took a breath and turned to face him. "This is just like what

I went through with my parents." I looked over my shoulder and into the foyer where the steps stretched to the second level of the house. "I can't put Gavin through that."

Colton pressed his lips into a hard line and nodded, like he remembered me talking about it on our first date all those years ago.

I released a heavy sigh and took Colton's hand in mine. "I am sorry I didn't tell you the truth. It was stupid."

"You're right, it was stupid. We have to be on the same team, Gail. Always. No secrets."

I nodded. "No secrets."

We stared at each other a moment longer, and I longed to feel his arms around me. I longed for peace and quiet.

"Can I hug you?" I asked hesitantly.

Colton didn't answer; he just pulled me into his arms.

The scent of his clothing was like home to me. It chased the odor of smoke from my memories and I inhaled gratefully. But regret still boiled in the pit of my stomach.

"Do you still love me?" I asked in a hollow voice.

His arms tightened around my waist. "I never stopped."

"Hey, buddy. Can we talk?"

Gavin looked up from his phone and scratched his arm uncomfortably before bidding me entry to his room. I crossed the carpet and sat down on his bed next to him. He watched me like a hawk.

"You need to clean those clothes," I said, nodding at the pile of laundry that apparently didn't make its way into his hamper.

Gavin just looked down at his phone with a muted grunt.

"Look," I said after an exhale. "All couples fight, but just because Colton and I seem to be at each other's throats some-times, that doesn't mean we don't love each other anymore. It's just...relationships can be a lot of work. As long as you work through your issues *together*, you should be okay." When he didn't answer, I added, "I'm sorry you had to hear that tonight."

"It wasn't just that. It's been *nonstop* lately." His phone buzzed and he texted a response.

"I know," I muttered. "Like I said, relationships have their ups and downs; that's normal. And you'll figure that out one day for yourself."

"It's okay, Mom. I just have other things on my mind right now, too."

I shifted so that I could face him fully. "What kinds of things?"

He tossed a glance up at the ceiling.

"Oh, come on," I pleaded. "Talk to me, I'm your mom. That's what I'm here for—to help you."

He peeked at me out of the corner of his eye. "Well, I had like, three tests this week, and they were all really hard, so I don't even want to look at my grades. And Coach has just been pushing us to our limits recently, saying we aren't doing the drills right, even though we *are*, or at least, I am. And..." His eyes flickered to his phone, and I caught the wary look that crossed his face.

"And?"

He swallowed. "I really, really like this girl. And I'm almost positive she likes me, too, but I'm too nervous to ask her out."

I smiled in spite of myself. "Can I ask what her name is?"

"Josie," Gavin said, and a blush painted his cheeks. "She was in my social studies class in seventh grade. That's how I met her."

I knew I should have been upset; he really was too young to dive into these intense feelings, but I was just so happy to be sitting here and talking openly with my son.

"What's she like?"

More color flooded his face. I had to keep myself from giggling. I'd never seen him act this way. "She's a gymnast, and she's *really* good. She always gets first place."

"Wow."

"And she's really smart, too. She gets straight As in every single class, and I'm pretty sure she's the president of the school's mental health club."

"Sounds like a very driven girl."

"She is." Gavin nodded. "And...really pretty."

I couldn't help it this time; I laughed out loud, and my son rolled his eyes.

"Relax!" I said. "I'm glad she makes you smile."

"Well, I hate myself 'cause I can't ask her out. I'm too nervous. Maybe I should just text her—"

"No!" I shouted and Gavin jumped. "*Never* ask a girl out over text. Trust me. Life's all about facing your fears. I suggest you take her out to dinner and ask her there."

Was I really giving Gavin permission to take a girl out on a date? It was like Colton had said—he was bound to experience it sooner or later. And I really did want him to be happy.

"But how do I ask her?"

"Son, listen to me 'cause this advice may save your life. Wait for her to go silent, and in that moment where you're both lost in each other's eyes, *that's* when you make your move."

"And she'll say yes?"

"Well, I would certainly think so! You are the most handsome boy in that school."

Gavin shook his head, but he was smiling now. "Okay, I'll ask her to go out for dinner on Sunday. Can I have some money?"

"Yes, yes." I waved the matter away.

He typed Josie a message and hit send, then sat up straighter and swallowed loudly. Not even five minutes went by before his phone dinged again, and a beaming smile broke across his face.

"She said yes."

I squealed. "I'm proud of you, Gav. You've got this. Just be yourself. Also...don't worry about me and Colton. We've just known each other for a long time, but we're very much in love."

"'Kay, Mom."

I pulled him in for a hug and squeezed him as he squirmed to escape my arms.

~

"My son's about to have a girlfriend," I whispered to Colton that night in our bed.

His arm was draped over me, shielding my skin like an extra blanket. "Five bucks he tries to impress her with his soccer skills."

I laughed and lightly pushed his shoulder. "I'd actually be concerned if he didn't."

"So, you're finally okay with it then?" Colton asked after a moment.

"Yeah, I think I am. I love my son more than words can describe. His happiness is literally everything to me, I...I can't explain it. I mean, sure, I want to protect him, but he can't stay young forever." My tone dipped on that last part. It was terribly bittersweet watching Gavin grow up. "I'm just glad you're here to help raise him."

"Yeah. I've actually been thinking recently." Colton shifted onto his back, and I snuggled closer to hear what he had to say. "I hate fighting with you, Gail. It's hell because I get so short-tempered when I'm stressed out, and I say things I don't mean. But then we walk away from each other, and it's like..." He shook his head. "I miss you so much." He squeezed my shoulder. "To be completely honest, I think I need you now more than ever, especially for...something important."

"What's that?"

A gleam shimmered in his eyes, visible only because of the night light spilling out from the bathroom. He looked perplexed, like his mind was churning to formulate words.

"Colton?"

He drew a deep breath, and I watched his belly deflate as he pushed all the air out. "I love Gavin so much, but I don't want to miss an opportunity before it's too late."

"What are you saying?"

He swallowed and turned to face me. We were nose to nose, and when he spoke, my heart turned to liquid.

"I want to have a baby with you."

Chapter Eleven

SARATOGA SPRINGS, NY

I had a lot of dreams growing up. I wanted to learn the violin and join an orchestra and make a life for myself that I could be proud of. I'd crafted those dreams when I was a young girl, way before Colton ever walked into my life, and I'd achieved them. But now, after everything I'd been through, and to have this man back in my life, I had a new dream, and I craved it.

"Yes," I said, over and over and over until the word sounded odd on my tongue, and Colton was laughing, and my heart was playing jump rope like a little kid. Like the kid I wanted with Colton.

I wanted it so bad, it brought on a physical ache of longing, stinging like the pierce of a moody hornet who was just having a bad day and happened to spot your flesh. I wanted this baby like a child who goes cross-eyed over the swirls of ice cream overflowing in a crisp waffle cone. There wasn't much of a difference between a want and a need here. In fact, they were synonyms. I *needed* this baby.

Colton's lips tasted so much sweeter tonight, sugar-coated in happiness, and I devoured them until my clothes disappeared and his hand was trailing down the skin of my abdomen. I wrapped my legs around his waist, locking him to me forever. And when his lips found my neck, and my fingers found his hair, the longing reached a fever pitch. I was a thermometer, threatening to burst. He whispered things to me—romantic things, dirty things, and things I couldn't even decipher, but it didn't matter. Because now I was gasping against his lips, and he was crumbling inside of me, and there was a moment when nothing else mattered. Nothing but him and me and the overwhelming release.

"God, I love you," Colton said, his voice stripped raw from all the panting and grunting.

I shook my head. "I love you more."

"Impossible," he whispered, and our smiles touched before he kissed me again.

A lot of things were funny in life. Dog videos were funny, reruns of *Family Guy* were funny, memes were hilarious. But nothing beat watching my son fidget in the passenger seat while I drove him to Josie's house on Sunday night. His leg was bouncing sixty miles a minute, and he kept checking his phone like it was going to explode in a shower of glass and orange sparks.

"Relax," I said, failing to hide my smile. "Things work easier when you have control of your emotions."

He nodded but tensed as we pulled up outside of her house. She emerged from her front door minutes later, and I leaned over to catch a glimpse of the girl who had captured my son's heart.

She had long tendrils of black hair and bangs that were pulled half back to reveal a lovely, petite face. Her skin was a dark amber tone, and when she got closer to the car, I noticed how stark and vibrant her hazel eyes were.

I unlocked the back door and said, "Hi, Josie."

"Hey, Mrs. Reeves." Her voice was light and clear as a bell. It was a voice that sweetened the air.

Gavin turned around to her, and they engaged in a little side conversation while Josie's mom came down the porch steps to greet me. As I reached out to shake her hand and introduce myself, it was clear that Josie was a spitting image of her mother.

"I'm Tanya," she greeted me cheerfully. "And you must be Gavin." She peeked into the car at my son.

He nodded and offered a polite grin even though his cheeks were scorching pink. "Nice to meet you, Mrs. Acclow."

"I could nawt pull my dawghter away from her phone fah *weeks*," Tanya gushed as our kids dove into a conversation of their own. She smiled, and her lips stretched over her gums, revealing perfect square-shaped teeth. "It's nice tah know she has someone tah talk to."

I put my elbow on the car's windowsill and leaned out a little further, intrigued by her accent.

"Is that a...Jersey accent I'm hearing?"

"Kinda close." Tanya clasped her hands together. "Bawston."

"Boston!" I exclaimed. "Of course! Did you just move here?"

"Moved heuh when Josie turned two. So about...thuhteen yeas now."

"Oh, wow. Well, it's so great to meet you."

"Yeah, yeah, and you! Gosh, while our kids hang out, we should, too! Oh, *tell* me you've had lawbstah rolls."

"I don't think I—"

"We need tah fix that *right* away! Yah totally invited over fah dinna, Gail."

I laughed. "Thank you so much."

"Be good, Josie!" She called into the car. Then she smiled at me again and scurried back up the porch steps.

The whole way to the restaurant, Gavin was an inflated version of himself—talkative, humorous, fidgeting with the music. Josie got a kick out of everything he did, giggling to herself in the backseat, which only served to feed my son's behavior. It was like watching history repeat itself.

"Text me when you're finished," I told Gavin when I dropped him and Josie at the door to the Brook Tavern.

He gave me a thumbs up and then held the door open for Josie. Through the window I watched the hostess grin at them and lead them to a booth, and my heart gave a fond squeeze. Oh, yes. I knew this story like the back of my hand. I just hoped these were where the similarities ended.

Cara called me on my way home.

"Gail!" she shouted into the phone. I had to pull my ear away from the speaker. "Guess what!"

I turned the car down another street. "What's up?"

There was a muffled conversation, and I could hear Beau's voice in the background. He sounded equally ecstatic.

"I'm pregnant," Cara declared.

I almost slammed on my brakes. "*Shut up!*"

I must have been on speaker phone because Beau chimed in. "Yeah, we talked through it and the time just seemed right."

"I wish I could hug you guys," I whined. "I'm so unbelievably happy for you. Congratulations."

"Would you come out to Michigan for a baby shower?" Cara inquired.

"Of course!"

She proceeded to tell me all the party details, from the food she would have to the color and style of decorations. I explained all the joys of pregnancy and how holding her baby for the first time would be the best moment of her life. Our conversation lasted all the way home; I even walked through the door still pinching the phone between my ear and shoulder. I found Colton in the living room, absorbed in a book.

"Well, congratulations again, guys. It's about time!"

"Who was that?" Colton asked after I hung up. His eyes were glued to his book, and he slurped a purple blueberry smoothie.

"Cara." I put my phone on the coffee table. "She's pregnant."

His eyes instantly cut to mine.

"That's crazy timing," he muttered after a moment.

"Tell me about it."

Colton cleared his throat. "How are *you* doing?"

I shrugged and collapsed down on the couch next to him. "We had sex two nights ago. I don't feel any different."

"I know, I'm just excited." He turned toward me, and the sparkle in his eye was so desperate, so beautiful, I wanted to snap a picture of it and never look away. "*Me* as an official dad." He extended his arms from his side. "That'll be so *amazing*!"

I was giggling now and pulling his arms around me. "If I'm being honest, I cannot wait to see that. But it was just a try."

"I mean, we could try again right now." His finger snaked into my shirt and hooked under my bra strap.

"God, you're tempting."

The shared grins led to kissing, which led to clothes flying off in every direction, and suddenly, his poor book was forgotten. We stumbled up the stairs. His lips teased my neck at the edge of the hallway, and I yanked him into our bedroom, wanting nothing more than to trap him in my arms. I wanted our muscles to get tangled in each other and form gorgeous knots that were impossible to undo. I wanted him in ways no one else could fulfill.

His lopsided grin was like kerosene for my heart that was already slicked in gasoline. He pulled the covers over us, and we vanished into our secret world of tangled limbs, savory kisses, and perfection.

～

Josie had said yes. I could tell by the way her shoulders brushed Gavin's as they trudged toward my car. Their cheeks were such a bright pink, I could've spotted them from the main road. Another dead give away: Gavin climbed into the backseat next to her instead of claiming shotgun like he had since he was twelve. I didn't say a word. I just mashed my lips together to keep from grinning and maneuvered the car out of the restaurant parking lot.

"Mom, let me connect my phone," Gavin said a whole thirty seconds later.

"No way. This is The Weeknd. 'Afterhours' is one of the best songs ever created. It was huge when I was a senior in high school."

"What's The Weeknd?" Josie asked, her alto voice clear and gentle and innocent.

At the red light, I stomped on the brakes a little too hard. "What's the—did you just ask—did she just ask—?" I turned around, peering at Gavin with my jaw on the floor.

He rolled his eyes. "The Weeknd's an artist my mom loves. He's just some old guy from back in the day."

I didn't think it was physically possible, but my jaw fused through the bottom of the car and landed on the concrete of the road. "Are you kidding me right now?"

Josie laughed and tucked a curtain of hair behind her ears.

"Mom, can I connect my phone now? The new Paynaur song dropped today, and it's *so* good."

"Oh my gosh, I've been listening to it on repeat all day," Josie concurred.

I flipped my palms up. "Who the hell is that?"

Josie laughed harder this time, and Gavin laughed because Josie was laughing. In the end, there was no winning with a fifteen-year-old, so my sweet "Afterhours" was replaced by a moody synth topped by indecipherable lyrics.

That was the first time I consciously felt thirty-nine years old.

And it sucked.

When we arrived at Josie's house, she swiped her hair over her shoulder.

"Thank you, Mrs. Reeves," she said as she climbed out of the car, her spotless white sneakers hitting the ground with a small *thump*. "Bye, Gavin."

"You gonna come sit up front or stay back there and drool?" I asked after Josie disappeared into her house.

Gavin sighed and climbed into the passenger seat.

"Okay, Mr. Romeo. Tell me *everything*."

I didn't remember ever seeing him smile this much. "She's...wow."

"Look at you." I glanced over at him quickly before focusing back on the road. "You're smitten."

His smile grew. "We just talked the whole time—about life and school and music. She's really funny, Mom. Like she's so..." He gestured with his hands. "Witty. That's the word I'm looking for. And smart. God, she knows everything about everything. I'm like *holy cow*. And her *laugh*—"

It was one thing that my son was going on and on about a girl, but what was music to my ears was the fact that he was talking to me at all with this much emphasis and emotion. The most I could get out of my teenage son these days was a few "yeahs" and "cools." Maybe the occasional "I love you, Mom." So this moment was definitely going in my sky-blue journal the second we got home. It was a momentous event and needed to be recorded.

"—looked at me, and that was it. I knew it. I told myself, *It's now or never*."

"So, you did it."

"I did it. And she said yes." He sat back in his seat, elbow resting on the console, probably feeling like the coolest guy in the entire world.

My heart wiped its tears. I couldn't help myself. "Aww, my little baby's growing up."

The cool guy retreated. "*Stop.*"

I laughed, and Pauzner—or whatever the hell his name was—filled the silence with dramatic beats.

"Josie actually has a gymnastics meet in two weeks," Gavin said as we pulled into the driveway. "Can we go?"

I killed the engine and that disgusting music. "You got lucky. Tod canceled rehearsals that weekend 'cause he's going to a funeral."

"Great!" Gavin frowned. "I mean, not great, but great. Schedule's free then. Can Colton come?"

"Why don't you ask him yourself?" I suggested, holding the door open for Gavin.

"Too late," he muttered.

Colton was sound asleep on the couch—one arm propped up behind his head and his mouth dangling open.

~

If Gavin had a superpower, it was finding a way to work Josie into every conversation he had with someone. I told him to finish his math homework, and he gave me, "Yeah, I was stuck on this one problem, but Josie helped me through it. She's amazing at math." I asked him how soccer practice was after school, and he said, "It was good. Josie hit me up and said how cool my cleats look." At some point in the following two weeks, I was reduced to just smiling and nodding.

I couldn't blame him. It was the rush, and I knew it well. The rush of having someone to passionately cling to for the first time. The influx of all these new emotions that hoisted you up to the tip of Mount Everest and let you breathe a new kind of intoxicating air. The air of first love. And my Gavin was being transformed by it.

On Friday afternoon, Gavin walked into the kitchen with a noticeable bounce in his step, and an uncharacteristic button-down shirt—zero wrinkles. He'd changed out of the pink Nike T-shirt he wore to school. This was clearly a move to impress Josie at her gymnastics meet tonight, but if it meant my son was ironing his clothes, then I wasn't opening my mouth to complain. Gavin pulled a box of goldfish out of the pantry.

"Blueberries are in the fridge," I reminded him pointedly. "Just in case you're in the mood to make a healthy choice today, too."

He sighed and trudged toward the fridge.

I glanced back down at my calendar and flicked my pen between my pointer and middle fingers. Since I had the day off from playing in the orchestra, I figured I'd start planning ahead. But there was so much coming up that it felt overwhelming to even begin tackling the list in my head. For one thing, Cara had scheduled her baby shower for this upcoming March, but way before that, I had to start planning Colton's fortieth birthday party, which was a mere two months away in January. He'd insisted that he didn't care for anything massive. But he had *also* said that the big four-oh was a massive milestone for him, given everything that he'd been through in his unnecessarily chaotic life. So, whether he liked it or not, I was throwing a party.

I was drafting up a list of potential guests when a heavy weight materialized in my stomach. It burned, sort of like a case of afternoon heartburn. I cleared my throat, hoping it would ease my discomfort, and of course, it didn't.

"Coach was all like, 'Andre! Either focus up or give us a mid-practice performance of a hundred pushups,'" Gavin was saying, deepening his voice to match his coach's baritone. "It was hilarious." He brought his goldfish and the blueberries over to the table. "So, anyway if Colton gets off work at four, can we—" He paused as our eyes locked. "Mom? Are you okay?"

The chill in my stomach grew more intense. "I think I'm going to be sick."

Gavin balked and tossed a nervous glance at the trash. "Uh."

I tried to swallow the acid that was crawling up my throat, and after a few tries, it was clear it had no intention of dissolving. I stood up and made a beeline for the bathroom, clenching my hand against my lips. I couldn't get the toilet seat up fast enough before the vomit spilled from my mouth. I wrenched and convulsed until my stomach was empty. It actually hurt—-how hard the muscles in my throat squeezed. I was basically puking up a lung or my esophagus. Or both. Once I was sure the bile would stay in my stomach, I sank down to my knees and inhaled through my nostrils.

"Was it something you ate?" Gavin asked, and I jumped. I didn't realize he had followed me.

I reached for toilet paper to wipe my mouth. "No. I just had a cup of strawberry yogurt."

"Gross." Gavin leaned against the door frame. "I've never liked strawberry yogurt."

I sighed. "You've never liked strawberry yogurt because I—"

My body froze, and my lips parted in shock. Or no, not shock. Realization.

"Are you gonna puke again?" Gavin asked in a voice that said *give me a warning so I can leave.*

"You probably don't like strawberry yogurt because when I was pregnant with you, just the site of that stuff made me gag."

Gavin gave me a clueless look. "Wait, is that how that works?"

"Doesn't matter."

I got to my feet and brushed past him. My heart had its hands cupped around its mouth and was screaming so loud the rest of my organs had to plug their ears. I took the stairs two at a time and barged into the bathroom in my bedroom.

"Mom, what's going on?" Gavin called from behind me.

I pulled the small rectangular box out of my medicine cabinet and bit my lip.

"What is that?" Gavin asked, his eyes flicking between the box and my face and back again.

"A pregnancy test," I murmured.

All confusion left his face like it had been sucked out by a vacuum. I was scared his eyes were going to pop out of his head.

"Just give me a minute," I assured him and gently closed the door.

I didn't know what I was feeling exactly. Thrilled. Nervous. Nauseous. Excited. Scared. Scared at the idea of another human being growing inside of me *again*, as if my body could handle that kind of stress a second time. I wondered how I even did it a *first* time. Pregnancy wasn't a hop and a skip over a rainbow; it was hard. Except maybe God was ready to have me walk that path again.

And I knew deep down, I would in a heartbeat.

I paced the tile between the shower and the sink, imagining a little nursery and a crib, which led to a memory of that horrible night eight years ago when our house was broken into. Suddenly, my hands were sweating, and I wanted to yank Gavin in here with me so I could protect him. *God please! Just calm my brain—*

The device showed one word on the screen:

Pregnant.

My brain instantly shut its mouth.

"Mom?" Gavin knocked three times.

Breathe, my subconscious demanded. I swallowed and picked the test up from the counter. Five deep breaths later, I opened the door.

Gavin's throat bobbed, and his eyes reflected a kaleidoscope of emotions. Above all, there was a question written in the crease between his eyebrows. I smiled and showed him the test result. Gradually, a grin smeared across his lips.

"So, I'm gonna be a big brother."

I nodded, letting my smile grow and flourish along with his.

Not four seconds passed before the front door opened and closed.

"Where is everyone?" Colton hollered. "Doesn't Josie's meet

start soon? I thought Gavin would be down here pacing in front of the door." He was climbing the steps now.

Gavin turned his eyes back to me, and I read the look on his face instantly, but I wasn't fast enough to catch him.

"Colton! Colton! Guess what!"

Chapter Twelve

MAY, 2082

Kota shoved the spoonful of cheesecake into his mouth and draped his arm around his girlfriend with a lazy smile. "Success tastes sweet."

"You got a little frosting on your nose," Finnley gushed, swiping her finger across Kota's nose.

They'd been dating since junior year of college after Kota bought her a drink and then spilled it while gesturing dramatically during their conversation. According to Finnley though, he'd had her at hello. The drink had also missed her dress, which saved his life.

Abigail slid a card across the table, and Kota did that thing where he tried hard to keep his cool, but his deep grin betrayed him.

"Congratulations, college graduate," he read. "Even though you're so stinkin' rich with knowledge, here's a few extra bucks to make your day." He held up the crisp hundred dollar bill. "Thanks, Grandma."

"That's meant to be split between you and Finnley," she replied and winked at Finnley.

"Hey, wait. We didn't get a hundred bucks when we graduated," Trinity chimed in, gesturing between herself and her twin sister, Andrea.

"You each got fifty." Abigail shrugged. "That makes a hundred."

Andrea and Trinity exchanged a look, but Gavin chuckled under his breath. His daughters were always seeking fairness and perfect balance between themselves—even as adults.

"There's something else," Aliana said, gesturing to the card. "Did you finish reading?"

Kota frowned and picked up the card again. His lips moved silently as his eyes grazed over the words again, and then his jaw split in half.

"What?" Andrea cried.

"We're going to Venice, Italy!" Kota gasped.

"All of us are," Abigail clarified.

There was a moment of shocked silence at the table, and then the kids were all out of their seats, screaming. Neighboring tables offered confused looks, but Abigail didn't care. This reaction was what she'd been waiting for for weeks.

It had been too long since she'd been to her favorite city in the world, and this time, she was sure, would be her last. Abigail wasn't what she used to be—now a withered temple of a body with aches, pains, and an ounce of wit left. Why not Venice? That was the question she'd posed to Gavin and Aliana when they discussed their annual family vacation.

"Are you sure you can handle that flight?" Aliana had asked.

Abigail remembered glancing over at her with a crooked eyebrow and a *how old do I look?* expression. She was going to Venice with them whether they liked it or not because Abigail may have been old and frail, but her heart was sixteen. Sixteen and in love and happy...even if the man she loved was now dust in the wind.

Oh, but he made the wind beautiful, she reasoned. He made it colorful and playful, and sweet, like a gentle caress or a passionate kiss. And if she could, she would stare at the wind until she became part of it.

"I have to go shopping to get a new swimsuit," Trinity exclaimed, whipping out her phone that still had the sticker of Towson's tiger mascot on it. She and Andrea had graduated last year, but they were still always decked out in college apparel.

Abigail smiled at them warmly.

Kids grew up so fast. It felt like just yesterday, Gavin had been riding a ripstik down the sidewalk, and Abigail sat watching from the porch swing, her belly big and swollen with her daughter. Now they were adults and sitting across from her, grinning at their own children.

"I might get a new suit, too," Gavin's wife Hope murmured.

He placed a quick kiss on her temple.

Yes, it was truly a gift to be sitting here with the people Abigail adored most. They filled a void in her that she never even knew existed until she had kids.

Outside, pink Azaleas lined the window, smiling at her and performing a dance in the breeze. The sky was that perfect blue that made you want to go home, pour a glass of lemonade, and just gaze out into the beauty of the world. It was spring now after all. Things always felt lighter in the spring. And for the first time in a long time, the tightness loosened its grip on Abigail's heart.

Chapter Thirteen

SARATOGA SPRINGS, NY (2040)

The floor of the arena was dotted with mats, balance beams, and bars. We were in New York City to see Josie in her first gymnastics meet of the season, and Gavin couldn't sit still. I was just about to tell him to stop shaking his leg when Tanya, Josie's mom, leaned forward in her seat and gestured between me and Colton.

"So, how long have you guys been togetha?"

"It's kind of a long story," I said with a small laugh.

"Are you kidding?" Colton draped an arm around my shoulder. "It's the greatest story of all time."

Tanya's eyes flicked between us, so I clarified. "High school sweethearts."

"Wait!" she gasped. "So, he's ya first love? Oh, that is so *adorable!* Simon, did ya hear that?" She slapped her husband's arm.

Simon glanced over at us. "Now *that's* what I call commitment. Nice." He held up a fist for Colton to bump, and suddenly the two were best friends. Tanya rolled her eyes.

"It's even better now though," Colton continued. A grin the size of California spread across his face. "We've got a little one on the way."

Earlier, when Gavin had spilled the beans, Colton had dropped to his knees in front of me, mouth agape and completely speechless.

"I'm gonna be a brother!" Gavin had shouted, jabbing the air with his fists like he'd just won the lottery.

Colton had simply stared at my abdomen. "Don't joke about this stuff."

"You think that's a fabricated reaction?" I'd asked, pointing at Gavin.

And then he'd wrapped his arms around my waist, pressed his forehead against my stomach, and cried while Gavin bounced off the walls.

Tanya's mouth fell open. "Shut. Up! Simon! Did ya—"

"I heard, I heard. Congratulations."

"I can't believe I'll be a dad," Colton murmured.

"Yeah, man. It's fun until they stawt havin' boyfriends," Simon posited.

Gavin's head snapped up. "Oh, come on, Mr. Acclow. I thought we were cool!"

"Oh, we're the coolest," Simon assured him and glanced at me with a shrug.

I laughed and turned my focus back to Tanya. "Yes. Colton and I have been in love for a long time. Gavin is my son from another marriage though."

"Yet ya found ya way back to each otha." Tanya pressed a hand to her heart. "That sounds like a fairytale! Meanwhile, Simon and I met at the gym." Her high-pitched laugh was easily contagious. "I'd love tuh hear the whole story sometime. Ya should write it out."

I cocked my head at her. "What do you mean?"

"This might be a me thing, but I'm a sucka for romance stories."

"Ain't that the truth," Simon muttered.

"You mean like, write about how we got together?"

"It doesn't have tuh be a published novel! But maybe jus' fah memory's sake. Yunno?"

Dani Caldwell flashed to my mind then. Once upon a time—several lifetimes ago—Evan's sister had said, *Everyone has a story, so don't think yours isn't worth writing.*

"I think that's a great idea," Colton declared.

Tanya turned toward Simon. "Will you eva' write somethin' about *me*?"

I didn't catch his response because an idea was starting to churn in my mind. *Write about my story, about how Colton and I—*

"She's up! She's up!" Gavin announced and pointed to the balance beam. And all talk of love stories was forgotten.

Josie approached the beam, and in her bright red leotard, she looked like a firework—beaming and impossible to look away from. For the first time since we'd arrived, I felt a pang of anxiety for her.

Before I could overthink her safety, she had gracefully lifted herself onto the beam and swung her legs underneath her to stand up. Except she didn't stand, she crouched with one leg extended out and her arms preparing to propel her.

My heart squeezed. "She's not going to—"

Josie twirled on her single foot. Her head whipped around with each turn, and even from here, I could see the intense focus in her eyes. She caught herself perfectly, and the audience cheered. Tanya and Simon were out of their seats. Gavin was gripping the railing.

Josie stood up fully then and executed one back-handspring and backflip before I could even process that she'd moved. And with the following leaps and one switch leap, my poor heart had climbed up to cower in my throat. But she was extremely good. This seemed like child's play for her.

She stepped toward the end of the beam, and I knew this had to be the finale of her routine because Tanya was screaming, "Come on, Jose! Ya got this!"

Josie took a visible deep breath, then forced her arms up and flipped backward again and again before hoisting herself into the air and twisting like her body was weightless. Her feet came down on the mat with a resounding *slap*, and she threw her arms up in the air.

Everyone was out of their seats in an instant, screaming for her. Her smile was electric as she turned toward her coach and accepted the bottle of Gatorade. I didn't know what I'd been expecting, but this girl was *good*.

Later, when Josie was finished competing, Gavin towed us through the crowd to reach her.

"You are phenomenal," I gushed.

Josie ducked her head to hide her smile. "Thank you, Mrs. Reeves."

"What do you say we keep this party going with some Farsca's Pizza?" Simon suggested, high-fiving his daughter.

Oddly though, the thought of pizza suddenly made me want to hurl. The sensation spiraled to the pit of my stomach, and I glanced nervously at the nearest trash can. *Not this again.*

"Gail, are you okay?" Colton asked, pressing a hand to my back.

"I just feel sick all of a sudden."

"That's the baby talkin'." Tanya beamed. "And it could also be that chicken ya had earlia. I always say, 'Never trust food trucks.' I always say that, don't I, Simon?"

I leaned into Colton when the nausea tied my stomach into a double-knotted ribbon.

He wrapped an arm around me and said, "Maybe some other time with that pizza."

"Wait, no," Gavin whined. "Can I still go?"

My son and his girlfriend clung to each other, refusing to part.

Tanya smiled. "It's no trouble. We can drop him off on our way home."

"If you don't mind, that would be great," Colton said.

"Of course, any time. Feel betta, Gail."

I smiled weakly, but before Colton could lead me toward the exit, I pulled Gavin aside.

"Behave yourself," I warned.

He gave me a solid salute. "Always do." He took Josie's hand and they raced for the doors.

∽

I felt worse on the ride home. It was like my intestines were being stretched apart and blowtorched.

"The chicken tasted fine when I ate it," I grunted.

"You are also pregnant," Colton offered. He looked over at me, and the smile on his face almost cured me.

Once we got home, I collapsed into bed. Colton slid off my shoes and adjusted a blanket over me before going to retrieve a trash can—just in case.

"Might be that damn stomach bug, too," I said. "I heard that's been going around."

"You are *also* pregnant." He pulled the comforter up to my shoulders.

"Really? I hadn't realized."

He laughed quietly and brushed a few strands of hair off my face. "Just wanted to remind you."

For a moment, we smiled at each other. They were smiles we'd exchanged at least three hundred times over the years, but then the flecks of gold in his eyes drew my attention, and before I knew it, I was lost in them. Lost in him.

"Can you stay?" I whispered. It made me feel young again somehow, like we were the only ones in the universe.

"Absolutely." He touched his nose to mine.

I let his fingers continue to caress my skin until fatigue grew stronger than the pain in my stomach. I didn't even remember closing my eyes, but when I woke up sometime later, my surroundings had changed entirely. The room was pitch black now, and Colton was asleep beside me in the bed. One look at the clock alerted me that it was just after midnight.

"Holy crap," I said out loud.

Colton jerked awake. "Are you okay?"

"I was out for *six hours*?"

My husband yawned and groggily rubbed the sleep from his eyes. "Yeah, you passed out. How's the stomach?"

"Better. I'm even kind of hungry. Please tell me Gavin's here."

"He got home around eight. I think we have some leftover vegetable soup. Do you want me to heat some up for you?"

"Yes, please."

When he returned, I downed the bowl in a few quick slurps, and it was as if my stomach clapped its hands. I wanted more.

"So, I guess you'll be eating like a horse from now on?" Colton asked as I finished my second helping of soup.

"Eventually."

I laid back down in the bed with a full, satisfied tummy, and reached out for Colton.

"If you feel funny in the morning, I can call and see if Jake can take my shift—"

"No." I shook my head. "Are you crazy? I'm pregnant, not dying."

I could see his hesitance even in the dim lighting, but the bills wouldn't be paid by my job alone. Plus, I had a three hour rehearsal tomorrow for the Saratoga Strings' mid-winter concert in a few weeks. Attendance was mandatory.

"Relax," I whispered. "I'm okay."

Still unconvinced, Colton laid down beside me and we drifted off to sleep together. In the morning, my head was throbbing. It felt like my brain had two fists and was beating at my skull to escape. I swallowed some Advil with my breakfast and tried to massage my temples in the peace and quiet before practice.

"Mom, I'm going to Andre's tonight," Gavin said, pouring himself a bowl of Raisin Bran.

"Sounds good."

"You okay?"

At the sound of my son's concern, I sat up straighter and forced a smile, which only made my head spin more.

"Yeah," I lied. "Good as always."

I must have been a bad liar because he didn't seem convinced either. "Text me if you need anything."

"That's kind of you."

He shrugged and disappeared into the basement.

Unsurprisingly, rehearsal just instigated my headache.

"Gail, you look like you're in some serious pain," Seth observed between songs.

By then, I was gritting my teeth just to stay in my seat—angry with a short fuse that had already burned out. I turned toward him and hissed that I was pregnant. His jaw immediately dropped, and Veronica's eyes almost dislodged from her head.

"I assume you're happy," she whispered as Tod addressed the orchestra about measure 40.

"Ecstatic," I deadpanned.

"Why are we just now hearing about this?" Seth whisper-shouted back.

"Because I just found out yesterday."

"Instruments up, please. Let's give it a try." Tod raised his baton, and our conversation was cut short.

Two hours and fifteen minutes later, my bones had turned to ash, and my mind was deflated into a pile of gushy nothingness. I lugged my violin case toward the door.

"What are you gonna name the baby?" Veronica asked.

"We haven't talked about it yet."

"Demetrius and I are thinking about adopting. Did I tell you that?" Seth's deep brown eyes twinkled. "I've always wanted a daughter."

"Me, too, honestly." I felt my heart surge a little at the thought, but I'd realized a long time ago that gender didn't really matter. What did matter was the fact that my body had the ability to conceive and carry a human being—*twice*.

"That's amazing, Seth," I went on. "I feel like this has been a long time coming for you and Demetrius."

"Uh, says *you*," Veronica retorts. "You've known Colton since 600 AD."

"I forgot you were a historian." I grinned at her and held the door open for them to pass through.

"I'm just saying," she continued. "You and Colton having a baby is like...rain in the middle of April."

"What does that even mean?" Seth laughed and took a sip of his nearly empty Starbucks coffee.

"It means it's inevitable," she clarified. "And, therefore, not surprising. But we are *very* happy for you." We stopped beside my car, and she gave me a gentle hug. "Just don't forget us when you're planning the invites for your baby shower."

"Shit, we have to get gifts then." Seth bumped her arm.

My lips twitched. "Thank you guys so much. That actually means the world to me." By now, the pain was subsiding slowly— praise God, hallelujah in the highest—and I placed my violin case in the trunk. "Well, I filled you in. Now you fill *me* in." I turned back to Veronica. "What's going on with you and Connor?"

The cello player exited the building right on cue, head down, auburn hair billowing slightly in the wind. When he looked up and noticed Veronica, he smiled and waved. I'd never seen Veronica's face look that elated or that red.

"Things are great." The smile was glued to her lips.

"She's in love," Seth forced between coughs.

"Don't you have somewhere to be?" Veronica demanded.

"Good point. Demetrius is probably already at the sushi restaurant. See you guys!"

"I really am happy for you, Gail," Veronica said then. "You and Colton deserve this." She flashed me a friendly smile and turned on her heel, conveniently running into Conner just as he passed.

It wasn't until I climbed into the driver's seat that I noticed the text message on my phone. It was from Elijah.

Miraculously, I'm off work today. Wanna have lunch and catch up?

Immediately, I responded with four exclamation points.

"So," Elijah said, swirling the lemonade in his glass and pinning me with his signature smirk. "Baby number two."

"Baby number two," I confirmed and chewed on my straw.

I was grateful that my migraine had kicked the bucket because I hadn't seen Elijah in what felt like forever.

"You think you can handle it?" he challenged.

"I'm a superhuman." I shrugged. "What's another pregnancy?"

"I'm not talking about the birth. Imagine taking care of a newborn and dealing with a lovesick teenager."

"Gavin's fine," I retorted, and he laughed.

Elijah and Brie had never had children. With Elijah's job as a journalist and Brie's hectic hours as a nurse, neither of them had the time or the energy. But they never complained either.

I looked out the window for a moment and spotted two teenagers bundled up and walking down the sidewalk. Something about the way they laughed with each other took me back to my years in college at the Curtis Institute of Music. Where I'd met Elijah.

"Do you think you'll ever play cello again?" I murmured. When he transferred to Ashford University, he'd promised me that he would never stop, but that was decades ago.

He shrugged. "It doesn't really cross my mind anymore. Why?"

Outside, the male teenager made a dramatic gesture, and the girl burst into laughter. I watched them with a heavy fondness sinking through my stomach.

"I don't know," I answered in a distant tone.

Elijah leaned forward with his elbows on the table—a motion that told me to continue.

I met his eyes. "I'm thirty-nine, Elijah. What the hell is that?"

He tried to suppress his smile. "Yeah, and almost forty. Isn't it great?"

By now, the teenagers had crossed the road and disappeared.

"I don't know," I repeated. "Sometimes it is and sometimes it isn't."

A waitress passed our table with a full tray of food, and when she set it down in front of a family, the little girls squealed.

"Well, I don't know about you, but I *never* wanna go back to my twenties." Elijah curled his lips distastefully. "All the ridiculous drama with my parents about college, the exhausting *does she like me? Does she not?* The Pulmonem Fever—*ugh*. Count me out."

"But what about the freedom?" I argued. "We weren't locked

into anything. We could do whatever we wanted when we wanted."

Elijah gave me a look. "What land were *you* living in during your twenties?"

"I just mean that we were still young, you know? Like our futures didn't revolve around...reminding your fifteen-year-old son to finish his homework or cleaning every inch of the house just to have it be messed up again in the next twenty seconds."

"I feel a vent session coming here."

I smiled at him softly.

He hadn't changed much over the years. He still had ready and willing ears.

"I just feel like I'm losing time. Hell, I'm already pregnant with my second kid."

"And that's a miracle," Elijah intervened.

"Yes." I touched my stomach softly. "But Gavin's already fifteen. And Colton's turning forty in a couple weeks." I placed my palms flat on the table and bored my eyes into Elijah's. "*Forty.* I knew him when we were *eleven*. This is just insane."

"Okay, okay," Elijah said. "I can tell you're having a lot of anxiety over this. Are you still on medication?"

"Of course," I grumbled. "But what's that have to do with it?"

"Nothing. I just want to make sure you have it under control. 'Cause if you don't have *you*, everything goes haywire. Especially for the baby." He sat back in his seat and glanced up at an abstract painting on the wall. "Nostalgia's normal, Gail. We all go through periods where we wish we could be young again. But if you think about it, there's a lot of beauty in growing up. Wisdom, for one thing."

I shrugged. "Fair point."

"Is there something deeper here that you're not talking about?"

I hesitated for five heartbeats before saying, "I guess I'm scared of losing myself in the monotony."

"Ah. Do you feel like you already have?"

"See, it's yes and no again. Because Colton and I have been through shit, and that doesn't feel monotonous. I'm still scared someone's gonna break into my house to this day."

Elijah nodded, and his eyes screamed sympathy.

"But then I'm always practicing my violin and cleaning and cooking and organizing and planning, and God, I *feel* like I need something crazy to happen!"

As soon as the words left my mouth, heat burst into my cheeks.

"You feel like you need something crazy to happen," he repeated slowly, dragging the words out and squinting his eyes.

I reached for my glass and downed half the water.

"Crazy as in...fill in the blank," he encouraged me.

"Not dangerous," I clarified with a bit of a bite in my tone. "But out of the ordinary. I'm just getting sick of doing the same routine over and over again."

"Is that why you're having a baby?"

"No, I—" The words instantly died on my tongue.

Was it?

No, I wanted a baby with Colton because we'd been dreaming of this for years. And because I really wanted to witness him holding his own child. But then again...I'd been so quick to jump into the idea.

"Stop." Elijah shook his head. "I know what you're doing, so stop."

"What?"

"You're taking what I said too literally and trying to break it down from every angle. Except it's not a black and white matter, Gail. You can have lots of reasons for having a baby. Take a breath, you're okay."

I sighed. "My anxiety is so bad."

"Monotony is no fun, I'll give you that. But you have to find one good thing in your day and hold onto it like it's the only thing that exists. Gratitude can be a drug."

"Okay, um...I'm grateful for this conversation right now."

"There you go!" His smile faded slightly. "Listen, Gail, it's true. We're growing up. So be it. But while we are, wouldn't you rather plant some roses to smell along the way?"

"Were you just born this smart, or did you fall into a vat of acid that gave you pure wisdom?"

"Nope. It's just life experience." He tapped his temple with another smirk.

I took a deep, calming breath. "So, gratitude. That's the answer?"

"Gratitude for everything," he confirmed. "Especially the small things."

"Can I take your orders?" our waiter asked, materializing out of thin air.

Elijah turned toward him immediately and didn't miss a beat. "Yeah, I'll have the crab cake meal with some extra asparagus please. And another lemonade when you get the chance."

I smiled at him and glanced down at my menu.

Chapter Fourteen

SARATOGA SPRINGS, NY (2041)

I really did not like January. I hated it because the sky was the color of spit, and the trees were decaying skeletons, and the ground was practically a demolition zone coated in several sheets of ice. It was a time of brittle smiles, snot-smeared noses, and paper pale skin. January was my least favorite month, but I was prohibited from hating it entirely because Colton just so happened to be born on January fourteenth.

His birthday was this coming Saturday. It was a surprise party, which meant I'd had to work my ass off to schedule distracting activities beforehand. I couldn't wait to see the look on his face when he would find all of our friends huddled in the living room. Plus, I could finally announce to everyone that I was pregnant.

Meanwhile, we were seeing a lot more of Josie. She came over for dinner most weekends, and afterward, she and Gavin would disappear into the basement where I *liked* to think they were just watching movies by the fireplace. She was steadily making her way into my heart. I liked how driven and polite she was, complimenting my cooking and saying the house wasn't that messy when it was a literal pigsty. And she made my son smile like no one I'd ever known.

It was an understatement to say that Gavin was utterly taken with her. He worked harder in school and at soccer just to impress her, which I couldn't complain about. He *showered* her with affection and from what I could tell, she was returning it just as much. Most times, Colton tried to embarrass Gavin with stories of when Gavin was younger, but Josie just blushed and laughed along with us.

When they were together, no one else existed. It was almost odd watching it from an outside perspective, but I had *no* room to talk. I lined them up in front of the mantle on the night of the big winter dance, snapping picture after picture until Gavin groaned and warned me they would be late.

"Is this really what young love does to people?" I asked Colton that night after the kids left. My voice was drenched in sarcasm. "Make them go crazy for someone?"

Colton smiled before placing an arm around my shoulder. "Gosh, who can say?"

Of course, with Gavin's flourishing love life, his other relationships were taking a hit.

"Haven't seen Andre in a while," I commented Tuesday morning as Gavin lugged his backpack toward the door.

"He's fine."

And that was it.

I squinted at my son over the rim of my water bottle. "Just fine?"

"Mhm." Gavin reached for his phone, and I had to be a dimwit to miss the blush in his cheeks. It was a text from Josie, no doubt.

"When was the last time you and Andre hung out outside of school?"

Gavin sighed, clearly not interested in the conversation. "I don't know. Like, three or four weeks ago?" He shrugged.

"You should ask him to hang out soon."

"'Kay."

I got up from the couch and grabbed his lunch box and my car keys off the table. "Don't burn your friendships over a relationship. That's a very tough hole to get out of."

Gavin scoffed. "You act like Josie and I are gonna break up."

I didn't say anything else. I just climbed into my car and opened the garage door. Gavin immediately connected his phone, and the car flooded with unintelligible rap lyrics. He mouthed every word.

"It will be so nice when you get your license," I joked.

"Speaking of, can we go to an empty parking lot this weekend? I wanna practice."

"Well, not Saturday 'cause that's Colton's party." I glanced in my rearview and then at Gavin.

"Can Josie come to that?"

"How about Andre?" I suggested.

"Mom."

"Gavin."

He rolled his eyes and typed something on his phone—probably a text to Josie.

It *was* difficult raising a teenager, I couldn't lie. Sometimes when we got into meaningless fights over dirty laundry or dishes, and he quickly snapped back with a harsh comment, it made me wonder how I *ever* had the bravery to talk to my own dad that way. Because I definitely had. But now things were just in razor sharp focus.

I pulled into the school drop-off line, and spotted Andre standing on the steps in a beanie and navy blue coat.

"Oh, perfect!" I exclaimed. "Go talk to him."

Gavin's jaw flexed, and he was clearly biting back an acidic response, but for whatever reason, he swallowed it. "Bye, Mom."

I craned my neck to see if he approached Andre or not, and to my immense relief, he did. Andre lit up when he saw him. The two walked into the building together, and a small part of my stress dissipated.

On the way to rehearsal, my dad called me—speak of the devil.

"Hey, Dad."

"Hi. I'm just calling about Colton's party this weekend. When should we be there?"

"Noon's fine. I'm taking him to a late breakfast, so we'll be gone for a while. I think Elijah and Brie are coming early, too, to help set up. And Gavin promised he'd help decorate, so we'll see if that actually happens."

"Hey, is Gavin surviving without that girl?"

I pulled into the rec center parking lot and pulled my keys from the ignition. "Hardly. I'm trying to raise a lovesick teenager."

"Been there," he muttered, and I laughed. "But even though I saw less of you the older you got, I'm still grateful for those years. It's something you have to learn to cherish because before you know it, they're gone."

"Please don't remind me, Dad."

"Ah, I won't. I'm just saying. Although sometimes I think you grew up a little too quickly, what with all that business between Colton's father and the breakup and the drama. Those days *sucked*. I felt like...I couldn't do anything to help. Those types of things can just scar you for life. It's crazy how times change."

"You did help," I assured him. "You taught me how to stay strong. I wouldn't have made it through that chapter of my life if it weren't for you, Dad."

"Well, me and music." He chuckled. "But I'm glad. You know the older I get, the more grateful I feel."

Elijah's words floated through my mind: *Grateful for everything, especially the small things!*

"Yeah, that's the way to live."

I'd taken Elijah's suggestion seriously, and for the past month and a half, I'd filled my sky-blue notebook with lists of random things that made me happy throughout the day. Sometimes, the lists were two items long. Other days, they exceeded ten. I wasn't sure if it was the power of the placebo of just writing something, but a part of me did feel lighter.

I wondered about that a lot these days—what treatments or activities I could do to silence the monster inside me. I had therapy, and writing, and medication—even Benzos for when I was feeling *extremely* anxious and had to dodge a panic attack. And now gratitude. But I was still anxious. It wasn't anywhere near what it had been after the break in or when Colton's father had almost killed him. But it was always there, sitting and twirling its thumbs, waiting to cut off my oxygen.

I wanted answers now more than ever since I was pregnant. I didn't know the exact percentage of increased risk for genetic predisposition, but it didn't matter. Gavin had gotten really lucky in that aspect. But what about this baby? Would he or she inherit my anxiety and live life overthinking every little decision? The thought made me nauseous. What kind of person was I to even take the chance on handing someone this hell? Then again, guilt didn't help much either. So, to deal with the overthinking of my overthinking, I listed things I was grateful for every day in hopes of appeasing my mind for even five minutes.

"Each day is a blessing," Dad said. "I mean, look at me! I'm still chuggin' along! Sixty-nine is just a number."

"You got that right." I spotted Veronica and Connor walking inside with their instrument cases, giggling over some private joke. "Hey, I'm at rehearsal now, Dad, but I'll see you on Saturday. I have some big news, too."

"Does it have to wait till then?"

"Yep." I grinned to myself as I retrieved my violin case from the trunk. He was going to freak out when I told him he would have a second grandkid.

"Fine. Have a great rehearsal, sweetheart."

"Thanks, Dad."

Just as I hung up, Seth appeared beside me, looking fresh in a button-down flannel shirt.

"Veronica's drooling over Connor, so I need a new buddy to walk inside with."

"Good thing I'm here!" I smiled at him.

"It beats third wheeling."

On Saturday, I took Colton out for breakfast for his birthday; at least, that was the excuse. Meanwhile, our friends were invading our house, and I'd left Elijah and Brie in charge to welcome them. The massive line of cars was a dead giveaway though, so Colton pretty much had it figured out the moment we stepped into the house.

"Surprise!" everyone yelled.

"Happy forty, you old head," Ashton Rinoven shouted, slapping Colton's shoulder affectionately. He and Colton had been friends since the sixth grade, and as soon as Colton saw him, a massive smile split his face.

I spotted Gavin and Josie through the crowd and moved toward them.

"Grandpa's not here yet," Gavin informed me.

I furrowed my eyebrows. "That's not like my dad. Did you call him?"

"We can," Josie assured me. She gestured to Gavin's phone, and they disappeared into the other room.

"Nice party," Erica said.

I hadn't seen her in ages and almost yanked her arm out of socket to hug her. "God, I missed you. You're not gonna believe the news I have."

"What, did Gavin have his first kiss?" My friend clasped her hands together. "That's adorable!"

"No," I said, then thought about it. "Well, I don't know. Probably. But that's not the news."

Cara appeared, her amber-golden hair now cut to shoulder length and layered in the front. It somehow made her look older and even wiser. Her warm doe-eyes twinkled even brighter than I remembered. And her stomach was just barely beginning to show. Beau smiled at me and waved. He was secured to Cara's side.

"Oh, good, you're just in time," Erica announced. "Gail was about to spill some news."

"What's up?" Cara asked.

"No, you guys just have to wait," I insisted.

Erica threw her arms up, frustrated, but Cara narrowed her eyes at me. I could practically see the lightbulb flash in her brain.

"You're pregnant, aren't you?"

I tried hard to suppress a smile. Erica's hand shot to her mouth.

"Wow, talk about timing," Beau said, squeezing Cara's hand.

"Shh!" I hissed. "It's supposed to be a surprise." I was mainly talking to Erica because she was wide-eyed and clearly five seconds from jumping up and down.

"I can't believe this," she breathed. "That's amazing, Gail."

I opened my mouth to respond, but Gavin tugged on my sleeve.

"Grandpa didn't answer," he said.

Frowning, I checked my phone and saw that it was 12:15 pm. Dad was never late—especially for birthdays.

"Uh...all right. Maybe he was just reading and lost track of time or something. We'll call again in a bit."

Gavin shrugged and pulled Josie off through the crowd. My father still hadn't shown up, and by one o'clock, we had to get on with the festivities.

The afternoon brought laughter and delight as we all sat around the table and recalled our best memories of Colton. Ashton described the moment he walked in on teenage Colton kissing a poster of Ariana Grande, which made us all laugh so hard we couldn't breathe.

"Here you go," Elijah said, dropping a small present in Colton's lap.

Colton pressed his lips into a line. "I really didn't need any—"

"Just open it!" we all cried in unison.

He sighed and tugged at the blue wrapping paper. It was a personalized keychain with his initials on it and a picture of us on our wedding day. I leaned across the table to get a better look at it, and Brie just shrugged.

"You two have one of the best love stories ever. Elijah and I figured...why not take it with you wherever you go?"

"Thank you so much," Colton exclaimed. He stared at the picture, particularly at me.

Elijah laughed. "We're competing to see who has the best gift."

Colton shook his head. "Nah, nothing could beat the gift that Gail has for me."

I shot him a look because I hadn't been prepared for him to say that. He waved his hand, urging me excitedly, and then gave me a thumbs up and a breathtaking smile. I felt my heart flip flop in my chest as I stood up from my chair.

"Everyone, I have an announcement to make."

"Oh, finally!" Erica squealed.

I looked around at the faces crowding my kitchen table and smiled. "Everyone...Colton and I are—"

The shrill ringing of the house phone cut me off midsentence, and I glared at it until it stopped. In the silence that followed, I tried again.

"I'm pr—"

Another round of ringing.

"Oh, for Heaven's sake. Gavin, would you please see who that is?" I sat down, flustered by the interruption.

My son excused himself from the table and took the phone

from its cradle. After greeting the caller, an odd expression crossed his face.

"It's Jamie."

"Here, let me have it," Colton offered. He took the phone. "Hello?"

My stomach lurched when horror pinched his face; his mouth dropped to the floor.

"Oh my God...No, don't worry. We'll be right there. Thanks for the update." When he hung up, my heart was hammering for a different reason. The room was deathly quiet before he said, "We have to get to the hospital. Gail, your dad just had a heart attack."

Chapter Fifteen

SARATOGA SPRINGS, NY

How did this happen?" I demanded. "He was perfectly healthy! He never smoked, never drank, never had *any* underlying conditions!"

"Ma'am, please calm down," the nurse said.

"I want answers!" My voice broke on the last word, and Colton had to put a hand on my shoulder to calm me down.

"Ma'am, all I can tell you right now is that he is in emergency surgery. Further information will be released when the operation is complete."

"Is he going to die?" I asked bluntly.

The woman gave me a bewildered stare. I couldn't imagine having her job, having to break the news to a victim's family. She paled slightly and swallowed. "Like I said, we can't know for sure until the operation is complete."

"Gail," Colton murmured. He squeezed my shoulder in a way that said, *Don't push this. All we can do is wait.*

I strode into the waiting room of the hospital, even though waiting was absolute torture. My leg bounced fiercely as I glared at the doors that blocked me from my father. Colton pinched the bridge of his nose and laid a hand on my leg to stop the incessant shaking.

"I'm sorry," I heard myself say. "For having to cut the party short. But—"

"Don't apologize," he said. "I'm not mad, Gail. I'm scared." His eyes dropped to the tile under our feet. "Your dad accepted me back into the family after everything that happened, and he took care of Gavin when we couldn't. For a while, h–he was like my dad, too..."

"What about Sean?" Colton's stepdad had replaced his monster of a biological father who *should* have been rotting away in prison for beating him all those years ago but had gotten out. God knows where he was now.

"Sean's great, but your dad really gave up a grudge for me. That said a lot about his character."

Pain seeped into my heart like a plague. Of course Colton loved my dad as much as I did. The *world* loved my dad. He was too kind, too gentle, too loving; if anything, we didn't deserve him.

"D-do you think he'll...?" I couldn't even bring myself to say it.

I didn't realize Colton was crying until a stray tear caught the light and scurried down his cheek. My eyes started to burn for the fourth time in the last hour.

Colton sniffled and cleared his throat. "I don't know."

The air was as thick as an invisible fog. It curled around us, pressing in on our chests like the pressure of water. For a moment, I watched Jamie converse with the same nurse before a twinge of nausea curled through my stomach. I shifted in my seat, which snatched Colton's attention instantly.

"Are you okay?" His eyes flickered toward my stomach.

Not now, I wanted to whine at the universe. *But okay, yes now.*

Bile boiled at the base of my throat, threatening to shoot up and out. I twisted in my seat again.

"I don't remember feeling this sick with Gavin." For a second, I was sure I was about to puke right here on the floor, but it was a false alarm.

"Maybe we're having a girl," Colton said. My eyes snapped to his, and he smiled softly. "I'm going to go get you some water. Hold tight."

A girl...My heart pounded at that realization. What a blessing she would be.

Colton returned seconds later, and I took the water bottle from him, sipping slowly until the rolling nausea faded. As it did, the hospital came into my awareness again, as did the grim realization that my father was enduring emergency heart surgery. Was he alive? Would he make it?

"My dad should be there when our kid is born," I whispered.

"Nobody lives forever, Gail."

"It can't be my dad's time yet."

"That's not your call to make."

When I dropped my head into my hands, Colton draped an arm over my shoulder.

"Look," he whispered. "Whatever happens, we'll make it through. We always do. We did even when we didn't have each other. Your dad wouldn't want us to put our lives on hold if he decides to go."

"I don't *want* him to go."

Colton's only response was a troubled sigh.

Some time later, Jamie sat back down in the row of chairs across from us. I stared at her, waiting for some kind of reassurance that Dad was fine, but she just shook her head and closed her eyes.

"They're not telling me anything."

We sat for a long time in utter silence. Outside, the sky expanded into a waterfall of colors on the horizon. Under other circumstances, it could have been a beautiful sunset, but my leg was shaking again, and my neck had developed a nasty cramp. How long did emergency heart surgery take?

"If I don't eat soon, my stomach will eat itself," Colton said eventually. "I'm going to the cafeteria. Can I get you ladies anything?"

"No, thank you." Jamie smiled weakly.

I really wasn't hungry, but I didn't think I could casually skip meals now that I had a human growing inside of me again. "Salad, please," I told him tonelessly.

He kissed the top of my head and disappeared into the elevator.

"Jamie, if you want to go home and get some sleep, I can stay here. It's no trouble. Gavin's with Josie, so I don't have to be back yet. In fact, I'm sure he'd love it if I stayed here all night. But I'll send Colton to pick him up." I rolled my eyes at the thought of my son spending the night at his girlfriend's house. That was *not* happening.

"Oh, no, I couldn't leave." Jamie shook her head. "I need to be there when Albert wakes up. Assuming he does."

It dawned on me then that my father was like Jamie's Colton. She loved him as much as I loved my husband.

"Albert is such an amazing man." She sighed. "You know, at first he was just another doctor in the clinic, but he was the only one who genuinely made me feel welcome when I became a nurse there. And I'm a real sucker for gentlemen, but your father is the kindest man I've ever met."

"Thank you." It was so nice to hear stories about my dad.

"I'm the lucky one." She chuckled. "For some reason he chose me, and my heart has belonged to him ever since."

"To tell you the truth, I've never seen my dad so happy. Even with my mom, I doubt he felt like himself."

This brought a shy smile to Jamie's face. "I think he may be the love of my life. Took me a little while to find that person, but

I'm more than grateful it's Albert. Plus, I never had any kids of my own, Gail. My ex-husband was very abusive. We had a lot of financial issues, and he took his anger out on me. Called me names, smacked me across the face." She shuddered at some memory. "But your father is the complete opposite of that, and it shows in how he raised *you*—such a strong, beautiful woman."

"I'm grateful for you, too, Jamie." I reached out to take her hand.

Sometimes, a simple gesture like that could act as a lifeline.

"And...if he doesn't come back, I...well, I just want you to know that he loved you, Gail. More than anything else in this world. You were his biggest achievement."

Before I could respond, Colton came back with the food. I picked through my salad like a bird while the sky turned to an inky black. It was getting late, and I knew Tanya wouldn't be too excited to roll out a sleeping bag for my son either. She was very conservative when it came to that, as was I.

"I can pick him up," Colton offered. "And then I can come back here and pick you—"

"I'm not leaving." My tone left no room for arguments.

"Well, then I'll bring pillows and blankets."

I leaned in to kiss him.

"Did you tell Jamie the news?" Colton asked then, glancing down at my abdomen.

"No, we should tell her together."

Jamie questioned us with her eyes, and when we told her, her mouth quivered until tears leaked down her cheeks. Something in me soured. How could I talk about bringing someone into the world when my father was possibly about to leave it?

Colton had to leave to pick up Gavin, and when he did, the empty chair next to me somehow made the whole waiting room feel colder. More dreadful.

Jamie and I sat in silence, and I looked back up at the sky, only now, I was counting the stars. An hour passed before I noticed that Jamie had dozed off. Even in sleep, she looked troubled with her eyebrows pulled together and a frown sagging her lips. Exhaustion was tugging on my bones, too, but I couldn't sleep. I was too worried.

It was five past midnight when a doctor stepped through the doorway. He was wearing a surgeon's cap with a mask down around his neck. My entire body became a block of ice. He crossed the waiting room toward us in four quick strides.

"Jamie?" His eyes flickered between us. Jamie rose from her seat and tiredly shook the doctor's hand. "Ah, hello. I'm so sorry about the wait, but these emergency surgeries can take up to six hours."

"Is my dad okay?" I demanded.

The doctor turned his eyes to me, and I could see the regret plain as day. It was mixed with sorrow and pity. I wanted to beat my fists against his chest before he said, "Albert is resting in a room upstairs, but...he may not make it through the night. The harshness of the attack was too much for his body to handle. We did everything we could."

"So, he might not wake up?" Jamie asked, pressing a hand to her heart.

"It's hard to say. This type of heart attack is typically referred to as the Widow Maker." Guilt quickly crossed his face. "There was a blockage in his LAD artery, and when that's the case, oxygen can't get through at all."

I wanted to scream, wanted to pick up one of these chairs and throw it out the window. I wanted to collapse and cry. What was life without your parents? How did you go on? I tossed a threatening look at the receptionist, imagining what she would do if I trashed the place in a rampage.

"Will we get to see him?" Jamie asked.

"Of course."

He must have sensed my heightened hysteria because he quickly beckoned us toward the elevator. Somehow, the hospital seemed a lot quieter up here in the hallways, like this sector was where patients went to wait to die and people were only silent out of respect. The thought disturbed me. I cupped my clammy hands around my elbows.

"He's in here," the doctor murmured.

Jamie practically threw the door open and lunged inside. I was quick at her heels.

Seeing Dad with a bunch of wires poking out of his skin didn't look right at all. He was sickly pale, almost as pale as the sheets he slept on, and a ventilator wheezed in the corner. It was kind of like walking into the Twilight Zone. My father never got sick; he never needed this kind of attention—it didn't make sense. But it dawned on me that the only reason I felt this way was because I'd always thought my father would be here. There are people in your life that you never expect to disappear, and then one day, they end up in a hospital bed with IVs protruding out of the veins in their arms. And the sight is incredibly frightening. *Nobody lives forever.*

Jamie brushed a strand of silver hair off my dad's forehead and then collapsed into the folding chair beside the bed. She had fresh tears now, and they made her eyes swim and glimmer. I moved forward slowly, feeling as if one quick movement would snap my body in half.

"Dad?" I whispered.

No answer. Not even an acknowledgement. He simply laid motionless, as if locked in some epic dream that wasn't worth waking up to miss. At least that was what I told myself. Jamie mumbled some things, but I hardly listened. I couldn't get over how *pale* he suddenly was. After a while, Jamie encouraged me to say something, and I had to dig down deep to find my voice. There was so much to say that I didn't know where to start. How did you say goodbye to someone who had been there all your life?

"Start small," Jamie encouraged, like she'd read my mind.

I shook my head. "I-I can't believe this is happening. I..." My voice choked into a whisper, and I felt the tears come at last.

If I wanted to say something, I needed to say it now because the time was ticking, and what would I do with myself if I never told him what he meant to me? I had to do it now, while that heart monitor was still pulsing.

"When I was young, y-you used to read to me," I began, hating the way my throat constricted around the words. "You said...'Maybe if I read her Shakespeare, she'll grow up to be a famous playwright someday.'"

Jamie laughed, tears cascading down her cheeks like two waterfalls.

"W-when I was older, you let me bring a boy home, and I know you hated seeing me walk away with him, but you also knew that he made me smile, and my happiness was your happiness." I sniffled, and the words surged out of me now. "You were there for me during my first heartbreak and my divorce, and you were the best grandpa my son could have ever had. Thank you for believing in me when no one else did."

"Why don't you tell him?" Jamie said. "About your big announcement."

My hand involuntarily touched my stomach. I drew a deep breath. The statement was hanging on the tip of my tongue. My father continued to dream.

"I'm pregnant, Dad. Colton and I are expecting."

No response, yet somehow, I knew he heard me. It was like a change in the air, a tiny thrill of excitement, of congratulations. For one moment, all three of us were happy.

But it didn't last long.

The heart monitor skidded and stuttered, filling me with horror. Jamie was on her feet at once, screaming for a doctor, and just like that, the silence of the hallways erupted into fits of shouts and commotion. Doctors and nurses clamored around the space, and I felt someone's hands grip my shoulders. I didn't turn to see who it was because suddenly, the heart monitor plateaued and a shrill ringing filled the air.

The world moved in slow motion then. Jamie's head fell into her hands. The nurses retrieved a defibrillator. My father's body convulsed under the jolts of electricity. People were shouting, but I couldn't hear anything over the whine of the heart monitor. All the while, someone was towing me out of the room. I had one last look at my dad, and once I was in the hallway, the world reared into motion again.

I shoved and kicked my way out of a male nurse's grip. He must have been in training because he looked so young. His eyes were wide with terror and anguish. It might have been his first experience with a patient's death.

My father's death.

I stumbled through the hospital, not caring that my sobs were loud enough to disturb the other patients. I groped the walls for support but I couldn't feel anything. All I could think was that yesterday, my father was alive and healthy.

"It's not fair, it's not fair," I mumbled through my cries.

I wasn't talking to anyone in particular, except maybe God. I couldn't help it. I was angry at him for taking my father, and so quickly and unexpectedly. It wasn't fair at all.

I burst through the doors and froze when I saw Colton standing in the waiting room with a pillow and blanket in each of his arms. He froze, too, and I knew my appearance said it all. He tossed the pillow and blanket into a nearby chair and caught me when I fell into him.

The next thing I knew, I was leaning over my kitchen sink at home, tears slipping off my nose and down the drain. Gavin stood by the table. I could almost see his heart breaking. I pulled him into my arms just as Colton encased me in his own, and the three of us sobbed quietly. Sobbed for the raw gaping holes in our hearts.

~

One of the hardest moments of my life was watching my father's coffin being shut. It was beautifully adorned with piles of roses, but I had to look away when they lowered the casket into the ground. Tears burned furiously in my eyes. Gavin was an absolute mess. Jamie sat hunched over like the weight of the loss was too much for her body to handle.

Afterward, there was a small Celebration of Life reception held at a nearby restaurant where they offered tables of tiny sandwiches, baked chicken, sweet corn, and every dessert under the sun. Dad had always said life was better with a full stomach.

My aunts and uncles sat together, lost in conversations, and my cousins gave me shoulder squeezes before moving toward the dessert table. Several of my father's old coworkers were also in attendance; they filled their plates and shuffled to open tables. Gavin, Colton, and I went to sit in the back corner.

"What do you think Grandpa's doing?" Gavin popped a cherry tomato into his mouth. "In heaven, I mean."

Though it was an innocent question, my lips trembled, and my appetite vanished. Sensing my discomfort, Colton took the reins.

"I bet he's sitting with Jesus and eating the biggest feast ever."

Gavin nodded, somewhat satisfied. We ate in silence for all of five minutes.

"On the bright side," Gavin said slowly. "I'm gonna be a brother."

Something in his tone made me glance up from my plate and look at him. Really look at him. His smile was a little crumpled at the corners, and it was obvious he was trying to lighten the mood and make us feel a little more whole. It was actually working. I saw my son in a bit of a different light at that moment because he suddenly looked and sounded so mature. He wasn't my little baby anymore. He truly was growing up.

"Yes, you are," I replied with a nod.

"Have you thought of any names?" Colton asked. Ketchup was smeared across his bottom lip.

Gavin bit back a grin. "How about Mordeki?"

"And for a girl?"

"Uh, Jazelyn."

"Those are some wild names," I said after taking a sip of water.

"They're from my new favorite video game." His eyes twinkled. "Deathtron."

I shook my head, and Colton jumped in. "I think those names are pretty great. We'll keep them in mind."

I had to laugh when Gavin shifted in his seat with a wide grin. He was happy. Maybe even ecstatic, and it felt like a giant weight had finally left my shoulders. For the first time in weeks, we sat as a family should—laughing and discussing the blessings that were yet to come.

I realized that maybe I *could* survive my father's death. Little moments like these made it slightly easier to breathe. I wasn't going to collapse after all. The future was still bright, and like Colton had said, my father wouldn't want me to put my life on hold just because he was gone now. I was pregnant, and it was time to start planning. As our little family continued to fantasize about the baby's gender and name, I knew that my father was somewhere up in heaven, blowing me one last kiss.

By the end of March, my abdomen was starting to grow. I'd been to the doctors a couple times, and the best part was that unlike Evan, Colton stayed by my side through it all. He drove me to every visit, sat through every mood swing, held my hair while I vomited, and kissed my ballooning tummy every night before bed. He was also my very handsome date to Cara's baby shower, where she and I posed together for a picture I now had framed and hanging above my mantle.

Colton took it upon himself to build an entire nursery in the spare bedroom. On his off days, he still worked, covering the hardwood with carpet, assembling a crib, and selecting the best type of furniture for me.

"For when you breastfeed," he explained, carrying a rocking chair to the corner of the room. When it was in place, he wiped his forehead on the sleeve of his arm. "For when you want to bond with our baby."

His tone was so light, so delighted. He was just as excited about the baby as I was, maybe even more so, and it made my heart beat sideways. I crossed the room and pulled him into a hug.

"You will be such a good father."

"That's the plan." He chuckled.

I kissed him feverishly. His touch sent flames licking across my skin, and just knowing that he still thought I was beautiful with a protruding stomach, my desire heightened tenfold.

"Hey," he murmured against my lips. "You're already pregnant. We should probably take a break—"

"Shut up and kiss me."

His laughter swelled. "Yes, ma'am."

My son was also preparing for the birth of his sibling. He said he planned to teach him or her some tricks on the soccer field, thus securing their popularity the moment they entered high school. Gavin's enthusiasm brightened my days as I endured countless headaches, nausea, and mood swings.

"I definitely wasn't this sick with you," I told Gavin one afternoon as I flopped down on the couch with a bowl of chocolate ice cream.

"Like I said, we're having a girl," Colton nearly sang.

"Awesome," Gavin said from the other chair. "I can teach her to ride a ripstik so she can show everyone else up."

"Won't you have anything better to do than trying to harm your baby sister?" I asked.

"I wouldn't harm her," he appeased me. "I'd be right there to catch her if she fell, and yes, actually. I'll be too busy marrying Josie."

I looked up from my bowl of ice cream at the same time Colton looked up from the TV.

"What?" Gavin asked.

And so it began. The blissful future planning. The endless imaginings of a perfect lifestyle. It was natural, I knew that, but it scared me. How hurt had I been when my young heart had been broken for the first time? How hurt had I been when my future with Evan dissolved into nothing? It was always nice to fantasize, but most times, it was just dangerous.

I knew Colton was too nice to take the leap, so I exhaled and said, "Son, I know you love Josie. We love her, too. But don't give up on your own future."

"Well, she is my future."

"What about soccer?" Colton urged. "You're an *incredible* soccer player."

"I can do that on the side." Gavin shrugged.

My husband and I both knew that "on the side" meant never again. He was planning to demolish his whole life for a girl he'd met in high school. I kind of felt guilty for thinking this since I was sitting right next to my high school sweetheart. But that was *rare*, and I didn't want my beloved son to get hurt. To have his dreams crushed. He had his whole life ahead of him. He just didn't see it yet.

"We just want to make sure you're making the right decisions for you," I noted. "When it comes time to choose colleges in a few years, don't just follow Josie because you think—"

"Because what?" Gavin said, his tone souring. "Because we're gonna break up?" His chuckle lacked humor. "I love her."

"We didn't say you didn't," Colton tried, but Gavin was livid now.

"Josie is the best thing that's ever happened to me, and I love her. It sucks that you guys can't be happy for me."

I pressed a hand to my forehead. The best thing that's ever happened to him? He was only fifteen! It truly was different hearing these words from an adult perspective. Colton switched the TV off and turned to face my son with a hard, father-like stare.

"Gavin, sometimes you have to walk alone to really figure out what is worth living for."

I couldn't have said it better myself, but this statement was not something the lovesick teenager in the house wanted to hear at all. Gavin shot up from the chair and bounded up the stairs, slamming his door like an exclamation point. I knew what he would do. He would go for a run or play some video games—anything to cool off—and then he would rebel against Colton's words. He would try his absolute hardest to prove that he had this love thing figured out.

That was what teenagers did after all: rebelled.

"He thinks I don't have faith in their relationship," I realized, and it hurt to say out loud.

"Or he just really wants us to be happy for him."

"I *am* happy for him, Colton, but they're just...so young."

"Well, speaking from my own experience, you can't really tell them not to fall in love, no matter how old they are. The heart wants what it wants. I mean, who knows, maybe they will end up together someday. It's too soon to tell."

I ate my ice cream in silence, pondering his words.

The summer came eventually and brought boiling days. On our days off, Colton forced me out of the house and into the blistering heat for long walks, and I came back with a sweat-soaked shirt every time. He claimed that this was good for me and our baby. The more physical exercise, the easier birth would be. He must have done a lot of Googling in his free time. He also became the chef of the house, cooking healthy dinners each night, claiming a nutrient-filled body meant a nutrient-filled baby. His devotion was adorable.

I was getting bigger, and with the added weight, my cravings were unbearable. Colton restocked the fridge with ice cream almost every night, and then he would hold me while I downed delicious bowl after delicious bowl.

At my next appointment, the ultrasound technician informed us that we were in fact having a girl. So, after Colton kissed my hand and wiped his tears away, he went pink happy, ordering pink blankets, decorations, and toys. The nursery became so pink, it nearly blinded us.

"A baby sister," Gavin echoed wistfully when we told him. "That's awesome." He was in awe for all of ten seconds before his phone buzzed.

Truthfully, I didn't see much of Gavin, but when I did, Josie was attached to his side.

I really had to hand it to my son. He had attended every single one of Josie's gymnastics competitions in the spring, brought her flowers for congratulations, and became a hero when she was tired or upset. If anything, I was proud of the man he was becoming. Girlfriend or not, Gavin was going to be an amazing person. And Colton was rubbing off on him more and more. They bonded over the construction of the baby's nursery, and the fight about the future was temporarily forgotten.

"We really do need to start thinking about names," Colton announced one night at dinner. His pencil was poised on paper. "Any name. Go."

"I told you," Gavin began. "Jazelyn."

"What about Jenna?" I said, stuffing my mouth with cooked cauliflower.

Colton wrote these names and then added *Renee* to the list.

"I think Rosie is a pretty name," Josie suggested.

"No, we should name her something really futuristic and cool," Gavin said. "I'm telling you. Jazelyn is the way to go."

I shook my head. "You play too many video games, son."

"I always liked the name Casey," Colton shrugged.

"What about Phoebe?" Josie chimed in, waving her fork at the list.

"Aliana," I said. It was just the next name to pop into my mind, but it was followed by a satisfied silence.

"I think we have a winner," Colton beamed.

"Whatever," Gavin murmured, turning his attention back to the chicken on his plate.

"So, when are you due, Mrs. Reeves?" Josie asked.

"The doctor said August 12th."

I thought I would be nervous for the pain, the long hours, the stress. But I would have Colton with me this time, and the thought made every knot of tension in my body dissolve completely. I really didn't fear the birth at all.

And so, life continued on in its blissful dullness. The days trudged by, bringing warm breezes that tickled the lush green leaves, and aside from my terrible morning sickness and moodiness, it was one of the nicest summers ever. Calm in the sense that life hadn't thrown us any wrecking balls recently. And much to Colton's happiness, Sandy and Sean were coming around a lot more. With the news of their granddaughter, our house quickly became theirs—more so than normal. I didn't mind the company. It gave me more opportunities to practice my violin for our guests. Sean loved string instruments, and Sandy claimed she'd missed my playing almost as much as she'd missed me.

But Gavin and Josie were an ebullient, rebellious force. They came and went as they pleased and spent too much time in the basement. Colton strode into our bedroom one evening to announce that he'd just caught our two young lovebirds in the midst of a makeout session.

"Really?" My eyebrows shot up.

"Well, when I went down to get my laptop, she was in his lap and their heads, like, snapped toward the TV." He sighed, collapsing onto the bed. I noticed the smirk playing on his lips. "Should I give him the talk or do you want to?"

I laughed now, realizing the irony. We'd done the same thing as teenagers. "I think he'd rather hear it from a *guy*. If you don't mind."

Colton shrugged. "Not at all."

"They're just like we were," I whispered, trailing my fingers down his chest.

"Those were the days, huh?"

I climbed on top of him, but my baby bump prohibited us from a comfortable kiss. I had to strain my neck all the way down just to meet his lips, and we ended up laughing at our sad attempt until the doorbell interrupted us.

"Oh, that's Mom," Colton said, shifting out from under me and extending a hand to help me up. "I think the meatloaf is almost done."

"'Mkay, I'll go fetch our little daredevils. But if Gavin's shirt is off, I'm calling it out right away."

"Be nice, love," my husband urged. "They're just kids."

"Doesn't matter," I retorted and turned to waddle out into the hall.

Thankfully, my son and his girlfriend were fully clothed, but their cheeks were flushed pink and their lips were red and slightly swollen. I didn't broach the topic, just called them for dinner, and they slipped out from under my gaze and hurried into the safety of the living room.

Gavin called Sandy Mammaw now, and the two greeted each other warmly.

"God, you're getting so tall!" Sandy complained. "Do me a favor and stop growing up. Hi, Josie." She fluffed her silver curls and then waved her withered hand at my son's girlfriend.

"Hello." Josie's voice was light and sweet like a thin ray of sunshine.

Sean immediately gravitated into the kitchen to help Colton finish dinner, and soon we all sat down to a meal of sizzling meatloaf and steamed asparagus. Colton led us in Grace, and we dug in.

"What are your plans for after high school, Josie, honey?" Sandy asked.

"Mom," Colton muttered pointedly. "Let the poor girl eat."

"Oh, hush. A dignified girl like her, I'm sure she has her whole life planned out."

"Actually no," Josie smiled, seeming a little flustered by being in the spotlight. "I'm torn between biology and psychology."

"What about gymnastics?" I wondered.

She shrugged. "I love it, but it's not something I want to pursue. I'll never be good enough for the Olympics, and it's kind of just a hobby anyway. Besides, I'd rather help find a cure for cancer."

I cocked my head at her. It was wild to see someone who, despite her young age, was already this mature and considerate of others. She wasn't like the typical narcissistic girls I knew in my day, but far more poised and moral. My respect for her increased even more.

After dinner, Colton and I cleaned the dishes while Gavin entertained our guests with videos of his past soccer tournaments and Josie's most recent competition from last June. Their laughter carried in from the living room.

Colton smiled. "It's nice having everyone together."

"I agree." I scrubbed one of the plates harshly with a sponge. "I just wish my dad was here. Next time, we should have Jamie over, too. It's not her fault she had a Bible study tonight, but I feel like she's still really upset after...what happened with my dad." I swallowed to keep the emotions at bay.

"Done deal." Colton placed a newly dried plate in the cabinet and turned to kiss my forehead. "We'll get Jamie feeling better as soon as we can."

Our moment was cut short when we noticed Sandy standing in the threshold of the kitchen, her eyes flickering fondly between us. Here in the near dim lighting, she looked much older, and it made my heart sag. But her mind was still sharp as the crack of a whip and her comments equally witty.

"You need a haircut, son." She tugged at a strand of hair that was curling behind Colton's ear until he ducked away from her.

"Yeah, yeah." He flashed me a grin and then disappeared into the living room.

Sandy turned to me. "Can we talk for a little bit? There's something I've been meaning to tell you."

She wasn't ever one to pull me away from a crowd, so this strange request made my anxiety flair. But her smile was kind and patient, meaning no harm. I swallowed the fear that was lodged in my throat and followed her into the dining room.

Sandy eased herself into a chair with a mild grunt, and I sat across from her, wondering what all of this was about. She turned her emerald eyes on me, and I was stunned, yet again, by how much they resembled Colton's.

"Is everything okay?" I asked.

"Oh, yes." She waved her hand dismissively, the new wedding ring on her finger sparkling in the light. "I just feel like you and I haven't gotten to talk in a long time. And I was thinking recently...that you deserve to know what happened."

"With what?" A frown etched itself into my lips.

Her expression dimmed slightly. "What happened with Colton and his dad all those years ago. You should know how it played out in the end."

Chapter Sixteen

SARATOGA SPRINGS, NY

I assume my son never told you?" Sandy asked.

"Not really." I shook my head. "I didn't want to make him talk about it more than he was comfortable with."

She nodded and leaned back in her seat. "I can't even tell you, Gail. I can't put into words how scared I was when I found out."

"How did you?" I asked. I'd always been curious how things actually went down on her side.

"Well, first of all, I didn't even know what happened. That day you called me while Colton was home from school, he told me he had a bad migraine, and I didn't question it because he had a lot of stress from school and volleyball back in those days."

"Right." I recalled attending many of Colton's volleyball tournaments while we were in high school.

"But then he started acting weird. He was snappish, and he was walking funny." She grimaced. "And then one night I asked him if you were coming over for dinner any time soon 'cause I hadn't seen you in a while. Mind you, dear, I was still working at the time, and my head was in the clouds."

I feigned a smile as she patted my hand apologetically.

"But by then, I guess you two had been broken up for a week. And when he told me that, I thought he was joking. Of course, he wasn't, and then I started freaking out. I didn't get to say goodbye to you, or even...talk to you one last time! I figured the breakup may have been why he was acting so strange until..." She blinked several times, and tears glistened in her striking eyes.

I didn't push her because now I was remembering the day *I'd* found out about the abuse. Junior year, the burning asphalt of the student parking lot, the ghost-like look in Colton's eyes, and those God-awful purple streaks slashed across his back. My eyes were suddenly drowning in tears. That had been one of the darkest days of *my* life, let alone Colton's.

Sandy inhaled and released the breath through her nostrils. "He was sitting at the kitchen table doing homework, and all of sudden, he just started...bawling his eyes out. I was in the kitchen cooking dinner, and I heard him and rushed in. It was *horrifying*, Gail. I didn't know why he was crying. He wouldn't say anything, he was just shaking and sobbing. I pulled him into my arms and then he jerked real hard, like he was in pain. And...that was when he told me."

My lungs strained, and I realized I wasn't breathing. For four long heart beats, we stared at each other, reliving the bloodcurdling memories. What had I been doing when all of that occurred? Probably moping around in a zombie-like trance at the loss of my love. But this went deeper than typical heartbreak.

"I was terrified," Sandy continued, her voice barely a whisper. "I mean, Ramon could have *killed* him. I wasn't happy with Colton going in the first place, but I never thought Ramon would do this. He was a drunk and an asshole, but he never physically touched either of us. So, to hear that he *beat*...his own son—" Her voice choked, and she pressed a hand to her mouth.

I extended a hand to rest on her shoulder. I was crying, too, and my heart was screaming for Colton.

"Ramon had PTSD his whole life," Sandy spat. "His own dad was an abusive prick. I tried everything I could to help him while we were married. I tried to get him in counseling, AA, you name it." She shook her head. "He always went back to that damn bottle. That was why I left—'cause I couldn't take it. And I took Colton with me. There were...times when Ramon would call and ask about Colton or say that he was...a changed man, but...it was all the same. He loved alcohol more than both of us.

"And the *things* he would say to me, *God*." She flinched. "I can hear them to this day. 'Sandra, you're a bitch! You're a whore! You can't do anything!'"

"He said those things to you?" My mouth hung open in utter shock.

She nodded with a miserable look on her face.

I felt my frown deepen. "But why didn't you—"

"Leave him sooner?" A sad smile played at the corners of her lips. "Because of the rare moments when he *wasn't* drinking. He would...come home and kiss me and love me. He bought toys for Colton. They went to the park together and passed the volleyball around. I think for a time, Colton actually kind of looked up to Ramon. But that was because I worked my ass off to keep his abuse under wraps."

I gave her a questioning look.

"I wasn't gonna let my kid see that stuff," she insisted as if it was obvious.

And just like that Sandra Reeves became my definition of a superhero. That couldn't have been easy by any means.

"And Ramon really didn't act out in front of Colton either. It was like he almost had a heart sometimes," she added sarcastically and rolled her eyes. "But anyway, after Colton told me what happened, I called the cops immediately, and he stood there screaming, 'Don't call them! Don't call them! He'll kill me!'"

I had to let my head fall then, and my tears created circles on the fabric of my shirt as they fell.

"Except it all happened so fast," Sandra continued in a distant tone. "Ramon confessed like *that*." She snapped her fingers. Maybe a part of him really regrets what he did—God, I hope so. He was arrested that night."

"Good."

I remembered trudging into the living room at home and seeing Mr. Reeves' face up on the TV screen with the news anchors speaking in the background. It had been terrible to *see*; I couldn't imagine the hell Sandy and Colton must have been through.

"I got Colton into therapy eventually. Oh, Gail, the kid was scared of everything. He would even back away from *me*—his own mother. As if I was going to hurt him. It broke my heart, let me tell you. I wanted to *kill* Ramon, so much so that our neighbor, bless her, she stayed over some nights just to calm me down. Make sure I didn't do something stupid. 'Cause seeing my son after his therapy appointments and seeing the tormented look in his eyes...I wanted revenge *badly*.

"But then Ramon was sent to jail, and Colton finally started to heal—physically, at least. And after a while, I think...your name started to come up in his therapy sessions. Since the shock was finally dying away, I think he realized that he missed you a lot. And truth be told, Gail, honey, I don't know why he ended things between the two of you, but...I also think it was for the best. For the time being at least. But good Lord, did he miss you. And so did I."

She reached over to give my hand a fond squeeze.

"There was one night in particular where shit really hit the fan," she went on. "I asked him what happened between the two of you. I didn't know if he was ready to talk about it, but he wasn't eating or sleeping, and I was gettin' real tired of the one-worded responses. So, when I asked, he just got real anxious and started saying things like, 'She's gone! She hates me now!'"

"I didn't hate him," I cut in quickly, leaning forward in my seat for emphasis. The desperation in my tone was clear as day. God, I would've given anything to go back in time and prove to him that I didn't hate him.

The amount of problems that could've been solved had we had one *conversation.*

"Well, I just let him sit there and yell. He was crying his eyes out—it hurt so much to see. And when he finally got quiet, I asked him if he could text you and make things right. He just shook his head and said, 'No, she hates me now.'"

"I didn't!" I insisted in a wavering voice.

"We didn't know, honey," she said. "The situation was messed up from so many angles. I asked him if he regretted it. And he said yes instantly."

I didn't know what to take from that. Granted, I hadn't been the one slashed with a belt buckle by my own father, but I had been wounded, too, just in a different way. I thought Colton hated *me*. And why would he not? I'd been the one to suggest going to his dad's house in the first place. Even after all these years, I still couldn't forgive myself for that.

"I think you were the one of the best things that ever happened to my son. And after everything started to calm down, it was *hard* to believe that you were actually gone. I'm usually against kids dating so young, but you two were something else. Believe me, that breakup affected all of us. And every girl that he brought home after you..." She shook her head distastefully. "I didn't like any of 'em."

I giggled in spite of myself, yet my vision was still blurred from crying.

"Especially that Beverly." Sandy gagged. "She was *never* a good fit for my Colton. I don't know *what* he saw in her. But something told me that you two would find each other again. I just felt it coming. He never stopped loving you."

Aliana gave a friendly kick in my belly, like an exclamation point to Sandy's remark. The movement caught Sandy's eye, and she smiled.

"Life is funny," she murmured, her eyes focused on my ballooning stomach. "All I can say is that when I got to the hospital after Colton's car accident and they gave me his phone, and *you* were calling...I knew God truly was looking out for my son after all."

"And I'm grateful," Colton said from behind me, making me jump.

Turns out they were all standing there: Colton, Sean, and the kids. Gavin and Josie looked traumatized as they gazed at Colton, and I suddenly realized I'd never mentioned Colton's tragic past. But it wasn't my story to tell. They were bound to find out someday. Colton wasn't looking at them; his eyes were trained on me, and the fond smile I loved so much tugged at his lips. We'd been through so much just to get here.

"And we can be thankful that little Aliana is healthy," Sandy said, patting my stomach. "A miracle."

Colton's hand appeared on my shoulder, and he kissed the top of my head.

"All's well that ends well," Sandy declared, lifting her glass of lemonade. "I'll drink to that."

She was right; life *was* funny. All the ups and downs, all the tragedies and the triumphs, they were plot points in the perplexing story that was life. Moments of growth that God embedded in our personal adventures. And if I'd learned anything, it was that you never really understood happiness until you had experienced a crushing low. And I'd had my fair share of those, which made this moment of togetherness that much sweeter.

∾

Two weeks after Gavin's sixteenth birthday, I turned forty, and on that day, my own nausea woke me up. I barely made it to the toilet in time, gripping the sides for stability as vomit streamed from my lips. Colton risked being late to work just to hold my hair.

"This sucks," I groaned, falling back onto my bottom and away from the toilet. I leaned against the tub and wiped my mouth with a towel.

Colton sat down across from me. "But you're one hell of a trooper. Give yourself some credit, love. It's all for a good cause."

I wasn't in the mood to play nice when my night shirt was stained in puke, and I was now officially yet another year older, so I just stared at him.

He sighed. "I stocked up on chocolate ice cream last night."

This made me smile. "Good, thank you."

"Mhm." He laughed. "Happy birthday, gorgeous. I gotta run, but I'll see you tonight." He winked and leaned in to kiss me, but froze inches from my lips. "I'll just see you later." Instead, he gave me a quick Eskimo kiss and disappeared out the door.

It was a Saturday, so I assumed Gavin was going to be with Josie all day, but he surprised me when he announced that he had plans with Andre.

"I'm glad to hear it," I said, watching Gavin scarf down a plate of eggs. "Is my advice finally getting to you?"

He shrugged. "We're just gonna skateboard at the park."

I thought his tone seemed a little melancholy, but I couldn't be sure.

"Everything okay with Josie?"

He nodded, but there it was again—a flicker of sorrow.

"Gav, you can talk to me."

"Everything's fine," he snapped, and I cocked my head at him. He never acted like that.

He sighed. "Everything's fine." Calmer now, more controlled. He tossed his plate in the sink and then moved toward the stairs, but not before calling, "Happy birthday, Mom."

I stared after him for a moment, not sure what to think.

Were Gavin and Josie having issues in their relationship? Were they strong enough, smart enough to work through those issues? I hoped the answer was yes. I loved Josie, and the last thing I wanted was my son's heart getting broken. But they were just kids. I didn't *want* to have to give Gavin the breakup talk yet. He was still too young.

By the time Colton got home later that night, I was sick of overthinking. He found me in the living room and held up an iced cookie cake in one hand and a bouquet of deep red roses in the other. He then proceeded to sing a terribly offkey rendition of "Happy Birthday," and I gave him a grimacing smile until he was finished.

I couldn't even get a word in before he exclaimed, "Let's have sex!" He danced all around me, making me wheeze with laughter.

"Are you kidding? We can't. Gavin's not spending the night at Andre's, he'll be back soon. Besides, I carry your child and all you give me as a birthday present is sex?"

"Hey," he stepped toward me, wearing an impish grin. "I could give you one hell of a present." I started to roll my eyes and laugh again, so he took my hand. "And it's *our* child, Gail. You're just the brave one."

"I should say so."

We stared at each other for a moment until we burst into giggles again. For a moment, I felt like I was sixteen. A young girl who was lost in the presence of her first love. Until Aliana jabbed me with her foot. Seeing our baby kick, Colton sank onto his knees and pulled my shirt up over my belly, exposing the pale skin underneath. Then he gingerly brushed his lips right where Aliana was cradled in my stomach and whispered, "I love you, sweetheart."

I watched him with a broad smile.

"For the record, no, I did not just come home empty handed for the love of my life," Colton said, standing to face me again. He reached into his pocket and retrieved a small velvet pouch. "Happy birthday."

I took the pouch, ran my fingers over the smooth surface, and shook its contents into my hand. A single stone plopped into my palm—olive colored and oval-shaped. I peeked at Colton, but his smile told me to keep inspecting it. So, I turned it over and on the opposite side were the words *To the one I love: Abigail Reeves. Here's to now and forever.*

"Is this what I think it is?" I asked, testing the stone's weight.

"Mhm. A prayer stone. Custom made." His self-assured tone was so adorable, my heart sighed.

I pressed the stone to my chest. "I love it. Thank you so much."

"Of course. I wanted to give you something to hold on to forever, even when I'm not here. It's a reminder that wherever I am, I still love you."

"You're never going to disappear," I insisted, shaking my head vigorously.

I had convinced myself that everyone else would leave someday. My father, my friends. Hell, even me. But not *this* person. Not this man whom I loved more than life itself.

But instead of responding with words, he placed a protective hand on my stomach and kissed me fiercely.

I didn't like when Colton talked about going away at all. It made me nervous. And so, for the rest of my birthday, long into the evening, I held my husband a little tighter, kissed him a little harder, fearful of the moment that would separate us.

To my immense relief, Josie came around again, and the two romantics disappeared into the basement that acted as their private fortress.

The summer faded, sucking all the humidity from the

atmosphere until we were granted perfect weather by the end of August. It was Gavin's sophomore year of high school, but he was highly unwilling to return to the classroom. He would much rather be on the field.

"Soccer tryouts are on Friday," he explained on the morning of his first day.

"Think they'll let you start on varsity this year?" I beamed.

Gavin was such a good soccer player that he'd been bumped up to varsity by the second semester of his freshman year, but he wasn't a starter or striker. That was the new goal.

He shrugged, trying to conceal his burning desire. "Hopefully. But how are you feeling?" He stared at my protruding abdomen.

I was due in ten days.

"Honestly?" I brushed a few stray hairs out of my face. "I'm bloated and feel like an oaf. I also kinda miss being able to reach down and tie my own shoes."

My tummy was so swollen by now that my back had started aching and the morning sickness had become a daily chore. The doctor told me I was right on track, but this routine was getting a little incessant.

Gavin laughed. "Well, you're almost there." He grabbed the keys to my car. "Can I take the Subaru?"

He hadn't wasted a second on getting his license. The day of his birthday, he marched me right into the DMV and buckled up to take his test. It had been hell for me letting him drive when he had his permit alone, but that was because I had a talent for worrying about every little thing that could go wrong. Gavin had favored driving with Colton over me by a longshot.

"You are a two-week old driver," I reminded him. "Be careful. Watch for bikers and buses. Stop at every stoplight."

He groaned and took my keys off the hook. "I'm not stupid, Mom, I know."

"And text me when you get to Starbucks!" I called after him.

"Tanya will have my life if you crash with Josie in the car, and I'm gonna have *your* life!"

"Yeah, yeah!" He disappeared into the garage and seconds later, I heard my Subaru purr to life.

This was a whole new ballpark for me. I'd been afraid when he was seven and riding a scooter down the driveway, so *this* was next level fear. In order to distract myself, I checked my email and found the most recent one to be from my conductor.

Hi Gail!

Just checking in to see that you and your husband are resting well and preparing for your daughter's arrival! The orchestra sends love and positivity your way!

Congratulations again!

Tod Niles

I'd had one last performance with the Saratoga Strings before stepping away on maternity leave, and it had been a blowout rendition of old rock songs, including Aerosmith's "Dream On," which had sent the crowd into a frenzy. Colton had even said it was one of our best performances ever. But now I was taking the time off that I needed, and my violin sat in its place in the corner, waiting patiently for my return. It wasn't like I was gone completely though. Veronica and Seth texted me nearly every day, updating me on the orchestra's next concert, asking me how I was feeling, and wishing me congratulations at least five times in one text.

This email from Tod really played the strings in my heart. Something about him resembled my old college orchestra conductor, Professor Autrie. Though Todd wasn't a French immigrant with a thick accent and gray hair, he had the charisma that it took to move people with music. He lived for the music, and he lived *because* of the music. Losing Professor Autrie had been worse than hell. I had idolized him through and through, and my anger had cost me relationships with other conductors. But Tod brought out the best memories of Professor Autrie. Because of them, my dream of someday being a conductor was resurrected. A part of me wondered if I truly would ever get there—to the point where I could command an orchestra myself and inspire another young instrumentalist. That was the cycle of life. I hoped I still had a foot in that cycle.

August twelfth was stormy and cold, but I tried not to take offense to Mother Nature's mood swing. It did come in handy though, as Gavin's soccer meeting ended up being canceled because the coach lived thirty minutes away and was stuck with a flood warning.

Sandy and Sean arrived early in the morning with bright, beaming faces. Jamie was at our house, too, with a batch of home-made cookies to celebrate. She seemed to be getting a little better, but she was still quiet these days, likely to be found gazing out the window with glassy eyes. I knew how she felt. It was days like these that I *really* wished my dad was here.

I wished he could give me a thumbs up for luck, like he did when I was little and tried to ride a bike for the first time. Like he did when I gave birth to Gavin. Though it felt like a rock sinking through my chest to think about, I was sure he was sending his love from Heaven this time.

Truthfully, I wasn't nervous. Colton never left my side. Every time I moved, he tensed, but that was to be expected. He was going to be a first-time dad.

"Relax," I whispered, curling my fingers through his. "God's on our side. It'll be okay."

"I know." He smiled. "I just can't wait to meet her."

We were all excited, *especially* Gavin. He had spent so much time in that nursery with Colton, putting the final touches on the walls and the furnishings. And today, he was a firecracker, bouncing off the walls to meet his baby sister. He even canceled plans with Josie for this, and *that* was monumental.

The day was normal. I sat in front of the television with a bowl of chocolate ice cream and binge-watched several movies with my family. For a while, when I was lost in the plot of the shows, I forgot that I was supposed to give birth. But sure enough, around four-forty pm, Aliana got tired of waiting. Gavin actually laughed when my water broke, unlike Colton who went into mission mode and started ordering everyone else around.

My husband drove me to the hospital himself, with our parents and my son in the car behind us. I gripped my seat belt anxiously, already measuring out my breaths. Colton took my hand.

"You okay?" he asked.

I nodded. "Just pregnant and about to give birth. You know how it is."

"Yeah, I've been there, too."

That made me laugh hard, and it removed some of my anxiety.

The doctor was expecting us. I was immediately wheeled to a reserved room while Colton continued to hold my hand the whole way, reminding me to take deep breaths.

The air was light, tension-free, much different from the first time I'd given birth. I wondered if that was just a stereotypical, second-time-mom thing. I knew what was coming now, and I didn't fear it.

"Your baby has a clean bill of health from the looks of this," the obstetrician continued, examining what must have been my medical charts. She let the clipboard fall onto the counter beside my bed. "A true miracle."

Colton squeezed my hand.

I figured it was going to be a while, so I settled in and patted my stomach, to which Aliana replied with a painful kick. I winced, and Colton eyed me nervously.

"It's normal," I assured him. "Geez, if you keep looking at me like that, I'll have to call the doctor in for *you*."

"Sorry." He cupped a hand on the back of his neck. "I just hate feeling helpless."

"Tell me a story," I said suddenly. He glanced back at me. "Tell me a really good story. It'll help calm us both."

He sighed and gazed around the room until his charming eyes lit up.

"Okay, okay. I've got one. Once upon a time, there was a boy who lived in this huge castle. He was very rich, but very humble, and he was in love with this girl."

"Real original."

"Shh. So, this boy...we'll call him Joe. Joe was head over heels in love with—" Colton pressed his lips into a tight line as he thought and then continued, "—in love with Lucy. He had all the wealth in the world, yet she never noticed him. And it made him sad, like, really sad."

"That's a lot of sadness."

Colton rolled his eyes playfully. "But before he was crowned king, Joe needed a queen. So, he tried to get Lucy's attention, but every time he tried, he would chicken out. It wasn't until they were matched by the royal council that she finally noticed him and started liking him. Their relationship lasted a year and a half, but just before their wedding, they had a huge fight."

"About what?" I wondered aloud, wincing through the pain of a contraction.

Colton shrugged hopelessly. "Nobody can recall. But Joe reacted badly and threw her out of the palace before their future could unfold. Twenty years went by, bringing the fiery destruction of a dragon and huge financial issues for King Joe and his subjects. He solved the problems eventually, yet his heart still belonged to his lost love.

"Luckily, fate was on his side. As he was venturing through a neighboring kingdom, he stumbled across a magnificent orchestra, with his beloved Lucy playing in first chair. Thankfully, she was thrilled to see him, and the heartbreak had changed them. They had grown and matured tremendously. The very next month, they got married. A year later, they had a child and lived happily ever after."

"Huh, that plotline sounds a little familiar," I mused.

"Does it?" Colton scratched the back of his head. "I've never heard it before."

"So, am I your queen then?"

The kidding drained from his face, replaced by a look of loving devotion. "You always have been."

His kiss was a temporary painkiller, but Aliana was ready to join this world. It almost felt like she was beating her tiny fists against my abdomen, looking for a way out. Sandy and Jamie joined us just as my contractions started to worsen, and Dr. Pearson positioned himself at the foot of the bed.

"Say goodbye to your credit card," he warned Colton.

The room relaxed into loud laughter. Sandy's booming laugh echoed off the walls, and I laughed too, despite my extreme discomfort. The pain only increased. Invisible knives stabbed my womb, tore at the flesh of my legs. I pinched Colton's hand tightly, but he barely noticed the pain. Instead, his lips were at my ear.

"You can do this," he whispered. "I'm right here, and I love you more than anything else in this world."

A scream tore from my lips as fire licked its way up my skin. The ceiling blurred with my tears, and Colton kissed my sweaty temple. Another round of pain rippled through me, just as Doctor Pearson adjusted a mask onto his face.

"Show time," he declared in a silly voice to lighten the mood.

But I was gone.

The room faded around me until there was nothing but

Colton, who continued to whisper into my ear. I couldn't hear what he was saying, yet he was so vibrant beside me, like a glowing, prominent force. His body seemed to be exerting some sort of energy because it consumed me. I turned my head to look at him. He was staring straight back at me, those gold-green eyes an endless abyss of beauty. His lips moved frantically. A wrinkle creased the skin between his eyebrows, but he wasn't forty-years-old anymore, he was sixteen. The boy from our youth kissed my head again.

A hundred memories replayed in my mind: our first kiss in the hospital after his near-fatal car accident, how my heart jumped for him when he appeared through the crowd at my performance, the wretched taste of anguish when I saw him with Beverly, the first time he'd touched me and sent my body through a whirlwind of pleasure, the immense heartbreak after he left me in high school. Our first kiss. The first time I looked at him and noticed him that day in English class. Like the characters from his story. Just two young kids, completely unaware of the future.

I heard our youthful laughter. I recalled my screams of heartache when he was gone. My pulse jumped at the memory of his lips on my neck. Tears touched my eyes at the memory of his wedding ring sliding onto my finger. Our baby...

How could you grow to love someone so much?

The memories faded when Colton gasped beside me. It was then that I came back to the present. My hand was still clutching his to the point of breaking a bone, but a shrill cry caught my attention. Reluctantly, I tore my eyes away from Colton and glanced down at Doctor Pearson. There was a very beautiful, very pink, baby girl in his arms. She screamed, wriggling her little arms around, as if trying to find a home. I stared at her in amazement as Colton cut the umbilical cord.

Aliana Reeves.

If I was still in pain, I didn't notice at all. All I could see was the squirming, little figure in the doctor's arms. Jamie and Sandy were already in tears. They clung to each other, sobbing joyously.

My arms didn't seem to work, pinned to my sides by pure exhaustion. Colton took the baby instead, and I eagerly looked back up at him. A ribbon of fading sunlight streamed in through the window, dousing Colton in a shade of gold. The light danced on our baby's fair skin. And in that moment, my heart stopped. The sight of my husband holding our daughter made fresh tears sting my eyes. Time seemed to slow, and I watched him smile down at her, watched her miniscule hand reach up to him.

Colton was radiant. A glimmering angel. His eyes oozed sparkling tears. His lips stretched to both cheeks, and he glanced over at me. A blistering energy passed between us. Something far beyond happiness.

My eyes dropped to little Aliana then. She cried and cried, reaching for something in the distance. Reaching for me. A tear trickled down my cheek. Our little miracle had no idea what her parents had been through to get her here. It had been a love story like no other.

Chapter Seventeen

SARATOGA SPRINGS, NY (2041-2042)

Click!

Sean's camera flashed and captured the moment Gavin held Aliana for the first time. Gavin's smile was whole and utterly overjoyed. He loved his baby sister so much. It even took a half hour just to convince him to let other people hold her—particularly Josie, who fell in love with Aliana the moment she saw her and was obsessing over her rosy cap and tiny pink pj's.

Our daughter was like this little ball of delight, always giggling, always smiling. She hardly slept, much to mine and Colton's dismay, but there was so something so wonderful about her aura.

We took at least a hundred family photos that Halloween, and Gavin insisted that I snap a few pictures of him and Josie as well. They wore matching zombie costumes, smeared in gallons of fake blood, which was a large contrast to sweet little Aliana, who we'd dressed up as a pumpkin. The pudgy orange costume and pumpkin cap fit her perfectly. I scrunched Colton's shirt up in my fist and squealed at how cute she was.

It was the perfect night, full of sweets and laughter and love. Aliana cried when I pried a Snickers bar from her tiny fist. As I patted her back to lessen her sobs, Colton kissed the crown of my head.

"Our miracle," he murmured.

I nodded happily.

"Hey, Colton, have you ever seen *Paranormal Activity?*" Gavin called from the living room.

"Uh, I don't think that's appropriate—"

"Best scary movie ever!" Colton shouted, cutting me off. "Are we watching it?"

Josie's laughter carried in through the living room, followed by a "Heck yeah!" from Gavin.

I cradled Aliana closer to my chest and turned toward Colton. "If my son wakes up from nightmares tonight, I'm blaming you."

"Don't worry." Colton kissed me again. "I'll just offer some funny commentary the whole time so that it's not that scary."

"Well *I'm* not watching it," I insisted, lifting my chin to seem tough. But in reality, watching scary movies on Halloween was a no-no for me anyway. I was the definition of a scaredy cat.

"That's all right. I think Aliana's getting tired anyway."

One look at our daughter's drooping eyes confirmed his statement.

"Keep the screams down, will you?" I asked, one foot on the stairs, a hand on the banister.

Josie nodded, but Colton and Gavin were already settling in with bowls of candy. I rolled my eyes and climbed the stairs.

Aliana squirmed in my arms, trying to find a comfortable position, and I adjusted her accordingly as I sank into the rocking chair. I placed the pacifier between her lips and began rocking.

Memories swirled in my brain of another time and place, when Gavin was the one in my arms. When I'd been alone and uncertain and scared. When my future was nothing more than a fading dream. But Aliana possessed that same twinkle in her eyes that Gavin had. She stared at me with those big eyes, like she was trying to commit my appearance to memory. I was attempting to do the same. With Gavin so grown up now, it brought tears to my eyes to remember the good old days when he was young like this. But I wasn't alone with Aliana; I had Colton. I'd survived the fire just to get our daughter here, just to have this moment alone with her.

I would give her the world, just like I was going to give Gavin. I would provide for them both until my dying breath.

Gavin's scream raced up the stairs, followed by a round of shushing and muffled laughter. I shook my head at their buffoonery and grinned down at my daughter. Aliana watched my reaction and smiled too, illuminating the whole room. It left me breathless for a second, seeing my miracle light up like that, and I wished Colton were in here to see it, too.

I rocked my daughter until her little eyes slipped closed, then I carefully lowered her into the crib. Exhaustion swept over me, making the tiniest movements burdensome, so I retired to my own room and curled up in bed with a good book.

Time passed, and on the week of Thanksgiving, Gavin was in a mood again. I didn't understand where these tempers were coming from since they were completely uncharacteristic of him, but they had gotten more frequent over the past month. He trudged through the house as if the entire world was annoying him. I tried to make conversation and ask what was going on, but he shrugged me off with a grunt and a glare.

"He might just be tired and stressed with school," Colton muttered.

"'Kay, well this behavior has to stop before Thursday. We're having everybody over for Thanksgiving dinner."

Colton nodded. "Yes, I know. I know."

We were both drained from a week of zero sleep, thanks to Aliana's nighttime sobs and her idea that when dawn woke the sky, everyone was supposed to get up. So Gavin's moodiness was pushing us past our edges.

"You have to do something," I told Colton. "Gav won't talk to me."

Colton ran a hand over his face and then extended his arms, frustrated. "Did you not just hear me? He's probably tired. What do you think I can do?"

"Maybe it's a guy thing."

"Or a common teenager thing," Colton argued.

"Help me get this house in order so that I can at least be a *little* grateful on Thursday, dammit!"

We stared each other down, nostrils flared, hands curled into fists. Eventually, he heaved a sigh, rolled his eyes, and stomped off to change Aliana's diaper. My eyes trailed after him for a moment, and I was still fuming when Gavin emerged from his room.

"Hey," I said, pressing my hands to my hips. "What is wrong with you?"

His eyes betrayed him, reflecting a sense of gloominess. He leaned back against the wall and shoved his hands into his pockets. "Nothing." His tone was harsher than his gaze.

"It's Thanksgiving, a time to be grateful," I reminded him. "Tell me what has you down, so that I can fix it."

He just shrugged. "You wouldn't understand."

I laughed humorlessly. "Try me."

He seemed to think it over, but then shook his head.

"Everyone's gonna be here at three on Thursday. Is Josie coming over in the morning like we talked about?"

The gloom in his eyes deepened. "I think she's busy."

Something in my heart twitched. "Honey, if something happened between you two, you can tell—"

"Nothing happened," he assured me. But his tone said otherwise.

Before I could ask more, he disappeared into the bathroom and the sound of rushing water filled my ears.

I was sure a Thanksgiving party would be medicine for all of us. We needed it; the tension in the air was like a poisonous fog hanging over the house. But come Thursday, things hadn't really calmed down. Gavin was still lost in his daze.

We opened our house up to everyone: Cara, Beau, and their beautiful baby boy, Colton's parents, and Jamie of course, Elijah and Brie, our high school friends, and Seth and Veronica, who contributed a homemade casserole to our feast. It was a grand celebration—one for the books.

Our guests stayed long into the evening, too happy (or drunk) to drive back home. Cara and I serenaded with a violin-voice duet, and then we all played Apples to Apples until eleven-thirty, trying our best to keep our voices down so as not to wake the baby. But it was hard. Ashton kept dealing the funniest cards, and I couldn't even look at Erica without bursting into giggles. Togetherness was our pharmaceutical, curing the stress and short-temperedness in our hearts.

But not for Gavin.

He sat in the corner, faking smiles and staring off into the distance until excusing himself to go to bed around midnight. Colton and I shared a concerned glance as everyone else waved goodbye to him. Something really wasn't right.

Over the next couple of days, I expected him to bring Josie over to introduce her to our friends and family, but he remained in his room, only coming out to hold Aliana. It seemed his baby sister was the only person who made him smile for the rest of the week.

"Any school dances coming up?" Sandy asked him on Sunday after church.

Gavin shrugged. "There's one in January."

"Ooh, I bet you and Josie are the cutest couple in the whole school. You know, in my day..."

It was obvious Gavin had zoned out. Cara asked if he was okay, to which he just nodded and went to tend to Aliana again.

"It's Josie," I told Colton that night. We were in our bedroom —the only private space to talk in our fully occupied house. "It's gotta be her. Usually she's here every single day, and he was so excited for her to come this week."

"Let's not jump to conclusions." Colton sighed, but his tone was hardly convincing. I could tell he was assuming the worst, too.

"Oh, no," I whined, wringing my clammy hands through the air. "What are we going to do? You don't think they..."

It dawned on me that I might never see Josie again, and my stomach churned. Loss was difficult from all sides.

"We don't know anything. Maybe they just had a fight." Colton took my hands in his so that I would stop shaking. "Sometimes teenagers drag things out, but I say give it till December. I bet they'll be back in each other's arms even before then."

It was a long, tortuous wait. We felt everything Gavin felt, only five times worse. When he was forlorn, Colton and I were absolutely dismal. When he was angry, we were red hot. We felt every emotion in stunning clarity, but the pressure of uncertainty only made it worse. This made it extremely difficult to raise a baby.

In the meantime, we tried to talk to Gavin, but he only pushed us further away. I ended up asking Pastor David to help us pray for him. I was worried sick, and God couldn't answer our prayers fast enough.

All through Christmas and through the beginning of January, Gavin was up and down. He would cry laughing some days and yell at me other days. Josie didn't come around much anymore, but my son threw us for another loop when he announced he was taking her to the winter dance. The emotional rollercoaster soared upward again.

"Hi, Josie," I greeted her warmly on the night of the dance.

When she smiled at me, I realized just how much I'd missed her face around here.

"Hi, Miss Abigail." Lightly said, as pleasant as ever. She turned to face Gavin, and the skirt of her sunflower yellow dress swished with the movement. Her dark skin shimmered in the fading sunlight.

She gazed into my son's eyes, and the two looked like they were head over heels for each other, silently promising forever. Colton and Josie's father snapped pictures of the kids while Aliana squealed in my arms.

"Oh, she's adorable," Tanya gushed, peeking over at my daughter.

"Thank you."

"It makes me miss holdin' a little one. Simon, let's have anotha' baby!"

Josie's father scratched his eyebrow, and we laughed. "Sorry, but I think I'm busy."

Everything seemed okay. Josie was here; Gavin was in good spirits. Aliana managed to make it through the day without a screaming tantrum. For now, everything was fine.

But little did I know that that was the last time I would see sweet Josie and her wonderful family. It was the last time I would see my son gaze into her eyes with as much affection as he did in that moment. It was the last time I would give Josie a hug and send the two of them off to a high school dance. Because the very next week, Gavin returned home in a whirlwind of fury.

"Whoa," I said, watching him throw his backpack onto the couch and storm into the kitchen.

He didn't even say hello to his baby sister. I followed him and stood by the table.

"Is everything okay?" It was a stupid question, I knew, but when he rolled his eyes, it hurt.

"Josie and I broke up."

And suddenly the world lost its light.

~

Aliana sensed that something was wrong. She squeezed my hair in her tiny fists until I was forced to release her from my arms, and she quickly crawled toward Gavin. He lifted her up onto the couch and rocked her back forth, but his expression was still distant, still remorseful.

It had been a week since the breakup...a very long, very emotionally draining week. Maybe a week from hell. But Gavin went about his day in a silent world of solitude. The only one who seemed to bring him to life, if at all, was Aliana.

We didn't speak of Josie, but her absence filled us all. It was like Sandy had said about me and Colton—the breakup was affecting everyone. We couldn't bring ourselves to talk about it. We simply moved around in this darker reality and suffered quietly.

Colton and I worried about Gavin. He seemed to be okay, but I wasn't so sure that his content façade stayed when he was behind his closed bedroom door. He was bottling his emotions, and I wanted so badly to take all the pain from his heavy heart and demolish it. I wanted to know what happened; I wanted to *help*. But I didn't push him.

I knew from my own experience that pushing only made things worse.

Tanya called twice, wondering what was going on. She was just as confused as me and Colton. The only ones who knew what had happened were the kids, and I assumed all of their friends as well because Gavin opted to quit social media for a long time. He said he didn't want to deal with other people's input right now.

So, as I watched him cradle Aliana in his arms and smooth her thin blonde hair out of her eyes, my mind was burning with dozens of questions. Colton sat beside me, hunched over in his seat with his hands folded under his chin. We both knew the sting of heartbreak so well.

"How was school today?" Colton asked in an attempt to make small talk.

Gavin looked up from his baby sister, his eyes darkening at the question. "Fine."

I almost shook my head and yelled at him to stop shoving his emotions to the side, but that was probably the worst thing I could have done. Instead, I sat frozen.

This same exchange happened every night for the next four months, but Gavin's responses were getting curter, weaker, like his life energy was draining with each response. Tanya didn't call anymore. It was like the Acclow family had disappeared off the face of the earth. Maybe that was a good thing. Better for healing purposes.

One night, I found Gavin in his room bent over his laptop and copying bullet points into a spiral notebook. He didn't move or acknowledge my presence, even when I leaned over his shoulder to examine the notes.

"What class is this for?" I asked.

"History, but right now we're studying a more recent event."

"Which is?"

"The...Pulmonem Fever outbreak?" He shrugged and continued scrawling away into this journal.

Sour bile touched my taste buds. In an instant, I remembered the hysteria of quarantine all those years ago. The uncertainty that the world would never get back on track. Endless movie marathons with Cara. Walks around the block in Philadelphia, which served as my only access to fresh air even though I had to wear a mask.

"We know all about that," Colton said from the doorway.

Finally, Gavin looked up. "You do?"

"I was twenty-two years old," I recalled tonelessly. The memories were so fresh. They sent my stomach spiraling to my feet.

"Worst year ever." Colton shook his head. "But also one of the best...if you look at it from a progressive medical point. It taught the World Health Organization a very valuable lesson."

Gavin copied this down into his notebook and then shoveled a hand through his hair. "The worst year ever?"

It was funny. He probably thought *this* was the worst year ever. But he didn't know what it was like to endure heartbreak during quarantine. "Yeah. It sucked."

Colton's eyes touched mine, and I knew he recognized the bitterness in my voice.

For a long time, Gavin was silent. He stared at the wall, but I knew he was walking back through his own breakup, rewinding to that terrible moment, to the end. I realized then that it didn't really matter whether there was a global pandemic or if aliens were invading earth. Breakups were just flat-out terrible.

Finally, he sighed and said, "I think I'm ready to talk."

Colton walked further into the room and sat down on the bed beside me. I was grateful Aliana decided to fall asleep and stay asleep tonight because this conversation was long overdue.

Gavin slid his hands down the fabric of his shorts and exhaled. His lips twitched several times, and his eyes jumped all around the room, like the words were hidden somewhere. He sighed again before saying, "I-I don't even know where to start."

"Well, how did you break up?" Colton's voice was gentle, coaxing.

Gavin glanced at him, and something like frustration flickered across his face. "We'd broken up several times before."

"What?" I shook my head, trying to process this.

"Well, more like *she* broke up with *me* and then missed me, so we got back together."

"Josie?" I inquired, shocked. It didn't sound like the sweet, innocent girl I'd come to know.

He gave me a *duh* look and nodded. "She would say that she was getting bored, or that the spark wasn't there anymore. That when she kissed me, she felt nothing. She actually *told* me that."

My heart quivered, bracing itself for the impending break.

"But I really liked her, so I respected her need for space and tried to focus on other things when she was gone, but then I always got the text that she wanted to hang out again. It just got...really confusing."

"How many times did this happen?" Colton asked, crossing his arms.

Gavin shrugged. "Maybe four times?"

I felt my eyes bulge out of their sockets. He'd been through this *four* times? And he never came to us with the issue? Something about that offended me, but I shoved the thought away.

"And...she got really jealous over time. I would just be *talking* to a girl before class started, and she'd be all over me for like, trying to cheat on her or something. Which wasn't the case at all."

"No, of course not." I fully believed him. No son of mine would cheat...not like his father did.

"She didn't even talk to me for a week and a half before the winter dance, but when we went together, she was all lovey again. I thought I could stick it out. I-I thought I loved her beyond all of that confusion, but...it just got to be too much. I couldn't take it anymore."

"So, *you* broke up with *her*," Colton clarified, and Gavin nodded, suddenly seeming guilty.

"Why didn't you tell us?" I asked in a hollow tone.

"I thought I could handle it on my own," Gavin admitted. "I didn't want anyone to worry. But...I don't know, I just had to end it."

"Did you ever feel like the spark was going out?" Colton asked.

"Hell no. I loved her."

"So, how'd you do it?" I muttered.

Gavin drew a shaky breath. "We both knew that the end was coming. I mean, we sat together at lunch on Friday and didn't say a *word* to each other. And then while I was in math class later that day, she texted me and asked if I could meet her in the library during our study hall period. I said yes, of course, 'cause I missed her." He said the last part a little sheepishly.

"But when I saw her, I knew that it wasn't going to be a normal conversation. She looked sick and...exhausted maybe? I don't know. But we sat together, and she apologized for everything. For being distant and saying mean things and...breaking up with me all those times. I wanted to believe her *so* badly. She took my hand, and it was like she never wanted to let go again. But something in my gut just didn't feel right, and I couldn't lie to her. So I...ended it.

"To be honest, I feel like a giant weight has been lifted from my shoulders, you know? I don't have to *deal* with her anymore, with all that confusing bs. I'm almost happy that I did it. But..." His eyes filled with fresh repentance, and his shoulders hunched over again. "I guess a part of me really misses her."

Colton and I looked at each other.

It was so familiar it was almost painful. The initial shock, the cutthroat pain, the way your chest seemed to heave every time it crossed your mind. The thoughts seemed permanent, like you were doomed to endure the never-ending cycle of grief forever. My heart squeezed at the memory, and I inhaled to clear my mind.

"It's normal to miss her," I murmured gently. "Everything you're feeling is normal."

"At least I can hang out with Andre now without Josie constantly hammering me about the details."

"Was this her first relationship, too?" Colton asked.

"Yeah."

All the pieces fell into place then.

It was no excuse for her behavior, but it did shed some light on her motives. First love was a wonderful, enlightening, terrifying thing, but it all came to an end for the same reason: the uncertainty that there was something bigger and better out there in the world. The fear of commitment. Perhaps Josie was overwhelmed by that promise of affection and by her own feelings. Maybe she was confused, as any young teenager would be. After all, she'd dated Gavin for a year and three months. That was a long time for their age. They had yet to learn.

I pressed my hand to my forehead and tried to massage away the onslaught of a headache.

My son had finally reached the fork in the road, where he would have to choose how to go about life from now on. But he wasn't about to fade away, not if I had anything to say about it.

Gavin was telling Colton about all the things he wanted to do now that he was single, and I caught the last part of his statement.

"I wanna let loose and have a good time. I don't want to be hurting anymore."

I knew Colton was about to respond, but I beat him to it. "Forgive Josie then."

They both stared at me, and the silence was deafening.

"Forgive her." There was something in my tone that had never been there before—a sort of wiseness. An unmistakable ring of integrity.

Gavin didn't like this suggestion. "Forgive her? Are you kidding me?" He scoffed and rolled his eyes. "Why would I do that when she *hurt* me so many times!"

"You said you didn't want to hurt anymore," I challenged. "But the only way to truly heal is to forgive."

"But I—" Gavin's eyes shifted between us, and a look of helplessness crossed his face. "I'm angry at her. She ruined my life. She's a bitch!"

"HEY!" I snapped, pinning my son with an intense glare. Colton reached out to touch my shoulder, possibly to hold me back, but I shrugged him off. If heartbreak pushed Gavin into the real world, then I would treat him so, and he needed to learn this. "Some things are unforgivable. Lying, cheating...but Josie didn't do any of those things. I don't care if she spit fireballs near the end of your relationship. Do not curse her name. *Ever*."

Gavin cocked his head at me. "I can't believe you're taking her side."

"I'm not," I insisted firmly. "But she's not a bitch, and you know that deep down, that's just the hurt talking. Besides, this was the first relationship for you both, and she didn't know any better. She has her issues, you have yours. But you did love her."

"She really hurt me!" Gavin yelled, throwing his hands up.

"Then you *take* that hurt and you learn to grow from it!" My voice was strong, authoritative. Even Colton shrank backward.

In the following silence, I stared my son down until tears welled up in his eyes. He let his head hang so that the tears could drip down to the carpet. I swallowed the stinging lump in my throat and watched him cry for a few moments. He was finally letting it out. He sobbed until his poor eyes were bloodshot and his mouth couldn't stop quivering.

Eventually Colton said, "Your mother's right. You can't get anywhere in life holding onto that anger."

Gavin pinched the bridge of his nose, and more tears trickled down his wrist. His sniffles were the only sound in the room, but I would rather have had it this way as opposed to him trying to bottle up these beautiful emotions. And they *were* beautiful. Feeling led to healing; Gavin just didn't know that yet.

"I-I..." He seemed to be choking on his own words. My hands twitched to comfort him, to take the pain away. He continued, "I'm angry b-because I can't...get *over* her." More tears, more heartbreak.

But the confession was a start.

"Gav, sometimes breakups are like going through withdrawal after an addiction." My tone was softer now, almost like a comforting caress. "They suck, but...they're opportunities to grow. Like for example, you might try to communicate better in your next relationship."

"I don't want anyone else," he spat. "Just Josie."

My next response slipped away from me, and I let my eyes drop. I knew that feeling all too well.

"I'll tell you what you're *not* gonna do," Colton said then, calling our attention back. "Don't have a rebound relationship. Those types of relationships never last, and it's unfair to both you and the girl that you would be with. Instead, focus on *yourself.*"

"I just hope I made the right decision." Gavin sighed after a while, raking a hand through his hair. His cheeks glimmered with tears.

"Well from what it sounds like, I think you did," I replied. "You're both so young, and you need a chance to live in that youth without the stress of a relationship for a little while."

I knew the look in his eyes quite well: the horror that you may never recover what you had with that person. I sighed and finally reached out to take him in my arms, and for once, my teenage son didn't protest.

"Forgive her," I whispered, patting Gavin's back as he convulsed with sobs. "I bet you a hundred percent that she's just as upset as you are."

"She can't be," Gavin managed. "She never loved me anyway."

"Now you *know* that's not true," Colton insisted, shaking his head. "You two were so close."

Gavin pulled away from my arms and dragged his hands down his face. "I don't even know how to forgive her. I mean, I can't *do* anything without thinking about her. I-I can't play soccer 'cause she used to be in the stands supporting me. I can't do homework 'cause she and I used to do it together. I can't get on social media without checking her profile page." He rubbed at his eyes like he wanted to scratch them out.

"I never said forgiveness was easy," I responded. "*I'm* even still learning. But you can get through this, Gav. One day at a time, one hour at a time." He looked like he might burst into tears again. "One moment at a time."

"There is life after heartbreak, buddy. Trust me," Colton placed a hand on Gavin's shoulder. "And you'll see it eventually."

"You just need some time," I added, and my heart screamed sympathy for this small, grief-stricken boy whose sadness was a knife in my abdomen. "Focus on soccer. That's your passion. And your baby sister needs you."

Gavin looked back at me, his piercing blue eyes like two ferocious oceans. "I don't think I can be friends with Josie, Mom."

I shook my head slowly. "Forgiveness doesn't mean going to hang out with that person next weekend like nothing ever happened. It means acknowledging the issue but no longer passing judgment. It's in the past for a reason, Gav. God's got a plan for you, so don't stop praying just because someone's gone."

"I'm not ready to talk to her." Gavin's tone was drenched in fear.

"That's okay," Colton answered for me. "You don't have to any time soon. Take your time."

"And just because she's gone, that's no excuse for you to start juuling or drinking or partying in any way," I warned. "You have too much to live for to throw your life away like that."

We had another stare off before Gavin sighed and nodded, and I knew he wouldn't trail down that path. He would be stronger than that, even when feeling his emotions sucked worse than smoking them away.

"You're okay," I asserted. "You will be okay. This pain is temporary."

One final tear oozed from his eye, but he wiped it away this time and offered me a weak nod. It was a feeble response, but I accepted it. Now, the healing could begin.

~

"Hey, Gail?" Colton stepped into the bathroom just as I finished brushing my teeth.

"Yeah?"

He folded his hands together, looking terribly uncomfortable and out of place. Curious about his body language, I turned to face him fully.

"What's wrong, Colt?"

"Nothing." He shook his head and jammed his thumb over his shoulder. "Just...what you said to Gavin tonight...you really are an amazing woman, and I..." He swallowed, and his eyes reflected his pain. "I'm sorry for hurting you all those years ago. I know we agreed that it's in the past, but sometimes I can't shake the feeling that you've outgrown me and are too good for me now."

I placed my hands on his face, swiping at a runaway tear that was scurrying down his cheek. "Shh. Don't apologize."

Confusion pinched his features. "But you said—"

"It was painful when you left," I told him. "But you taught me the importance of self-awareness and gave me the opportunity to chase my own dreams for a little while. Besides," I said, rubbing another one of his tears away. "You were man enough to admit your own mistakes and for that, I know we still deserve each other. You are perfect for me, Colton Reeves. In every single way."

He sniffled and then kissed the palm of my hand. "Thank God I didn't stray too far away."

"Thank God," I agreed and then touched my lips to his.

Chapter Eighteen

SARATOGA SPRINGS, NY–NEW YORK CITY, NY (2042)

Gavin stayed busy.

In the fall of his junior year, he played striker on the varsity soccer team and was even voted team captain by his teammates. He went out with Andre a lot more, usually to the pizzeria in town or to the gym, which was slowly becoming Gavin's new drug of choice.

I hardly heard another word about Josie except for the occasional, "She was at the color-run today." Or, "I saw her out with some friends on Friday."

"Are you okay?" It was my go-to question.

He would inhale through his nostrils, pull his shoulders up with the movement, and then exhale. "I think so."

And if he wasn't, he would go out and jog for two hours.

Time was moving too quickly. Not only was Gavin seventeen and taller than me, but there was an air of independence in him now that screamed blossoming maturity. It kind of made me sad in a way. When I came home after rehearsal and found that he'd already cooked himself dinner or powered through two loads of laundry or volunteered to watch Aliana while Colton or I showered, it made me miss the days when he was younger. When I could still hold him. But he was a vine, growing up and up and up, further out of my reach. Growing closer to a man. I wondered if this was how my dad had felt while raising me. I wondered if he, too, suddenly felt useless at times, or if it was more a sense of accomplishment.

In spring of that year, we began touring colleges for Gavin. There was a big debate over what he should major in, but it was becoming abundantly clear that soccer was turning into more of a hobby. The dream of playing pro was fading into the background. In April, Gavin chose business. We toured at least five colleges over the following months, and Gavin would hold Aliana as we walked, pointing out the prestigious buildings and making her giggle.

"Okay, top three choices," he announced in early May. "Syracuse, Albright, and Penn State."

Colton pumped his fist into the air. "Yes! That's what I'm talking about! We are!"

"Penn State," Gavin deadpanned and forked through his mashed potatoes.

"PSU! PSU!"

I cut my husband off and said, "You still have a year to commit, Gav. You've got time."

"I know, but I feel like everyone's ahead of me. Andre's dead set on Pitt already, and Sam said he's gonna sign with Michigan for soccer."

"This isn't about them," I insisted. "This is about you and *your* journey. Take your time. The world isn't going to end if you don't have a decision by tomorrow."

Gavin rested his chin in his hand and glanced at Aliana in her highchair. She was staring back, crushed peaches smeared across her chubby, rosy cheeks. Her green eyes were big and round. They could hold all the light in the room and then maybe some of the sun as well.

If there was anyone who kept this family intact, it was Aliana.

She kept me up at night, wanting to be everywhere but in her crib. She liked to toss her food across the table instead of eating it. She liked to be held all hours of the day. And she liked to scream in the grocery store. I should've been fed up with the lack of sleep and the puke cleaning and the diaper changing, but I honestly wasn't. Because for as exhausted as I felt in my bones, my daughter was still one of the best things to ever happen to me.

Colton was at her side constantly, jiggling her toys and making silly faces. She even giggled more around him than she did with me. Watching them interact resurrected something in me that I didn't realize was missing.

It happened one night as Colton was stretched out on the living room floor, teaching Aliana how to play with the interactive cube in front of her. It made noises when she pressed the buttons, and to her, that was the coolest thing in the world. Colton pointed to a button. The cube beeped, and she squealed with delight. The glimmer in her eyes was nearly blinding.

The smile Colton gave her was a smile I'd never seen from him. It was faint but overpowering. He looked completely in awe of the baby girl in front of him. I tried hard to find the right words to match his expression. Adjectives cartwheeled and back-flipped through my brain without ever standing still. Eventually, I snatched my sky-blue notebook from the kitchen table and opened it to a blank page. It was almost full now.

Colton reached out and tapped Aliana on the nose. She giggled again, and he pulled his hand back. His shoulders bounced as he laughed.

I began writing without even thinking about it. My pencil knew what to do as it guided my hand across the page. It was sloppy and basic—*Colton is a brand new father*—but it shushed my talkative brain, so I kept going. I wrote about the scene right in front of me, down to the way Aliana waved her arms when Colton wouldn't push the next button fast enough. I wrote and wrote and wrote, until the muscles in my hands screamed for a break.

Colton glanced up at me. "What'cha writing there?"

I stared down at the page for a moment and then twisted my lips. "I wanna take some writing classes."

Colton blinked and pulled Aliana into his lap. "This is new."

"I've just sort of always been journaling since college. It's nothing cohesive. Mainly bullet points about people in my life, depression, music, traveling. Hi, sweetheart!" I paused and waved back at my daughter. She bit down on her tiny fist and smiled.

"Am I in the journal?" Colton asked. I could practically see his ears perked up like a dog's.

"You will be."

"Awesome."

I bit my lip. "I want to take a writing class."

Colton bounced Aliana on his knee and made motor sounds until she was giggling and clapping her hands. "I say go for it. If it's something you're passionate about, don't hold yourself back. I know you'll be amazing."

"It'll be tight with rehearsal, but I'm willing to give it a try."

"You planning on writing a book or something?" Colton grinned at me.

"Not necessarily. But I have a feeling I'm gonna write something one day that will really resonate with the people I love."

～

"Writing classes, huh?" Veronica twisted one of the pegs on her violin and plucked the strings. "Do you mind if I tag along?"

I looked up from my sheet music. "Sure! I didn't know you were into writing."

"When I was younger, I wanted to be a screenwriter. That was before I started the violin, but the dream never really died."

"If you can help me find some writing classes open to the public, I'd love to try one with you."

"Let's check now then." She whipped her phone out of her back pocket.

The rest of the orchestra was still tuning their instruments, and Tod was answering Claira Heffen's question. We had time.

"Nothing, nothing." Veronica was staring lasers at her phone, eyebrows furrowed in concentration. She continued to scroll. "There are probably a ton of classes offered in the city. Let's check there."

"I'm just looking for something that'll give me some tips on how to—"

Veronica's unexpected gasp cut me off. It was so loud that the people around us turned to see if she was okay. Her eyes looked like they were trying to pop out of their sockets.

"What?" I demanded.

"DC is coming to New York City on a book tour!" Veronica slapped my arm repeatedly, and a breathy scream escaped her lips.

"What's DC?"

"You mean *who* is DC. She wrote one of the most iconic Sci-fi series of all time!" When it didn't click for me, Veronica shouted, "*Warning*! Five-stars on Amazon, number-one bestsellers list. Oh come on, Gail! Do you live under a rock?"

"Apparently."

She sighed and looked back down at her phone. "We're going. If anyone can offer us writing tips, it's her."

It wouldn't hurt to talk to a published author. I could learn a lot from her expertise. Maybe I'd even be lucky enough to learn how to gain control of the jumbled words in my head. Then one day, I could write about my husband and children. How I was going to write about them yet was beyond me, but the idea was a force from Heaven. It had taken me by the shoulders and refused to let go. I was not about to avert my gaze and pass up this opportunity.

"When's the event?" I asked Veronica.

"May 14th." Her lower lip protruded into a pout. "Please say you'll go."

"Oh, I'm going," I assured her.

The universe was practically patting my back and demanding that I attend. And when the universe tells you to do something, you do it.

Jamie agreed to watch Aliana while Veronica and I were in New York City. Gavin was busy assistant-coaching a young soccer program, and Colton was swamped with work. It was always difficult leaving my daughter, but she clung to Jamie like an introvert clung to safe solitude.

The entire ride to the city, Veronica filled me in on the details of the *Warning* series. It was about a group of aliens who go awol from their mothership and travel to earth to warn humans of the mothership's plans to take over the planet. Apparently, it was translated into five languages and had at least eight hundred reviews on Amazon. I didn't really get the significance of that, but if the book was selling, then good for DC.

"You *have* to pick it up," Veronica insisted. "It's not a suggestion, it's a command."

"I'm not a big reader," I admitted.

Veronica narrowed her eyes. "Weird dynamic. You want to be a writer, and yet you hate reading."

"I don't want to be a best-selling author," I argued. "I just want to write something special for my family."

"Like what?"

The Empire State Building and the World Trade Center

reached up and punctured the cloudless sky. New York City was dazzling from a distance away.

"I'm not sure yet."

The event was being held at a Barnes and Noble on 5th Avenue, so naturally, the line stretched out the door and down the sidewalk. Posters hung in the glass windows, advertising DC's latest edition to the *Warning* series. This was the third and final book in the trilogy.

I felt a little out of place standing in line amongst screaming fans and bookworms. All I wanted was to ask a few questions on how to get started writing. I wasn't interested in picking up the series at all. It almost felt like I should've been the last person in line so that all of these avid readers could get in there before me and meet their hero of an author. Veronica already had cash clenched in her fist to buy the book by the time we got to the doors.

There was a live Q&A scheduled with DC and then a signing session immediately after, and as the girls in front of me raved about the main character of this book and all her admiring qualities, I questioned how much of this was actually worth my time. DC, whoever she was, probably had an inflated ego.

We ended up sitting closer to the back, so I had to crane my neck to see the makeshift stage. Two chairs were set up, and the host was already seated. Cameras clicked and flashed; the volume of scattered conversations was a dull roar. At two o'clock sharp, the host stood up. She said a few words thanking Barnes and Noble for hosting the event and about how popular the *Warning* series was.

It dawned on me then that something about the concept of this series felt vaguely familiar. I racked my brain, trying to pinpoint where I'd heard something like it before. The host spread her arms in a welcoming gesture, and people started to scream.

I leaned toward Veronica. "Wait, what does DC stand for?"

Before she could answer, the host exclaimed, "Ladies and gentlemen, Danielle Caldwell!"

She sashayed around the corner, her blonde ponytail swinging with every step. She wore black-rimmed glasses and a sleek gray pantsuit. She looked professional; she looked accomplished; she looked...so grown up.

My heart was ice cold in my chest. I couldn't believe this.

It was Dani.

She's a successfully published author, Evan had told me at the dinner table all those years ago when I'd agreed to meet him and catch him up on Gavin's life. Except it didn't occur to me then what "successfully published author" could look like. And here she was—grown up and beautiful and radiant.

My throat squeezed shut.

The last time I saw her, Gavin was a newborn, and she was just graduating high school. I remembered the boxes of journals in her room and the twinkle in her eye. I remembered the way she always carried a notebook so that if and when an idea popped into her head, she could write it down. Sometimes, I missed her even more than Evan.

I hardly heard a word she said during the Q&A. I was so in awe of the fact that she was up on that stage at all, happy and funny and posing for pictures. She deserved this. All of it. I didn't know what had gone on in her life since I'd left, but one thing was for sure: she'd worked hard to get to this point.

Veronica leapt out of her seat with the rest of the crowd as Dani thanked them at the end of the session.

"Who has a copy they want Danielle to sign?" the host asked, and the audience went *nuts*.

I couldn't even react. My mouth was still parted in shock. My heart had disintegrated half an hour ago.

"I know her," I told Veronica as she towed me in line to get the book signed.

"The world knows her," Veronica replied.

"No, no. *Personally*. She's my ex-husband's younger sister."

"*What*? Your ex-husband's sister is *DC*?" Veronica shakes her head. "Why am I just now hearing about this?"

"I didn't know it was her!"

My fingers were shaking. What would I even say to Dani? A simple hello almost felt rude. What *did* you say to someone who you hadn't seen in decades but missed so much that their absence became a permanent hole in your heart? God, it was almost painful being in her presence. It pried open a box of so many memories, both incredible and appalling.

We reached the front of the line. Veronica lunged forward, holding her book out with an electric smile. But as soon as Dani's eyes locked with mine, her face went blank. She stood up out of her seat, momentarily forgetting Veronica's outstretched hand. We just stared at each other, gaping and blinking like two idiots. Eventually, I managed to step forward.

"Dani. It's so good to see—"

She held up a hand and stepped back.

"Don't." It was quick and to the point, but her voice was strained. She shook her head once and then turned toward Veronica with a pasted smile. "Hi, there."

Veronica glanced at me uncomfortably before acknowledging Dani. "Uh, hi. Listen, I'm a huge fan."

I didn't hear their conversation. All I could do was stare at Dani as she signed Veronica's copy with a swooping signature and posed for a selfie. She did not look at me again.

Something in my soul caught on fire. This was a once in a lifetime event, and if I was determined to catch it in my palm, then I was not leaving until Dani and I had a conversation.

"Gail, this is crazy. I don't know what happened in your past, but DC clearly doesn't want to talk to you. Can we please just go?"

"No."

We were seated in a lounge area. The line to meet Dani was

shorter now, and as soon as it ended, I was going to march right back up there. Too often I'd turned a cold shoulder on the possibility of reconciliation, but this was a gift from God; I was sure of it. Veronica shrugged hopelessly and went back to reading.

As soon as the last person left, I shot out of my seat. Dani spotted me and instinctively gathered her things faster.

"Dani, wait," I said once I reached her.

She turned to face me with a look of utter exhaustion, but it didn't seem to be from people-pleasing all day. It looked like mental exhaustion, like the thought of even dipping a toe into the past was impossible for her right now.

"What do you want, Gail?" Even her tone was tired.

I blinked at her. "That's not how you greet someone you haven't seen in ages."

"I wasn't aware I owed you anything."

Who was this girl? She seemed so far from the innocent, sweet girl I once knew. "Dani, I didn't mean to offend you in any way. I'm actually really glad to see you."

"Yeah, well." She sniffed and grabbed her pen and the rest of her display books off the table.

My heart started hammering. This moment couldn't end yet. Call it a burning desire for closure, but there was an actual ache in me to talk to her and catch up. To learn about her college experiences and her writing process and how she managed to chase her dream so effortlessly. I was fully aware that none of it was my business, not after how things ended with Evan. But that didn't stop me from wanting to make everlasting peace with the past.

My mouth opened and closed a few times before I blurted, "Wanna grab a bite to eat?"

Her icy blue eyes touched mine, and she scoffed.

My chest blazed. "Look, Dani, I know Evan and I had our differences, but I'm still the same me...just older now. And I still think you are an amazing person. I thought that when I met you, I thought that when Evan and I got divorced, and I *still* think that. I would be honored to eat with you. Not because you're a bigshot published author now, but because...I've missed you."

I knew it wasn't in my right to be saying these things. Yet they poured out of my mouth like a prayer.

Dani stared at me for a moment with her jaw clenched and her nostrils flared. A woman in a flowy white blouse and black pencil skirt came around the corner.

"Dani, we're ready to head out when you are. Remember you have that zoom meeting with your publisher tonight at eight."

Dani's narrowed eyes were still locked on mine. I could have melted under that intense gaze. I was already sweating enough as it was.

Finally, Dani turned toward the woman. "Cancel the meeting," she said. "Tell Lue I'll catch up with her on Monday. I have dinner plans tonight."

Chapter Nineteen

NEW YORK CITY, NY

I told Veronica I'd uber home. She wasn't happy about skipping a meal with the critically-acclaimed DC, but she understood the importance of this dinner.

"Just tell her I'm her biggest fan, and that I love every single one of her books, and that it was an honor to meet her," Veronica pleaded before dropping me off at the door of the restaurant.

"No problem. Thanks again, Veronica."

She waved and merged back into the hectic traffic of the city. Veronica had grown up here; the bumper-to-bumper chaos was just another day to her.

I met Dani inside. She was already sitting at a table, skimming the menu. The couple in the booth across from her was positively freaking out at the mere sight of her.

"Have you read my books?" Dani asked the moment I sat down. She didn't look up from her menu.

"Uh, no I haven't." I instantly felt guilty. "But I hear they're absolutely amazing. In my defense, I didn't know you'd choose

DC as a pen name. If I knew it was you, I would've picked up the series immediately." I wasn't a big reader, but I was a big supporter for the people I loved.

"It's Danielle Albrett now actually. I'm married, but I kept my maiden name for writing."

Married. God, the time flew by.

"Do you have any kids?"

"A daughter, yes." Dani finally glanced up at me, the light reflecting off the lens of her glasses. "Serena."

A tiny smile tugged at my lips. "That's amazing. What else have I missed?"

Her eyebrows pulled together as I asked the question, and her eyes flicked around the restaurant. "It's been a dream come true, but this didn't happen overnight. My first two books didn't sell well. I released them and nobody cared enough to buy them."

"Dani, I'm sure people—"

"No. My parents were the only ones who read them. It was a coming-of-age duology. Cliché, predictable, nothing special." She shrugged. "I didn't write anything for a long time after I released the sequel. I graduated college with a master's in education but never put it to use. I moved to Maryland but was evicted from my apartment because I didn't have a good paying job and couldn't pay rent. I basically thought my life was over. Do you know how embarrassing it is to move back into your parents' house at twenty-five? *Embarrassing*," she emphasized before I could answer.

"But while I was there, I came across some old journals and found the concept map for *Warning*. Worked my ass off to get a manuscript finished and submitted to a new publishing company, and God finally took my side."

I bit the inside of my cheek. "Everything happens for a reason. I'm sure that time of your life was difficult, but look where you are now."

She nodded, but something in her expression was still irritated. "Met my husband a year later in a café while I was going through my last round of rewrites. He, along with my Serena—they are the best things that have ever happened to me."

"That's great, Dani!" I didn't understand why she seemed so dismal and on edge. She was living a superstar's life.

She seemed to want to say more. Her lips twitched like she was at war with herself over whether to continue or not.

"Why didn't you ever call?" She asked it so quickly, I wasn't sure I'd heard her right.

"Call?"

"To say goodbye, Abigail." Her tone left no room for excuses. She was glaring at me now, lips sagging into a frown.

Oh.

I placed my elbows on the table and leaned forward. I should've been expecting this.

"I don't know." It was an honest answer carved from the depths of my heart. "The night Evan told me he...cheated, I just grabbed Gavin and left. I didn't think about what leaving would do to anyone else. I just needed to get myself out of there as fast as possible. I don't expect you to understand," I added when her eyes grew glassy. Her face held so much tension in that moment. I could see the muscles in her neck straining like wires. She really was upset.

"I..." She looked away and swallowed loudly. "I admired you so much. Not just for the person you were but for how you changed my brother. He was lost, but when you came into the picture, he became someone amazing. He actually started caring about things again. He was happier. More himself. I just remember thinking, wow, that girl's incredible. She brought my brother back."

My heart was cracking down the middle. There was so much hurt in Dani's eyes. So much confusion and anger—all directed at me. I felt sick.

"I don't talk to my brother anymore," she continued hollowly.

"The moment I found out what happened, I slammed my bedroom door shut and cried for hours. I was nauseous over the fact that he was stupid enough to cheat on you, but I hated you, too, for disappearing off the face of the earth. I..." She inhaled and clenched her fists even tighter. "I loved you like a sister. I looked up to you. I wanted you in my life. And the next thing I knew—" Dani flipped her hands. "You were gone."

"Dani—"

"And with my nephew, too," she interrupted, more acid spilling into her voice. "I can count on one hand, Abigail, how many times I've seen Gavin. *One* hand. How old is he now? He must be at least sixteen."

"He'll be eighteen next month," I said in a small voice.

Her face grew paler. I watched the color drain like it was funneling into a hiding place.

"Evan never had another kid, Gail."

"What?" I wasn't sure why that piece of information prodded my heart. "I thought he remarried."

"He did." She didn't say anything else, which made me think that Evan hurt just as much as I did at one point. If that kind of pain leads you to never have children again, was it possible that he actually regretted his decision?

"Have you told Gavin?" Dani asked, setting her lips into a firm line.

My soul shrank in my body. "I haven't yet."

She tossed her napkin onto the table and stood up from her seat. I started panicking as she shoved in her chair and started for the door.

"Dani, stop," I half-shouted, catching her wrist.

She looked down at me, clearly surprised by the gesture, and pulled free from my grasp.

"I'm sorry, okay?" I held my hands up, feeling hopeless and cut open and responsible for all the hurt in this girl's heart. "I'm sorry that I left out of the blue and took Gavin with me. I'm sorry that I never called to explain myself. The choice to leave Evan out of Gavin's life was one of the *hardest* decisions I've ever had to make. Because you're right." I shrugged as the tears started to tickle my eyes. "He's Gavin's father. He *should* be a part of his life. He should know you as his aunt, and he should know his cousins from Laine and Taryn. It is my fault that our families have split, and for that, I am so sorry." I shook my head. "But I can't be sorry for not trusting Evan after what he did to me. I just can't be. Whether you agree or not, Gavin deserves a father-figure who is going to show up for him and be proud of him a hundred percent of the time. And he finally has that."

Dani tilted her head. "What're you saying?" There was no judgment in her tone now except for a tiny slice of heartbreak.

I sighed. "I'm in love with someone, Dani. I've been in love with him since I was fifteen, and we just had a daughter together. I'm trying hard to process it and be present in this new era of my life, but the past just keeps coming back again, and again, and again. It's getting harder to fight every single day. Gavin's leaving for college in a year, and he still doesn't know who his real dad is. I want to tell him, and I want to explain myself, and I want to express how much I love my husband, Colton. But that's my problem, Dani." My voice was escalating. "I can't find the right words for anything. I'm too much of a coward to even begin to understand how to tell anyone the truth behind my feelings. That's why I came to your event today! So that I could ask you how you communicate your feelings so clearly on paper. I want to explain everything to my children. I just don't know where or how to start."

"You..." Dani shook her head. "You want me to help you write a book?"

"No. I just have so much I need to tell them. Maybe it'll be a letter. I haven't figured it out yet. But there's no way I'm just running into you by coincidence." I stared up at her, hating the way my breath was trapped in my throat. This moment would change everything.

Dani held my gaze for a second longer and then glanced up at the door. Her jaw clenched just like Evan's did, and if I had X-ray vision, I would've seen her brain flipping between each decision. I gripped the back of my chair so hard that my fingers were screaming. I figured I'd lost the battle, but she heaved a sigh and sat back down. I was weightless with relief. My mouth opened to thank her, but she spoke before I could get a word out.

"The thing about writing is that you have to write from your heart and not give a shit about what anyone thinks." Her voice was softer now, kinder. "Sometimes it's not about gorgeous sentence structure or mind-blowing plot twists. It's about the feelings that your words provoke in readers. Does that make sense?"

I nodded and retrieved my sky-blue notebook from my purse. Dani eyed it curiously, almost like she knew her name was scribbled on several of the pages.

"So, what exactly do you want your kids to know?" she asked.

"Everything. Gavin is in that phase where he thinks I've never experienced a breakup or dealt with hardship, but I want him to know that he's not alone. I've always sort of kept my past a secret with him, but I'm sick of that. And I know my daughter will ask the same questions someday. I want to give them something tangible that'll explain it all."

Dani nodded, and we were interrupted by a waiter to take our orders.

"You said you're in love," she murmured when we were alone again. She squared her shoulders. I couldn't imagine that this would be easy to hear after what happened with Evan, but I was grateful that she was even willing to sit and talk with me. "Love can be a great root when writing about tough subjects. So, tell me about him."

A smile touched my lips the way it always did when I thought of Colton. He was my sunlight, moonlight, and everything in between.

"Oh, boy," I said, and Dani actually smiled. "Where do I even begin?"

Chapter Twenty

SARATOGA SPRINGS, NY

Our waiter tried to communicate that we were overstaying our welcome by forcing smiles and gesturing to the crowd of waiting, hungry customers who could have used any extra table, but Dani and I didn't care.

After I stumbled through a lame summary of my history with Colton, Dani demanded to see my journal. We walked page by page, and I explained all of the names and situations I'd scribbled in over the years.

"You've certainly got a lot of material here," she said distractedly, leaning forward and squinting at Evan's name.

I remembered writing it in that exact spot. It was senior year of college when I considered Evan to be the cure-all for my depression and anxiety.

"My problem is that I don't know how to translate what I feel for Colton," I explained. "Every time I try, it feels basic."

Dani considered this for a moment and then gently closed the notebook. "Let's try something I learned in college."

I straightened, suddenly nervous. "Okay."

"One word descriptors," she explained. "Anything that comes to mind in one word." Her eyes bored into mine. "Colton."

"Handsome."

We smiled at each other.

"Okay, good," Dani said. "Keep going. Colton."

I pressed my lips together. "Kind. Considerate. Amazing cook."

"That's two words," Dani interrupted. Then she cocked her head. "No, it's fine, whatever. Continue."

"Not very organized. Obsessed with volleyball to this day. Dry but cute sense of humor." I nodded. More words were waiting to roll off my tongue.

Dani opened the journal and slid it across the table to me. "Write them now." She fished a pen out of her purse and handed it to me as well.

I hesitated. There was something intimidating about a blank page. Except everything else in this journal was mainly cluttered word vomit, so I had to remind myself that perfection was not the end goal. At least not in this notebook.

So, I wrote Colton's name as neatly as I could and fired off the things I'd just verbally listed to Dani. She sat back in her seat, sipping on her third lemonade.

We'd been sitting there for three hours now.

I pushed on, thinking of all the little things Colton did and said that I both loved and got annoyed with—even though I loved them, too, honestly because they made him who he was.

Has to have the car volume on an even number.

Would work all night if his boss let him.

The biggest reason Aliana smiles every day.

Speeds through books like nobody's business.

Fan of country music for some reason.

Fifteen minutes passed before I looked back up at Dani. She sat patiently with a dim sparkle in her eye.

"How's it feel?"

"Good," I admitted. "I need to do more of this exercise."

"You're welcome." She shifted in her seat. "Let me ask you something. What do you think you'll gain from writing this letter?"

"Peace," I answered immediately.

"Peace from what?"

"My anxiety I guess." The statement made me realize I was twisting my hands under the table.

Dani leaned forward. "Why don't you include that?"

"What, my anxiety?" My tone screamed *absolutely not.*

"Why not? I don't think you're going to get peace until you work through that stuff. And even then you might not." She cleared her throat apologetically. "But listen, writing is a fantastic coping mechanism."

"I know," I muttered, keeping my eyes glued on the open page.

"So, why not?"

"I don't want my kids to think I was some crazy—"

"I *highly* doubt they will, Gail." Dani sighed. "You want it to be a tell-all? Crack your shell open and give them what they deserve."

My heart was pounding. I'd never outwardly written about my anxiety, just the people who caused and cured it.

"One word descriptors," Dani said. I mirrored her when she took a deep breath. "Anxiety."

I blinked four or five times before answering. "Scary. Unbearable. Intrusive." I had to consciously pull my hands apart so I'd stop twisting them. When I stopped, I felt naked and exposed. "Heavy."

Dani's eyes touched the paper and flickered back up to my face.

I heaved a sigh and picked up the pen. Even the word "anxiety" was ugly on the page. My handwriting was sloppy; I had pressed too hard.

I didn't like this sinking feeling in my stomach. It felt like there were hands plunging through my skin and squeezing my intestines until they were about to burst. My breaths became shallower. Dani's eyes felt warm on my face.

I drew a line out from the word and listed the adjectives I'd already said. I wrote them quickly, almost like the mere act of spelling these words would physically hurt me.

When I'd been seeing Gianna, she would ask me if there was a live tiger in the office. It was an exercise meant to help me realize that nothing in the immediate environment was going to swallow me whole. I tried to think about that with this.

These words aren't live tigers. They're just words.

My hand went on, scratching out words like *embarrassing* and *sick*.

"How are you holding up?" Dani's voice made me flinch. Her eyes were wide when I looked up. "Sorry."

"It's okay." I shook my head and swallowed.

"Did you...used to have anxiety like this?" she ventured.

"It was more depression back in the day, but yeah."

Instead of apologizing like I expected most people to do, Dani licked her lips and shrugged.

"Did you know some of the best writers had mental health issues?"

The question caught me by surprise. "No."

She nodded and didn't say anything else.

I wasn't sure why, but that small statement felt more like therapy than any psychologist had ever given me. Sometimes it only takes the right person to remind you of something.

I wasn't alone.

We finally gave in and decided to leave once the sun was an orange blot on the horizon. I was sure the restaurant staff was cheering in the back.

Outside, Dani caught me by surprise when she pulled me into

a hug. We didn't say anything. We just held each other, desperate to put the past to rest.

"Stay in touch," Dani said, and her voice had a warning in it. She'd already put her number in my phone before I paid the bill.

"Absolutely. And thank you so, *so* much." I gripped the notebook to my chest with one hand.

Dani smiled. "I want updates." She tapped her phone and then her face grew serious again. "Just remember. Be you and your writing will shine."

This could have been the end. Our conversation could have ended right there on a busy sidewalk in New York City, but the thought of walking away made me feel sick to my bones. Something was nagging me, something massive and clearly important. I knew exactly what it was, and it was fighting its way up my throat and onto my tongue.

"Dani," I said just as she turned away. "I want you to see him."

Her eyes widened. "You mean..."

I nodded. "Gavin deserves to know you personally. You're right. How are we ever going to heal if we keep running?"

It was the first time since she was seventeen that I'd seen Dani's face come to life. Color rose in her pale cheeks. Her blue eyes twinkled. Her lips stretched into a ginormous grin.

"How long are you on tour?" My chest felt cold and hollow, but it was strangely relieving. Years of pent up angst, fear, and regret were slipping right off of me. The weight difference left me breathless.

"Until June 2nd."

"Call me then, and we'll set something up."

I was not prepared for her to dash into my arms again, so when she did, all the air left my lungs.

"Thank you, Gail." Her arms were iron. "Thank you so much. I'll be in touch."

Aliana grew into a lovely little girl. She'd inherited Colton's green eyes after all. The specks in her irises were copper-colored, but when the light illuminated them just right, they appeared gold. Her hair resembled mine—wavy caramel locks spilling down to her shoulders. And her smile was a tiny slice of Heaven.

Gavin took on a parenting role as much as Colton and I did. He looked out for his sister with his life. Sometimes, I even found my children knee deep in playdough in the living room. In those cases, when the pink goop was smeared through the carpet, I glared at my son with clenched fists until he would say, "Don't worry, Mom. I'll clean it up."

Aliana also helped Gavin through his senior year of high school. She cheered him on during his final season of soccer, gave him a hug for good luck on the morning of his SATs, and jumped up and down when Gavin announced his commitment to Penn State. Colton was more ecstatic than any of us. He had graduated years ago, but his motto was "Once a lion, always a lion."

"And now you're one, too!" He high-fived Gavin and yanked him in for a hug.

Gavin had clearly climbed the food chain during his senior year. He had somewhere to be every Friday night—either with Andre or the rest of his soccer team. He even went out on three different dates. I figured that was reasonable. These days, Josie's name was a flicker of a ghost. Gavin didn't really connect with any of these other girls, and I was secretly grateful for that. At this point, I just wanted him to get through high school. No more heartbreak.

When his graduation rolled around, I was a mess. After orchestra rehearsals, I spent my time combing through old photos of Gavin when he was young. There were all of his baby pictures that Evan had taken. There was the time he'd soared on the tire swing in our front yard when we first moved here. That

Halloween he'd dressed as a vampire cowboy with Andre. Soccer photos, school dance photos, photos of us on the beach and in the car and in the house.

If I learned anything from Evan, it was that pictures were time capsules for our hearts. Magical memories to resurrect beautiful emotions. Looking at Gavin's pictures now, there was a tightness building in my chest. It was an ache for the past. Fortunately, my past would be meeting my present any day now.

Dani and I had been texting a lot the last few weeks. She asked me how my writing was going, and I gave her updates on Gavin's life. Right now, my soul-searching and brainstorming were on pause because of Gavin's graduation. My son didn't know about Dani yet. I wanted it to be a surprise.

We're having a grad party for him next Saturday, I texted Dani as I sat back down with my scrapbook. *I'd love if you could make it.*

It's funny you think I would miss it, Dani replied seconds later.

I smiled and flipped open my scrapbook again.

Aliana climbed up on the couch next to me and peered down at the photos.

"Look at your brother," I said, passing her the school picture of Gavin in his cap and gown.

"Yeah, what do you think, Aliana?" Gavin asked, shuffling in from the kitchen.

She smiled down at the photo and then leapt off the couch into her brother's arms. "Yay, Gavy!"

Colton's hands were trembling softly in his lap. They always did that when we were at the high school—it didn't matter how many times Gavin played in the home games. This was where our lives changed all those years ago, so I couldn't blame Colton. Just like he couldn't blame me for nervously twisting my hands together every five minutes. These days those mannerisms were unconscious, but the memories still lurked in our brains.

Sandy and Sean sat on Colton's right. Sandy was dressed in a floral pink blouse, white capris, and a floppy sun hat. Jamie sat on my left with her ginormous sunglasses and peach-pink lipstick. She was holding Aliana and rocking her back and forth.

The school orchestra began "Pomp and Circumstance."

"Gavy!" Aliana clapped her hands as the graduates appeared.

Gavin was near the front of his class. When we spotted him, our hands went up, and we shouted his name. Even from high in the bleachers, I caught the blush in his cheeks. He peeked up at us under his cap and gave a small wave.

Despite the heat of the dazzling sun rays, the ceremony was wonderful. I cried the moment Gavin walked across the stage to accept his diploma. It felt like an exclamation point after everything he'd been through during high school. The future was so near and so bright.

"One more picture! Andre, scoot in a little," I ordered after the ceremony.

Andre clamped an arm around Gavin's shoulder, and I snapped them as they laughed. They clung to each other, seemingly afraid to part. But then Gavin's gaze flickered across the field, and he bit his lip tentatively.

Ah. Of course. On the 30-yard line, Josie was posing with her friends. Her inky black hair was curled to perfection, and her sleek white dress was covered in elegant pearls. I knew this moment well. When their eyes touched, the connection was almost visible. But it didn't last long. Gavin high-fived one of his other soccer buddies, and suddenly the whole team was swarming my son for a picture. The past was temporarily forgotten.

≈

My front yard was dotted with lawn chairs and tables that were covered in half-empty pizza boxes, veggie trays, fruit trays, and bowls of every kind of chip. Music played from Colton's portable speaker, and my son and his friends were kicking a soccer ball around. The whole team was here, plus other friends from school in addition to family and neighbors. Even Elijah and Brie stopped by for a little while. A customized *Congrats Gavin* banner hung above our garage door—courtesy of Jamie early this morning. She was seated near the garden, giggling with Aliana. Everyone was in such good spirits, but now that it was drawing closer to one o'clock, I was getting nervous.

Colton knew about Dani. We had discussed it one night while I was organizing my reading nook and he'd been trying to read.

"It's for the best," I had told him.

He'd just stared at me in disbelief. "No way Gavin's aunt is Danielle Caldwell. I mean, what are the odds?"

Luckily, his adoration for reading and authors outweighed his simmering hostility toward anyone associated with the man who had cheated on me. Today was about forgiveness. Or at least... taking a few steps *toward* forgiveness.

Dani was due here any minute now. My fingers were shaking slightly. I watched Gavin steal the soccer ball away from Andre and kick it toward their makeshift goal. When he scored, he pumped his fist into the air.

Gavin *didn't* know about Dani. I only told him that someone very special was coming to the party today, and he seemed fine with that. Excited even. I hoped he would still be as excited when he found out that Dani's blood was his blood.

When her white Audi pulled to the curb, no one noticed. No one turned their heads to gaze at the blonde-haired woman with the chic black heels as she stepped out onto the sidewalk. It wasn't until she was halfway up the driveway that one of Gavin's female friends—the bookworm, as he called her—gasped and nearly spilled her soft drink. After that, everyone swarmed her, even a couple of Gavin's teammates.

Gavin was clearly confused. He pushed his way through the crowd and peered down at me. He was a full head taller than me by now.

"Why'd you invite a famous author?"

I sighed and glanced at Colton. He nodded softly.

"Gavin, honey, why don't we step inside for a second?"

They stared at each other, and the resemblance was almost spooky. The same blue eyes, the same golden shade of hair. Even the same arrowhead nose.

"So," Gavin said after three painfully long beats of silence. "I'm related to someone famous. Cool."

Dani laughed, and it sounded more like a sigh of relief. "Well, I can't believe my nephew's a soccer star bound for Penn State. You know, that was my second choice school back in the day."

"Where'd you go instead?"

"University of Delaware. That's where my family lives."

I saw it in Gavin's eyes; his heart skipped a beat.

"I wanted you to meet her yourself, Gav," I said. "I know you have questions. Go ahead."

Sounds of laughter carried in through the open screen door. Colton was entertaining the rest of the seniors with an old school volleyball tournament. On the sidelines, family and friends hollered. From the looks of it, they were having a blast.

Gavin stared at his untouched cup of lemonade. "What... what was my dad like?"

"A bit of a slob." Dani rolled her eyes, and Gavin laughed. "No, he was very athletic actually. In high school, he was like the king of the track team. Everybody loved him. Everybody wanted to be around him. Mr. Popular." Dani paused as a smile crept across her lips. "Today though, he's a professional wedding photographer. Lives in New Jersey with his wife, Amanda.

"Oh, gosh. He was hilarious though. When I was kid, he used to barge into my room and dance around like a monkey just to make me laugh. This one time," Dani pressed a hand to her mouth and snorted. "This one time, he came in wearing these *ridiculous* hot pink glasses and shorts that were way too tiny. He'd stolen one of our mom's purses, walked into my room, and said, 'All right, I'm headed out to the grocery store. You need anything?'"

Gavin burst out laughing. I did, too. I liked talking about these memories—the happy ones, the ones where Evan was his younger goofy self. There had still been a taste of that humor when I first met him. It's what drew me to him like a magnet. Our parting in New York City all those years ago still weighed on my heart, but with conversations like these, I found myself struggling to hold onto any malice at all. As Gavin's eyes crinkled and his laugh echoed off the kitchen cabinets, I realized that I really hadn't been holding malice for a long time now. I only thought I was.

"There are so many stories." Dani's eyes glimmered. "He made a few *really* stupid mistakes in his life, but...I've since forgiven him, you know? We didn't talk for a long time until I realized how much time I was wasting by being mad at my own brother."

Gavin nodded, going a little pink in the cheeks.

"For example..." Dani turned her empty lemonade glass in a little circle on the table. "You. You were never a mistake to him."

"Does he know you're here?" Gavin asked.

Dani glanced at me. "As a matter of fact, he does."

My heart jolted with so many emotions. Predominantly, fear that I'd made a mistake by keeping Evan out of Gavin's life and regret that I had.

"He didn't...want to come?" Pure disappointment painted my son's face. My hand instinctively settled on his shoulder.

"He didn't just want to show up out of the blue and ask you to accept him into your life. But he told me to tell you something."

"What?" Gavin leaned forward.

"He said, and I quote, 'Gavin, son, take care of yourself and make good decisions. I'm proud of you and I always have been.' He also mentioned that, when you're ready in your own time, you can meet him. But it's only up to *you*." Dani smiled at her nephew. "He said he won't take offense if the call never comes, but you can decide what you want."

Tears stung my eyes. This was the part I'd been waiting for. Next month, Gavin would be eighteen and allowed to undo the mistake I'd made. I'd been waiting for so long. It was a low boil beneath my bones, somehow undetected, or more likely, avoided. Gavin should have been the one to decide all along. I was too afraid I would lose him.

"Wait, I don't understand," Gavin said. "What did he do that would make me not want to call him?"

Dani's eyes shifted to me again.

"We just had our differences," I offered with a small smile.

"Trust me," Dani said. "He's matured a *lot* in the last few years."

I wasn't sure if that remark was directed at me or Gavin, but it didn't matter. My son was smiling now. Smiling so big, I had to wipe a tear before it could escape my eye.

If people continued to hold onto their hatred—like I had done for far too long—their hearts would become poisoned, misshapen, and gnarled organs. Seemingly incapable of love. But I couldn't do that anymore. I couldn't be that person with a son and daughter looking up at me. Every choice I made was for them. As it turns out, letting go made me happier.

"It's up to you," Dani repeated. "I won't be offended either. I'm just grateful to be sitting with you right now."

Gavin smiled faintly. I knew he was working the decision over in his brain. He chewed his bottom lip, folded and unfolded his hands, and bounced his leg. The clock ticked away the seconds.

"You know what?" Gavin looked up at me with a growing smile. Hope shimmered on his face. "I want to do it. I want to meet my dad."

Chapter Twenty-One

SARATOGA SPRINGS, NY

We made a plan: Gavin would meet Evan the first week of July. Dani and I would go with him. Colton said he was proud of Gavin for wanting to take a leap, but the whole idea of going to meet his father turned Colton's insides. He wanted no part of it other than to support from a distance. Besides, someone needed to stay with Aliana.

In the meantime, with Gavin gone for Senior Week, my violin stayed glued to my hands. I played furiously, releasing all the intense emotions that were buzzing around in my brain. Having little Aliana around to act as my audience made it even better. When I played, she twirled in time with the music as if she were a ballerina.

"You're quite the dancer, aren't you?" I said one morning.

She nodded with a smile and continued to pull a brush through her baby doll's hair.

"Are you gonna dance in front of people someday?"

"I dunno." She flashed me a grin.

When I was not attached to my instrument, I was writing. Intense emotions cultivated new descriptor words, and I listed them into my journal. One by one—like pebbles cascading from a cliffside.

Anxiety: burning, bright, constricting.
Gavin: smiling, growing, perfect.
Aliana: golden, adorable, innocent.

By small doses, I was beginning to dissect the massive tangle of emotions floating in my brain. The pages in my journal were crammed tight.

On Thursday afternoon, Tod announced that he was cutting our practice short because he had a big announcement.

"Do you think he's adding another piece of music?" Seth mused, eyeing the stack we already had.

"Doubt it." Veronica shook her head.

Our midsummer concerts were usually an hour to an hour and a half. Adding another piece would only lengthen our performance time. As we finished practicing our last song, Tod cleared his throat and placed his baton down on the podium. He looked a little pale, like whatever he was about to say was going to be tough to get out. I swallowed nervously.

"I have been a conductor for thirty-three years," he began with a gentle smile. "In that time, I have met some of the most amazingly talented people, so I am extremely grateful for all of you. However," he went on with a dip in his tone, "my wife and I have been talking about moving back home to Tennessee for some time now. At first, I was against the decision because my love for this orchestra has just grown tremendously over the years. Saratoga Springs is as much my home as Tennessee is. But I'm also getting older. I find that I'm missing my home state more and more with each passing sunset. I figure it's a wise time now considering I've worked a full life. That being said...this midsummer concert will be my last concert with you."

Gasps spurted into the air; some hands shot up to cover mouths. Seth gripped the back of my chair, as if to steady himself. But my eyes were cast downward, stuck to my violin. I focused hard on the instrument. On its curve and fading color, on the rosin dusted over the strings, on the way it fit so perfectly in my hands. Doing this helped me avoid a panic attack. I didn't like losing people. It scared me to death. But a part of me also wanted Tod to be happy.

"We'll miss you!" Jesabell Abrams called from the viola section.

The affection started raining down. Tod blushed and bowed his head.

"It was not an easy decision!" he reiterated, wagging his finger. "I am going to miss you all beyond words."

The rehearsal was emotional. We could hardly practice without getting sidetracked by someone shouting another sweet memory of Tod. This orchestra was my second family.

"Gail, may I speak with you?" Tod asked as I zipped my case shut two hours later.

"Sure."

I followed him out into the hall and away from the rest of the orchestra.

"I am sorry for pinning this news on you so abruptly," he said sympathetically.

"We all want you to be happy, Tod," I said with a small smile. "If Tennessee is where your heart is, then I'm all for it."

He laughed quietly, and his shoulders bounced up and down. "I actually brought you out here to ask you something, Abigail."

I felt my eyebrows raise in question.

He planted his hands on his hips. "Will you take over for me?"

My mouth instantly dropped to the ground. "Wait, like...conduct?"

"Yes," he answered, a grin splitting his face.

"I mean, if you trust me to—"

"You are a *phenomenal* violin player, Abigail. One of the best I've ever heard. Your work ethic and intonation are incredible. You're very professional." He shrugged. "You're perfect for the position. If you want it."

My mind was spinning. I could picture it now—the audience screaming for me as I sashayed across the stage, the exhilaration of conducting a full orchestra like a captain governs a ship. The opportunity to be like Professor Autrie. My face must have been priceless because Tod started to laugh.

"I-I would *love* to."

He clapped his hands together, then launched into a speech about time and commitment, but I couldn't keep my mind from drifting.

Me. A conductor. At long last. I could almost feel Professor Autrie's delight from all the way down here on earth. I could almost hear his hearty laugh and see the sparkle in his eyes. My heart jumped wildly in my chest.

"Thank you so much, Abigail. I wouldn't want the Saratoga Strings falling in anyone else's hands."

I left rehearsal with my stomach doing happy cartwheels. The moment I got home, I went straight for my notebook.

"What are you doing, Mommy?" Aliana asked, climbing into my lap at the kitchen table.

Colton glanced over at us from the stove. I didn't understand how he could make stirring a pot of rice look so handsome. He grinned at me.

"I got an awesome surprise at work," I explained to my daughter. "Your mother's gonna be in charge of the orchestra now!"

I didn't think Aliana knew what that meant exactly, but she

wrapped her arms around me, and it was the first time since Gavin left on his senior vacation that I felt even slightly whole.

"Your mother and I have some fun plans tonight, too," Colton said, grabbing some plates from the cupboard.

"Oh, we do, do we?" I winked at him.

Aliana's eyes flickered between us, asking a dozen questions. I jumped in before she could attempt to ask any.

"What story do you wanna hear tonight after dinner, sweetheart?"

Her face lit up. "How did you meet Daddy?"

"Oh, what a story!" Colton exclaimed. "Full of love, and twists, and turns, and bad guys. But there are some events you may be too young for, missie." He brushed a curl off Alianna's forehead on his way to the table. "Your mother and I have known each other for a *long* time."

I laughed at Colton's enthusiasm.

"Tell the story!" Aliana chanted.

"Well, it hasn't always been a cake walk," I admitted sheepishly.

Colton's eyes touched mine. "Whose life has?"

For a moment, I stared into Aliana's unknowing eyes. She was so sweet, so innocent. She would grow up someday, too, and face life's vexing tribulations. She would need a guide, something to remind her that she could get through it. If I could, she definitely could.

I looked down at the sky-blue journal with pages and pages of life experiences. It was a tangible reminder of growth, and one day, I would turn that growth into a letter for my children.

Aliana's curious gaze brought me back to the present.

"Someday, I'll explain all of it," I promised. "I'll tell you how I met your father. And I'll tell you how music saved my life. I'll tell you about all of these other amazing people who made me who I am. And...I'll tell you how it all came back around."

Aliana frowned. "Why not now?"

I looked at Colton, my heart skipping when he smiled that damn perfect smile that had captured me from day one.

"I'm just not ready yet," I answered softly. "Sometimes healing and processing takes a long time. But for tonight," I grinned at Aliana. "How about I read you *Sleeping Beauty*?"

Chapter Twenty-Two

NEW YORK CITY, NY

For the first time in over a decade, I was not afraid to see Evan. I was not angry. I was not choking on depression or regret. I simply was. My brain was quiet as I maneuvered my way through the bustling city crowd beside Gavin and Dani.

Gavin walked with his shoulders back and his chest puffed out, but there was a rosy blush coloring his cheeks that hinted to me that he was nervous after all. When he had called Evan for the first time, their conversation lasted forty-five minutes. Gavin went on and on about soccer, senior week shenanigans, and his friends. He laughed a lot. He smiled even more. I'd only heard Evan's muffled voice on the other end, but I knew he was cracking jokes *and* taking a breath to listen to his son.

I knew this would all be okay. God was on our side.

When we reached the agreed upon restaurant, Gavin inhaled, ballooning his chest. Dani was practically bouncing on the balls of her feet. She hadn't seen her brother in almost three years.

It took all of five seconds to spot Evan seated dead center at a table and scanning a menu instead of his phone. He was wearing glasses now. Prescription, clearly, from the way he was squinting at the menu. He had grown a dusting of a beard that stretched down his jawline. His blond hair was slightly disheveled. He looked like himself but also like a total stranger. When he looked up, his sharp blue eyes landed right on Gavin.

I'd never seen him smile like that.

"Dad?" Gavin's voice wavered.

"Hi, son."

They didn't know whether to hug, shake hands, or just stand there and smile at each other.

"Please," Evan said after a moment. "Come and sit down."

Dani sashayed to the head of the table, grinning as she caught Evan's eye.

"Nice of you to clean up for once," she joked.

"Nice of you to *show* up for once," he shot back.

They grinned—two siblings. Two peas in a pod once more. I was so happy when Dani explained that they had made up. In a way, it set the world right again.

Finally, Evan turned his eyes to me. They were still just as icy blue as I remembered, but the ice appeared to be melted now, softer and shimmering. Healthy. Matured. I hoped my eyes looked the same way.

"Hi, Gail." It was a voice from my memory, from a time when he was my everything.

Every muscle in my body unclenched. "Hi, Evan."

"What's good here, Dad?" Gavin eyed the menu curiously.

"I've never been here." Evan chuckled. "But whatever you want, it's on me. Same goes for you two," he added, gesturing between me and Dani.

"Okay, great. In that case, I'll take a glass of red wine, a large Fettuccine Alfredo, and a cannoli for dessert," Dani declared.

Evan glanced at her. "Yes, ma'am, and when I become a famous rich author, too, I'll just buy you this whole restaurant for Christmas."

"Oh, thank goodness!"

They giggled at each other from across the table. Gavin laughed, too, his eyes flicking between them with an expression like wonder. He was having *fun*. I finally allowed myself to smile.

By the time our drinks arrived, we were easily the loudest table in the restaurant. Dani and Evan shouted, trying to out-do each other by sharing hilarious stories from their childhood. Gavin detailed the most exciting soccer game from his senior year when he scored three goals and almost got a yellow card for cursing at an opponent—something I pretended not to hear. But I jumped into the conversation as well, explaining that I was days away from being a new conductor and that my daughter was turning into a ballerina. We laughed, screamed, listened, shared.

It felt like I'd left my body at the door and was just floating here, lost and tangled up in the Twilight Zone. But it felt good. It felt good to let go.

"All right, kid. Fess up." Evan wiggled his eyebrows at Gavin. "Where's your girlfriend at?"

"I don't have one," Gavin replied, shrugging modestly.

"All the girls want to be with him," I posited. "You should've seen the way those girls were looking at him at the graduation party."

"Mia and Claire are just friends, Mom."

"Aw, don't say that. You'll break their hearts."

Dani laughed until she snorted.

Sometime later, after we'd had our fill of Italian cuisine, Evan grabbed the check and paid. Just as we were headed toward the door, he touched my elbow.

"Gail, can we talk for a second?"

Dani grasped the hint. "Gavin, let's go check out that saxophone duet across the street."

As soon as they were gone, I turned to Evan. Such deep-set, familiar eyes evoking so many emotions. After a single deep breath, I was able to quiet them.

"We did good." His smile was full, unthreatening. "Or...you did good, I mean."

"He was so excited to see you," I said.

"I can't believe I got so lucky. But Gail—" His eyebrows pulled together. "—I just want to say...I'm sorry. I was young and stupid and blind. You didn't deserve anything that happened, and if I could go back, I would, a hundred times over. And what I said to you...about Colton. That was *completely* out of line. I never should have opened my mouth at all." He glanced at the ground. "I know I don't deserve your full forgiveness, so I'm not going to ask for it. Trust me, I've had a *lot* of time to self-reflect and realize what a douche I used to be, but I've worked my ass off to be better. I just need you to know that I'm sorry."

His words washed over me. Waterfalls upon waterfalls. The lump in my throat grew two sizes larger.

"I'm sorry, too." Tears made my vision wavy. "I shouldn't have run off and cut you out of Gavin's life. That wasn't fair to either of you. And I've said things that I regret, too. It's okay, Evan." We stared at each other—into each other's souls for the first time in a *long* time. "I forgive you."

Evan blinked, breathless. He was such a man now, and I was such a woman. Time was scarily good at its job.

"I know Colton's right for you," he said, smirking lightly. "You guys belong together."

My smile blossomed. "Well, hey. I bet you and Amanda are a perfect match."

He laughed and stuck out his hand. "Friends?"

The earth stopped rotating. *This is it,* I realized. *This is the final step.* I could be happy after this. Totally and entirely happy.

"Friends," I said and shook his hand. "You can see Gavin any time you want, but it's up to Gavin."

"Thank you *so* much," he whispered, "for letting me meet my son."

Chapter Twenty-Three

SARATOGA SPRINGS, NY (2042)

The end of August loomed on the horizon, and Gavin's car was already packed with the last of his things for college. He'd spent the remaining days of summer at the pool with Andre and FaceTiming his father every week. Colton and I had helped him move into his dorm, and he was on his last transfer trip, the backseat of his car jam packed with the last of his clothes in suitcases as well as soccer posters he refused to part with.

"Call us if you ever need *anything*," I sobbed. "And don't be stupid."

"I won't, Mom."

Gavin stole Aliana from my arms and pressed a dozen kisses to her cheek until she giggled uncontrollably.

"Stay here, Gavy," she whined when he went to release her.

"If I could, I would, but I gotta go earn a degree." He offered her a high five instead, and she clapped her small hand against his.

"Hey," Colton said, drawing my son toward him. "Go kick ass at University Park."

"Colton, Aliana is—"

"Go kick *butt* at University Park." Colton rolled his eyes and Gavin laughed as he leaned in to hug him.

It was bittersweet, but I knew Gavin was more than ready to go. He'd had enough of high school and old Saratoga Springs. He craved the college life now. He squeezed my hand one last time and sank into the front seat of his car, the engine grunting and wheezing as he turned the ignition.

"Make good decisions!" I hollered as he backed out of the driveway. "I love you!"

His brakes squealed as he stopped at the intersection at the end of the street and turned left, out toward the main road. There was a gaping hole in the driveway then, and I stared at it blankly. Colton patted my shoulder soothingly.

I turned toward Aliana. "Never grow up," I pleaded, and she gave me a twinkling smile.

Life without Gavin was strange, but in the following weeks, we slowly fell back into a rhythm. I spent most of my time on the phone with Dani and organizing my plans for the Saratoga Strings. Conducting itself was a breeze; it was the extensive music selection that tripped me up half the time. I didn't know how Tod so effortlessly chose our music for each show. I ran through composition after composition, comparing and contrasting.

During rehearsal, we tried sample pieces. I tried to do my job and properly keep the orchestra's attention, but my daughter ended up stealing the show. We'd agreed to allow open practices every now and then for our family members, and today, Aliana was twirling to the music. Colton tried to reach out to her, but she skipped to the center of the room, right behind my podium, and resumed her swaying. Her arms fluttered at her sides. When she leapt into the air right on beat, the small audience gasped in delight. I peeked at Seth and found that he, too, looked surprised. At the end of the piece, Aliana swooped into a deep bow and the entire room exploded into applause. Aliana smiled at the attention, her cheeks filling with color. My husband stood at the side of the room. His mouth was agape.

"Okay, Gail," Seth said as the room filled with motion. "Your daughter's literally a dancing queen."

"She dances all the time. We turn on reruns of *America's Got Talent*, and she's up and moving like an actual contestant."

"Two words." Seth held up his fingers. "Dance. Lessons." He raised his eyebrows for emphasis. "I think she could be a real star."

"I guess I could sign her up for a few classes."

He nodded vigorously. "When she makes it big, *she'll* be paying the bills, Gail. It's a win-win."

I laughed and turned toward Colton. Aliana stood beside him —a smiling ray of sunshine.

"You were amazing, sweetheart," I tickled her stomach and her laughter peeled through the air. "How would you like to join a real dance class?"

I felt Colton's eyes on me, so I looked at him. His expression was bright, imaginative. I knew he was on board with the idea.

Later that night, we researched dance studios in the area. Surprisingly, there were quite a few, all with great reviews. One stood out to me: The Elite Club—*award-winning dance studio, five-time winner at the World Championships, dedicated coaches and students. Specializes in all genres.*

Colton squinted at the screen. "One class a week is forty-five dollars? That's pretty expensive."

My eyes trailed over the genres that were listed in pink on the website: *ballet, tap, jazz, acro, hip-hop, contemporary, robotic-element, musical-theater, fusion...*The list droned on and on. I didn't know so many types of dance even existed.

"And I guess it would be even more if we had to buy her, like, ballet flats or something."

"She doesn't strike me as a ballet dancer." Colton wrinkled his nose distastefully. "But regardless, we need to stack our paychecks before sending her to this place."

"Well, it's either the Elite Club or Rhythm Dance of Saratoga Springs." I glanced at my husband. "I want her to have the best training."

"What if she's not even a dancer? What if she's just going through a phase but is actually an amazing volleyball player?"

"Get your head out of your butt, the girl's clearly a dancer."

Colton's shoulders sagged for a few seconds before he said, "Wouldn't it be sick if she was a hip hop dancer?"

I cocked my head. "She doesn't strike me as a hip hop dancer either."

We both looked at each other and laughed.

Sure, the Elite Club was bound to be extremely expensive, but I was willing to put a few bucks aside if it meant my daughter could be in her element. My wallet, on the other hand, was already in tears.

"Go in there and try your best, honey. I'll be right out here the whole time."

Aliana's hand was clamped nervously around mine as we stood in the lobby of the Elite Club's studio. It was a place that screamed success with too many medals and trophies to count. They hung from the walls and were showcased behind the glass of the receptionist's desk, and if you moved a certain way, the light would catch them and blind you for a second. The lobby was bustling; girls in leotards strutted this way and that, and a cluster of boys in baggy pants and backwards Snapbacks cluttered by the vending machine. Aliana was a minnow in this ocean of bigger fish.

"She'll be in studio two with Julie King," the receptionist informed us kindly, pointing down the hall.

Autographed pictures of who I assumed were famous choreographers lined the walls, and a girl in pointe shoes scurried past us like she was late for class. My nerves settled when I noticed other toddlers around the corner. They, too, were hanging onto their mothers.

"Hello, lovelies!" the instructor, Julie King, declared. She was a medium-sized woman with impressive biceps and frizzy red hair —not someone I would expect to teach a beginner contemporary class, but the children flocked to her like moths thirsty for light. Aliana seemed to lose her wariness because she bounded straight for the door with a large smile.

"Have fun!" I called after her, but she was already inside.

There was a small sitting area just outside the studio door, so I flopped down into a seat and craned my neck to see in through the window. The other moms huddled together, gossiping and laughing, and I tried to focus on Aliana—the little part of her that I could see through the partially closed blinds. She seemed to be having the time of her life.

Even though Dani did not know Aliana as she knew Gavin, I texted her often, updating her on my daughter's life. When I told her that we enrolled Aliana at a dance school, Dani demanded videos and pictures. I tried my best with what little view I had.

When the hour was up, the door flew open, and a sea of toddlers spilled out in the waiting area. Julie King stood to the side, a sheen of sweat glistening on her brow. For a moment, her eyes trailed after Aliana and then flickered away.

Aliana *loved* it; her mouth moved nonstop the full fifteen minute ride home. It was clear that we'd found the proper hobby for her.

Every night, she practiced her steps and followed the stretching routine that Miss King had taught them. She leaped all around the living room, extending her arms and her feet, careful to make sure her toes were pointed. When Sandy and Sean were over, as they often were on weeknights, Aliana would put on a show for them.

"You are a natural born star, pumpkin," Sandy expressed. "You know, when I was little, I loved to dance too, but..."

Colton rolled his eyes and blurted that the dishes needed cleaning. It was his typical line to escape from his mother's endless stories. But Aliana listened intently to her grandmother, her smile growing with each passing second.

~

A couple weeks after her third birthday, Aliana participated in the Elite Club's annual Halloween parade. It was an extra charge, of course, and I felt my wallet thin again as I coughed up an extra fifty bucks, but Aliana looked so cute in her flowy ghoul costume and makeup. The studio performed a routine to the Ghostbusters theme song and won an award for Best Float.

Aliana really was very talented. She moved in a way that the other little girls couldn't. Aliana had fluidity in her movements, gracefulness. Even her facial expressions reflected the tone of the dance. And her talents weren't going unnoticed. Several members of the Saratoga Strings asked when they'd see my little dancing daughter again, and Sandy came over almost every afternoon just to watch Alianna twirl effortlessly.

After Aliana's next practice, Julie King approached me through the crowd.

"I assume you're her mother?" Her voice was a little shrill, and I didn't know how Aliana put up with it.

"Yes."

"Well, I just have to say that your daughter is amazing. She gets the technique down like it's already second nature. I really think she's ahead of the others in the class."

"Thank you," I breathed.

Aliana sat in the chair behind me, replacing her turner flats with light-up Velcro sneakers.

"I know you're new to the studio, but we do have a competition team," King continued. "The minimum age we require is four, but if you're interested, I'd be happy to sit down with you and discuss terms."

"A competition team?"

"Yes." Her corkscrew curls bounced as she nodded. "Our Elite dance team travels all over the states to compete, and we usually end up snatching a spot for the national and World Championship lineups. Aliana would be on our mini team until she turns eight."

"Well..." I glanced behind me at my daughter.

It was an incredible offer. I wasn't afraid of Aliana going onstage. She possessed more star quality than anyone else I knew. but I was worried about the commitment since I had to run the Saratoga Strings.

"I'm not sure," I said eventually. "I think she's a little too young yet."

Julie King nodded politely. "Totally understood. The spot's always hers if she wants it. I've worked with a lot of kids over the years, but Aliana is definitely one of a kind. While some people have to *work* to get that first wave of technique into their bones, your daughter was born with it."

I had to hand it to this woman—she knew how to make her customers feel cherished.

The money was the biggest problem. Colton and I weren't poor, but we weren't exactly comfortable. We had to work our butts off, with extra hours put in every week just to pay bills by a reasonable time. And dance was the expense that made us sweat a little more every month. We had to combine our paychecks just to pay off the monthly fee.

"Why didn't you put anything down for December yet?" I asked him one afternoon. Bitterness seeped into my tone.

His eyes snapped up from the checkbook. "What does it look like I'm doing right now?"

I shrugged. "Don't know, especially since *I'm* always on time to pay my half, and you always wait."

"How?" He had that *you're exaggerating this out of proportion* tone. "Because as I recall, I always have it done by the end of the week."

"We agreed Monday was always the pay day for her dance stuff."

"When did we agree to that?" He threw his hands out and pinned me with a confused glare.

"When she started in October!" I yelled, glaring back.

"If you think she's gonna be able to keep this up, you're fooling yourself, Abigail." He gestured to his checkbook and shrugged. "How will we pay for this and her schooling, *which,* mind you, she hasn't even started yet! We should be saving our money!"

"She loves dancing, Colton! It makes her happy."

"I never said it didn't. I'm saying it's a crunch for our savings."

I let my head fall into my hands and bit into my lower lip. Maybe we should have waited to enroll her in a class. Maybe then we wouldn't have been sinking our financial battleship. But then maybe it would have sunk either way.

"Excuse me for wanting to encourage our daughter's hobbies."

"This is not just about you, Abigail," Colton said, ripping the check from its binding. "This is about our ability to stay afloat in the world. In case you haven't noticed, money doesn't grow on trees."

"Do you think I'm blind?"

"I think your head is in the clouds."

He rose from his seat, scraping the chair across the linoleum, and then stomped toward the stairs. I didn't feel bad. Not yet at least.

Needless to say, Aliana didn't get the Barbie dreamhouse she so desperately wanted for Christmas.

Time crawled by. Colton and I hardly spoke. We were too wrapped up in our own whirlwinds of stress to even attempt peaceful conversation. Aliana was the only one to speak, talking about her love for dance class like it was her biggest dream come true. She was so happy most nights at dinner that I almost smiled, too. Almost. Until another monthly payment came.

"I'm really tired of this," Colton said one morning as I hogged the mirror, brushing through my hair.

"If you need to stare at yourself, go to the bathroom downstairs," I retorted.

It had been bad enough sharing a bed with him recently, let alone the rest of the house. We'd just gotten on each other's nerves so much, and for what reason, I couldn't even say.

"Gail." He took me by the shoulders and spun me around so that I was facing him. I glowered at him for a moment before he said, "Just stop."

"Stop *what*?" I went to shrug out of his grasp, but his hands locked me into place.

"Stop pushing me away," he answered, and his voice was hollow, almost inaudible.

I stared at him again, something crackling in my chest. "If this is about the money, I told you I'm—"

"Forget the money for a second," he pleaded. A muscle rippled in his jaw; his eyes were liquid emeralds. "I just want my wife back."

I was tense in his arms, and the air was thick and quiet between us. His eyes bored into mine.

"I'm sorry for being such a dick recently. But I really need you back on my team. Please."

My mind was split. The grudge-holder in my brain persuaded me to walk away. But when Colton looked at me like that, like I was the only person in the world who could hold him up, my heart broke into its usual sprint. His hand found mine and our fingers slowly intertwined. I'd missed him deeply.

"I've been putting in a lot of hours with our new project at work," Colton said. "A lot more than most people. Maybe I can talk to my boss about a raise, so that we can keep Aliana in dance where she belongs."

"Colton, that would be amazing."

We were inches apart now, our noses brushing with each subtle movement. I wanted to feel this energy forever. It was the kind of energy that I only knew with him. The kind that got my heart pumping, head rushing, skin prickling. I smiled against his lips and felt him do the same. When he kissed me, I melted. It healed my heart, and I wrapped my arms around his neck, determined to keep him trapped here with me forever.

Not only were we able to keep Aliana in her contemporary class, but we had her successfully admitted into preschool the following year as well.

I waited in the pick-up line after her first day, staring off into space and drumming my fingers against the steering wheel. I waited for all of the other kids to shuffle out to their parents, and then there was my little Aliana. I watched the assistant teacher escort her out, her oversized backpack bumping with every step. But she wasn't alone. Aliana was holding another little girl's hand, and when they were forced to part, the two girls reached in to hug one another.

"Who was that?" I asked my daughter as she climbed into the backseat.

"Estelle," Aliana said merrily. She retrieved a multicolored fidget cube from the side pocket of her backpack and began toying with it. "She's my best friend."

Chapter Twenty-Four

SARATOGA SPRINGS, NY (2043-2054)

Estelle Westmore became my daughter's favorite person in the whole world. What started out as a couple Saturday playdates became an attached-at-the-hip friendship. The kind of friendship that produced matching bracelets, shared Barbie dolls, and constant laughter.

Estelle was an artist. She never went anywhere without a sketchbook and small box of crayons. She turned our kitchen table into an art studio, teaching Aliana how to draw blue flowers and maroon sunsets while their forgotten cups of chocolate milk spoiled in the afternoon sunlight shining in from the windows.

They wore matching princess gowns on Halloween. They made glitter turkeys for Thanksgiving. They constructed a fort of pillows and watched *Rudolph* the day before Christmas Eve. Estelle even came to Aliana's End of Year dance performance, posing for several pictures with my daughter after the show. They became Aliana and Estelle. Estelle and Aliana. Best friends forever.

It warmed my heart. I was happy that my daughter had found someone to confide in, even if their only worries spanned from making handshakes to learning how to read together three years later.

On the other hand, Gavin was living the college life. Over the next three years, he worked his butt off with internships and job applications in the business field. He played in too many soccer games to count, several of which we were able to attend. He even met a girl: Hope Garrison. A sweet-faced Kentuckian with glittering green eyes and thick, copper-colored hair. A psychology major with hopes of becoming a licensed professional counselor.

Gavin met her at the gym during his junior year. She'd caught his eye after powering through forty-five push-ups, hardly breaking a sweat before reaching for her multicolored gallon water bottle. Apparently, she'd smiled back at him.

Gavin and I talked for two hours on FaceTime the next month after he'd taken Hope out on their second date.

"I'm nervous," he admitted at the time. "I haven't really dated since Josie."

"It's okay to be nervous," I had assured him. "You are in a time of your life where the possibilities are endless. If you like the girl, go for it!"

I met her the following year, at the first of Gavin's soccer games as a senior. It was by accident since Aliana had been yanking on my arm to take her to the concession stand before the game, and Hope just happened to be waiting in line for a pack of Swedish Fish.

Gavin had shown me pictures of her before, but that was nothing compared to actually standing next to her. She was five-foot-five of pure muscle. She could have easily snapped me like a toothpick with arms like that, but her smile was warm, and her tone was gentle. A duality no one would expect.

She came home with Gavin for Thanksgiving that year and came back again for Christmas, lugging a bag of silver presents.

She'd gifted me an apron with little violins on it, and I suddenly wanted my son to marry this girl. Sure, Hope was model material with a killer GPA and was an avid Penn State enthusiast (much to Colton's delight), but there was one quality that stood out above all others: she made Gavin smile. *Really* smile. The kind of smile that sinks in through your mouth, slides down your throat, and cannonballs into your heart.

She was the one.

Several months later, after we'd watched Gavin accept his diploma at college graduation, he came to find us through the crowd. Evan and Amanda wrapped him in a hug before Dani got a hold of him and wiped her tears on his graduation gown. Eventually, Aliana reached for Gavin, and he kissed her cheek.

"Are you and Estelle still going strong?" he asked.

She nodded vigorously. "*Super* strong."

"*Super* strong?" Gavin grinned. "Keep super strong friends close, okay?"

"I will. I love you, Gavy."

Evan suggested a big celebratory family dinner.

"Are we going, too?" Aliana patted her stomach and groaned. "I'm hungry!"

"Why not?" Colton smiled at Evan.

It had taken a year or so for Colton to get used to Evan. They weren't best friends, but they were mature enough to have civil conversations. That was all I asked for.

"You pick the place, Gav!" Evan exclaimed.

Gavin was too busy beckoning Hope over for a hug to hear his father's suggestion. When he was with his girlfriend, lost in her eyes, no one else existed. I had to clear my throat to grab his attention back.

Gavin turned to us. "What? Oh, yeah. There's this great

restaurant called Charlie's. They have pretty much everything, and yes, Aliana, they have French fries."

Aliana squealed.

"Should I make a reservation?" Amanda offered, retrieving her phone from her floral-patterned purse.

Amanda and I weren't close. In other words, I was never itching to be in her presence, but she was kind enough with her thin, dimpled smile and exotic, colorful jewelry. Like Colton and Evan, we could play nice, too.

"Absolutely," I answered her and tacked a kind smile onto the end of my statement.

Time went on.

Gavin found a job at a marketing company in State College, Pennsylvania. We helped move him there permanently and eventually helped Hope move in *with* him. Three months later, he confessed that he was going to propose to her.

I couldn't wrap my head around the fact that my son was nearly six hours away now with a diamond ring hiding in his back pocket. I couldn't believe Aliana was suddenly in her final year of elementary school. I didn't like how the time between the Saratoga Strings' fall and winter concerts felt like the blink of an eye.

I tried to be aware of the passage of time. I tried to watch the sunset each night and consciously take it in, describing the colors in my notebook like Dani suggested. I stayed on top of Elijah's proposition and listed small things I was grateful for. I listened to Colton's progress with the Witker project at work. Conversations became cycles. Sunsets faded into the expenses of black, star-speckled skies. No matter how hard I tried to hold on, time slipped through my knuckles.

The June before Aliana started middle school, Gavin and Hope got married.

The wedding was Penn State themed with and white decorations galore. Even the cake was vanilla with navy blue swirls of icing and a Nittany Lion figure on top. The entire family was there, crowding the dance floor, the bar, and everywhere in between. After I successfully choked through a toast, Gavin and Hope took Aliana out for a dance. Aliana's knee-length pink dress swayed with every motion. In the meantime, I held Colton's hand and tried my hardest not to tear up.

Two weeks after Gavin and Hope got back from their honeymoon, Colton and I took the kids to the Florida Keys in July. We spent nearly sixty percent of our time either in the water or sunbathing on a beach that resembled paradise. Estelle tagged along, keeping Aliana company as they swam with dolphins and collected orange seashells from the surf. Meanwhile, Gavin and Hope enjoyed romantic dinners and wine-tasting before returning to walk the beach at sunset.

While we were sitting on the shore, listening to the waves crash and fade, I fell in love with Colton all over again. I fell in love with the way he held my hand—with a comfortable pressure as a promise of forever. I fell in love with the crook in his smile that appeared whenever he watched the kids attempt to boogie board on an incoming wave. I fell in love with his soul. His wholesome, golden soul that managed to stay rosy and pure over so many years.

My thoughts were temporarily silenced when Aliana and Estelle splashed out of the water and started back up the beach toward our umbrella.

"What's up, buttercups?" I asked, handing them both bottles of water.

"The waves are getting pretty big," Estelle explained.

I looked out just in time to see Gavin and Hope dive under a massive wave.

"Perfect time for a snack," Colton chimed in. He reached for the cooler.

"I think I wanna live here when I'm older," Aliana said once she and Estelle were settled on their bright pink beach towels.

"Like on the beach?" Estelle asked.

"Miami."

"We should get a house together!" Estelle exclaimed.

Colton rubbed soothing circles across the back of my hand, and eventually, I fell asleep.

As the summer winded down, we figured Aliana had waited long enough to join the Elite Club's competitive dance team. She'd all but talked our ears off about how badly she wanted to audition. Colton promised to take more hours at work just so he could see his daughter get to live her dream. Aliana made the team, of course, and Julie King was ecstatic to have her join the other dancers.

When the school year began, it came roaring. Aliana had school all day and then one of us, usually Sandy, drove her to dance rehearsal almost every night. I tried to make sure I always packed a few extra snacks for her to take because she was absolutely spent by the time she got home.

This season the main coach, Reese Fisher, announced that there would be *two* contemporary dances: one more modern-based and flowy and one that would reflect a societal issue.

"Coach Fisher says that choreography isn't good unless it tells a story," Aliana explained after practice one day.

The story, as it turned out, highlighted the negative effects of addiction since Reese's step-brother had suffered an overdose the previous year and passed away. The song was a painfully gorgeous cello piece, and the dancers, Aliana in particular, moved in a way that was robotic yet sluggish. With each crescendo, another dancer would drop to the floor. They fell like dominos until the last one standing, my daughter, pretended to inhale an invisible substance and dropped to the ground as well. It was only a rehearsal, yet they had played their characters so well, I felt tears jab my eyes.

Coach Fisher clapped frantically. "That was probably the best time I've seen you guys run the dance. Great. Aliana, make sure you watch the angle of your foot at this one part..."

After she released the kids, I grabbed a hold of Aliana. She tried to squirm out of my embrace—the suddenly too-cool tween she was now—but I held her tightly.

"Don't *ever* do drugs, do you hear me?" I whispered.

Her tiny, muscular body convulsed as she laughed. "It's just a dance, Mom."

Competition season began that March, and after several painful attempts to pull Aliana's hair into the required complicated braid, she learned how to do it herself.

Gavin and Hope traveled to attend Aliana's highly anticipated performance. We met them in Albany, along with Sandy, Sean, and Jamie. I shouldn't have been surprised to see Estelle and her family there either. We all sat together in the crammed auditorium.

I squeezed Colton's hand. "I'm nervous for her."

"Same," Colton muttered, his eyes taking in the large stage in front of us.

"I'm not worried," Sandy shook her head. "My granddaughter is the best dancer on that team."

When the judges announced their routine, the dancers took their places on the stage, falling into their starting poses like butter melting on a hot plate. Their performance was flawless. Colton and I were perched on the edge of our seats, and Estelle had placed her hands under her chin in awe. Gavin was tense at my side. The whole audience seemed to be at a standstill, collectively holding their breath as each dancer collapsed to the poison of their addiction. When Aliana went down, there was a blaring silence, and then one of the judges shot up from his seat and clapped, bringing on a thunderstorm of cheers from the audience. Tears sliced my eyes again. I spotted Reese Fisher in the front row blowing a kiss to her dancers.

The other contemporary dance was just as gorgeous, yet everybody knew that the addiction one was a winner. At the award ceremony later that afternoon, the female judge stepped forward to announce that Reese Fisher had won the Outstanding Choreography Award. The judge then announced that the Elite Club dance team won the highest scoring routine of the entire competition. We all screamed until our throats were raw.

"Amazing," Colton said afterward in the lobby, dipping to kiss his daughter's head. "Just amazing!"

"Thanks, Dad."

Sandy congratulated Aliana a dozen times before the two demanded to have their picture taken in front of the competition's logo banner. Aliana wanted a picture with Estelle. I snapped and snapped, capturing their beaming, smiling faces.

The two girls turned toward each other and embraced in a strong hug. I took a picture of that, too, but when Estelle pulled away, something changed in Aliana's expression. It was hard to decipher, especially with so much commotion going on around us. Eventually, Estelle waved goodbye and left with her parents.

We went to Pizza Kingdom to celebrate, but Aliana was quiet all of a sudden, like the dizzying triumph of her win had been sucked out of her bones. She kept trying to catch Gavin's gaze, and when she finally did, she said, "Do you wanna go to the arcade?" Gavin made a face, but Aliana seemed insistent. "I have to tell you something."

They didn't return for some time. When they finally did, they both looked normal. Chipper even. Aliana seemed happier.

"What did you guys talk about?" I asked Gavin that night while Aliana was in the shower, scrubbing layer after layer of stage makeup off her face.

My son shrugged. "Just stuff." He looked over at me. "Everything's fine, Mom. Stop worrying."

I swallowed loudly. "You know me, I always worry."

"She's just growing up," he said. "It's life stuff."

What could be so important that Aliana would tell her older brother before her own mother? I tried not to take offense to that.

Aliana wanted to go shopping. Apparently, her graphic Tees and ripped light wash jeans weren't good enough anymore, so she dragged me into stores with designer clothes instead and pulled the most risqué pieces off the shelves.

"Absolutely not," I said as she held up a skimpy, see-through lace top.

"Why not?" she pouted. "All the cool girls wear this stuff. If I'm going to be popular, I need to dress like them."

I stared at her, eyebrows raised. "Honey, you don't need to dress like that to be popular. Who told you this?"

"Carmine Birgons," she said. "She's the most popular girl in school."

I sighed. "Aliana, you are a sixth grader, not someone who jumps on a bandwagon."

She wrinkled her nose. "*What*?"

"If Carmine jumped off a cliff, would you?"

"It's a simple outfit, Mom." Aliana rolled her eyes.

After a twenty minute compromise, I ended up purchasing $200 worth of new clothes. They weren't as risqué as the kind she wanted, but they weren't as concealing as the kind *I* wanted. It was a happy medium, if you could even call it that.

As time ticked on, Aliana did seem to develop a following at school. Soon, my daughter and Estelle were attending sporting events and so-called parties and whatever else the popular people wanted to do. She even got a call from Carmine Birgons at one point, and the two went shopping at the most expensive stores in town. Thanks to Carmine's wealthy parents, the thirteen-year-old was already loaded.

Aliana's life quickly became friends and dance. I wasn't sure how she kept her grades so flawless.

Estelle practically lived at our house, and the girls spent most of their time up in Aliana's bedroom with the door hardly cracked open. Their giggles drifted down the stairs, and I could never quite catch what they were talking about. When I was that age, I'd finally started noticing boys, but I wasn't hearing any guy names on Aliana's lips yet. Maybe she was still too concerned with learning how to French braid.

Nowadays, it was difficult to focus on anything other than my children's lives. Church was the only thing that brought me back to earth. Pastor David suggested I take up a new hobby to tame my mind, so while I wasn't conducting, I began scrapbooking. It worked like a charm. When I was pasting pictures into the booklet, I was no longer obsessing over what decisions my daughter was making.

I sent three pictures to the printer and made myself a cup of tea while they processed. Aliana was still at school, and Colton had a late shift, so the house was almost eerily quiet. But for once in my life, I didn't feel like I was drowning in the silence. I figured I could make friends with it instead.

I pulled the pictures from the printer and collapsed back into my chair at the dining room table. My scrapbook lay open, decorated with all sorts of colored shapes and swirls. I was going to add the pictures of Aliana's first dance competition.

There was the one with Aliana and Colton in front of the dance banner. How Colton managed to look so handsome in the dim lighting, I didn't know. There was the photo of Sandy squeezing the dickens out of my daughter, and then there was the one of Aliana and Estelle. They were going in for a hug, eyes locked, smiles glittering. But then I noticed the twinkle in Aliana's gaze.

My eyebrows furrowed as I leaned in to take a closer look.

I was young once; I knew what love was. I could recognize it in someone's gaze from a mile away. It had been in my eyes when I went on my first date with Colton all those years ago. It had been in Gavin's eyes when he talked about Hope for the first time. And it was clear in Aliana's eyes as she looked at Estelle. Suddenly, it was so clear why she looked dismal after Estelle had left the competition. And why she never seemed to talk about any boys.

With my heart pounding, I glued the picture into the book, though it was slightly off-center thanks to my shaking hands.

The panic in my bones wasn't stemming from the thought that my daughter might be a lesbian. I was nervous about how to approach the situation. I'd heard terrible stories of kids growing up in households where the family was only as strong as the common genetic makeup of their blood. Too many stories of parents caring way more about their reputation than their own child's happiness. I wanted us to be different. I wanted to be there for Aliana and support her every step of the way.

The more I considered this, the more my panic bubbled into excitement. It didn't matter if Aliana's eyes twinkled for a girl or a guy. She was having her first crush. My heart swelled at the thought.

When Aliana got home from school that day, I stood idly by while she got ready for dance and pulled her hair up into a disheveled bun.

"What, Mom?" she inquired, slipping past me to shove her turner flats into her dance bag.

I swallowed. "How're you doing?"

She glanced up at me and shrugged. "I'm fine, why?"

"Are you and Estelle okay?"

Her gaze was scrutinizing now, suspecting. "Yeah."

"Honey, you can talk to me about anything, okay?" I was positively a hundred percent certain this was more awkward for her than it was for me. I pasted a kind smile on my face, trying to ease the tension.

She hauled her dance bag up onto her shoulder. "I know."

I leaned back against the wall. "And I just want you to know that I support you, always."

"Mom, I—"

She was cut off by the chime of her phone, and her face blanched when she read the message. "Crap, Wilma says Coach is in a terrible mood. Someone probably gave her attitude during practice again." Aliana nodded toward the door. "Will you please drive me to rehearsal before she bites my head off, too?"

"Sure."

The moment was gone. And I wouldn't get another one like it because Aliana always had something on her to-do list. Talking wasn't one of them. I figured it was unhealthy to suppress such emotions and not open up to anyone about them. Although that wasn't entirely true. She had Gavin. He was always one text message away for her. And, of course, she had Estelle.

The competition season ended with a blowout performance at the World Championships in August, which we had to travel to New Jersey for. Our team placed second to a hip hop group from Pennsylvania. Still, second in the whole world was something to celebrate. It had been an incredible season from start to finish. Aliana worked hard for this achievement, and she deserved it.

When we got home the next day, Sandy, Sean, and Jamie

showed up with a cake to congratulate their star-studded dancer on her big win, and Estelle appeared with a celebratory card she'd made herself. The two girls sat at the end of the table, leaning close and giggling. I made sure to watch them out of the corner of my eye—watch for anything that would confirm my suspicion of their romantic connection.

"So, Mom, did you hear back from the doctor yet?" Colton asked.

The question made me freeze, and I glanced over at Sandy. "Wait, what happened?"

Sandy's mouth was full of cake, so Sean answered for her. "She had a lump removed last week."

"Left breast," Sandy added eventually. "The doctor has yet to call us back."

"Oh, my God." I'd been so focused on my daughter recently that I'd forgotten to acknowledge the health of others.

Sandy's announcement traveled to the other end of the table, and now Aliana was looking at her with horror-filled eyes, too. It was quiet before Sandy waved the matter away.

"Don't worry, sweetie. I'll be all right. You know me, tough as iron." Her smile was kind. It crinkled her face.

But I could feel the apprehension radiating from Colton beside me. His shoulders were slumped, and his face was chalk white. The gloomy shadows underlining his eyes weren't simply from a lack of sleep.

Why hadn't he told me? I suddenly felt stupid for not realizing something was off. Here I had been, obsessing over Aliana's love life, and not catching the fact that the woman who had given birth to my husband was possibly sick.

This woman...who had taken me in at the fragile age of sixteen...who had cooked for me, paid for me, accepted me into her family based on the judgment of her son, was facing a major health concern. Yet she seemed content, unbothered. Cancer wasn't something that could agitate Sandra Reeves. She would continue to go about life, forever undeterred.

"Wait, you're okay, right, Mammaw?" Aliana demanded.

"Healthy as a horse, sweetheart," she replied with a wink.

But from the looks of Sean and Colton, I didn't know if that was the truth.

Chapter Twenty-Five

SARATOGA SPRINGS, NY (2054)

"Breast Cancer," Colton hissed. He paced back and forth through our bedroom, shoveling his hands through his already unkempt hair. "She has stage-four breast cancer!"

I sat on the edge of the bed, staring down at my shaking hands. When I spoke, my voice was thin, hardly audible. "Calm down, Colt."

"Calm down?" he screeched, turning to me with a fiery, wild look in his eyes. "It's my mom, Abigail. I didn't tell you to chill when your dad was in the hospital."

"No, but you were there for me," I said. "And I'm here for you—"

"They gave her six months," he bellowed.

"That's better than six days," I pointed out.

"They put a time limit on her life, Gail." His voice broke, and he shook his head vigorously. "They're not supposed to do that. Th...they can't...take her away."

I sprung off the bed and took him in my arms just as he broke down. For a moment, he was tense, frozen by the onslaught of emotion, but then he let his head fall to my shoulder and wrapped his arms around my waist, trembling with each sob. I held him tightly, afraid to let go for fear he would break in half.

"Shh," I soothed him, but it was extremely difficult to pretend to be strong.

Tears were biting my eyes, too.

Sandy grew thinner and thinner each time we saw her; she'd taken to wearing hats just a month after her first chemotherapy treatment. For the extent of winter—which was an unusually harsh one—she was forced to stay indoors. The doctors feared that if she contracted the seasonal flu or the Pulmonem Fever, it would catalyze the cancer's sinister plans. So, Colton risked his own life, driving on icy slick roads in the middle of blizzards just to go be with his mother.

He became tired and antsy, tossing and turning every night like he was being strangled by some vicious nightmare. Some nights he would snap at me, other nights he held me close and reminisced about all the beautiful memories he had of his mother. And I let him talk for hours because I liked to hear the stories, too.

Sandy never acknowledged how sick she was. Her spirits were sky-high. On the days when we FaceTimed with her, she would smile and laugh without a care in the world, and I had to excuse myself from the call just so that she wouldn't see me cry.

Aliana, on the other hand, bottled her emotions. She was in seventh grade now, and Estelle was her outlet from the stress of middle school and the hardships of home. I was very grateful for that.

Gavin called once a week, seeking an update on his grandmother, though we never had good news. I told him he should come home to see her before it was too late, but the snow separated us.

"This is all happening so fast," he said. He sounded sick to his stomach.

I was seated at the desk in my bedroom, and the muscles in my neck were screaming. My head was down a lot these days because my body seemed to lack the energy or the motivation to keep it up. My chin was pressed in the palm of my hand. My fingers were pinching the bridge of my nose. My eyes were red and puffy with fresh tears.

"I know," I replied. Not even my voice sounded like my own.

"How does that work?" Gavin asked. "How do things like this just pop up out of the blue?"

My stomach churned. I was sick of having this conversation. I tried to tell myself all the time that life came in waves. It was a coping mechanism that Giana had taught me all those years ago after our house was broken into. Life came in waves, and emotions accompanied those waves. The takeaway was that they would pass. And that there was beauty in *every* moment—not just the good.

There's beauty in every moment. There's beauty in every moment. There's beauty in every moment. My brain repeated the phrase, but all it did was stab my eyes with tears.

"Life is crazy sometimes, Gav. Curveballs are everywhere."

It was a while before he responded again. "I'll FaceTime Sean tonight so that I can see Grandma."

"Sounds good." I couldn't even smile at my son. I was so upset.

It was one of the harshest winters we'd ever seen. Aliana's school was canceled for two weeks. I'd canceled multiple rehearsals with the Saratoga Strings, and the dance studio closed for the safety of its students. There was an endless gray sky, almost like Mother Nature was mourning the condition of Sandra Reeves as well. And each day, it grew colder and colder.

"She doesn't have much time left," Colton muttered one night.

Our house was dark, save for the dim light hanging above the kitchen table, and it was quiet enough to hear a pin drop all the way from upstairs. Colton, Aliana, and I sat with bowls of steaming soup, yet we didn't eat. Our faces were void of emotion, and we stared off into space.

"I saw her today," Colton added. "She was all skin and bones."

Aliana flinched and pushed her bowl away, the sound of it scraping across the table almost too loud to bear. Colton heaved a troubled sigh, and I reached out to squeeze his hand. The rest of the house was empty, but an agonizing presence loomed over our backs: the inevitable. The near future. Possibly the Grand Reaper silently urging us to say our goodbyes to Sandy.

The very next day, she was gone.

Sean informed us that she had died comfortably in her sleep, but I didn't think *comfortable* was the correct adjective. Not where cancer was concerned. At least she didn't have to suffer anymore. It was the coldest day of the year: a bone-chilling seven degrees. Unlike Colton, who was an absolute mess, Sean became a shell of his former self. We called him after they removed Sandy's body, and his voice was not his own. It was gravelly and toneless.

Aliana cried all through the funeral, and I began to think the sight of her mammaw in a casket was too much for her. As it was too much for me.

The sun didn't touch our house for four months; we were trapped in this dark oblivion of loss. I was angry with the weather for gradually improving because a part of me thought that I was supposed to be healing, too. That we all were. But it was just a lie.

Colton was lifeless. His breathtaking internal light had been extinguished. It took all of my energy just to make him sit down and eat dinner some nights. And when he spoke, he spoke of his mother.

The only person who seemed overly eager to return to normalcy was Aliana. She'd taken up another technique class at dance, even though her technique was already flawless enough. When she wasn't at dance, she was at Estelle's. I still hadn't gotten the opportunity to talk to her about her feelings. Then again, I was sure she was on an emotional rollercoaster like the rest of us right now.

She went to more and more gatherings with the people at her school. Estelle's mother often came to pick Aliana up, and I noticed just how closely the two girls sat together in the back seat. How the tiniest bit of distance seemed unbearable to them.

As time went on, Aliana developed a bit of an attitude with me. I understood that teenagers often grew their own backbone, but Aliana was hurtfully snappish. Several times I questioned her about what was wrong, but she shook me off and told me to get out of her room instead.

"It's grief," Colton muttered. His voice was hollow and broken. It tore my heart to shreds. "She doesn't know how to deal with the loss."

"Should we...try going to a family therapist?"

"I would, but I doubt our thirteen-year-old daughter would approve of going to see a...shrink." He emphasized the last word with air quotes. "It would cramp her style."

"I don't give a damn," I retorted. "This is for her well-being. I'm worried that she's falling down the wrong path."

"I'm worried, too." Colton sighed. Then he looked at me with those piercing gold-green eyes. "Life doesn't really feel like life right now, and I'm sure Aliana would concur."

For a moment, we were quiet, and the TV droned in the background.

"You know Aliana's in love with Estelle, right?" Colton whispered.

I turned to face him again. "Yeah, I know. Did she talk to you about it?"

"No," Colton shook his head. "But I can tell. And honestly, I don't really care as long as she's happy. She seems confident in who she is and who she loves."

"She's known Estelle her whole life. I guess it's not really a surprise they've fallen for each other."

"As long as she has someone." He leaned over to press a tender kiss to my forehead.

Togetherness was what helped me and Colton get back to normal—whatever *normal* was. But that was all we could do. Just take it day by day, moment by moment and trust that things would get better. Ever so slowly, sunlight crept into our house again.

In April, Gavin and Hope came to visit. It was nice to have the house full again; it made the harder moments slightly less gut-wrenching. But not even my son and his lovely wife could fully restore my content.

"Hey, Mom, where's Aliana?" Gavin asked.

"Estelle's," I answered somewhat harshly. I wasn't happy with the fact that she had skipped this family dinner to be with her friend, but Estelle had claimed that she had big news that couldn't wait. I sincerely hoped they weren't going to elope somewhere.

"Oh, no. I've missed Aliana," Hope said disparagingly.

"She'll be back," I said. And if she wasn't, I was going to place a reward on her head.

As if the universe read my thoughts, the front door swung open. I went to put the last dirty plate into the dishwasher when I heard Colton dash across the room.

"Are you crying?" he demanded, pulling Aliana into his arms. Gavin and Hope froze a few feet away. "Sweetheart, what's wrong?"

"What's going on?" I called, nearly dropping the plate in my haste to be at my daughter's side.

When Colton pulled away, Aliana appeared with swollen,

bloodshot eyes. Her nose dripped, and I reached for a box of tissues.

"Estelle." She wiped her tears on her arm. "She's moving to Nevada."

∼

Sometimes I asked God why life was like stepping out of a frying pan and falling straight into the fire.

Fresh off our loss from Sandy, Colton and I now had to watch our daughter spiral. She was hardly home and always claimed that she'd simply *forgotten* to text us where she was. I was shocked when Coach Fisher called to inform me that Aliana hadn't been in practice these last two days. *So, she was skipping now?!*

I knew what depression was; it was the insufferable nagging of loneliness and hopelessness that never seemed to relent. It made the simplest tasks twenty times harder. Watching someone else endure the pain was like being held under ice cold water. I was deeply worried.

Gavin and Hope extended their trip just because Gavin's presence alone seemed to appease Aliana's suffering, but even he couldn't help pull her from this rut. Like Colton expected, therapy wasn't Aliana's thing, and medication was next to useless. But what could I say? The poor girl had just lost her beloved mammaw and now she'd lost her first love. A terrible, dreadful double whammy.

Life could be extremely cruel.

"Where are you going?" I questioned Aliana as she trudged toward the door, a purple and green duffel bag strapped over her shoulder.

"Carmine's having a big sleepover tonight. She has a sleepover, like, every Friday night."

"You have a long rehearsal tomorrow, Aliana. Coach Fisher

isn't happy with you skipping this week." I planted my hands on my hips. "And neither am I."

She shrugged. "Apparently, it doesn't matter anyway. It's not like I'll be dancing forever. Look, Livia's mom is giving us a ride over, and she's almost here."

"Wait. Sweetheart, I'm worried about you. I get that what you felt for Estelle was more meaningful than you let on, but—"

"Whatever," Aliana hissed, pressing her eyes closed like it would block out the mention of her friend's name.

"It's okay to stay home every once in a while. Just look at Gavin. He never partied in grade school, and he turned out okay."

Aliana's bright green eyes flared. "I'm not Gavin though, am I?" She glanced over my shoulder at Gavin and Hope who were snuggled up on the couch in front of the television. Aliana looked like she might gag. "And it's a sleepover, not a party."

She spun on her heel and slammed the door shut. A red Toyota was parked at the curb, and Mrs. Maisley waved at me like she thought this was all a happily agreed upon arrangement.

"This is ridiculous!" I exploded. "Aliana is never home anymore! I don't know what's going on. I can't get a hold of her!"

Gavin sat up on the couch. "You're doing everything you can, Mom."

"Teenagers can be difficult to reason with," Hope offered tentatively, a worried look pinching her petite face. "Several of my clients are teenagers."

I sat down in the armchair like a deflated balloon. "I feel like everything is crumbling."

"It gets worse." Colton appeared in the hallway, and I could immediately tell by the paleness in his cheeks that something was wrong. "I was taking the trash bags out of the cans upstairs and look what fell out of Aliana's."

He held up a long, skinny object.

My stomach gripped its way into my throat, and Gavin dropped his head into his hands. Hope tossed me a nervous glance. Slowly, I rose from the armchair and took the object from my husband. He pressed his lips into a grim line.

The vape pen was cold in my hand. "Is this what I think it is?"

Colton leaned against the wall for support. He ran a hand over his chin, shaking his head as if to clear it. "Yeah."

"Since when the *hell* does my daughter vape?" I demanded.

The house was thrust into silence, and my face jumped six degrees until I was positively fuming.

This was bad. First, Aliana was skipping rehearsals, then she was constantly out with Carmine, and now *this*? I wanted to crush this vape pen in my bare hands. I wanted to destroy it for poisoning my daughter. Instead, I curled my fingers around it and decided to let her explain herself.

"She's grounded for the rest of the month," I muttered and stomped into the dining room.

Unsurprisingly, Aliana didn't take that too well.

"It isn't even mine!" she tried to reason the next morning. "It's Carmine's."

I actually felt pity for Aliana, and that nearly liquified my stomach. Here she was—a young girl who was damaged by her losses—making a sorry excuse for her motives to vape.

Now I could see the hollowness in her cheeks. Now I understood why she'd been suffering so many headaches recently. And she had the audacity to tell me it was Carmine's? Her eyes were frantic, nearly pleading, and I stared back at her in disbelief. Who was this stranger I was talking to?

"How long?" The question slipped from my lips and hung in the air.

"What?" She looked back at me with pink ears.

I repeated my question much louder. Colton pinched the bridge of his nose. Aliana watched him, and for a moment her face crumpled in agony, but she regained her composure all too soon. Her eyes flickered back to me, cold and emotionless.

"Since Mammaw died."

So, she'd been voluntarily poisoning herself since January.

"You're grounded until further notice. End of conversation. And no more vaping or sleepovers. You're lucky I don't tell Coach Fisher about your behavior. She'd have you off that team faster than you can imagine."

"That's not fair!" Aliana screeched.

I almost laughed; I couldn't believe my ears. "Life's not fair."

Colton, ever the peacemaker, stepped between us and gave me somewhat of a warning look. It said, *don't antagonize her and make it worse.*

"You're an athlete, Aliana," he said carefully. "You have too much at stake to throw it all away for a stupid decision."

"Stop talking like that!" she screamed, and Colton stepped backward, surprised at her outburst. "You act like all I'll ever be is a dancer! Like that's what I want my whole life centered around. I don't even care, I just want to have fun."

"Dance is a gift," I shouted. "And you're taking it for granted right now."

"So what?" She threw her hands up in frustration. "Everything dies eventually."

Colton looked like he'd been slapped. He froze at my side, lips slightly parted, a horrified look in his glazed eyes. His jaw clenched several times before he cleared his throat and strode out of the room.

"Dad," Aliana said, stepping toward him. "I didn't mean—"

But he was already gone, and her effort was wasted. She swallowed loudly and looked down at the kitchen tile.

I felt like I was going to throw up.

"What has gotten *into* you?" I whispered desperately. "Sweetheart, I know you're hurting, but you don't need to push us away like this. Vaping isn't the answer."

"Stop." Her lips quivered. "Just stop."

Aliana shoved past me and escaped to her room. Seconds later, her door slammed shut with a resounding *boom*. The vape pen sat on the table, looking utterly harmless. I glared at it.

I set a number of ground rules, demanding that Aliana be home from school at three-thirty sharp every afternoon and that she worked on her homework until dance at five o'clock. Shockingly, Aliana followed these rules, but she was not herself. She never spoke, and if she did, it was an inaudible mumble. She hardly ate, and her body was visibly changing. She became as pale as cream, and the look in her eyes resembled that of a starving zombie.

Withdrawal.

It was scary to watch. I tried to be patient with her and talk her through the struggle, but she always sent me away with the intensity of her glower. For the hundredth time in this long, miserable cluster of weeks, I felt powerless.

Aliana was slipping and each day, she fell further and further into oblivion.

One weekend toward the end of May, Aliana's phone buzzed with an invitation to another one of Carmine's legendary sleepovers. It had nearly been two weeks since Colton had found the vape pen. I told Aliana she wasn't going. She didn't fight me on this; she simply gave me an empty look and trudged up to her room.

"I think it's time we lay off," Colton suggested.

I was tuning my instrument, plucking the strings to match the pitch in my mind, and Colton sat next to me with a book in his hands. When I didn't answer, he turned to face me fully, and I couldn't avoid his gaze any longer.

"The poor girl needs more help than she's getting."

"I paid that therapist four hundred dollars, and she didn't do shit for Aliana," I spat, snatching my bow off the couch.

"Well, maybe she needs to go out with her friends again. I think she feels lonely, Gail."

"She shouldn't. I've been trying to get her to talk to me for weeks, and she hasn't opened up about any of it."

"Maybe she'd feel more comfortable around her friends."

"Estelle was her friend." As soon as I said it, the air changed. It was a tingle down our spines. I met Colton's scrutinizing gaze.

When Estelle told Aliana that her mother had gotten a new job in Nevada, the girl was gone by the end of the week. I always wondered why she didn't tell Aliana sooner, but maybe she couldn't bear the news either. For a moment, I wondered how *Estelle* was handling the split.

From the hallway we heard a stair creak, and I snapped my head in that direction. Aliana didn't appear from around the corner, and the house fell quiet again.

"Look, I'm just tired of seeing her so upset." Colton shrugged. "I feel...terrible. Like there's so much more I could be doing, but I don't...I don't know what *to* do."

I felt all the fear bubble up inside me at once. "I'm scared, Colt. I'm scared she's gonna disappear. If she could just *understand* that we love her more than anything else on this earth...would that change her? Help to heal her?" I let my head drop into my hands. "I never meant for this to happen."

"Nobody did," Colton responded. He placed a strong hand on my shoulder, holding me steady. "Life is weird sometimes. Things happen that are out of our control, and all we can do is pray that she recovers. God knows what's going on. He's well aware of our fears, but he has a plan."

I nodded, inhaling deeply to free my mind from the constant cloud of terror and anxiety. "I guess you're right. She needs to rejoin the world sometime. I'm going to talk to her."

Colton squeezed my hand. "I'll get dinner started. How about tacos? They're Aliana's favorite."

I flashed him a grin. "Good call."

The lights were off upstairs, so I felt my way up the steps, fumbling for the light switch. Aliana's room was dark, too, and my eyebrows crinkled curiously.

"Aliana?"

A faint glow caught my eye from under the bathroom door, and the steady rushing of water sounded in my ears.

"Hey, Aliana? Sweetheart, we need to talk." I knocked a few times, but there was no answer. I knocked louder. Maybe she had her headset in and couldn't hear me. "Aliana!"

My fingers enclosed around the door handle, and the coldness of the metal seeped into my fingers for one split second before I threw the door open. When I saw her, my scream tore through the entire house.

Aliana was lying motionless on the floor. Her skin was horribly pallid, and a blue tinge colored her sagging lips. Her eyes, which were still open, showed two constricted pupils the size of pinpoints.In her hand, she clutched an empty bottle of prescribed antidepressants.

I sank to my knees, trembling in terror. I shrieked my husband's name in a hoarse tone. My voice felt raw in my throat, like a hundred claws were scratching at my trachea.

Colton must have heard me because he nearly fell into the bathroom in all his haste to get there. I didn't hear what he said, but it sounded like he was screaming. I couldn't hear anything at all over the pounding of blood in my ears. My heart was in over-drive; panic pulsed through me at dangerous levels. I reached a quivering hand out to Aliana's arm and screamed again at how cold her skin was. Tears streamed down my cheeks, and a trail of saliva dangled from my gaping mouth.

This couldn't have been real. Colton wasn't rushing through the house, screaming into a phone. There weren't sirens wailing in the distance. Aliana wasn't right in front of me...unconscious.

Bile chugged to the base of my throat, and I lunged for the toilet, hardly making it before I vomited violently. The door was thrown open from downstairs, and I heard Colton guiding a crowd. Several pairs of feet pounded against the steps, and the paramedics appeared at last, speaking in quiet yet urgent voices. One of them touched his gloved fingers to Aliana's neck, checking for a pulse. And seconds later, the word Narcan filled my ears. I vomited again. When I looked back up, Aliana was in a gurney and disappearing down the hall.

Colton pulled me to my feet, towed me through the house, and hoisted me into his car, but my mind was still three steps behind. I didn't know where I was, or where we were going, or what was wrong. The tears burned as they poured from my eyes, and my shaking fingers scratched at my throat and chest, trying to locate the source of pain to rip it from my body. But I did so in vain.

Colton trailed the ambulance all the way to the hospital, and that was when the shock of this miserable event finally consumed me. I couldn't breathe.

As soon as he shifted the car in park at the hospital, I threw my door open and sprinted to Aliana.

"Please hurry!" I rasped when the paramedics rushed the gurney through the hospital doors.

They raced Aliana down several hallways, and I kept pace with them until a man intercepted me. We were outside of a pair of doors marked *Emergency*. The paramedics pushed Aliana through the doors and continued down the hall, and I tried to go after them, but the man—it took me several seconds to realize he was a doctor—stopped me.

"Ma'am, you can't go in there."

I fixed my wide eyes on him and slapped his hand away from my shoulder. "The hell I can't! That is my *daughter!* Now get out of my way!"

He stepped in front of me again, and a scream erupted from my quivering lips. I fought against him with every ounce of energy in my body, but his strength was unbeatable.

"Aliana!" I cried, banging my fists against the barrier between us, but the damn door wouldn't budge. "*No!*"

"They need to pump her stomach," the doctor insisted. "It will help to revive her."

Suddenly, a new pair of hands was hauling me backward. I tried to fight until Colton's voice touched my ear.

"Shh," he soothed, but I could tell he was fearful, too. He was sobbing and worried sick for our daughter. "Shh."

In all of my anguish and dread, my mouth remained open but no sound escaped. Just rivers and rivers of tears from my eyes. My knees buckled beneath me, and Colton held onto my body as we sank to the cold floor.

Numbness was a myth to me. I felt the sharpness of despair with each breath I took, terrified of the moment a doctor would emerge from the doors and deliver the news that would stop my heart forever.

Chapter Twenty-Six

SARATOGA SPRINGS, NY (2054–2059)

My bones were sobbing by the time a doctor pushed through the doors and scanned the waiting room. I had never held that much tension in my body at one time. It was five minutes past midnight, and I was still shaking from head to toe. The skin around my eyes was swollen from crying.

The doctor caught my bewildered eye. "I assume you're Miss Reeves' parents?" Colton and I nodded vigorously. The man cleared his throat. "Aliana attempted to overdose on prescription antidepressants."

My throat squeezed. "Attempted?"

The doctor nodded. "Yes, she's alive."

I nearly blacked out from the relief. Colton swept me into his arms, and our hearts pounded against each other.

"You both are very lucky you found her when you did," the doctor continued. "Otherwise, things could have been much worse."

I shivered. It was dizzying to think of what could have happened. I quickly shoveled the thoughts out of my mind.

"The only question now is why would she do this?" the doctor asked, his eyes flickering back and forth between us.

There was something accusatory in his gaze, and I recoiled. "Well, she's obviously been dealing with depression."

Colton added, "My mother died a couple months ago from cancer, and then a few weeks later, Aliana's...best friend moved away. It was too much for her to handle." He went on to explain all the methods we'd tried to help her and how they'd been unsuccessful.

The doctor crossed his arms across his chest and blinked at us. "Sounds like she's in need of some serious care, which we'd be glad to assist you with."

He informed us of several in-patient mental health treatment centers within the community.

"Food for thought," he added with sympathy pinching the space between his eyebrows.

"I never considered in-patient care before," I replied. I didn't like the thought of being away from Aliana, especially after what had just happened.

"It can be expensive," the doctor admitted. "But we want to see that she's getting the treatment she needs."

"What about lifestyle changes at home?" Colton asked.

"Returning to the same environment can trigger relapse, but if she has to, strong behavior modification will be key. Things like sticking to a healthier routine, weekly psychotherapy, exercise." He shifted from his left foot to his right foot. "She *can* recover from this, but it's important to make sure she's making the right choices."

"No helicopter parenting, I assume?" Colton offered.

I squeezed the back of my neck.

"Well, you'll want to show her your support obviously. Encourage normalcy. You know," he flashed his palms, "hanging out with a healthy group of friends, staying up to date in school. Stuff like that. We can talk more about this if you have any other questions, but your daughter should be waking up any minute now. We've been keeping a close watch over her, and she seems to be stabilizing more with each hour. I'm sure she'd want to see you guys." He beckoned with his hand. "Come on back."

It hurt worse than hell to see Aliana in a hospital bed. It hurt worse than heartbreak and childbirth and my own damn depression. She didn't belong there in the middle of buzzing machines and under generic cotton blankets. She belonged at home in her own bed with the neon green stars we glued to her ceiling and a million hugs from her parents. She deserved happiness and peace.

Somewhere along the way, I had really messed up.

"We also found traces of nicotine in her blood," the doctor said.

"She used to vape before we got her off of it." Colton's voice was stripped raw. He was already on his knees beside the bed, holding Aliana's hand.

My eyes didn't move away from my daughter. I needed to see her chest rise and fall. I needed to see her *breathe*, just to assure myself over and over again that she was alive. The heart monitor tried to help calm me down with every beep, but I still had to press my clammy hands together to keep from shaking.

I stared at her for the length of five deep breaths, and then she began to stir. When her eyes fluttered open, I gasped and joined my husband beside the bed. There was life in her eyes now; she was here, cognizant. *Alive.*

We didn't say one word to each other. Colton and I just clung to her for dear life.

"I thought you were gone," Colton breathed.

A tear glided down his cheek, and I realized how terrifying this must have been for him. It was what *his* mother had faced when Colton was beaten all those years ago. He shuddered and kissed Aliana's forehead.

I wanted to ask what the hell had been going through my daughter's mind, how she could ever consider such a rash action, potentially murdering me and Colton from the inside out. But that was a conversation to be had elsewhere. All I cared about right now was that she was here.

Her eyes touched mine with a look of sincere despair and apology, and that was when it dawned on me. Somehow over the years, we had become obstacles for each other. I'd put an end to her freedom and recklessness all because of a lack of trust. Perhaps she wouldn't have gone to the lengths she had if I hadn't raised hell. She was a teenager, for God's sake. It was in her nature to rebel. On the other end, she had pushed my anxiety to its limits, almost like a game. *How far can I push my mother today?* Now, after looking into her eyes and seeing the precious life they held, something in my chest broke. It was a wall finally crumbling to the ground.

"I'm sorry, Mom," she whispered.

I immediately shook my head and wrapped my arms around her again. "It's okay. I love you. You know that, right?"

She nodded against my chest.

My head swam with relief, and when I kissed Aliana's forehead, something told me that at long last, everything would be okay. God truly did work in fantastic, terrifying ways.

I stared into the mirror, detesting the wrinkles and mop of thinning hair that stared back. Time had changed me, forced me to age with hardship and experience. It was evident in every gray hair that peeked through the curtain of chestnut locks. It was clear in every freckle that vandalized the skin of my arms and legs. I scrutinized the knee-length purple dress that I was wearing, and as I oscillated in front of the mirror, I couldn't tell if those curves in my belly had always been there or if I'd just grown plump over the years without noticing. When the door opened, I was shaken from my thoughts. I turned to see Aliana, who was stunning in her white cocktail dress and high heels.

It had taken four years for her to look like that again—full, healthy, happy. It had taken several arguments and countless therapy appointments for her to even return to normalcy. And by that point in time, she was already a senior in high school.

Estelle became a dream to her—nothing but a distant memory that only caused a quick pinch of pain and then faded into the background. That progress alone took months and months of therapy. I figured she would always have some type of reaction though when Estelle came up, as was the curse of first loves. But Aliana would survive now. She had finally regained her strength.

"I can't believe you're graduating." I sniffed. "Feels like just yesterday I was holding you in my arms and rocking you to sleep."

She grinned. "Well, everybody has to grow up sometime."

"Why are both my kids running away to Pennsylvania?" I frowned.

"Mom, the University of Arts is a great school for dance. Besides, don't you know Philly like the back of your hand?"

A smile touched my lips. "Yeah I do. I have a lot of good memories from there."

"See? I'll be fine. Also..." She sat on the edge of my bed and her dress ballooned. "I know I've said this before, but I'm sorry I couldn't tell you about me and Estelle." I noticed how she still twitched at the sound of the name. "I just didn't know what I was feeling, and I didn't want to involve you or have you worry—"

"Sweetheart, you are allowed to love *whoever* you want. If you're happy, I'm happy. Just no convicts or anything like that."

Her silvery laugh echoed through the room like a bell chime.

"Hey, everyone's waiting," Gavin called from the hallway.

He looked so grown up and handsome in his navy-blue polo shirt and khaki shorts. Hope was one lucky girl. Not just because she was married to my son but because she was now pregnant with twins. I remembered the moment they surprised us with the news. I'd been drinking a glass of milk and had spit it across the entire kitchen table, only seconds before screaming and pulling my son and his wife into my arms.

I was going to be a grandmother.

"Coming," Aliana said, leaping up from the bed. "I'm really glad Hope decided to come. Are you sure she's gonna be okay?"

Gavin nodded. "She's a superhuman. Besides, she wouldn't miss your graduation. Are you kidding?"

I smiled at my children as they raced down the hall and escorted each other down the stairs. I followed them out and spotted Colton at the door.

Colton...

He beamed up at me, his breathtaking smile stirring something deep inside my chest. It was kind of unfair how flawless he still looked after all these years. Time didn't seem to touch his features, not in my eyes anyway. The kids would've claimed otherwise, but when I looked at my husband, I still saw the heart-throbbing boy from our youth.

As the kids piled into Gavin's car, I pulled Colton back and gave him a fierce kiss. He looked breathless when I pulled away, and a touch of pink blossomed in his cheeks.

"What was that for?" he asked.

I felt myself drown in those perfect, dazzling eyes. "I just love you. So much."

"I love you, too." He was beaming.

Before he could kiss me again, the blow of a car horn tore us apart. But I couldn't let go of him. I held Colton's hand all the way to the high school, through all the student speeches, and I squeezed his hand extra hard when Aliana walked across the stage to accept her diploma.

It felt like Colton and I had just finished a forty-year long marathon. After everything we'd gone through for the kids, they were finally set on their own path. They were their own people now, and it was finally time to settle down. Colton and I only had seven years until retirement, but those years would fly by faster than ever. We were getting older, and nothing could stop it.

After our daughter exited the stage I turned to Colton and asked, "Is this the end?"

"The end of what?" He shielded his eyes from the glaring orange sun that was setting across the football field.

"Like, is this the end of our road? Both kids are through high school. Gavin and Hope are having twins." I craned my neck down the bleacher to see Hope reach for Gavin's hand. "They don't need us anymore. What does that mean for us?"

Colton pursed his lips, and I watched the fading sunlight illuminate his features.

"Well, this is the beginning for Gavin and Aliana," he said eventually. "They have their whole lives ahead of them. They're both healthy and capable of doing great things. We've raised them well, Gail. Don't worry. It's just time for them to...leave the nest. That's what my mom used to say. But in the meantime," he took my hand in his and our fingers automatically linked, "you and I can sit back and smell the roses for a little while. Relax and let God carry us through what he will. I know that when we were young, we were always scared of growing up, but now...I actually want to embrace it."

I wondered what our sixteen-year-old selves would have said if they could see us now. Would they think we were boring? Too soft spoken? Or would they be fulfilled to know that everything had worked out in the end?

For a moment, Colton and I were the only ones in the world. The countless other bodies around us faded into nothing. There was only my husband and our glorious future.

"Can we go back to Venice? I asked, recalling the vivid memories of our honeymoon.

"I would love to." Colton smiled.

It was amazing how at fifty-eight years old, this man still had the power to make my heart bend over backwards.

I knew what I wanted then. I'd conducted more concerts than I could count these days, and my children were strong, independent people. My duty felt nearly complete. Now there was only one thing left for me to do.

"I intend to spend the rest of my days with you—gray hair, wrinkles, and all."

Colton laughed softly. "We're not that old yet. Plus, what about the writing project you've been dying to finish?"

My heart surged. "I need to actually sit down and write it. I've been so busy planning it out."

"I can't wait to read it."

Raising my pinky finger, I smiled at him and murmured, "To forever."

Colton's eyes bore into mine, and I could so easily see the young boy I fell in love with all those years ago. His pinky locked with mine. "To *now* and forever."

Chapter Twenty-Seven

SARATOGA SPRINGS, NY (2059–2063)

The following September our house felt empty, so I did what I always did in these odd times: I played my violin.

Despite the fact that the maple-colored paint had been scratched and the strings were permanently smeared with hardened rosin, my instrument was still capable of exerting the sweetest melody. I dabbled in Johann Strauss' waltzes again. The simple harmonies reminded me of simpler times. Before I was the conductor to one of New York's finest orchestras.

The formation of the Saratoga Strings had shifted over the years. Sadly, we lost our incredible head cellist Lester in July, but we gained a brilliant young cello player, whom I nicknamed Rush just because of how fast her fingers could skip up and down the strings. I wondered if this was how Tod and Professor Autrie had felt while watching their newcomers. They must have been proud and reassured that the legacy of their orchestras would be carried on through another generation. I could see that perfectly.

When I was at that podium, baton raised and ready, I was fully in my element. The music filled me in ways it never had before, throbbing beneath my bones and washing over me like soothing waterfalls. I felt alive in those moments; I felt young again. And best of all, I felt Professor Autrie smiling down on me and cheering, "*Bravo, ma chérie!*"

Once again, music healed me. It helped me to process the absence of my children and to accept the fact that I was, indeed, aging. But there was *one* thing sweeter than the music.

Colton.

We'd fallen back into a smooth routine: sharing mugs of coffee in the morning until we had to be separated for work. Then after, returning home to cook together and settle in so I could play my instrument and he could read until we were too tired to keep our eyes open. Of course, we did tend to argue a lot these days over the silliest things. But what could I say? I'd been connected to this man for more than forty years. Arguments were a given. Sometimes, I even left the house for a while just to cool off from his idiocy. No matter how much his ignorance infuriated me though, I couldn't stay away. Every time I left, I ended up coming right back home. We loved each other too much to ever turn away. He taught me to grow in ways I never could have imagined.

Every night, I held Colton's prayer rock tightly in my hands and thanked God for providing us such a fulfilling life. The rock was like an anchor, reminding me what was most important. I would crawl into bed and kiss my husband goodnight, feeling so utterly fortunate that this man was mine.

One day in late March, Colton and I rushed to a hospital in Pennsylvania to see the birth of our grandchildren. Hope lay in her bed, all sweaty and red-faced, but with a look of serenity on her face. Gavin stood beside her with tears streaming down his cheeks. And there they were: Andrea and Trinity Reeves—identical twin girls, only differentiated by the color of the blankets they were wrapped in.

My heart instantly melted at the sight of them.

The doctor jovially congratulated Gavin and Hope. And as Evan and Amanda peered down at the babies with wonder, Aliana pulled me into the hallway. She was a month away from finishing her first year of college now. Her hair was a tone lighter than the last time I'd seen her.

"I just wanted to let you know that I met someone," she said, crossing her arms over her chest like the topic made her uncomfortable, yet she couldn't hide the sparkle in her eye.

"Tell me," I urged excitedly.

"Her name is Mackenna." Aliana eyed me curiously as she said this, but I gestured for her to go on. "She's a dancer, too. We met at tryouts."

"Contemporary?"

"Hip hop," Aliana gushed, going red in the cheeks. "She's really, *really* good."

Her eyes popped when she said this—sparkling green irises catching in the light. I hadn't seen her eyes twinkle like that since Estelle, which both excited and terrified me.

Grief was a road full of detours, sharp turns, massive hills, swooping valleys, and dead ends. It was lined with orange warning signs. It was an insufferable journey. Happiness did not begin the moment you woke up after an unsuccessful suicide attempt. There was no euphoric epiphany of *I survived! I am perfectly okay now!* Happiness didn't begin five months after that either—when you had to go to therapy sessions even though finding peace felt like a sisyphean task.

The hardest lesson Aliana had to learn was that happiness was not a place. She kicked, and she cried, and she spit out excuses.

"I'm fine! I'm better now! I don't need to keep going to therapy." Arms raised out from her sides, eyebrows arched, a plastic smile. She was clever and persuasive until a memory or a trigger yanked her back down the funnel.

I had to watch this happen over and over again. I had to watch my daughter walk down that tangled road of grief and face every obstacle.

At times, I didn't understand it. I didn't understand what was holding her back from letting go. Was there a human capacity for how quickly someone could move on from massive losses? If so, what made it harder for certain individuals?

The answer was that there was no answer. Healing was not a black and white matter; it was gray territory. Uncomfortable. Uncertain. It was learning to unclench your fist in a fight or flight situation. It was hard work.

Five years of hard mental work.

So, as I was listening to Aliana tell me about Mackenna, my soul smiled. My heart lifted its arms in victory. At long last, she'd reached the other side.

"She sounds wonderful, sweetheart," I said and wrapped my arms around her.

~

The years flew by faster than I could turn the pages of my scrapbook.

We took several trips to the University of Arts to watch my daughter perform, and Mackenna was so phenomenal my jaw dropped. I remembered the first time I saw her dance. Much like Aliana, she commanded the audience with every snap of her arms and every pop of her chest. Hip hop might as well have been created *for her*. Her smirk was bona fide, and her eyes were like stars. She had the crowd out of their seats and screaming by the time she bowed.

"Mr. and Mrs. Reeves," Mackenna had said after the show, all confidence and zero fear. "It's an honor to meet you."

"Tell us the truth," Colton had insisted. "Are you a robot who has to recharge every night?"

Mackenna laughed. "If you count collapsing after a full day of rehearsal, then I'd say so."

That had been the beginning of the girls' sophomore year. From that point on, Mackenna—Mack, as we now called her— was as much a part of the family as Hope, meaning she tagged along on family vacations and was welcomed to gorge with us on the holidays.

In the meantime, Aliana FaceTimed me often.

"I think I might love Mack," she confessed one evening. She didn't look at the screen as she said this. Instead, everything about her was cast down: her eyes, her mouth, the tails of her eyebrows. She still struggled with this anxiety.

"It's okay to love someone," I reminded her gently. "That's a good feeling to have."

Aliana finally looked up at me, green eyes popping with concern. "When do I tell her?"

"Why not right now?"

"Because she might not be ready to say it back."

I took a moment to gather my thoughts. "Aliana, sweetheart, if you truly know deep in your bones how you feel about this woman, then tell her. It takes a lot of guts to be vulnerable with someone like that, but if your heart is telling you to say it, you need to say it. What do we always say? Come on," I urged when she pulled away and rolled her eyes. "Come on! What do we say?"

"We are not guaranteed tomorrow," she muttered. A trace of a smile tugged at her lips.

"Exactly. Honey, you deserve to be happy in every sense of the word. If she's not ready to say it back yet, that is okay. At least you can be confident in the fact that you spoke your mind."

Her smile grew wider. "Thanks, Mom."

"Don't mention it. I charge forty dollars per therapy session." I winked at her, and that finally earned me a laugh.

∿

Andrea and Trinity came along to Aliana's college graduation, dressed in little matching yellow dresses. Gavin had become the best father in the world. He did more for those girls than any other parent I knew. Except maybe myself.

Aliana had taken up bartending during her last two years of school so that when she graduated, she could take Mackenna to Miami, Florida. She claimed it was for the sunshine and dance opportunities, but I knew her desire went deeper than that. I recalled the time our family had traveled to the Florida Keys, and Aliana had said she wanted to move there someday. Back then, Estelle had still been around. It seemed like a way for my daughter to finally make peace with the past, and I was proud of her...even if I detested the distance.

At our celebratory family dinner for Aliana and Mack's graduation, Andrea and Trinity kept Colton's full attention. They wanted him to color with them, wanted him to tell them another cheesy joke. They couldn't get enough of him. Beside me, Gavin chuckled.

"Thank God for Colton," he murmured, watching his daughters cheer and clap when Colton showed them his mediocre drawing of an orange cat.

"Absolutely."

Gavin shifted in his seat. "I mean...thank God that he came into my life. He was the first person to show me what a good father was like."

I stared at my son for a second, taking in his grown-up appearance of close-cropped hair and the touch of a goatee stretching around the perimeter of his mouth. I leaned in and planted a kiss on his temple. He smiled at me, glancing back at his children.

"Yes, thank God for Colton." I took a deep breath as a confession crawled onto my tongue. "I'm writing something."

"Writing?" Gavin eyed me curiously.

I nodded. "Your aunt Dani's been helping me for years. I'm writing something for you and your sister." I glanced at Aliana, who was immersed in a conversation with Hope and Mackenna. "It's just taken me a long time to figure out what to say and how to say it. You know I love you both *very* much."

"Yeah, of course."

I smiled. "Sometimes my writing has to take a back seat though. I had to raise you kids and pay a thousand bills, practice my music, conduct the orchestra."

"You're a superhero. We know that." Gavin laughed.

"I'm better than a superhero. I'm a mom."

Chapter Twenty-Eight

SARATOGA SPRINGS, NY (2066)

Retirement snuck up on me like the space gray Subaru who tails you on the highway: undetected until you check your mirrors.

I had been busy the last few years, watching my twin granddaughters grow up and start first grade. Hearing about my son's work as a marketing director and laughing at the stories of his supposedly eccentric customers. I took time to visit my daughter in Miami and tearfully clutched her hand as she showed me the diamond ring she planned to propose to Mackenna with. I was busy attending their wedding, straightening Colton's tie and towing him onto the dance floor. I was busy conducting the Saratoga Strings, which had grown substantially in the last two years.

I was busy. Retirement decided it was time for a break.

"Scoping out the new members, huh?" Veronica asked after rehearsal one day.

Her charcoal hair had lightened. Her golden skin had wrinkled. Her eyes, though, were just as vibrant as they had always been.

Conducting was a stressful job, and she had been my right hand woman for so many years now. An expert at pep talks. An organized life-saver. An exceptional friend.

"I have to," I replied forlornly. "Somebody here has to take my place and conduct."

Members of the Saratoga Strings moved around us, chatting amongst themselves, unzipping and zipping instrument cases. There were so many choices staring me in the face.

There was Linea Shombs—impeccable cello player who had studied music at Berklee College. Jaxon Yuvano, Julliard grad with more performances under his belt than anyone else I knew. And Wesley Bucken, a genius violinist from the Curtis Institute of Music.

"I vote Jermaine," Seth insisted, crossing his arms and nodding at the young bass player.

"Jermaine doesn't even know what day it is," I disagreed with a wide grin. He was the orchestra's comic. Unbelievably hilarious, but not a match for this conductor puzzle piece.

"Anyone here would be honored to have the position," Veronica reasoned. "They wouldn't take it lightly."

My eyes narrowed at the crowd of instrumentalists in front of me. I tapped my finger against my chin like a self-obsessed philosopher. This was a hard decision.

"You'll figure it out," Veronica assured me with her signature sweetheart smile.

"I still vote for Jermaine," Seth said. "The guy had me in tears last week with that bar joke."

Fifteen minutes later, after the majority of the group had left for the evening, I gathered my laptop, car keys, and unfinished bottle of tea in my hands. Just as my purse slipped down my arm, a young man rushed to get the door for me.

"Oh, thank you, Wesley," I breathed.

His eyes crinkled when he smiled. "No problem. Have a great rest of your day."

He was our newest member, added a year and a half ago after I heard his exquisite, shortened rendition of Beethoven's Violin Sonata No. 9, which, in my opinion, was one of the greatest violin pieces ever composed. And Wesley had blown right through it like it was child's play. I knew from the moment I met him that he was a must-have for the Saratoga Strings.

"You, too."

I turned to head out the door until something in my heart made me freeze right there on the blacktop. It was something nostalgic and whole. Bright and brilliant. It was Professor Autrie and Tod Niles. It was Elijah and Cara. It was the Curtis Institute of Music and all of the beautiful memories I had there. Similar memories, I was sure, to Wesley's experience.

"It's you," I cried, turning back to Wesley. He was halfway down the hall when I caught up with him.

He jumped when I grabbed his shoulder. "I'm sorry?"

I couldn't unsee it. Wesley was perfect for this position. He had the *spark* in him. He let the music move him, *consume* him. It was the reason I'd rewarded him with first chair. He practiced and worked harder than everyone else because he understood that even with all his talent there was still room for improvement.

"Would you take my place?" The question burst from my lips before I could stop it, and I kind of wished I could've taken it back and restated it more professionally like Tod had done. I was just so excited.

Wesley's eyes became saucers. "Seriously?"

I knew that look well; I had *worn* that look.

"Yes! Absolutely. W-when do I start?" He cleared his throat and tried to contain his emotion but failed drastically.

"Two weeks," I replied. "Meet me after rehearsal tomorrow, and I'll go over everything you need to know."

It still felt bitter to have to pass the torch along, but at least I knew the Saratoga Strings would be safe and well guided with Wesley. All of us old-timers were getting ready to step down anyway. Now it was up to the fresh faces, and Wesley was God-sent to lead them.

~

Colton surprised me on my sixty-fifth birthday by throwing a party with all of my old friends, most of whom I hadn't seen in years.

The first face I saw was Cara's, and I gawked at her. Her once pale blonde hair was now a creamy silver. She'd cropped it to her shoulders, and it took me a minute to accept the fact that we were as old as we were. I had to laugh at Beau. Gone were the days of his chiseled features; they were now replaced by worn skin and thinning hair. Erica and Spencer still looked like they were forty instead of sixty-four, and a small part of me despised them for it, but my affection overwhelmed my jealousy. The sight of Elijah and Brie almost brought me to tears. We were all finally together again. It made my heart swell with happiness.

The real surprise came when I was directed outside and onto the driveway. I hadn't been allowed into the garage all day, so I became suspicious when Elijah, Beau, and Colton squeezed through the side door and slammed it shut before I could peek.

"Don't tell me it is what I think it is," I warned my girl friends.

They shared a meaningful look with each other, and the grin on Erica's face practically gave it away. When the garage door opened, Cara rested a hand on my shoulder.

"Happy sixty-fifth, Gail!"

Sure enough, the entire garage had been cleared except for a sleek, navy blue 2066 Jeep Wrangler. My eyes bulged from my head as everyone cheered.

"What the hell is this?" I breathed.

"Your birthday present." Elijah smiled.

The car glittered in the afternoon sunlight, nearly blinding me. "W-but...how did you afford...who got—"

"Oh, shush!" Erica gave a lazy roll of her eyes. "We all chipped in."

"You drooled at the TV every time this car commercial came on. It was perfect." Colton looped an arm around my waist, clearly satisfied with himself.

Spencer tossed me the keys. "It's all yours, Gail."

"Well, come on! Let's take it for a spin!"

Driving this car was like gliding through butter. I even stomped on the gas pedal, and we took off to a heart stopping seventy-five miles an hour on a desolate forty-five mile per hour road. From the back, my friends squealed with excitement. I gripped the steering wheel until my knuckles were white and the adrenaline sizzled in my chest. It was then that I decided sixty-five was just a number.

Nostalgia creeped in as the day went on. After all my friends left, I retired to my bedroom, happily stuffed on red velvet cake. I went straight to my desk drawer and retrieved the old sky-blue journal, which was now stained and withered from forty-some years of use. It only had two blank pages left. I flipped through the book and grazed a finger over my own handwriting, taking note of how it was rougher in some places than others.

There was Katy Marsh and Professor Autrie. I'd written Cara's name for the first time with a pink pen. I had *scribbled* my mother's name for the first time because of the fury she used to bring me and my father. So many people, so many connections.

I lowered myself into the chair, wincing at a sharp pain in my hip, and reached for a pen. I wrote Colton's name. I wrote each letter carefully in my best penmanship because this was the name that had meant everything to me since I'd met him. Slowly then, I wrote a small description beside the name: *the man who captured my heart and never let it go.*

"Hey," Colton said, entering our bedroom sluggishly. "I'm exhausted, so I'm going to bed."

I grabbed his hand before he could move to the bathroom. "Thank you for everything. Today was amazing."

He shrugged and failed to hide a blush. "It's no trip to Venice."

"Doesn't matter. I love you."

He kissed me slowly, It still packed a punch to my heart. "I love you more."

I didn't think that was possible.

My first month into retirement was so boring I considered recalling Wesley and stepping back into position as conductor.

"No, Gail." Colton shook his head and laughed. "You're retired now for a reason."

We sat at the kitchen table, munching on chewy roast beef and seasoned green beans. I was proud of the dinner I'd made tonight, even if the beans were a little overcooked. Cooking was the only thing I did now that I couldn't go to the rec center and lead rehearsal. The thought made me bitter, and I stabbed a piece of beef with my fork.

"What the hell am I supposed to do with my life now?" I demanded.

Colton laughed again, and I glared at him.

"You find peace," he managed through his chuckles. "You find peace and take up new hobbies."

"Like what?"

"Like..." Colton took a sip of his water and glanced all around the dining room while he thought. "Like joining me for charity meetings at church. They're actually pretty fun. Donating makes you feel good. Or...what about writing? You're always bent over that journal, Gail. *Something's* gotta come from that."

"Something *is* coming from that," I confessed. "I'm nearly done drafting the story now."

"What story exactly?"

"Our story."

He sat back in his seat, lips curling into a smile. "Good idea. People might learn something from it. It might even become a bestseller. You should dedicate it to me." He winked.

I had to laugh. "It's for Gavin and Aliana. Something for them to hold onto forever." I paused, considering his earlier suggestion. "I'll come to the next charity meeting with you. I think it'll do me good."

And that's exactly what happened. Colton and I became a lot more involved in the church. Pastor David had retired two years before, leaving his son to take over and preach to the congregation instead. I liked Gabriel; he was very animated like his father and had a talent for keeping the congregation on the edge of their seats.

Some Sundays, when Colton helped behind the front desk, I would wander out into the gardens behind the church and sit on one of the stone benches. There was a statue of an angel there. It always brought me comfort.

I pictured Colton—something I always did when I wanted to center my thoughts—and when I pictured his beautiful eyes, I realized that I could do it. I could find peace with him beside me. He was more than enough. And writing to my children was something I would accomplish before I left this earth.

My phone rang on the way home from church that day. Colton was driving, so I was able to pick it up. Aliana's picture flashed on the screen.

"Hey, sweetheart," I greeted her.

"Mom, you're not gonna believe what I'm about to tell you." Her voice was loud, overflowing with excitement.

"Go on then."

"Mackenna and I...are adopting!"

My shout of glee filled the car and Colton nearly slammed into a guard rail. "That's amazing!"

"His name's Kota," I heard Mackenna call from the background. "He's from Vermont."

"Apparently, his parents died in an accident, and he didn't have family around to take him in. Thank God we found him."

"Kota," I repeated the name, adoring the way the syllables fit together.

Colton couldn't take the suspense any longer and demanded to be let in on the story. When I told him, he screamed louder than I did.

Chapter Twenty-Nine

MIAMI, FL—SARATOGA SPRINGS, NY (2066–2081)

H urry up, Gail! I wanna see my grandson!" Colton was bouncing on his feet, jittery from both the two Coca-Cola's he drank on the flight and because his newest wish of becoming a grandfather had finally come true. We were about to meet Kota.

We'd just landed in Miami, and already the heat was gluing my hair to the base of my neck. Colton towed me through the terminal, surprisingly fast for a sixty-six-year-old. We purchased a tiny goldfish of a rental car and then sped down the coast. I was a chatterbox. By the time we got to Aliana's house—a cottage-like home with off-white vinyl siding and a dark pitched roof—I had successfully talked Colton's ears off.

Gavin's rented blue Sonata was already parked in the driveway. The front door swung open, and Andrea and Trinity sprinted down the two concrete steps.

"Hi, sweethearts!" I gushed, pulling them into my arms.

They were identical—down to the glittering ruby color they

painted on their nails. The only way to tell them apart was by the earrings they wore. Trinity had emerald studs. Andrea wore sapphires. They hugged Colton next and then pulled us inside.

"Kota's so cute!" Trinity exclaimed.

Inside, there was a winding staircase and varnished wood floors. Aliana and Mack were seated on the plush L-shaped couch, and in between them sat a little boy with bright red curly hair and an ivory face. His cheeks were stained pink. His eyes were bright blue. He looked to be about five years old. Andrea and Trinity crowded around him, making silly faces. Kota seemed to relax then and smiled a gap-toothed smile.

Colton's mouth was fixed into an O shape. I could practically see his heart beating out of his chest. Mine was, too.

"Girls, give Kota some space so Grandma and Grandpa can meet him," Gavin said from the opposite end of the couch.

His arm was draped around Hope, and she was clutching her hands to her chest. Hope adored children.

"Kota, this is your grandma and grandpa," Aliana murmured to him.

"The best of the best," Mackenna added with a wide grin.

Kota blinked at us, those wide blue eyes equally curious and shy. He was so tiny sandwiched between his mothers like that. I'd never wanted to hug another human being so badly.

"Hi there," Colton said, bending down so that he and Kota were eye to eye. He held his hand out. "What's up, little man?"

Kota stared at his outstretched hand and then reached out to shake it. His tiny hand was lost in Colton's, but something twinkled in Kota's eyes then. The smile started on the right corner of his mouth and dragged the other half up with it.

"Hi," he said in a little voice. My heart screamed.

"Hey, Kota." I stepped forward, waving down at him.

He smiled at me, too, but kept looking back at Colton like he wanted to know everything about the man in front of him. I knew they were going to be best friends.

The week was full of beach days under a cabana, hours walking through markets, eating in tropical themed restaurants, and making our grandchildren laugh. Kota stayed close to Colton, holding his hand and pulling him into the crystal pools and into the ocean, just to where the waves could splash against his knees and Colton's calves.

I was sitting under our tent with my gigantic floppy hat, sunglasses, and layers upon layers of sunscreen even though I was in the shade. In my hand was a spray bottle with a fan attached to it. It was eighty-six degrees today, and I was praying the fan's batteries wouldn't die on me. Colton was out in the water with Kota, lifting him above the waves. They'd been out there for an hour. Trinity and Andrea were further out, dipping under waves with their mother and father.

"That's cute," Aliana murmured, lifting her sunglasses. She gestured to Colton and Kota.

"I didn't know Colton still had that much energy," I replied.

"Yes, but I mean that Kota already idolizes him so much. They just met. He's not even that close with me."

Mack was outside the tent, stomach-down on a beach blanket, lathered in tanning oil. She raised her hand. "Or me."

"We're a very close family," Aliana continued, still watching her son splash around in the waves. "But Dad's just brilliant. You know, I watched him convince Kota to eat broccoli the other night," she said.

Mack's jaw dropped. "We have to bribe him with TV time!"

"It's my dad." Aliana held up her hands, like *I don't know how he does it*.

Maybe because Kota was surrounded by amazing women all day, he needed to spend some time with an amazing man every once in a while, too. I looked over at my daughter.

"Yes, your father is incredible."

Aliana laughed quietly. "I should ask him for some tips." Her voice was soft, almost desperate and a bit sad.

I cocked my head at her. "Are you doubting your abilities as a mom?"

She shrugged.

I turned my fan up another notch and resituated myself in the beach chair so I could face her fully.

"Honey, that's part of parenting. I can't even tell you how many times I doubted myself. Probably every day. But you *learn*." I smiled at her. "You experience and you learn. If you ask me, I'd say you're off to a pretty great start. I'm kind of jealous actually."

"Why?"

"'Cause you didn't have to deal with the luxury of changing diapers at two am and tend to a crying infant and wean them off breast milk. You know, Mack," I called, "your wife here had me up every morning at five am so she could play with her toys! Can you believe that?"

Mack slapped the beach towel and laughed for a whole minute.

Aliana grinned. "How can I make it up to you?"

I watched Colton lift Kota above another wave. My grandson's excited squeal was fresh music to my ears. "You can buy me new batteries for this fan so that it never dies."

Retirement wasn't so boring after all. In the fifteen years that followed, Colton and I returned to Venice, *this* time with our whole family, which made for an even more exciting trip.

Gavin liked sightseeing. Aliana loved the shopping, and we couldn't keep Mack and Hope away from the water for more than five minutes. Kota and the twins kept busy with snorkeling and adventuring around the city. And Colton and I got to dance on the balcony again. Slower this time, since we were both in our very early eighties, but our hearts still swayed right along with the music. It was a vacation I would never forget. Unfortunately, we had to return home sometime.

It was brought to my attention that Colton's health was deteriorating.

The month after our vacation, he started experiencing a lot of unexplained dizziness, and it became difficult for him to walk on his right leg. The doctors found nothing wrong with him but promised to keep an eye on his condition. Ever the optimist, Colton's spirits ran high. He reminded me to be grateful for every moment. Each night before bed, I held his prayer rock, and we thanked God together.

It was for this reason that I was finally finding peace. I found it in the marigolds that grew in my garden, and I felt it on the warm evenings when we sat outside on the porch swing with glasses of peach tea.

I was okay with the life I'd had. And I was okay with leaving it behind whenever God felt the need to bring me home. But that was where the serenity ended.

Underneath this placid lifestyle I'd recently acquired, a great fear still clung to my heart. A terror beyond terrors: the loss of my husband. Never in a million years did I consider living one moment without him on this earth. Even as teenagers, when we'd broken up, a portion of my tattered heart was still okay because he was still alive. But if he left this world before I did, I didn't know how I would handle it. I wasn't ready for that, even if he was turning eighty-one this coming January. He was still the boy from our youth; he was still my Colton. I couldn't give him up. Not yet.

Stubborn as I was, I even prayed for more time, begging God to either let me go first or let us go together. Anything else just wouldn't be fair. Of course, when would I learn that life was far from fair?

The thought of losing Colton for real gave me nightmares, and every time I jolted awake I would reach for Colton in the darkness, and he would hold me tightly and assure me that everything was okay.

Maybe this was the hardest part to life. It wasn't teenage heartbreak, or childbirth, or divorce. Maybe it was losing the one you love forever. Knowing that...you could no longer see them. That they were permanently gone.

"Death scares me," I admitted to Pastor Gabriel one Sunday after the church service.

Colton was helping to hand out T-shirts for vacation Bible school, and Gabriel's door just happened to be open. I slipped in, retrieved a cookie from the tray in the back, and took a seat. Gabriel didn't mind at all.

"Why does it scare you?" he inquired patiently.

I stared at him like the answer was obvious. "I'm scared of the grief. I'm scared that I'll never get over the loss." I remembered finding Aliana blue-lipped and unconscious on the bathroom floor, and a violent shudder ran through me.

Gabriel sat across from me, steepling his fingers under his chin. "Would you agree if I said death was an open door?"

I sighed. "Yes."

"Gail, everything that happens is under God's control. Just because you lose someone doesn't mean you'll never see them again. You *will* see them, in a place *far* better than earth."

"How can I be sure? What if I can't even find my dad up there?"

Gabriel smiled at this. "Something tells me you will. Don't fear death, Gail. It is only the gateway to our next life beside the Father."

Through the glass doors, I watched Colton place a neon green T-shirt in a young boy's hands. The smile on Colton's face was magical. It brought me back to reality. Gabriel followed my gaze and nodded his head as if he could read my thoughts.

"All we have is here and now, Gail."

Colton laughed at something the little boy said, and my heart gave a loving squeeze. "You're right."

Andrea, Trinity, and Kota always came to visit in late June, so when they arrived the following week, I took Gabriel's words to heart and paid attention to every little moment I had with my grandchildren. They were old enough to drive now and were entering college this coming fall, which made me feel even older, and meant I had to do everything I could to slow time.

Colton and I took them to the pool and out shopping at some of the stores in town. We also took them to the Brook Tavern and forced them to listen to the story of our first date here. Trinity crinkled her nose at that and mentioned how *old* this restaurant was.

"It's been here since we were kids," Colton said.

My grandchildren balked at him and glanced around again at the polished wooden floors and ceiling. It wasn't long before their phones chimed and their faces were glued to the screens.

"Are you still talking to Bode?" Andrea asked her sister.

Kota leaned in and elbowed Trinity mockingly. My eyebrows lifted curiously. I hardly got to see them, so I wanted to be in on every aspect of their life that I could.

Trinity's cheeks reddened. "We've been Coast Chatting a lot, and he followed me on Flashgram, but I don't think things are gonna take off."

I frowned. "What's Flashgram?"

Three pairs of eyes locked on my face.

Andrea burst into giggles. "It's like, the biggest social media platform in the world right now."

I glanced at Colton for help, but he looked just as clueless as me.

"In our day it was Instagram," Colton grumbled, reaching for his glass of water.

Kota scoffed. "Nobody's used Instagram in forever, Grandpa."

"Please tell us you know what Coast Chatting is," Trinity pleaded.

I suddenly felt very excluded and out of the loop. More so than ever before. That was another disappointment of getting older: suddenly your grandchildren knew more than you did. "Can't say I do."

This time Kota started laughing, and when I shot him a look, he pressed his hand to his mouth to muffle the sound.

"It's basically where you snap pictures and videos to people from all across the world," Andrea said.

Colton and I shared another confused glance. "You mean like Snapchat?"

"Like what?" Trinity asked, her face pinching in a perplexed manner.

"Lord help us." I pressed the heel of my hand to my forehead and began massaging.

"It's okay, Grandma," Kota assured me.

"Like hell it is." I rolled my eyes and glanced back at my giggling grandchildren. "Whatever you do, don't get older."

The summer was coming to an end. I'd spent most of my time in church, hosting vacation Bible school and sticking around after services for charity meetings with Colton.

Last August, the church's support team had traveled to Uganda to build three schools—an impressive improvement over the previous year's single money supply to fund medical research. It was announced that *this* year, the support group was taking volunteers to travel to Venezuela to help run a blood drive at a children's hospital. And Colton was more than eager to help.

"Sign up with me," he encouraged as we walked through the church's rose garden after today's service.

"In case you forgot, sir," I said, patting his arm, "we aren't twenty anymore. We can't just pack up everything and go to Venezuela."

"What do you think all those car wash fundraisers were for back in spring? To my knowledge, *you* were part of the group that organized those. The trip is paid for, Gail."

"Still, I don't know."

We parked ourselves on one of the cement benches near the angel statue. Her arms were spread open in a welcoming gesture.

"Think of the impact we could have!" Colton exclaimed. "We could save a child's life."

"We've done that already," I answered.

It was one thing to see pictures of a third world country, but it was another thing to actually walk the streets of one. To see the makeshift shelters and the trash-filled streets and the skin-and-bone children. It would be a mentally-jarring trip.

Colton read my thoughts. "You're scared. I get it, I am, too. But God's calling me to do this, and...I would love if you came with me."

There it was—that dazzling, no-good smile that weakened my resolve. I blinked and laid my head on his shoulder so I wouldn't have to see it.

"How are you such a good person?"

His shoulders bounced as he laughed. "Would you rather I be a selfish asshole?"

"No!" I sat up to glare at him. "I mean...you're just so *good*. Not a lot of people would willingly go to a third world country just to have a blood drive. Come to think of it, not a lot of people would be involved at all."

"I just want to help." He shrugged. "No kid should have to go through what I went through, and even if it's not parental abuse, I still want to give them a good life. Show them that...it's worth sticking it out for."

I laced my fingers through his. "You're an angel, Colton Reeves."

"I wouldn't say *that*."

But I could see it in his eyes—the pureness, the desire to do good and spread love to this callous world.

"Do you ever think God sent you here to find me?" I asked. "Sent you as...my personal angel?"

"It's entirely possible," Colton murmured, kissing the tip of my nose. "But I think I would've remembered being an angel."

I shrugged. "God works in mysterious ways."

～

The trip to Venezuela was scheduled in exactly three months: November twentieth. My husband's name was clearly printed on the sign-up sheet. All I could focus on was our upcoming trip to visit Gavin and Hope.

Hope's research on determinants of pessimism among college students was finally cleared for publication. It was an accomplishment entirely worth celebrating, so I decided to go out and buy some sparkling champagne to crack open once we got to their house.

It was a gorgeous day in August. The sky was a limitless blue dome overhead, smeared through with a few wisps of lazy clouds. A gentle, sweet summer breeze swept through the screen door. It twirled my hair as I went to grab my car keys.

"Hey, Gail?" Colton called from the sofa.

His dizziness had returned harshly today, so I'd insisted he stay put on the couch.

I sat down beside him. "How are you feeling?"

Colton shrugged. "My head's still kinda spinning, and that pain in my right leg is back."

"Should I schedule another appointment with the doctor?"

"Nah." He rested a reassuring hand on my arm. "Don't go through the trouble, I'm all right."

I wasn't convinced. "Keep drinking water. Here, you're out, let me get you some more."

"I'm not a hundred, Gail," he laughed. "I'll get it myself. Go on and get the champagne, I'll be fine. Oh and also, get some more Mint Oreo cookies if they have them, please."

"'Mkay." I nodded, standing up and fumbling with my keys. "I'll see you later. And drink water!"

"Wait, hold on," Colton called me back.

"What?"

The way his eyes bored into mine at that moment, a dozen emotions coursed through me. The whites of his eyes were slightly bloodshot, surrounding large pools of gold and green. His eyes shimmered. I tried to decipher the look on his face, but I couldn't name the expression.

"What is it, Colt?"

He shook his head—a tiny, almost invisible movement—and his lips pulled upward into a dazzling smile. "I just love you. So much."

"I love you, too." The response was magnetic, automatic. I said it to him every day. "I'll be back soon, okay?"

I risked hurting my back just to bend over him and kiss him, but it was worth it because every time our lips touched, my soul elevated in my body. Kissing Colton always made me happy. I even drove to the store, scream-singing one of my favorite songs from when I was a teenager.

The supermarket wasn't crowded at all. I moved down the aisles, still dancing from the music that was now in my head.

I was so excited for this upcoming week. I couldn't wait to see Gavin and Hope again. And Colton had promised we'd go see the

Saratoga Strings, who were set to perform in Philadelphia while we were there. I floated down the aisles and collected two bottles of Rosé before circling back around for Colton's cookies.

"Ooh, is someone having a party?" the particularly chipper cashier asked.

I passed him my credit card. "Yes. A party with my family."

"Aw." The boy grinned. "Well, I hope you have a great rest of your day and a great party."

"Thank you!" It wasn't every day that you encountered nice people like that, and I danced out into the parking lot, happier than ever.

There were days in my life when I had random surges of euphoria. I didn't complain though. I would take this unexplained delight over the crushing weight of depression *any* day.

Traffic was light on the way home, so I made it back with record timing. Still singing the music that was lodged in my brain, I collected the groceries and kicked through the screen door after unlocking it.

"Colton!" I called, smiling cheek to cheek. "I got the—"

My statement was cut off by a sudden knife to the chest. I'd rounded the corner into the kitchen only to find Colton unconscious on the floor. He was flat on his stomach, arms stretched out to both sides, and in his one hand was the empty glass. The glass he'd insisted he would fill himself.

Something crashed and shattered on the ground, but I didn't register what it was.

I collapsed onto my knees beside Colton and started violently shaking his body, screaming for him to wake up. Screaming for God to do something. When Colton didn't stir, I turned him over and pulled him into my lap, shrieking at the way his lifeless body slumped in my arms. His eyes were closed, blocking me from the vibrant colors of his irises. But I refused to think I wouldn't see them again. My stomach was roiling; my heart screeching. He wasn't waking up! *Why wouldn't he wake up?!*

It suddenly occurred to me that nothing would change until I called 911. Cursing, I set Colton down and went to grab the phone, wincing when I heard a sickening crunch under my shoes. One glance at the floor confirmed that I'd dropped the bottles of champagne, and now there was a mess of shattered glass and liquid all over the floor. But I couldn't deal with it now. I had to get help.

My hands were shaking so violently I was afraid they'd dislodge themselves from my body. When the operator answered my call, I bellowed into the phone, my voice echoing furiously off the walls.

I couldn't even look at Colton; I couldn't open my eyes. My body was going into shock. Soon I would pass out, and part of me hoped I would. Anything to put an end to the pain that was now searing me in half. *Don't take him from me*, my heart wailed. *Please don't do this!*

My feet were already moving before my brain acknowledged it, and soon, I was holding him in my arms again. I didn't plan on moving then because moving even the smallest muscle would make the pain so much worse. My only hope was to assume that this was a nightmare. My tears flowed freely down my cheeks, slipping into my gaping mouth, and I choked. I screamed again, releasing every last ounce of oxygen from my lungs, and then gasped for air. The pain was intolerable, and I thought I might burst into a million pieces.

"You're not gone, you're not gone," I chanted, though I didn't know what I was trying to do—bring him back or convince myself he never left.

But I knew...There was no pulse thumping in his neck. There was no color to his skin. He was growing colder by the second. The white walls faced me, quietly drinking in my sorrow until sirens squealed in the distance.

~

"I'm glad you came to the service today, Gail. I think the message was very appropriate for your situation right now."

I gave Pastor Gabriel a stoic look. I hadn't been feeling anything the last two months, but Gabriel knew me better.

He sighed. "How are you holding up? For real."

I shook my head slowly, searching for words and failing tremendously. But anything that exited my mouth would have been a lie anyway. I didn't know how I was holding up. I didn't even know if I was alive.

In the last couple days, my friends and family had sent text message after text message of condolences. Even Evan had reached out with an apology. Dani had sent her prayers.

"Do you want to talk about...what happened?" Gabriel asked.

Blazing hot tears stung my eyes, and I licked my chapped lips.

"It was a stroke," I answered angrily.

I recalled the doctor's words when he broke the news to me: *Your husband suffered a stroke, caused by a blood clot that blocked blood vessels to his brain.* It broke my heart right in half.

Gabriel squeezed his eyes shut for a second and then looked back at me. "I am *truly* sorry, Gail."

"I should have gotten him the damn water. I should have just stayed home. He wasn't feeling well for God's sake. I should have *known* something was going to happen."

"You couldn't have known," Gabriel replied softly.

"Colton was always dizzy! The pain in his leg was unbearable. Some days he couldn't even walk! What wife am I to not take those things more seriously?" I demanded. "The doctor said those are signs of a..." I blinked furiously, feeling my face redden with agitation. With guilt. "Signs of—of a stroke. He said that *months* ago!"

"Listen," Gabriel said, leaning forward in his seat. "You *cannot* blame yourself for what happened to Colton. Doing that only puts you on the should-cycle."

I shook my head vigorously. "The what?"

"The should-cycle," he repeated firmly. "It's a part of the grief. You should have done this, you should have done that. No." Gabriel shook his head, boring his eyes into mine. "You *couldn't* have. It was God's will. He was ready to bring Colton home."

"*I* wasn't ready!" I retorted sharply.

The following silence was so thick it was almost tangible. I shrank back in my seat and drew in a ragged breath, which burned my lungs.

"Look," Gabriel said after a moment. "I really am sorry for your loss. I understand that you've known him for a long time and those relationships are always the hardest to say goodbye to. But...you should take comfort in the fact that he is in a better place now. He's no longer suffering or in pain. He's okay, Gail."

I was trembling with my sobs now, and I realized that it was the first time I'd cried in two months. Not since I went numb that one dark evening alone in my house after the funeral.

"I-I just want...him here with...me." I pressed a hand to my mouth as Gabriel's figure blurred with my tears. "I *miss* him."

"Of course." The pastor's voice was low and soothing. "You're *allowed* to feel that way. He was the love of your life."

I pictured Colton in all his aging glory: a lump on the couch, chuckling at something on the TV. All of our late-night talks on the porch while the sun was bleeding into the horizon. His comforting arms around me...

I sniffled. "I met him when I was eleven years old, you know."

"I did not know that." Gabriel smiled politely. "And you were together all these years. That's incredible."

"Well, not quite," I corrected, and a single laugh burst from my lips. It all seemed so distant now.

"But your love won in the end. Is that not something to celebrate?"

My head dropped, and I stared at my hands that were folded in my lap. There was my wedding ring with the two diamonds secured to my finger. I stared at the pair of diamonds, thinking there should only be one now, but I was grateful they remained together.

"Let me ask you this," Gabriel said, bringing me back to the present moment. "If Colton were still here, what do you think he would be doing?"

I blinked. "He would probably be out there in the support group meeting. And he'd probably be helping to plan the trip to Venezuela." A single tear trickled down my cheek. "He wanted to go on that trip *so* badly. He even asked me to..." I trailed off as the realization struck me.

Gabriel's beaming smile lit up the room. "Sign up sheet's right out in the hall. I think Colton would really love it if you went on his behalf."

For the first time in a long time, my heart started to race.

"I'm scared," I whispered.

"All of life's greatest adventures stem from fear, Gail. That's what makes the story worth telling. If you ask me, I think God is trying to show you something with all of this. What might that be?"

I swallowed, suddenly seeing everything in crystal clarity. My bottom lip quivered. "That no matter who you lose, you will be okay."

"Colton's proud of you." Gabriel nodded. "I can feel it. You should, too."

Slowly, I rose from the chair and trudged into the narthex, feeling my heart pound with every step. There was the sign-up sheet. And there was his name. A perfect signature full of swoops and curls. *Who cares if we're eighty now?* he'd said one evening not three months ago. *That just makes me want to go even more and see the world before it's too late.* I held the pen in my trembling hand and carefully signed my name below his.

It took me a moment to come to terms with the unexpected rush of contentment that filled my bones. It was like I had been revived. I could breathe again. I had to do this for Colton, and now the truth was that I *wanted* to do it.

I dried the last of my tears on the sleeve of my shirt and turned toward the door. Pastor Gabriel smiled kindly and waved goodbye.

Chapter Thirty

SARATOGA SPRINGS, NY (2082)

G ood morning and merry Christmas!"

"Merry Christmas!" the congregation sang back to the assistant pastor.

The hall of worship was brilliantly decorated with low-hung wreaths and shiny silver stars that hung from the ceiling. In the corner, there was a gigantic tree covered with faux snow and adorned with large golden bulbs. It was a winter wonderland. The perfect setting for the perfect day.

I sat in one of the front pews, surrounded on both sides by my children and grandchildren who had come home for the holidays. Aliana held my hand as the assistant pastor smiled at us.

"Before we begin worship on this glorious Sunday, the birthday of our savior, we must highlight the work that was finally completed in Uganda by our very own church support group. This project was organized two years ago by Malinda Brown, Jake Westbrend, and Colton Reeves. It is my pleasure to announce that the schools have all been built."

An uproar of cheers rang out from the crowd, and I inched my chin higher as a smile blossomed on my lips.

"I would also like to highlight that it has officially been two years since our *first* trip to Venezuela for the blood drive, and the people appreciated our help so much that they have asked us back again and again."

Pictures from the trip flashed on the large TV screens in the background. And there I was—an elderly woman, standing amongst young civilians, our fists raised as if to say *we can overcome anything that comes our way!* Aliana squeezed my hand, and Gavin flashed me a gleaming smile.

The assistant pastor pushed his glasses back up the bridge of his nose. "I must make a shoutout to Miss Abigail Reeves, who is sitting right here in the flesh." I laughed at his tone. "She was our oldest traveler, yet she donated the most blood and even ventured into one of the villages to visit the less fortunate children."

More cheers echoed off the sanctuary walls.

"Thank you for your contributions, Mrs. Reeves. God bless you. Now then, if you would please join the band in singing *The First Noel.*"

"Dad would've loved to have seen those pictures," Aliana whispered to me as the lead singer stepped up to the mic. "I think he's happy that you went."

"Oh, I know he is," I responded and couldn't help but giggle at the memory of his eagerness.

My eyes flickered to the massive cross that hung in the back of the sanctuary. Today it was bathed in red and green lights. I said a silent prayer in that moment, thanking God for this wonderful day. *And another thing,* I said in my mind. *Please tell my husband that I love and miss him very much.*

～

After the service, the narthex was swarming with people. The church usually had its largest turnout during the holidays, so it wasn't a surprise seeing this many faces. I elbowed my way through the mob to grab a sugar cookie from the long line of baked goods.

"Miss Abigail, looking lovely as ever."

I turned to see Blake Walker, dressed handsomely in his church clothes and Christmas tie. He ran a hand through his quaffed silver hair and regarded me the way he always did. With a kind, flirtatious smile. It made me laugh. Here we were, two old fossils, yet Blake's boyish charm was still alive and well.

"Enjoying the holiday so far?" he asked, reaching around me for a chocolate chip cookie.

"Yes, I am. And you?"

"Oh, I can't complain. My grandchildren are in from Santa Barbara, and my son brought home his new wife. I think they'll work well together." His eyebrows danced. "Like you and me."

I scoffed and tossed my napkin into a nearby trash can. "How many times must I tell you my heart belongs to someone else?"

"I could give you the world, Abigail, darling." He smiled coyly.

"Good thing I've already seen it."

We smiled at each other. After a moment Blake held his hands up in defeat.

"Someday."

"I'm already eighty-two. Don't hold your breath."

He kissed the back of my hand and flashed me a determined look. "Merry Christmas, Abigail."

"Merry Christmas."

Luckily, Kota had driven his large SUV to New York, so I watched my family duck into the back seats before easing into the passenger seat. Aliana and Mackenna sat in the back row, and Hope had to sit on Gavin's lap. Not that she minded, I was sure. In the way back of the SUV, Trinity's boyfriend, Bode, was squished between the twins. What a large, dysfunctional, *beautiful* family I had.

That calming sense of euphoria was returning at long last. It had taken approximately a year and a half to even come to terms with what had happened. And if I dug deep enough, I was sure I'd find that ugly emptiness again. But I was better now. Time was a trickster. It murdered you and then revived you. Even at eighty-two-years-old, I still couldn't determine whether I hated time or appreciated it.

I was so busy considering this that Kota startled me when he said, "I think you got a package, Grandma."

"What?"

My grandson pulled the SUV to the curb outside my house and sure enough, a cream-colored package stood up against the front door.

"It's Christmas," Gavin said. "The mail shouldn't be running."

"Maybe it didn't come from the mailman," Aliana suggested.

I gathered everyone inside before retrieving the package. It was light and small.

"What is it?" Andrea asked once I'd gotten inside.

Everyone was staring at me with the same question in their eyes.

"Let's see," I answered distractedly.

I ripped through the plastic and felt the rectangular shape and smooth texture of a novel cover. I pulled the book out and stared at it, confused.

The Warning was printed in large, drooping letters across a midnight blue cover.

"Hey! It's great-aunt Dani's first book!" Kota exclaimed.

"I read it and loved it," Trinity piped up. "I love telling all of my friends that my great-aunt is a best-selling author."

I pressed a hand to my mouth to stifle a laugh. Oh, Dani.

"Wait, what's that?" Kota said, gesturing to a page that stuck out from behind the cover.

I pulled the small card from the book and laughed out loud this time. Dani had even taken the liberty to write me a note.

Dear, Abigail,

I know you never picked up *The Warning*, ya big liar. Do me a favor and read it. Enjoy it, hahaha. Think of it as an ode to the good old days. I know time is passing, but I want you to understand that I'm still grateful for you every day. If you hadn't dated my brother, I never would've gotten this amazing friendship. Everything happens for a reason. I hope that this letter finds you in good health and good spirits. I know Colton would be proud of you. He was an amazing man. You better be writing, Gail. That story is worth telling! I love and miss you. Happy holidays.

Best wishes,

Dani C.

I adored Dani more than words could express. She always knew what to say to give me the necessary kick in the pants.

I'd spent years brainstorming, pausing to reflect, filling the spaces of my journal with one-word descriptors. It was time to start writing. I wanted my children to read the letter, and I wanted my grandchildren to read the letter. *Their* children, too. I wanted them to know that if *I* could get through life's trials, they definitely could. I *needed* them to know they weren't alone in their pain.

This was what being human was all about. Everyone wanted to be acknowledged, accepted, and loved. It was my turn to pay it forward.

I could feel this epiphany pulsing in my body; it lit my heart on fire. A young Colton flashed in my brain. He zipped around the four-square patch while I quickly crossed the monkey bars.

Oblivious of each other, yet forever connected. My children had no idea just how deep this story went.

"I need to get some paper," I said urgently.

"For what?" Gavin asked.

"The letter I've been preparing to write for decades."

I climbed the stairs one at a time, moving slower than ever before. The memories were weighing down on me. There was so much to say; it was extremely overwhelming. But there was also a sense of peace that pervaded this idea. I could feel it growing stronger with each step I took.

In my imagination, Colton waited at the doorway to our bedroom, and the smile on his face was so beautiful it made me freeze for a second in awe. He waited patiently, ever the chivalrous gentleman from my memories. Slowly, I came back to myself.

"This one's for us," I told him as I passed the threshold and walked straight for my desk.

The sky-blue notebook was right where I'd left it—beside Colton's prayer rock. I retrieved a blank piece of paper from the printer and carefully set the pencil tip down. Colton stood over my shoulder, and I could feel his love and affection surging through my body at unexplainable wavelengths. With this feeling, I gathered my courage and began the letter.

Dedicated to the one I love...

The Ending

SARATOGA SPRINGS, NY (2083)

Aliana Reeves dabbed a tissue under her eyes, hoping her mascara hadn't smeared while she was crying. But it probably had. The emotions were almost too much to process. Her brother Gavin pulled her in for a hug, and even though she wasn't facing him, she could tell that he was just as affected.

"Wow," he breathed, his voice shaking slightly. "I'm..."

"Amazed?" Aliana suggested. She sniffled and shifted to glance up at him. "I can't believe Mom wrote all of that just for us."

Gavin was speechless. His lips opened and closed at least four times.

A breeze swept through the area, ruffling nearby leaves and blowing Aliana's hair around in her face. She scooted closer to Gavin on the bench and laid her head on his shoulder.

"I'm happy you got to meet your dad," she said after a moment.

"Me, too," Gavin said softly. "I just never knew the depth of the situation. How he cheated on Mom. The things she said to him. How hard they worked to forgive each other. And all of it for me."

"They loved you very much."

"They loved you, too," Gavin insisted.

Aliana felt a reply die on her tongue. She realized she didn't want to say anything. She wanted to leave that fact floating in the silence. It felt good to just be in this moment, like nothing else mattered at all. She hugged the thick collection of pages to her chest and bit her lower lip. Not every person on this earth would write such a lengthy thing for the people she loved. It just made her mother shine in an even brighter light.

"It's funny," Gavin mused. "I never would've guessed Mom and Colton were as close as they were. When he started coming around, I was only like, five. I just assumed they'd met at a coffee shop or something."

"Well thank God they *did* meet. Otherwise, I wouldn't be sitting here right now," Aliana said.

Gavin grinned at her. "Everything happens for a reason."

Aliana thought back to when she was a little girl and all the hours she'd spent playing with her dolls and going back and forth between her house and Estelle's house. She'd never heard from Estelle again after she left for Nevada, and to this day, Aliana didn't know if that was a good thing or a bad thing. All she understood was that that loss had corrupted her mind, played with her emotions. It had almost taken everything from her.

"What's wrong?" Gavin asked, sensing her gloom.

"I'm such a dumbass." Aliana shook her head in disbelief. "I only cared about popularity in high school, and it...practically took my life. If I wouldn't have gotten involved with Carmine, and if Estelle hadn't—"

"What?" Gavin interjected. "If Estelle hadn't what? She was always going to leave, Aliana. Remember what Pastor Gabriel told Mom? Get off the should-cycle. You were meant to go through that. It changed you."

"But it hurt everyone involved. I was just so angry, so *over* it. I wish I wouldn't have—"

"*Stop*," Gavin said. "God's plan was written. He wasn't gonna let you go that easily. Clearly there was more you needed to do. And there *was*. You needed to keep dancing to meet Mack. And you needed to meet Mack to adopt Kota. Now look at your son! He's a freaking historian for a museum! Without you, he *never* would've had that opportunity. Don't sell yourself short just because of one bad bump in the road. Take it from Mom." He tapped the front page of her letter. "For every bad day, there's a good one waiting just around the corner."

The siblings stared at each other.

Gavin was right. Aliana wasn't that girl anymore. She was stronger now, more self-aware. And that was all that mattered. The future was finally here, and she had every intention of walking into it with her head held high. If her mother could get through it, so could she.

For now though, she glanced around at the gorgeous summer trees and found peace in their swaying leaves. It was quiet. The kind of quiet that could put you to sleep if you allowed it to. And for a second, Aliana wished she *could* sleep. She was so mentally exhausted. But Mackenna would call her soon, wondering if she was okay. And Hope had to be concerned about Gavin by now. The two siblings had been out all day.

"Do you think they're okay? Mom and Dad?"

Gavin tossed his head back and laughed. "Something tells me they've never been better."

"I miss them a lot. I really hope they found each other."

Another breeze kissed Aliana's cheeks and she inhaled, hoping to steady her nerves. The loss had been so hard for her and trying to block the pain only brought it right back.

"I miss them, too," Gavin murmured. "But I'm *positive* they reunited. With a love as strong as theirs, nothing could stand in its way. It's impossible."

"I remember Mom was *so* devastated when he died. It was like...the life had been *sucked* out of her. Mackenna and I obviously love each other, but...what Mom and Dad had...that was almost otherworldly."

It took Gavin a moment to answer, but when he did there was a faraway look in his eyes. A certain gleam that Aliana couldn't quite place.

"You never really part forever. I mean, sure, death is scary, but...one day we'll all meet again in a place through the stars, higher than the sky. *That's* where you reunite." He looked over at his little sister. "And I bet you all the money in the world that when Mom got there, Colton was waiting right at the gate."

Just imagining such a thing, Aliana felt her eyes heat up with fresh tears. She knew it in her heart. Her parents were running hand-in-hand in a glorious field together as they were speaking. In fact, this thought filled Aliana with so much joy that her heart nearly exploded.

Gavin's phone buzzed, and he pulled it from his pocket. "It's Hope," he said, gazing down at the screen. "She wants to know how we're doing and when we'll be home."

"Well," Aliana exhaled and squeezed the stack of bound papers between her hands. "I guess that's our cue."

Gavin's eyes fell to the ground in front of them. "It's always hard to say goodbye."

"But we have so much to look forward to. Take it from Mom." Aliana grinned, proud of herself for stealing Gavin's statement from earlier.

Gavin chuckled and stood up. "So, this chapter of our lives is officially closed and finished?"

Aliana accepted her brother's outstretched hand and pulled herself up off the bench. "Apparently so. But here's to the future."

The siblings linked their arms and walked off into the distance, leaving the majestic orange sun to set on the beautifully adorned graves of Colton and Abigail Reeves.

Acknowledgments

If you're reading these acknowledgements, my heart goes out to you, thank you. You are a phenomenal human being. I hope you enjoyed Abigail's story as much as I enjoyed writing it.

There were a lot of ups and downs I experienced while writing this sequel, let alone the duology as a whole. That is why the list I'm about to chuck at you is so lengthy. It would be longer, but unfortunately, I don't have the ability to thank every single person who has shaped me into the person I am today. Regardless, the people on this list deserve more thanks than I could possibly articulate with words.

First off, my incredible publisher Jodi Jackola. I tell you all the time in our unending chain of emails, but you have changed my life by taking a chance on Abigail and Colton. I am so unbelievably grateful for your support, expertise, and compassion. You have helped me achieve my biggest dreams—so much so that I am dreaming up new ones. Even bigger ones. You have helped me rekindle my love for writing time and time again—you and my contract, hahaha. THANK YOU.

Next, my parents. I know you both want your own shout out, so here you go: Hi, Mom! Hi, Dad! You have been waiting for this sequel for a *whole year*. Don't worry, I've been polishing it up for you. Writing and rewriting and rewriting again. I'm a real author now, what can I say. I have to do real author things. So, I'm sorry for making you wait, but the time is finally here. Enjoy and use this one to hold you over until my next book comes out. I love you both more than life. THANK YOU.

A few honorable mentions: my sister, my grandparents, all my aunts and uncles and cousins on every side of the family. Of course, this list would be nothing without mentioning the lovely, *incredible* friends I have made thus far in college. I love you all so much. Your support means the world and more. THANK YOU.

Lastly, I want to take a few moments to thank some of my best friends as well. The people who have seen me at my best and my worst but continue to love me all the same. In no particular order:

Emma Tibbett. Aside from literally helping me put words together to describe setting, you have been my voice of reason throughout this whole process. It is nice to have a friend who understands the struggles of a writer. The writer's block, the gaps between writing, and the influx of ideas—or lack thereof! Gosh... but look at us. We persevere time and time again. I hope you know that I am eternally grateful for our friendship. You are such a light in my life. Never change.

Cross Lawrence. As of this moment, you are across the world in Paris, but thanks to Snapchat, you are well aware of how much I miss you. Cross, the moment I met you, I knew we were going to be friends for life. God knew we needed each other. I'm so honored to be friends with you; you are an inspiration in countless ways. Thank you for helping me keep my head screwed on right throughout this process. It is comforting to know that no matter where we are, our friendship will always hold strong. I wish you endless love, peace, and success. COME HOME SOON PLEASE! I MISS YOU!

Nick Richardson. I could just say "You da best, Chief" and leave it at that because...'nuff said. But you know me. I can't keep my mouth shut. Nick, you are everything to me. Everything. You have carried the weight of my anxiety and depression for years now. You have carried *me* in my entirety—all my silliness and sorrow—for years. And not *once* have you pushed me away. You saved my life so that I could write this gosh darn sequel and achieve my dreams, dammit! I adore you more than words. But you know that. 'Nuff said.

Lastly, my readers. I love you, I love you, I love you. I can't say that enough. Without you, I am just a few words on a page. You make my work worth it. You remind me why I do it. I hope you enjoyed this sequel! Lucky for you though, I was born to be a writer. New projects are on the horizon! Stay tuned.

About the Author

Born and raised in Pennsylvania, Avery Volz knew she wanted to be a writer when she received her first journal at the tender age of eight. Today, she adores crafting stories that explore what it means to be human and what it means to be in love. Her mission is to make each individual feel seen and understood through the rocky roads that her characters walk. Outside of writing, Avery is an accomplished hip hop dancer. She also finds solace in her favorite romance novels, in her friends and family, and in her dog, Izzy.